The Immigrant's Treasure

James L. Glasoe

PublishAmerica
Baltimore

First printing

ISBN: 1-4137-3114-7
PUBLISHED BY PUBLISHAMERICA, LLLP
www.publishamerica.com
Baltimore

Printed in the United States of America

*A fact-based fictional biography of my grandfather,
Michael M. Bernhard Glasoe, [1865 – 1940],
including his original writings*

Poems by Bjornstjerne Bjornson, reprinted with permission of The American-Scandinavian Foundation. I searched in vain for a source from which to gain copyright permission for Bernhard Gabrielsen's poem, "Jul De Hjemme," Arne Garborg's verse, "Noreg," as well as the names of authors for various other poems included in my grandfather's writings.

Please Enjoy!

I dedicate *The Immigrant's Treasure* to every Norwegian-American who traveled thousands of miles across unfriendly waters, struggled with a strange new language and settled in mid-America, making it the heartland of this country. We, as your descendants, are both proud and grateful for your courage, your sacrifice and most of all, your accomplishments.

Thanks to all of you, especially Michael, Emma, Peter and Anna, my grandparents. This is for you.

Introduction

Dear Grampa Michael,

I just wanted to let you know that I have written a biography of your life. Yeah, me, little Jimmy; do you remember me? I used to climb up on your lap, and you told me stories about Norway. I was only 5 years old when you died.

Well, I'm now 68 years old, just a little younger than you were when you wrote your letter which began, "That which I will now write down... I intend it for my children who could read Norwegian."

Do you remember that letter? You started to tell your children about your life as a young boy growing up in Norway. I got a copy of the translation when I was in my 40s. That letter sparked an interest in me to find out as much as I could about you and your life.

I have to be honest, Grampa, I did not remember you or Gramma, but I wanted to. I wanted to know all about Norway and your life there. I wanted to know what brought you to this country. I wanted to know what your life in Minnesota and North Dakota was like. I don't know why this became important to me, it just did.

I have a wonderful wife, just like your Emma. Her name is Nicole Marie, but I call her Nikki. In 1984 we made the trip that I believe you wanted to make so badly, our first visit to "your" Norway to celebrate our 25th wedding anniversary. I know when you immigrated to this country in 1866 the trip took many days. Can you believe that it took only about 12 hours for us to fly from Minneapolis to Amsterdam, Holland? The next day we boarded a big ship, the SS Norway.

During the second night, we sailed into Geirangerfjord and anchored. When I woke up in the morning and went up on deck, what I saw took my breath away. The water was absolutely calm and as smooth as glass. The mountains that rose up majestically on both sides of the ship were mirrored in the water. Along the shore in some places and on all the peninsulas there were patches of green with a cluster of buildings on each. There were wooden fences within which sheep and cows and other livestock were grazing. I noticed one farm where a mountain stream descended into the backyard, forming a small cascade before reaching the fjord.

At that moment, I realized how proud I was that you and all my other ancestors came from this beautiful place. I was in awe of this land, and wondered why anyone would ever leave.

When we returned home, I resolved to find out about you by discovering exactly where you were born and where you lived. I didn't know how, but I knew I would have to find a way. I hoped that maybe your home had been one of the farms along the shore. I didn't know many Norwegian words and naively made up a theory that our name, Glasoe, was from, "glas oie." or glass island. I could envision a farm that looked across the "glassy" fjord waters to a verdant island in the middle. Using a map of Norway we acquired on our trip, I searched it in great detail for such a place, but in vain.

My first clue came from your letter where you mentioned Beistad Sundet and Fjord. Later, a cousin sent me some family history that got me moving a little further along in the right direction. So, now I knew your birthplace was somewhere around Beistad, and your letter had been more precise saying, "There, where Beistad Fjord flowed into Beistad Sundet, lay 3 farms, North, Middle and South Rones."

It took a long time, but I latched onto a more detailed map of Norway that showed the smaller Norwegian communities. There, in a county called North Trondelag, I found Beistad. My excitement was unbounded, and I was ecstatic when I saw there was a road to get there. I resolved at that moment to return to Norway, find that road and discover the "Nord Rones Farm" where you had said you were born.

Grampa, we now have a device called a computer. It is similar to the telephone, but instead of voices, we can send typed messages back and forth that show up on a little screen in each home. To send or receive something, most times, takes only a few seconds.

After I retired, like you did in the 1920s, I also had more time to read and write. I sent a computer message all the way to Norway asking for any information of any kind about you. I gave your name, the date of your birth and where you were born. Within days, a lady from Oslo sent me a message in English and said, "Well, Jim, what do you want to know?" From there she was off, sending me page after page of places, people and dates, all relating to your mother and father and their forebears dating way back to the 1600s.

In time, I also found out about Gramma Emma's family and then all my mother's ancestors. I started a "Family History" file that contained your letter and I began to develop a family tree. To make sense out of all the names, dates and places, I began to put what I had into narrative form. It was in the midst of this project that I discovered you were a skilled carpenter, a hardworking farmer as well as a gifted writer.

I wished, many times, that you had written more about your life than just that letter. After I sent a draft copy of my Family History narrative to some of my cousins, I got the unbelievable news back that one of them had 6 blue notebooks that were filled with your writings. My wish had come true; there was more.

In time, I got copies of those notebooks and their translation. I assumed the notebooks would pick up on your life where you left off in your letter. I soon discovered that what you had written was not the continuing saga of your life; instead, the notebooks contained some of your favorite poems, a beautiful description of the Norway you remembered and finally, a delightful fantasy about the heroic, "Ole Fjeldbonde,"—"Ole The Mountain Farmer." To me it was the pot of gold at the end of the rainbow—your treasure, hidden away in a box, in a closet, for over 60 years.

I knew immediately, Grampa, that I wanted to publish your writings so everyone in the family could read them. I finished my family history and published it myself under the title *Children Of One Thousand Years*. The title came from a verse by Knute Hauge: "Ingen er barn of idag, du er barn av dei tusen ar:" You are a child of a thousand years, not merely a child of today.

The longer I worked on getting it into typewritten form, the more I thought what you had written was so delightful that it deserved an even larger audience than just the Glasoe-Holte descendants. It should also be presented to all of those Norwegian-Americans whose ancestors had also immigrated to this country. I needed to find a way to publish "The Writings of Michael M. Bernhard Glasoe," for them also. First of all, however, I felt they should know something about you.

Here then is the conundrum: before I can introduce you to others, I have to get to know you myself. Getting to know someone I could not remember was, to say the least, an interesting experience. To accomplish that, I would have to depend on a few photos, a hodgepodge of anecdotal material that I researched or received from other family members and finally, most importantly, what you revealed about yourself in your writings. From that base, I decided I would create you in my mind and write the biography you started to write, but never got finished. I would continue where you left off. The burning question loomed, was I up to that challenge? I decided I would never know unless I gave it a try.

To help me with this task, I had my file full of ancestors' names, birthplaces, birth dates, spouses, marriage dates, children, homes, occupations, immigration dates and settlements, even dates of death. These were facts, verified over and over again from various sources. Sometimes dates and ages didn't always jibe, but that was not the big issue.

The next hurdle would be to bring all of what I had to life; you and Gramma; your parents; your brothers and sisters; your children, including my father and finally, the people in the various communities where you lived. You and all these people from your past had to become living, breathing beings.

I would start with you first, and give essence to the man who had written the letter "to those children who could read Norwegian." I decided to use that letter in the first chapter. That experience would become your present and I would figure out a way to bring in your past.

Next, settings would have to be established, people given character, situations developed, conversations created, everything must be done to bring your childhood, youth, middle age and final years to life. It was a bit of a challenge, but an interesting exercise in using my imagination to bring you and Gramma and other people to life on paper. While most of the others were family or relatives or people from historical documents, some people I had to make up entirely.

With a vague memory of your home, Grampa, I decided to make the opening setting for the biography your kitchen table, next to windows on the south side of the house. Set dressing would include your glasses, a pen, a notebook and, of course, the coffee cup, a saucer and a bowl of sugar lumps. All the older men, I remembered as a child, drank their coffee out of huge white cups, usually pouring a little in their saucer to cool it fast and then drank from that saucer. I imagined you did the same.

The garden on the lot north of the house was remembered more than vaguely. I had been scolded there for taking one of Gramma's spoons, sitting in the middle of the plot and eating black dirt by the spoonful. It would become a factor in my story.

The segue from the moment of you writing your letter to your past was a big obstacle. It was written and rewritten many times, until I decided to make those chapters, after the first few, the product of your memory.

Over time the book became a labor of love. All the characters became absolutely alive for me. I got to know them as family, my family: you, my grandparents, my parents, whom I of course knew best, my uncles and aunts, most of whose lives, like yours, ended, or were ending just when I was just getting started.

As I went on, it seemed that writing got easier. Through my acting experience in college and seminary, I learned to empathize with my characters, experience their joy and sadness, triumph and defeat, success and failure, challenge and victory, experiences and yearnings. Now I did it with the people in my book.

In the beginning, my hope was to make you and others in my book as real as possible. As I imagined and wrote about your final moments, Grampa, with Gramma by your side, I'm not ashamed to say that tears streamed down my face, just as if it were happening now, and I was sitting there by your cot in the dining room. At that point, I decided I must have done a good job.

I had gone off in search of facts that I could blend together with fiction and found, in my quest, living, breathing people: you, my grandfather, Michael, a proud Norwegian, a hardy pioneer, a loving husband and father, a skilled farmer and builder and last but not least, a talented author; my grandmother, Emma, faithful wife, dutiful mother, dedicated midwife and nurse, and church organist who seemed capable of surviving all manner of crises with the exception of your death; your relatives; people in the communities where you lived, some of them real, some of them invented by me; the Glasoe children, my father, Almer, and all my aunts and uncles.

In the year 2001, Nikki and I, along with my oldest brother, Harland, made a visit to your Norway. It was, of course, our second trip there, but Harland's first. From the Sons of Norway, I had obtained a very helpful map of North Trondelag that not only showed the small communities around Steinkjer, but all the farms as well.

I was able to locate Elnan, where I now knew your father was born; Nord Rones where you were born; Granhus where you lived as a young boy; Bartness, where you went to church and school and Glasè, now Gladsjo, the farm your father bought when he sold his boat and the name you took when you came to America. I was where I had yearned to be years earlier. We took pictures of the houses and the farmland. I can't tell you what a thrill it was to stand on ground where I knew you once stood and see all the sights you had looked at over 150 years ago. I also located Gramma Emma's parents' farms near Stod and Ongdalen.

We had made plans to visit the Trondheim area and see the Ydstie farm where my mother's mother, my Gramma Anna, was born and raised. We were thrilled to be able to also make prior arrangements to visit a farm, which was still in the family, where my mother's grandmother was born, the Sorte farm.

Finally, our goal was to travel down the Gudbransdal Valley that you described so beautifully in your writing, to Brottum, a tiny community just a little south of Lillehammer. There my mother's father, my Grampa Peter, was born and raised.

In putting your words into manuscript form, I tried to keep it exactly as you wrote it and as it was translated. In true frugal fashion, your script covered the notebook pages from top to bottom and side to side; no paper was wasted. I must confess, I did create some paragraphs and added some punctuation. I also put a title on your description of Norway, one I think you would like, *Norway, My Norway.*

I have been lucky or blessed, whatever you want to call it. I went to high school, college seminary and graduate school, 21 years of education. You, I'm assuming, went through grade school in a small rural community in Norway—that was it. Yet what a marvelous gift you had for writing. I am in awe of your skill. I suspect you must have read a lot.

I only hope that when you read what I wrote about your life, you will be as proud of me as a writer, as I am of you. Like you, I love to learn, I love to read and I enjoy writing.

Some day I hope to meet you again. Not quite now, however, as I still have many things to write.

Your loving grandson,

James L. Glasoe

Chapter One

The old man removed the wire rims from his ears and, with a sigh, laid his glasses on the blue spiral notebook next to the pen he'd used to record his thoughts. With thumb and forefinger, he massaged the bridge of his nose where the glasses had rested. Writing, he had discovered over the past few years, was a little more difficult than he might have anticipated.

Michael Glasoe could not remember a time in his life when he hadn't worked, beginning at age 7, herding cows for his uncle in Norway. In the succeeding years, he had labored as both carpenter and farmer, so his body was familiar with hard physical labor.

Since his retirement, he had discovered that the exercise of his mind, for days at a time, was an equally tiring experience. However, *when you enjoy doing something difficult, it's not so bad,* he thought. He did love to write; it gave him great satisfaction. It also took his mind off the pain, that dark visitor from the past that now had become the constant companion that never left his side and gave such urgency to his labors.

His current project was a letter to his children, telling them about his life in Norway as a young boy. His motivation had come during a recent visit from one of his young grandsons, Jimmy.

On that afternoon, Michael had been sitting in the living room while Jimmy's mother and his wife, Emma, talked in the kitchen. He had an afghan on his lap and was dozing, when a little hand gently touched his knee and a soft voice said, "Grampa, are you sleeping?"

"No, Jimmy, I was just resting my eyes for a bit. I'm sort of tired today."

"Are you sick, Grampa? Sometimes, you know, when I'm sick, I feel tired and get sleepy. Are you tired because you're sick, Grampa?"

"Yes, Jimmy, as a matter of fact, I am feeling kind of old these days."

The grandson had nodded, cocked his tow head to one side, looked up at him and, in a most serious voice, announced matter-of-factly, "You know,

Grampa, you and Gramma will die, and my mom and dad, too, because you're old. But not me, Grampa, I'm brand new." The blunt honesty of this young and innocent fledgling made him smile and shake his head in wonder. His little grandson was closer to the truth than he knew.

On the heels of his pronouncement, Jimmy was off to the kitchen. Back he came in a minute, with a saucer full of sugar lumps soaked in coffee. "Grampa, look at what Gramma Emma gave me. Do you think you're too tired to tell me a story?"

"Well, now, if you'll just climb up in my lap and let me have one or two of those sugar lumps, I just might work up enough energy to tell you about when I was a little boy like you. I'll also tell you about a very mean neighbor boy named Carl. Would you like to hear about that?"

Nodding, wide-eyed, Jimmy said, "Gramma told me I should share." He took a sugar lump and put it up to his grandfather's mouth and said, "Open wide, Grampa." Then he took two more lumps and put them in his own mouth, chewing and swallowing as fast as he could. Then up came another lump to Grampa's mouth. "Be a good boy now, Grampa, take your medicine." When it was chewed and swallowed, Jimmy said, "What do you think, Grampa? Do you have enough energy now to tell me about you when you were little like me?" He popped the last sugar lump in his own mouth, savoring this one slowly while wiping his hand on his overalls.

"Once upon a time, when I was just a boy like you, in a faraway country called Norway…"

"Is Norway a real place or is it make believe?"

"Oh, Norway is a very real place," Michael continued, "a very real and beautiful place," he added wistfully.

"And there was a mean boy named Carl there, right, Grampa? Was he a giant like Jack, of the bean stock?"

"Well no, he was bigger than me, but not as big as a giant."

Just then Jimmy's dad, Almer, came into the room and said, "Time to go home, Jimmy."

"Oh, but Daddy, Grampa was just going to tell me a story. Weren't you, Grampa? He was going to tell me about the mean neighbor boy, Carl."

"Carl?" Almer asked, "Who's Carl, Dad?"

"Oh, surely you remember Carl. He lived just across the road when we lived at Granhus. You must remember me telling you how "umulig" he was."

"I'm sorry, Dad," said Almer. "I don't remember anything about a Carl, and I've never heard of Granhus. This was in Norway?"

"Yes, when I was just a boy. I thought I told you all this years ago."

"If you did, Dad, I must have forgotten. Anyway, Jimmy, get your coat. Grampa can tell you his story about Carl the next time you visit."

"Norway's a real place, Daddy, a very real and beautiful place."

"I'm sure it is, Jimmy, but now it's time to go. Bye, Dad. Say goodbye to your grampa, Jimmy."

Circling his knees with his arms, Jimmy laid his head on Grampa's lap and with both arms he squeezed gently and said, "Bye, Grampa. I love you."

Now, weeks later, as Michael sat at the kitchen table with a fresh cup of coffee, he still couldn't get it into his head that Almer didn't remember Carl or anything he had told him about his life in Norway. In the following days after that encounter, as others of his children stopped by for a brief visit, he had asked each one of them in turn if they remembered him telling about his life in Norway, and they all shook their heads "no."

How could he have forgotten to tell them about his years in Norway? How could they all have forgotten what he told them, if he had? Well, he had concluded, one way or the other, telling his children about his mother and father, his own grammas and grampas, his sisters who had not come to America, all the places they had lived, the things they had done and the people they had known was a task that needed to be undertaken now. He knew time was getting short.

Michael had worked so hard all of his life that there had been precious little opportunity for reminiscence. In retirement, there was more time to remember, more time to think, more time to write. Since he had obviously, so far, failed in his effort to share his memories and experiences, especially those that had occurred before he emigrated here and then also those years before the children were born or old enough to remember, it was imperative now that he get them written down.

He was not a vain man, but he was humbly proud of his heritage and mildly pleased with his life's accomplishments, though he wished there might have been more. He had come a long way, both geographically and personally. He had created something to be passed on.

It was important to him that his family would have something to remember him by when he was gone—some written record. True, they were all grown now with families and homes of their own, some had even moved away. That didn't dampen the need to share the story of his life; in fact, it stoked the fire. With age, and now his health, as both impediment and motivation, he was determined to leave a written legacy of his life. Certainly, no one else was going to do it.

Michael's secret, life long passion had been his love of poetry, and soon after he retired, as a preliminary to his other writing, he had penned a few of his favorite poems into his blue notebooks. Poems! Much of the early history of Norway came from the poetic sagas he had read, at his father's urging, as a boy and as a young man. Poetry, he believed, had been, and still was, the soul of communication for the Norwegian. In Norway you learned two things—how to ski and how to write poetry.

His favorite book was the much-read tome, *Poems and Songs*, by Bjornstjerne Bjornson, with its well-worn pages and bright red cover. Because of the fragile condition of his copy, he had chosen to write down his favorites, with the thought that some day he would get them translated into English for his children. He knew that more than 20 years ago the American-Scandinavian Foundation had published an English translation of *Poems and Songs*, but the translator had made the verses rhyme in English, subtly changing the words and intent, just 6 years after the poet's death. Michael believed that to be an injustice; besides, he preferred the more poetic Norwegian language.

Bjornson had won a Nobel Prize for his works and, Michael felt, deservedly so. His poems were so richly descriptive, they made Norway come alive, and Bjornson's fierce nationalistic spirit and pride in Norway's independence from Denmark and Sweden became Michael's own. It was Bjornson who wrote the words to the Norwegian national anthem, "Ja ve elsker dette landet."—Yes, we love this land.

Now, he thought to himself, *I must remember where I put that notebook, find it and get someone to read and translate it into English before I'm gone and it gets tossed out.*

Inspired by Bjornson's poetry, he had written what he hoped was a somewhat poetic description of Norway, as he remembered it. As a child, he had been pretty much confined to a limited area of the country, but as a young man in maritime service, he saw the country from top to bottom. There was very little water touching the coast of Norway that he had not traveled on and what he saw, he remembered and what he remembered, he had committed to writing.

His homeland was such a glorious place, and he had kept the vivid images of its rugged beauty in his mind until this day. Oh, how he missed Norway! For him, the years had not dimmed, but instead had fired up the longing to revisit his homeland, as well as share that beauty on paper with his family.

He had never shared this feeling with Emma, but many times he wished that he had never come to this country. What he had so eagerly anticipated paled in comparison with the reality of what he experienced. True, he had done exceedingly well by the Norwegian standards of that time; he had created a farm of 320 acres. Sadly, however, Norway would always be glorious Norway, and North Dakota would forever be just North Dakota. From his homeland's mountains, fjords and valleys he had come to the flat prairies and plains of America.

As he grew older, it had become increasingly important for him to tell his children about the country he remembered so fondly, but they had never seen. To them, their world had always been flat and stretched for miles, filled with fields of wheat, oats and barley. It was all they knew, but he often thought of countryman Henrik Ibsen's words, "I will go further, higher, to the steepest peak—I will see the sun rise once more." Sadly, there were no peaks in northwestern North Dakota.

Ah, yes, Norway! His beloved Norway! Often, as he was writing, if he closed his eyes, he could see it, the majestic mountains, the glassy, mirror like fjords and the beautiful farms, often like green velvet, with sometimes a small waterfall in the backyard, and he would sing softly to himself, "Kan du glemme gamle Norge, aldrig jeg du glemme kan. Med det storte klippe borge, du er mine Fedres land."—"Can you forget old Norway? I cannot forget it. These proud cliff castles are, and will remain, my birth land."

Where had he squirreled that notebook away? He must remember to talk to Emma about his notebooks. She knew where almost everything was.

After he immigrated to this country, Michael's father, Ole, had made one visit to see him in Minnesota, but had not been impressed and returned to Norway to live out his life. Two of his sisters had also remained in Norway, and he corresponded with them over the years and knew that they were doing well. Sister Hilde had married Arnt Oldus Folden, and together they had farmed Metter Bartness and later Sparbu. Sister Lottie had married Peter Ystmark and they owned and farmed Ystmark in Malm, just across the fjord from where he was born.

If he had the money and his health was better, he would make a trip back to Norway tomorrow. How glorious it would be to walk that land one more time! Oh, that would be a wonderful visit. But in his heart, he knew it was not to be.

However, while he was unable to make the physical trip to Norway, he had found a way to go back through the use of his memory, his imagination and his pen and paper. After writing down his poems and his description of Norway, he had filled four notebooks with the fictional fantasy of Ole Fjeldebonde, "Ole The Mountain Farmer."

As his own fictional counterpart, Ole did not have to leave his beloved native land to find a homestead. He did not have to travel to a foreign land and learn a whole new language. Instead, this shrewd young son of a lowly "cotter" had boldly petitioned the Norwegian government to give him land up in the mountains, with the right to harvest trees for building and then to till the cleared land to grow the crops that would nourish his family and feed his animals. His request was granted, and the story unfolded like a dream, as Ole succeeded beyond his wildest hopes.

And, a dream it was—Michael's vision of what he wished might have happened to him, instead of the stark reality of what had occurred. Oh, how he had desired to have created there what he had here. Kan du glemme gamle Norge? Nei! Never! How could one forget such a glorious place?

He chose, from the beginning, to put all his writings in blue spiral-bound notebooks that he purchased at the local grocery store. Born of frugal means, he was a man who wasted nothing. His writing always began on the top line and he filled margin to margin down to the bottom line. Being a proud man, he also was careful to proofread each page and make corrections. Then, when he was satisfied, he took a clean notebook and wrote his final copy, error free, top to bottom, side to side.

His current task was to write his biography. What he had finished today was a good beginning, but he had a long way to go. He prayed his mind would stay sound and his hand steady.

He was a slight man, who never had to duck when going through a doorway, nor suffer through a diet. There didn't appear to be an ounce of fat on his body. Even as his mustache flourished, his hair on top thinned significantly, though it had not turned as silver white as Emma's. A strong and healthy man, he had avoided any serious medical problem until he had surpassed his 50th birthday.

At that age, Michael had experienced some minor prostate problems, first with frequency of urination and, over time, with minor pain. When the problem became severe enough that he missed some work, he finally went to the doctor.

The local doctor, J. Allen Smith, diagnosed an enlargement and a little inflammation of the prostate, prescribed some medication and suggested as a further course of treatment what he termed "watchful waiting." This course of treatment was characterized by regular exams to gauge any increase in the size of the gland or determine if any nodules had developed.

The doctor had reassured him that this is a relatively common approach for those who are better served by treating the symptoms, while out-living the problem. Curative treatments, such as surgery, were a final option. With time and medication, the problem subsided a little, but it never completely disappeared. When nodules developed he had eventually opted for surgery and, after a rather lengthy recovery, returned to work.

Just two years ago the pain had started to return. After another examination, Doctor Smith told him that there was a possibility that the cancer had returned. He matter-of-factly explained that over time it would spread; the question was, how fast? The choices again, as they were in the first round, were immediate surgery versus treating the symptoms with the hope of out-living the problem.

Having enjoyed good health all through his life, Michael was unprepared for major illness. He had to admit the prospect of further surgery at this age scared him. He took some comfort in the fact that even though his mother had died at a relatively young age, his father had remarried, was still producing children at age 70 and had lived to be 85 years of age. He chose to watch and wait, but the specter of death gave impetus to his need to write.

Just today, there had been one of those fierce episodes when the pain ripped through his body "full bore," burning like a prairie fire through his groin, sucking the air out of his lungs and bringing sudden and uncontrollable tears to his eyes. He was glad that Emma, his faithful and loving bride of 48 years, come just a week from Sunday, had not been around to see its effect on him this morning. Try as he might, he couldn't always hide these occurrences from her. Today she was upstairs and was not witness to his administration of the pain medication Dr. Smith had prescribed. Emma knew his pain, of course she knew, but he always felt better when she wasn't there to witness it.

Sitting today at the kitchen table facing east, he looked out the south window to his right and saw a glorious field of wheat. Unlike the constant beauty of Norway, the plains had a "hit and miss" approach to artistry. Today he reveled in the sun shimmering off the thousands of stalks of wheat forming a field of solid gold. In the distance, he thought he could see the dust cloud rising behind a "reaper." Good, he thought, the crop would not be lost. It was October, a very late harvest, a gamble with the weather to let the kernels dry in the sun. The flourishing field was a gorgeous sight, too seldom seen in his homesteading years. It was one of the few years that he felt justified in his decision to settle here.

Spring rains had been plentiful this year, and the promise for a good crop was high; the bushels per acre should run strong. The "dust bowl," a minor nemesis for him when the first mild hint of it appeared in 1919, was an absolute plague for his daughter, Lillian, and her husband, Al, when they took over the homestead in the mid 30s. Now it looked like it was finally easing its grip. He hoped the grain prices would not plummet.

In 1925, at age 60, he and Emma had made the decision to leave the homestead and move into Noonan. He rented the land out to his sons-in-law, Gust and Einar Roness. They did the best they could to keep things running, but drought, year after year, dried up absolutely everything in sight. It was a losing battle.

Michael and Emma's two-story house sat on a corner lot. The downstairs included an average-sized kitchen connected to a small formal dining room, leading to a fair-sized living room that faced west and then a small bedroom. The furniture was typical of what could be ordered out of the Sears-Roebuck catalog, and that's in fact where it had come from. Antimacassars guarded the backs of all padded chairs and the sofa. Crocheted doilies, held on by little screw pins, protected the arms.

The Glasoe home was only two blocks off the village's Main Street, which was typical of main streets in a hundred small North Dakota towns. As he reviewed that street in his mind, he started on the south end of town, where the grade school and the high school established a sort of southern boundary. If he walked north on the right hand side of the street, he'd first pass Gorder's residence (relatives by marriage), then the Clemmens' residence, which housed the telephone switchboard, a couple empty lots, the Catholic Church, not unlike his Zion, which he had built in 1915, followed by a couple more empty lots.

Memorial Hall, a red brick building of some size, sat on the corner. It saw multiple duty for the Noonan community: sometimes as an auditorium, gymnasium, a dance hall and now, on weekends, a movie theater. Noonan, like other small towns, was waiting for the epic movie *Gone With The Wind*, now making the rounds of the larger North Dakota cities. It would be in color and the rumor was it would be 4 hours long. If he walked in the door of Memorial hall, he knew he would immediately smell the odor of the chemically treated red sawdust compound used to sweep the floor. He was proud that two of his grandsons, Harland and Doran, Almer's oldest boys, were showing early evidence of being hard workers, taking on the job of keeping the Hall floors clean.

If he walked across the street going north, he would come to the business section. First was Stackston's Grocery, with its two plate glass windows, where he bought his blue notebooks, Tryhus Garage—the Ford dealership, Jenson's Safeway Grocery, Nelson's Photo Studio, a vacant tin-sided building and then Dunsford's Bar. Michael was not a drinker and had never spent much time in any of Noonan's bars, so when the doctor suggested having a glass of beer a day as a "tonic," he declined, with Emma's hearty approval. He preferred a dish of ice cream from Crum's Drugstore.

The next block was home to the stone-faced post office, with the bank behind. Attached to the post office, along the front wall, was the Traveler's Hotel, which doubled as the town's only restaurant and sported a front window room with a view of Main Street. Amusingly, it also provided the residents of the community with a view of those who had time to sit there and play cards. A visit in there brought the strong odor of tobacco smoke.

Mellum's barbershop was next, and Emma had told him about the trouble Jimmy got into there about a year ago. Jimmy and his friend, Marilyn, had been in the shop begging for money from the customers. Persistent, they would not take no for an answer, but told the customer to "dig deep in his pocket." George, the owner had finally called the mothers, and it was rumored the two were literally tied up at home for the day.

Then there was Lysocker's Shoe Repair, another open lot, then a tailor shop and finally, a beauty shop. Businesses came and failed in short order, so on any given day, you found either a new business or another vacant building.

Only a few places were left until he reached the north end of town: Hilde's house, then Henry Stafflen's Gas Station, the place his son Almer had first worked after he moved his family from Landa back to Noonan. Next there was a lot of open space and the railroad tracks. The coming of the railroad had originally created the town of Noonan, as well as dozens of other small communities in the county, the state and, in fact, the entire Midwest.

Across the tracks was the Farmer's Elevator, situated for easy loading of the grain bound for Minneapolis or Duluth, farther north in the sister state of Minnesota. Noonan was also a major provider of coal dug from the mine not far from town.

Now, if he crossed the street going west, he could see to the north Wissbrod's Service Station, which, together with the town depot on this side of the tracks, marked the village's northern border.

Heading back south, he passed the creamery, the place to go for the rich, thick cream needed to make "rommegraut." Then there were three small homes, the Smith Annex and brother Ed Glassoe's Pool Hall. Ed chose the Glasoe name but added an extra "s" for some reason. Nobody cared, so nobody ever asked why.

In the next block was Feeney's Bar, Crum's Drug Store with its soda fountain, a popular place on summer weekends when farm folks came into town, and the place he got his ice cream treat. On the corner was Noonan Supply with groceries, dry goods and a little bit of everything else. Just behind the store was Lindstrom's Hardware.

One more block south took him past Westland Service Station, an office building leased to an attorney or two, he thought, the Baukol-Noonan office where the local coal mine executives worked, the Catholic Rectory, which early on had been a dentist's office, the Noonan Miner newspaper office, Tandberg Auto and Nordstrom's Lumber Yard.

The corner of the next block was Noonan's "pride and joy"—the hospital. It was two stories, made of handsome red brick, with broad steps leading up to the front door. Next door there were 2 family residences. The Methodist Church came next, then another residence and finally, the tennis courts. A 15 to 20 minute walk would take him easily from one end of town to the other and back again.

As Michael mused, he thought, not a bad little Main Street. It had almost all of what he and Emma would need on an average day. They seldom found it necessary to go any place else. Family homes, including theirs, ran east and west of Main Street for two or three blocks on each side.

As Emma came into the room to check on her bread dough, bustling around, she asked what the smile on Michael's face was all about. Surprised it was there, he said, "Oh, I was just taking a little mental walk on Main Street, saying hello to some old friends. That way I save on the shoe leather."

Emma accepted his answer and poured him a fresh cup of coffee. He could have added that it was about the only way he got there lately, and he wasn't sure if he was saying "hello" or "goodbye." Wisely, he chose not to tell her that.

His gaze followed her around the kitchen. Like him, she was short in stature, but a little stockier. Her gray hair was pulled back into a bun—a popular hairstyle for all the local women of her age. She usually chose to wear a long, cotton dress, which was always covered by an apron, unless she was going out somewhere. Her most striking feature was her beautiful, blue eyes. Over the years, Michael had searched for a word that described their color. Baby blue was as close as he could come. Interestingly, the color was an exact match for his own eyes.

As he followed her movements, his thoughts strayed to his mother and the homes his family had occupied in Norway. He could remember them all, every nook and cranny. Instead of clean linoleum on the floor, there had been timeworn, unfinished pine boards. The couple's shiny gas stove and oven replaced the huge Norwegian open fireplace that sometimes took up a third of the kitchen. He admitted that even after all these years, he still missed the pungent smell of burning logs and the soft flares that lit even the most remote corners of the room as evening darkness settled in.

Emma, he thought, had it easier now that they had moved into town, and then chuckled to himself; she'd better not hear him say that. She was such a hard worker and hardly ever sat down during the day. In addition to raising and feeding a family, she had in fact, in their early years, been Doc Smith's "right hand," forever traveling with him out in the country to "mid-wife" or act as nurse for the sick. One time she had even been quarantined for three weeks.

Sorrowfully, he had to admit that after her bone cancer surgery, Emma had slowed down considerably, and she was no more the "Old Emma" than he was the "Old Michael." Time had and was continuing to take its toll on them.

After a while, he poured a little of his hot coffee from his cup into the saucer, blew on it a couple times and sifted it through his mustache. Emma's coffee was always good, and like little Jimmy, he knew how to make it better. He reached into the sugar bowl and took out two lumps. Dipping them into his cup and then sucking the sweet coffee out was a pleasure unknown in his homeland. His mother would have grimaced at such extravagance.

Michael reseated his glasses, picked up his tablet and flipped the cover over to the first page. He read the Norwegian script, translating most of the words into English, as he hoped his friend, Ole, would do when he proofread it. Norwegian was his choice for writing because it was easier for him. All of his formal education had been in Norwegian, the language of his parents and grandparents. English had been a requirement for survival in his new land, America. He could speak it, he could read it, but for writing—he preferred his native tongue. He began to read…

Noonan, North Dakota

October 17th, 1939

That which I will now write down is a little about my childhood and the times in which I lived, both here and in Norway. I intend it for my children who can read Norwegian. The time passes, the time runs hastily. Think about eternity in time, if the end is not to be sad.

There, where Beidstat Sundet begins to run through from Biedstatfjorden, there lies three beautiful farms on the south side of the sundet (bay) with the name Rones. There is in fact Nordre (north) Rones, Mittre (middle) Rones and Sondre (south) Rones.

At the time I was born, these three farms were owned by three brothers: Benjamin on the north, Daniel in the middle and Einar on the south. Benjamin was my mother's father. I was born on that farm, 16 September, 1865.

My parents lived there, together with my grandparents, until I was 6 years old. My father's name was Ole Magnus Elnan. My mother was Tale Margrete, born Rones.

When I was six years old, my parents moved from there to a farm not far away. The name of the farm was Granhus. The farm was owned by my mother's uncle, Kristopher.

I would now mention, before going further, that when I was a small child, my parents took me to Solberg Church to be baptized. They named me Michael Bernhard. I was named for my grandparents. My father's father's name was Michael. The Bernhard was for Benjamin.

Kristopher Granhus and his wife, Andreanna, had a son whom I cannot leave out of the story of my childhood. There were also three other sons and a daughter, all grown up at the time. The older ones were fairly decent human beings, but the youngest, Carl, who was born 12 years later, I must say, was an animal in human form. He was 10 years old when we came to live there and I was 6. My sisters were Hilde, 5, and Matte, 2. He did so much damage to me and my sisters, that if I should write like it was, it would take more than a year.

Carl was also mean to his mother. I saw him more than once push her to the floor and kick her when he didn't get what he wanted fast enough. The only thing his mother said was, "Now, Carl, you be a good boy." His father sat and watched and didn't say anything.

We lived in the "kaarhuset," a small house near the big house. On many occasions during the summer, Carl threw wet cow manure at our windows. As soon as my mother got them washed, he would come and throw some

28

more.

When we went to the wood shed to get wood for my mother's stove, Carl would follow and throw sawdust on us. He strewed it in our hair and stuffed it inside our collars. He was so strong; we could not do anything against him.

Sometimes he would take a rope and tie us up with it and put manure all over our bodies. Yes, Mother had a terrible struggle to keep us clean. He did this to us often, and then would stand and laugh with contempt. I have never in my life known another person so inhuman as that Carl.

On the farm there was a bull that was dangerous to handle. A young man who was hired to take care of the cattle had no trouble with the bull when he was with the rest of the herd. Carl refused to do any herding. All he could do was mischief.

One day Carl thought he would pull a fast one on me. He talked me into going with him up to where the cattle were. There was a fence on two sides where the cattle were grazing. By one of those fences lived a "husmann cotter" by the edge of the forest. Well, Carl's idea was to get me to a place where the bull would take after me. But Carl was slower than I and the bull caught him and took him by the horns and threw him high in the air. He tore his clothes and was scratched all over his body. It was lucky the husmann was close by and saw what was happening. He came running with a big stick in his hands and beat the bull with it until the bull left Carl. Otherwise, I believe that Carl would surely have been killed. Yes, so ended the wicked plot, and thereafter, the bull was made to stay in the barn.

One day Carl took me aside and told me I could ride a horse. I went with him to go and bring home a two-year-old colt that was tethered in the pasture some distance from the farm. Then he put a bridle on the horse, but did not fasten it properly. Then he lifted me up. The horse reared and threw me over his head. I landed on the ground. At the same time Carl let go of the bridle and the horse jumped over me. The horse could have stepped right on me, but didn't. If he had struck me on the head, it is doubtful that I would have lived to be sitting here telling you this. When I got up again, Carl was laughing at me in derision. "Did you fall off?" he said. "You should have hung on fast." Yah, that was a pleasant riding trip I received! But it looked like Carl had a lot of fun from it.

Later in the fall, my father came home from a sailing trip, planning to stay home for a few weeks. He had his boat anchored in the bay below the farm. One day when he was down at the boat making repairs, Carl took a rope and tied my two sisters by the barn wall. They were 5 and 2 years old. Carl had just begun to smear them with his usual ointment when my father came back and saw what he was doing. Father grabbed him by the neck before he could run away. He took him to the woodshed and, with a big stick, gave him a "rund juling," round spanking. I'm sure his rear was sore for a long time. Father said to him, "If you try something like this again, I'll report you to the "Landsmande" (sheriff), and you will be sent to reform school." Father then took him where my two little sisters were tied up and made him untie the knots. Afterward, Carl complained to his mother and she ran "rykkende sint" (smoking mad) and scolded him. My father let her keep on until she used up all her words. Then he told her that it was all her own fault that her son had grown so "udyr" (animal like). He said she had brought him up like that. After that, he left us in peace. He would go by and make faces, but did us no more harm.

In December that year, I was 7 years old and started to school. It was one English mile from where we lived. I walked with Carl every day until winter. He behaved fairly well except that after the snow was on the ground, he often grabbed me and threw me into the snow. Sometimes he took the cover off my lunch pail and filled it with snow. I put up with it and said nothing.

Our schoolmaster was an old grouch. His name was Martinius Zelen. I was so afraid of him; I hardly dared to look at him. Sometimes, he would come to me and put his hand under my chin and bend my head backward so that I had to look at him. "Look at me, I say!" That was my only winter at that school, the Bartness School. In the spring, my mother sent me to my father's brother.

My Uncle Edward's farm was at Skjeimebaken. I herded cows. That was the year I started to earn my own living. I surely found out that I had left my home and Mother. I was out with the cows from raining into sunshine, all the time. And very little was the food that I got. Edward and his wife were so stingy that they did not provide enough food for anyone who worked for them. They saved to put the money on the trunk bottom.

I stayed there for two years and life hung on in me. I went to school in the winter and was a cowherd in the summer. It was a long way to school, but I walked there every day. I had the same grouchy schoolmaster. He held school for a while at both Bartness and Hammersmoen.

My father's brother had no children to lay their love on. Money was their idol. It did not look to me as though it brought them happiness. They would always go around complaining and whining and looking darkly upon life.

They were dissatisfied with everything in general.

The last year I lived with them, they adopted a one-year-old boy to live with them. His name was Paul. In time, he inherited all they owned. None of their relatives got as much as one penny.

From there I moved to another of my father's brothers. His name was Amund Noostuen. His wife was Gurine. The distance to school there was not so far, so I had a little advantage there. But, otherwise, I cannot say that I had it much better. They, too, had no children. And they had the same greed. They saved on the food, at least as far as I was concerned. Their habit was to eat before I came home from school, so I had to be content with what was left over. Sometimes there was not much left over. I had two aunts who lived in the same house. Sometimes they took pity on me and sneaked some small bits of food. If it had not been for them, I would have very meager fare, "smalhans mikal."

Once in a while, it would happen that I had a free Sunday and could go home to my mother and my family. Then I was happy and forgot all my trials and troubles, "jenvordigheder." But that was not often in the summer. It was in winter, sometimes, that there was no school and I could go. At Christmas, I was allowed to stay as much as three days. Then I really had fun. I took my sled and slid down the hills on my way.

My aunts generally sent with me Christmas gifts for my mother and sisters. I believe I was more happy to bring them these gifts than they were to receive them.

But enough about that. I remember that those days, at least, were a good time for me. All my sorrows were forgotten while I was home at Christmas with my mother. Everything was happiness. But time went fast, thought I.
—Michael M. Glasoe

Memory, he mused, what a wonderful and awful faculty. Most of his were pleasant and made him smile. Other memories, like Carl, were probably better off forgotten, but persisted, no matter how he tried to forget them. That was strange, he thought. *I can wash the dirt off my hands after working the soil, but I cannot wash away bad memories that have persisted in my head.*

Lately, his daily way of living was sitting down with Emma's good egg coffee, some sugar lumps, reminiscing for a while and then putting those memories on paper. Doing this was the most important thing he could think of.

Over the next months, Michael planned to spend a lot of time in this exercise, thinking back and then writing down in his blue notebooks his memories about the rest of his life in Norway. He would also, if there were time, write about those years after he immigrated to America and settled in Starbuck, Minnesota.

He was lucky his memory was still so good, and the years of his life flowed easily across his mind like a motion picture, with himself as the main character. He recalled places, people, events and even the gist of a conversation or two. Through all his musings, he knew exactly what else he wanted to write down about his life. With these few pages, he had made a good start.

Now, it was time for a break. He would go out and see how the last of their garden vegetables were faring. The short summers and having to depend on others to till the ground and put in the seeds or starter plants meant late ripening and the possibility of frost damage if the cold came too early.

Much had already been gathered and canned for the winter ahead. Squash, a few pumpkins and a few straggler potato plants were about all he had to worry about now. Gardening was as close as he got to farming since retirement and, like his writing, he enjoyed it when he was feeling good.

As he stepped out on the back porch and surveyed the garden, he was struck by the size of the plot and laughed out loud. Even though it was just the two of them now, the garden plot looked big enough to feed their eleven children. Maybe next year he would cut back. But Emma so loved to share her canned goods.

Chapter Two

When he returned to the kitchen, he reread the pages he had written and smiled. This was a good start, but, oh, how tired he felt. He hadn't done much in the garden, but now-a-days, the slightest effort took its toll on his meager energy supply. He decided to go and sit in the living room until lunch was ready.

Closing his eyes in the quiet of that room, his memory raced on, his mind continuing its journey back through the early days of his life. When he paused to think about it, he was amazed by all the things that were stored in his head; it was like a whole library full of the history of his experiences. One had only to find the right shelf and the right book and the right page. He had always had the ability, given time, to pull out even the more obscure volumes. Today's tome was the one that held the information he had heard about his forebears, his experiences with them and with his father and mother in Norway.

Growing up in Norway had been a hard life for a young boy, but then it was a hard world for adults as well. Tillable soil, the lifelong quest for the farmer in Norway, was scarce in that land where rocky mountains and deep fjords prevailed.

He recalled that his father, Ole Magnus Elnan, was the second son of a cotter, Mikal Amundsen, and had no inheritance right to any land. By Norwegian law, unless the farmer divided a large farm into smaller ones, only the oldest son inherited family land. However, even if Ole had been the number one son, there was no land to inherit. As a cotter, his father was not much better off than the American slave, possessing little more than the clothes on his body, working from sun up to sun down to put money into his well-to-do employer's cupboard. Unlike slaves, cotters had the freedom to leave when they wanted to, but there was usually no place better to go.

Being a cotter was a hard life, working on a farm that at best provided you with a one room cottage, a small garden, if you had the time to work it, and a few kroner for pay that barely covered the family's food cost. If there had been any other alternative, Mikal would have taken it. Growing up in his father, Amund, and mother, Gunhild's, home, he knew well their cotter's life of frugality, but like them, he was helpless to escape it. In turn, he met and married Olava, a farmer's daughter with no inheritance rights, and became a cotter, just as his father had been.

To avoid duplicating his grandfather and his father's miserably harsh life and the lowly designation "cotter," Michael's father, Ole, was able to seize an opportunity on the nearby Beistad Fjord and as a young man he hired on with a sailor merchant whose business consisted of hauling goods from the large markets to the farms on his boat. Escape he did, but as Michael in his youth remembered his father, he was gone more than he was home.

To further escape the cotter stigma, Ole had also decided to take the farm name Elnan as his last name, rather than the patronymic option, Mikalsen [Mikal's son]. Though he was of the Elnan bloodline only through his mother, he could legally take as his last name the name of the farm where he had been born or on which he had lived.

In those days, as Michael remembered them, the roads that existed were little more than wagon ruts, and the most convenient means of transportation for those living on or near the coast was by water rather than land. The nearest large market for goods that Michael could remember was Steinkjer, almost in the middle of Norway, at the top of a waterway called Beistad Fjord, and only ten miles by boat from where he had been born.

The next biggest port was south in Trondheim, the third largest city in Norway, about one hundred miles away. There, by means of Trondheim Fjord, goods could be shipped in from several European ports and ferried north to Steinkjer and nearby small communities and large farms. This was the route Ole's benefactor knew well. Later it would become Ole's route.

In school Michael had been taught that ten thousand years before, his native country had been nothing more than a huge sheet of solid ice. Over the centuries, as the earth warmed, the ice melted and moved downward toward the ocean. The combination of moving ice and grinding glaciers forged out high rock mountains and furrowed out deep valleys where the water gathered into what the Norwegians named fjords. Along the coast, little land was created for cultivation, but what was available was put to the plow. More often than not, farms were no larger than 5 acres.

One of the largest farms on the merchant's route was Ole's birthplace in Elnan Valley. He had been born at Nauststua in West Elnan Valley. It was an old farm, Michael's grandmother, Olava, had told him, first established at least 500 years ago as Aelnom farm. Later it was called Elnadale and finally Elnan, before it was gradually split up into smaller farms. The name, she said, came from a small brook that ran through the valley west to east.

Next stops on the sea routes were west and then north on the coast of the smaller Beistad Fjord, where there were three farms named Rones, then two Granhus farms and finally Baertness, where there was also a school and a church. This time, from his grandmother, Marit, he learned that these also were very old farms that had at one time been a large single farm, Baertness. The presence of a church and school were evidence it had once been a very wealthy farm, somewhere near 2 and ¼ miles long and ¼ to ¾ miles wide.

The route continued on the other side of the fjord leading into Beistad Sundet, which was a sort of river or narrow lake that carried runoff water from the inland mountains to the fjord. Sometimes there were deliveries into the sundet, but more often than not, the turn around point was Malm, the biggest drop-off point of all.

To meet their needs, smaller farms in all these areas reached agreements with the larger farms for the delivery of supplies or brought their wagons to the dock to save the delivery expense. Once a contract was established, there was little chance it would be supplanted by an interloper. So first the merchant, and eventually Ole, faced no competition, and there were few days when their boat was not en route to purchase or deliver the necessities of life for the rural communities they serviced. The gulfstream that warmed the western coast of Norway ensured ports would remain open the year round.

One of the farmers who contracted with Ole was Johan Benjamin, owner of Nord Rones Farm. Two brothers farmed Mitra and Sor Rones. Johan became Ole's father-in-law when Ole married his youngest daughter, Thale Margarete. She had become Johan's only daughter when her sister died at age 8, just before Thale was born. So like his father and grandfather, Ole, too, became the husband of a farm owner's daughter—not a cotter, but a "logerende," newlyweds who live as lodgers, often with parents, until they get their own home.

By the time he could afford to propose to Thale, Ole was over 30 years old; she was 23. It was agreed that even though her parents were retired, the couple would live at Rones Farm. In return for food and lodging for his family, Ole, who was now the boat's owner, agreed to provide market goods for the farm at his cost.

When Johan retired, his only, and therefore oldest son, Torberg, inherited the farm by law. That law also specified that, in return for the farm, Torberg would guarantee to care for his parents for life. This inheritance had occurred just before Michael was born.

The farm was good land, but because it had been many times divided, there was not much of it—only twenty-one acres, which produced barley, oats and potatoes. Even with a productive garden, it was only a notch above subsistence living for Torber, his wife, their 4-year-old daughter and 1-year-old fraternal twins, his parents, the Elnans and 3 servant girls.

A couple dozen sheep provided meat and wool for clothing; a half dozen cows provided milk, butter, cheese, beef and leather hide; a lone goat also provided milk and brown cheese; a pair of hogs provided pork and hide; two horses turned the land over and sometimes provided transportation.

Breakfast, Michael recalled, was served at 6:00 A.M., and usually consisted of flatbread, "gammelost" (old cheese), "primost" (brown goat cheese) and whey soup. Lunch was served at 10:00 A.M. and consisted of barley meal porridge with milk. The "middag" (afternoon) meal at 4:00 P.M. was Michael's favorite. Typically, this was the biggest meal of the day and consisted of herring soup, a meat dish like side pork or other pork or maybe sausage, vegetables in season, potatoes, peas or cabbage which was often creamed or boiled, and, of course, flatbread. Churned butter made the boiled potatoes and thin, crisp bread his favorite. If his mother would let him, he could make them his entire meal. The last meal of the day, at 8:00 P.M., was the same as lunch—barley meal porridge with milk.

Michael's reverie was interrupted by Emma's voice. "Michael, lunch is on the table." The fragrant smells from the kitchen brought him to his feet, however slowly, and he suddenly realized how hungry he was after thinking about all that food. That was unusual now. Most days he had a limited interest in food and ate only so Emma would not be suspicious.

He helped himself to the "labskaus," cut and buttered a slice of Emma's fresh bread and took a sip of milk, kept cool in their new icebox. The warm dish of chocolate pudding with a little milk would finish out his meal. Ja, this was definitely better eating than in Norway.

As he looked across the table, Emma's pale blue eyes fixed on his and she asked, "Is something wrong with the food?"

"No, no," he replied. "I was just dozing a little and remembered sitting by my grandmother's table when I was about six."

"Was her food better than mine?"

"No, no, in fact I was thinking how much better this lunch was than what I grew up eating. The food was always good, but nobody can cook as good as you, my Emma."

She couldn't hide her smile of pleasure, but still she chastened. "Well, eat then. It's getting cold."

He took a large forkful of the potatoes and bit off a chunk of the bread and butter, washing it down with a good swallow of milk before he continued. "While you were upstairs, I was out to look at our garden earlier, and I remembered when I was very young, I got my first experience in gardening by helping my grampa Benjamin in his garden on Nord Rones. I remember I asked him about all the different plants. If he knew—and he usually did—he told me where they came from, how to harvest seeds for growing next year and when and how they were planted. I learned a lot those days."

Between bites, he told Emma of how his grampa had also taken him into the house and took down the "calendar stick" hanging on the wall. "He showed me the summer side and the winter side and explained all the little carvings. Each small groove along the bottom of the stick, he said, represented a day. Above the little notches were carved figures that told about when to plant and harvest, as well as identify exactly when the Christian festivals, feasts and celebrations took place. It even showed the day for bringing animals down from the summer farm and when to begin shearing the sheep. Did your parents have a calendar stick in your house in Starbuck?"

"Not that I can recall, but then days and seasons there would be different than over in Norway. Knowing my father's need to do things right, I expect when he lived in Norway, he, too, might have had one."

"Anyway, out in the garden, I remembered asking Grampa about potatoes—my favorite, as you know." He took another bite of the labskaus as if to reinforce his words. "He was very patient with me and told me when they should be planted and how. He told me how he gauged the growth of the potatoes by the size and height of the plant. That knowledge told him when to harvest each plant. All summer long and into the fall, he took me out to look at the plants, until he said it was time to dig. I have never forgotten those lessons."

Michael cleaned off his plate, wiping up the last of the gravy with the last bite of bread. Then he continued. "After the harvest was over and the potatoes were stored in sacks in the root cellar, he told me what his father, my great grampa, Torberg Danielsen, from Skevik farm, had told him about potatoes when he was about my age.

"When potatoes first came to Norway in the 1700s, no one would plant them, even though food was very scarce. For hundreds of years they had raised grain, which grew on top of the ground. That was all right. However, potatoes grew underneath the ground, and that's where the trolls lived, so it was difficult to convince people about the benefits of the potato. The Norwegian people in that time were very superstitious and believed that growing potatoes would surely make the trolls angry, and they in turn might put bad things in the potatoes to make you sick, or do other tricks to make awful things happen on their farm."

With an, "Oh, such nonsense," Emma began to clear the dinner plates from the table and pour fresh coffee to go with their pudding. Sometimes on special occasions, she whipped cream for the topping, but today, they made do with a little milk.

When she was settled again, Michael continued. "Grampa Benjamin said that it wasn't until a very well known and respected preacher got into his pulpit and took up the cause of the potato in his sermons that things changed. Back in those days, if the "Preston," the Pastor, said it was OK, then, in fact, God must approve and would bless their crops. Once God blessed the potatoes, they were safe from the trolls. Grampa believed that it was very important for farmers to have God's blessing. In fact, in the old days, long, long ago, when people believed in many gods, he told me a craftsman would create a beautiful, ornately carved cart. Small images of all the various gods were also carved and put in the cart. The cart would then be driven through all of the farmers' fields, so the gods could bless each acre. I remember how proud I felt to have Grampa tell me all these important things, and I remembered them well."

"Did your grandfather really believe in these trolls? I never heard such foolish talk in our house."

"You know, Emma, to this day I really don't know, but he knew a lot of stuff about them. I remember I asked Grampa if he knew any more stories about trolls. He motioned to the bench sitting in the shade of the house, and we sat there while he smoked his pipe and talked."

"Eat some pudding before the trolls come and get it," Emma teased.

"Trolls, he told me, are huge and grotesque, and may only have a single eye in the middle of their forehead, and very often have three heads. They are terribly strong, but are also stupid and are easily tricked by a quick-witted person. They hate the sounds of church bells, and they have a liking for eating human flesh. Their homeland was the dark, ice-covered land of Trollebotn, the huge frozen bay which connected Greenland to north of Scandinavia."

"Uffda, Michael, I've never heard such nonsense."

"Do they really eat people, I had asked him? He told me that depended on whether they were real or just something a grown-up made up to scare children. I told him I thought they were made up, because I was 6 and I'd never seen one."

"Oh such a thing to discuss with a child, Michael. I'm not sure I can sit still for anymore of this."

"Wait now, don't go, I'm just getting to the best part. I asked my grampa to tell me more scary stuff, and he told me that there are, of course, the *nisse*, who were tiny little mischief-makers. They are related to the trolls, but they were not so dangerous. They are the ones who actually guard our houses and barns and will defend our farms against evildoers. They are very small, but very, very strong for their size. Then there are also *gaardvords*, who are giant nisse. They are so big they can rest their elbows on the roof of the house. They chase the bigger trolls away.

"Oh, Emma, I remember I was so excited and begged Grampa to tell me more. Then, I told him that night, when it is dark, I'd tell mama and scare her. Oh, then he got upset, and he told me firmly that I'd do no such thing and get him into big trouble. These stories were just for me and not to talk of them to my mother. I agreed and said, 'OK, Grampa, but tell me more,' and that's when I learned about the *huldre*. I didn't understand him, so I asked, 'Hul what?'

"He repeated, 'hull drah,' and said they live up in the mountains or the hills. They sometimes live in the cellars of the *seter*, the summer farms. They are much more like us than the trolls or the nisse or the gaardvords. They are often mistaken for men, and sometimes they steal Norwegian girls away and marry them, especially those who are left alone in the mountain seters to tend the animals. Sometimes they try to fool them into sharing some dangerous food or drink. At my age, I knew I had never seen any of these things, but wondered with all his years if he'd ever seen any huldre. To kind of answer your question about whether he really believed in trolls, I remember he got a very serious look on his face when I asked if he'd ever seen one. He told me he was over 70 years old, and he couldn't say that he had. Then he said we'd better get back to work before my grandma Marit came out and chased us back into the garden with her broom. Laughing, he said that maybe tomorrow he'd tell me about witches."

"Ja, his wife should have chased him with a broom and then washed his mouth out with lye soap for telling such foolishness to a young boy. If you ever tell these stories to our grandchildren, you're going to be in big trouble."

With that, Emma cleared the table and began washing their dishes in the sink. Mischievously, Michael got up quietly from the table, snuck up behind Emma, grabbed her shoulders and said, "Huldre's got you!"

She jumped a little and then laughing, splashed dishwater in his face. Grabbing a towel, he wiped it off with a grin and then began drying the dishes.

Later, back at the table, fresh coffee in hand and sugar lumps at the ready, he continued his musing from where he'd left off.

The fall in Norway, he recalled, was his favorite time of year. There were berries for picking and honey gleaned from abandoned combs. A real treat was thin, buttered pancakes with fresh lingonberries and syrup. While on occasion there were fresh fish to replace the dried meats, autumn was the time for slaughter and the only time of the year when there was fresh meat and "pulsa," sausage made from blood. They tasted so very good, and often gravy was made to put on his potatoes, instead of butter, or gravy along with butter if he could get by with it.

Next to the house was a place for storage, where salted or dried fish and dried meat hung from the rafters. Grains and flour were also stored here, so the building was raised off the ground and rested on stones with a sizable gap between the steps and the threshold—all of this to keep out mice and rats. The woman of the house had the only key. The law said if a husband took it, got into storage and ate any goods, that would be the grounds for divorce. By the same token, the main house had one cupboard that housed the Bible, money and the alcohol. The husband, only, had that key.

The working day, he recalled, was a long one, divided up so the horses and workers could rest. The men would always rest after a meal, sometimes including a short nap before they returned to their work. So a rhythm was established of work, food, rest, and then work again. That was life on the farm, always a job to be done, always people to be fed, always a need for rest.

Michael decided it was now time for just that, a short nap. With Emma gone to the store, he lay down on their sofa and covered himself with one of Emma's many knitted afghans. As he was resting, he recalled how quickly the next few years of his life had gone by and how little he remembered of those years.

By the time he was 9 years of age, two sisters, Othilde Massine, called Hilde, age 5, and Mette Marie, known as Mattie, age 2, had been added to the Elnan family. He remembered how one day he had heard his mother talking to her brother, Torberg. They were talking very quietly, but Michael heard Uncle Torberg explain to his mother that it was getting harder and harder to make ends meet, that there were just too many people to feed. His mother was crying, but he heard her say she would talk to Ole and they would look for another place. That night Michael went to bed with a heavy heart. He worried what would happen to his family. Where would they go? This was the only home he knew. Why was Uncle Torberg so mean?

The next day after breakfast, his mother was again talking, this time with her mother. When she began to cry again, Michael thought his heart would break and tears started to roll down his cheeks. He knew what they were talking about. When Gramma Marit put her arms around his mother and hugged her, Michael wanted to run into their arms, too, but he turned his head away, hid his face with his tears and stayed quietly in his place.

Later that afternoon, when the main meal was over and the dishes washed and put in the cupboard shelves, his mother, with a smile on her face now, took his hand. Putting on her bonnet and picking up Mattie, she told Michael to hold Hilde's hand and they would walk down through the field to the water. There was a good chance, she said, that their father would be coming home tonight. When they reached the dock, they took off their shoes and socks and dangled their feet in the water. Mattie's legs were too short, so every now and then his mother would hold her tight and lower her so her little feet dangled in the water, too. She would kick and giggle as the water splashed them all. The sun was shining and the sky was blue. Michael thought this must be the most glorious place in the whole world; he didn't want to leave.

After a little while, his mother pointed straight ahead, across the water, to the land on the other side and said, "You can't quite see the farms from here, but over there are the farms where my grampa Torberg Danielsen and gramma Marit Olsdatter lived and where my father, your grampa Benjamin, was born and raised."

Her grampa, she said, had come from a farm called Skevik and Gramma from a farm called Saugestad, but that was a long time ago. Then she added that way, way over there, farther than you can see from here, was where her grampa Torberg's father and mother were from. Great grampa was Daniel

Torgersen and his farm was called Ressem. Great gramma was named Beret Larsdatter and her farm was called Ystmark.

Then turning and pointing to the north, she explained that her mother, their grandmother Marit, had lived just up the road on a farm called Granhus. Michael listened carefully and did his best to remember all the names and places. He looked back across the water and wondered if maybe they would live way over there. It seemed so far.

Ole did not come that day or the next. When he did come, the Elnans all ran down to meet him. There was much hugging and laughing, but then solemnly, Michael's mother told Michael to take his sisters up to the house. She and their father had something to talk about, but would be along shortly. When Michael looked back, his father was hugging his mother and she looked like she was crying again. When they came in the house, however, they were holding hands and laughing. Everything must be all right, he figured, and he smiled, too.

Next morning, Ole took off early, walking north on the wagon trail toward Bartnes. Solberg Church, the place where Michael was baptized, was there, and Michael wondered if his father was going there to pray.

It was close to dark before he returned. He hugged Thale first, and then with a smile, hugged each one of them in turn. Michael heard him quietly say to his mother, "It is done." Her smile was so bright it lit up the whole room.

The next morning after breakfast, Michael's mother took him and his sisters aside and told them that the family would not be living here much longer, as their father had found them a house of their own. She explained it was not far away, in fact it was just a little over a kilometer up the wagon route. They could still come back to visit Gramma and Grampa and, of course, would see them in church on Sundays.

What the children did not know was their gramma Marit, had made the preliminary arrangements with her brother, Kristofer Granhus, their mama's uncle. Their father Ole, yesterday, had sealed the deal by offering the Granhus family goods with no mark up or delivery cost.

Michael's mind raced, so he never really napped, and soon Emma interrupted his thoughts when she returned from her trip downtown. Before she put the groceries away, she started a fresh afternoon pot of coffee. He must start to write these things down tomorrow. But that didn't happen, nor did he write the next day, or the next.

After the garden goods were in and the canning was all done, fall turned into winter and snow soon covered the harvested field to the west of the Glasoe house. Prices stayed stable, and it had been a year to make a little profit for the Ellisons on the homestead—one of the first since Michael and Emma had left.

Noonan, like many other small towns all over the United States in the 20s, had struggled to survive. Those had been equally difficult years for the prairie farmers, as World War I destroyed the European grain markets. Farmers depended on the export market for profit, and lower grain sales meant small town businesses also suffered when the farmers had little or nothing to spend. The stock market crash found even the average, hard-working Americans in breadlines without enough money for food.

Then came the terrible dust bowl years of the thirties. In those years, even if there had been a market for grain, there had been no grain to sell. Farms dried up and some were abandoned. Small town businesses operated on a limited margin or closed up. Jobs disappeared. No one had money to do any hiring. The economy shriveled up like parched prairie fields.

Michael and Emma had said goodbye to several of their sons who headed west, as far as the state of Washington, to find jobs. Some of the large cities there thrived, building ships and manufacturing arms. The population grew and homes were needed. *Thank God*, Michael often thought to himself, *working with him, his boys had acquired carpentry skills.*

One of the last to leave was Almer, who had just recently left his family behind and set out for Seattle, where his brothers had earlier found employment. Brother Ole had done the same thing, and his wife was with her family over in Bowbells. Even some of the grandchildren headed west to find work.

While the boys never wrote to say how they were doing, in early December that year, Michael and Emma received a nice greeting from their granddaughter Ellen Roness. She told them a little about where she lived, inquired into their health, asked her grampa about his writing and wished them a merry Christmas. They were both very touched by her thoughtfulness.

Michael felt his health slowly deteriorating as the winter stretched on. Emma, too, continued having health problems, but never let on that she was not 100% herself. She no longer performed her community nursing chores as she had done for so many years, starting out as a young midwife. Now, Michael noticed, she sat down to rest more often than in the past. When he inquired about her health, she said she was fine, just slowing down a little.

He would reply, "Me, too, I guess."

He, himself, spent more time in his room reading and, on a few days, not even getting up for meals. As he had put it honestly in his letter, *one day we are up and around and the next maybe in bed.* Those days made him feel guilty, because Emma had to bring him his meals, when she wasn't feeling good herself. So most days, he struggled to be up, dressed and at the kitchen table. He thought every day about writing, but just could not summon the energy, and so he merely continued to reminisce. That activity was the one bright spot in a world grown gloomy.

Chapter Three

Even as the world around him began moving into a springtime mode after a long and dark winter, Michael's memories moved across his mind from one of the most difficult periods of his young life to one of the happiest.

The Elnan's house was across a wagon road from the Granhus home. It was smaller than Grampa Benjamin's house, but with less people, it seemed bigger. For a short time, Michael recalled that he had shared his upstairs bedroom with his sisters and later his new brother, Edward Gustinius, born in 1874.

There was no building for animals, so they kept none. They maintained a small garden, but only as big as Thale, with Hilde's help, could manage. Ole would bring home food supplies from the market, but if he was delayed, Thale purchased food from her aunt and uncle.

At around age nine, Michael recalled sadly receiving the news that would turn his life into a bad dream. Even after all these years, remembering the pain of separation and the awful loneliness that filled his heart was as real as if it had been yesterday.

He had not been around when his father and mother had a long discussion about him going to work. His mother pleaded for Ole to wait a few years, but, remembering his own youth, he was adamant that all boys his age go to work. His brother, Edward, had no children and needed someone to care for his cattle. Michael would have a good home. Her protests were futile.

Separated from his beloved mother and being away from home and family, this was his life over three long and lonely years. He had already poured out that sorrowful tale in the letter to his children. It had ended as abruptly as it had begun, and now he could relegate it to his past. There was no need to remember it ever again, and his children and grandchildren could use that story as a measuring stick to gauge the joy or sadness of their growing up years. None of his children had ever had to be sent off to work, and he ventured their children would escape that loneliness, too.

At Christmas time in 1875, his father surprised the family by announcing that he was giving up sailing and was going to sell his boat. At first they all laughed and thought that was a fine joke, but Ole was serious. He said he thought it was time that they had a home for themselves, where they could all be together. When the snow was gone and before he sold the boat, he would take time off to look for a farm. He knew many farmers in the area and believed he could ask them what was available. It would not be big, he cautioned, but it would be theirs. That was a happy Christmas, but they told no one else.

Again, the children did not know that their parents had been encouraged to move. Uncle Kristofer, who was now 70 years old, was going to retire and planned to move into the karhus. He thought there was not room for two families.

During the winter, Michael remembered, Ole sold his boat, got a good price and made his first purchase—a wagon and a team of horses. In the early spring of 1876, he showed up one day at his brother's farm and announced he was taking Michael along to pick out a good farm, and he would not be bringing him back. The smile that erupted on Michael's face stayed there the whole day.

As they drove toward home, Michael was allowed to name the horses. The male horse he named Askr, the first man of the earth, and the female he called Embla, the first woman. His father had said to him that those were fine names.

At age 10, going on 11, Michael felt very grown up assisting his father with such an important undertaking as picking out the right piece of property to farm. It almost, but not quite, made up for those years of isolation. When asked, he suggested to his father that the best farm would be a flat place in a valley, where hay for animals, Michael's specialty, would be abundant. They would also need some land for tilling and, hopefully, an out building or two to shelter the animals that they should buy before winter.

Ole nodded and said that with three children and another on the way, it was very important also to find a good house that would accommodate the growing family. Michael agreed. Ole added, of course, they would hope for at least five acres of land for tilling.

Together, they traveled farther away from their current home than Michael had ever been, about 20 or more kilometers north, his father had said. The land his father was considering was a small Glasè farm that had once been part of a very large single farm, but over time had been split up into four large farms and five smaller ones. They were going to look at one of the five. Actually, his father had already seen it as he looked for farmland on one of his last trips around his delivery route.

From the farmer who lived next door, they learned the derivation of the Glasè name which, he said, was at least a thousand years old and was transferred to the farm from the nearby lake; Glasè meant simply, "the glittering, clear lake." The farm was first registered in about 1430 and was then spelled "Gladesio."

Michael thought the choice was good, as it was obvious that hay would be available by fall. The house was bigger than the one they had now. It was two stories high and had four small bedrooms upstairs. Each one had a window so you could see almost the whole valley. Michael thought his mother would like the big kitchen. Surprisingly, the house had acquired very little dust, and only a few cobwebs would need to be broomed down.

However, there was no place to house the animals they would purchase. Before winter, a barn would have to be constructed and a fence built as a corral. The former tenant had used the barn on the home farm, owned by his oldest brother. Now, he was gone to America, so a purchase agreement was reached with that brother.

It was fun to watch his father bargain with the farmer. Just when it appeared a purchase price had been agreed on, his father said, "I notice you have some nice fir trees on your property. Before I agree to your price, I want you to throw in enough timberland for us to cut down trees and build a barn. We will not be wasteful."

The farmer hesitated just a little and said, "Agreed, if you take those along the edge of my field. Then I will pull the stumps and create a little more tillable land for me. In fact, as I think about it, take as much as you want."

They shook hands, and 2,800 kroner changed hands. Michael had never seen so much money, but after counting off the bills, it looked like his father put more back in his purse than he'd given the farmer. The Elnans finally had their own home.

On the way home, Ole talked sadly about his father and mother and the harsh lives they had lived. How they would have loved to do what he had just done—buy their own farm.

"You're named after your Grampa, Michael. That's the way things have always been in Norway. When you get married, you'll name your first son after me. If you have a girl, you will name her after your mother." When he talked about marriage and babies, Michael giggled and his father grinned.

Ole also told him that his mother's name had been Olava, and that's why, as a young man, he chose to call himself Ole, even though his baptismal name had been Magnus. He didn't know where the name Magnus came from, as his grandfather's name had been Amund. He guessed later on that his parents didn't want him to bear the name of a cotter. He was the youngest child, just as his father Mikal had been. With older brothers, neither of them was eligible to inherit their father's farm.

Then he smiled and said, "My grandfather, Amund Johnsen, had no land to give anyway. He was a blacksmith by trade, and as I was told, a very good one, too, but all his life he suffered from the degrading title of cotter. My grandmother's name was Gunhild, and she was born and raised on a farm called Rennan. She had three brothers and two sisters. Her oldest brother gave the newlyweds a cottage to live in, in return for Amund's services.

As Michael listened carefully, he went on. "My father, Mikal, was also the youngest, and the best he could do was to also become a cotter, too."

Michael knit his brows and asked, "What's a cotter?"

His father patiently explained that in Norway, the terms cotter and husmann meant the same thing. As the number of people in Norway grew, the amount of land that could be farmed stayed the same. Some young men, if they were the oldest son, inherited their father's farm, and some young couples were able to purchase a farm, but not many. Those who could not had no choice but to become cotters or husmenn.

"Many were children, like your grampa, Mikal, who were by birth ineligible to inherit a farm, so they would find another farmer to work for. In return, the farmer would rent them a small house and pay them only a little money for working in the fields and sometimes, harvesting trees for building. Your grandfather was hired to cut down trees and trim them into logs that could be used to make houses or other buildings."

His father was silent for a while and then continued, with what Michael felt was a touch of sadness is his voice. "Life was hard for my father, because he and your grandmother had very little, and had to share it with me and my two older brothers and sisters. When my brothers turned 10 years, they also went to work and received a little pay. Times were better then because we had more money. When I turned 10, I went to work, too. My job was to work with my father, so I learned to cut down trees, make logs and build things. It was a hard job, but I learned a lot."

Michael had always been curious as to how his father became a seaman, and now he had the chance to ask him. Ole replied immediately, "Being a cotter was nothing but work from sun up to sun down for my father and my grandfather. When I became old enough, it was to be the same for me. There was no time for anything else. There was also no future; there was no land to inherit. When I grew up in Elnan, I could see boats out on Beistad Fjord and thought, that's what I want to do. They were so beautiful and moved so elegantly through the blue water. One day I asked my father about them. With a lot of pride, he explained that since the time of our ancestors, the adventurous Vikings, the words Viking and sailor have been synonymous; the word Viking literally means *men of the bays*. The ships with sails are called jaekt boats. Jaekt boats are of different sizes. They are made of fir, like the trees we'll be cutting down and trimming into logs. The larger the boat, the more hands it takes to sail it. Goods are stored in the hold, which increases in depth in ratio to the length of the boat, which is sometimes up to 60 feet. Some smaller ones are used as fishing boats. Jaekt boats are the lifelines of the rural communities.

"I asked my father once if he wished he was a seaman, and he looked at me, and in the most wistful voice I've ever heard, said to me, 'Every day, Ole, every day.' I knew then, it was in my blood.

"After my confirmation, when I was fifteen years old, I went into the navy and served for two years. It was almost like a *hoyskole* education. Hoyskoles are sort of trade schools where you go after you finish regular school, that is, if your parents are wealthy and can afford to send you away. Most of them are in Oslo or Bergen, so if you didn't live there, you also had to pay room and board.

"I learned many things about sailing that would help me when I finished my tour of duty. My job was to help the sailor who made repairs on the boats. It was hard work, but not as bad as some of the other chores. I was glad the day I threw my duffel over my shoulder and walked from Steinkjer back home to Elnan.

"I lived at home and did odd jobs carpentering for a little while, and that brought in extra money for my parents. One day my father asked me to go down to the dock to pick up the supplies the jaekt boat was delivering to the farmer he worked for. We unloaded bags, barrels and boxes, all labeled *West Elnan Farm*. Then the captain helped me load the goods on the wagon. I had a list of what was coming and checked the items off.

"When we were done, we sat down to rest a bit. He lit up his old pipe, and

I gave him a purse of money that the farmer had entrusted to me. As he counted it, he looked at me and said, 'You know, I'm getting older every day. I need a good strong lad to help me load and unload. I notice you are strong and a hard worker, would you like to come work with me?'

"I remember how surprised he looked when I answered immediately, 'Can you pick me up on the way back? I need time to tell my mother and father.'

"Puffing on his pipe, he smiled and answered, 'I'll see you right here in two days. Just watch for my sail.'

"When I told your Gramma Amundson I was going to be a sailor who brought supplies to the rich farmers, she smiled a big smile, hugged me and said, 'You be a good one, Ole.' I think she was very relieved that I would not have to be a cotter.

"When I told my father, he asked how much I was to be paid. I had been so excited I forgot to ask. My father said, 'Well, when the boat comes back, before you get on it, you ask him what you are to be paid. The captain is a businessman, so I'm sure he'll not offer you a wage, but ask what you think you're worth. You tell him you have worked hard since you were ten years old, and you served in the navy for two years making repairs on the ship. Tell him how much the farmers around here pay you now to do odd carpentering jobs, and tell him you need double that. Also, tell him you need an advance, so you can find a place to stay and have something to eat.'

"Two days later, after saying goodbye to my family, I stood on the dock as the boat came in. I did just as my father had told me, and the captain responded just as my father had said he would. I told him in the strongest voice I could muster exactly what my father had said. He took his pipe out of mouth, smiled, stretched out his hand and said, 'Agreed. Now let's be on our way.'

"The first evening, the weather was pleasant, so the captain pulled the boat in toward shore and anchored for the night. He brought out homemade biscuits, buttered by some farmer's wife he said. He also had some dried meat and he gave me a bottle of home brewed beer. We could never afford beer in our home and there was not time to make any. I once saw my father drink a bottle when we were invited to the farmer's house for Christmas. It was very strong for me, but it helped the food go down. I saved the bottle and the stopper to put water in the next day.

"We slept in the hold of the boat on folded canvas that was used to cover goods to keep them dry. The captain gave me an old worn quilt to keep me warm. It smelled musty, and I was glad it was dark so that I could not see how dirty it must be. The next day we were off to Trondheim."

Michael was very proud of his father when he related to him how he eventually became the captain of the boat. Over the years as the boat needed repair, the captain depended on his skill with wood to do the job. In ten years, almost every board on the boat was replaced, and it was constantly kept as tight and trim and seaworthy as the day he first got on it.

Ole laughed when Michael asked him where he got the money to buy the jaekt boat. He told him, "After sleeping in the hold more days than in a bed, eating food packed by farmer's wives, I saved up almost everything I earned.

"Also, by then, to make sure I wouldn't go somewhere else to work, the captain gave me a small percentage of the mark up of goods from suppliers to the farmers. I also learned how to be a good bargainer, and when the captain said he was going to sell his boat and rest his weary bones, I asked, 'How much for the boat?' He gave me a price—I offered less. His price came a little lower and mine a little higher, and so we kept on until we agreed. We both knew what the boat was worth, and what it would have brought if I hadn't kept repairing it."

Slapping his knee, Ole had exclaimed, "I got it for quite a bit less than half the price of a new one. I did all right, Michael, I did all right." Then he took a long draw on his pipe.

Memories of that long-ago life at Glasè were positive. Michael smiled to himself as he recalled that the years there had been the best ever. His mother was so thrilled to have a home that they actually owned. Now when they made money, they put it in their own cupboard.

Michael sometimes thought his mother had worked too hard to make sure the dream never ended, and that her labors might have contributed to her early death. In memory of her and those wonderful days, he adopted that farm name when he left Glasè for America. He discovered early on that other immigrants from Glasè, who had settled in Minnesota, had added an "o" to the name, so he felt it must be the right thing to do. The final "e" then became silent. Instead of being pronounced "glas-ay," it was pronounced "glas-o."

The first months at Glasè had been spent cutting down the tall pines, stripping their branches and hauling them home, where he learned from his father how to square them off, measure them, notch the edge and put them up, pegging them one by one. It was hard work, from sun up to sun down, and Michael soon discovered and was pleased by what a hard worker his father was. Even though his father never said anything, Michael knew the admiration was mutual

They stopped only long enough to cut, bale and haul the hay home. There had been no time to till ground for oats or barley, so they had to purchase them. Before the snow fell, the roof was on, the cattle were moved down from the field, the hay was in the loft and Michael had a new little sister, Lotte Gurina, later known as Lottie.

Lottie's birth that first year at Glasè came at a difficult time for Thale, what with moving and getting settled while carrying a baby. However, the birth had been a time of celebration for the family in their new home. One of the older Glasè neighbors was a midwife and was available as needed. Michael ran to her home when the time was right. He didn't dare stop to put a saddle on the horse or hitch him to the wagon, but, as it turned out, there was plenty of time.

That first Christmas was a happy time for Michael, knowing he would stay home after it was over. Not only did he not have to leave, but he also knew that he was needed on the farm and would be a big help there. When he was older, he read a poem that described his remembrance of that happy celebration, "Jul der Hjemme." He committed it to memory.

Before Lottie was born, Michael had received permission to stay up and spend a late evening with his mother sitting at the kitchen table. Those were cherished moments for him. Everyone else had already gone to bed and was sleeping soundly. In a hushed voice, Michael expressed his concern that they must be watchful for the trolls who might steal into their home and take the baby, leaving a "changeling" in its place. He offered, "Mama, if you want, I will sleep in the baby's room. And if I hear any strange noise, I will wake up and run to your room and warn you."

Brushing the hair back from his eyes, she gently replied, "Your father and I will have the baby with us when it is first born, and believe me, we will be watchful for any troll trickery. Where did you get this idea? Surely it wasn't in catechism."

"No, Mama, I heard this from Martinius. Sometimes when he got really angry with me, he said I must be a changeling. I didn't know what that meant until we had a lesson on trolls. Then I learned that a changeling is a baby from the troll world that is exchanged for a real baby. The switch is made when no one is watching the baby, usually in the middle of the night. After the exchange, you know it's a troll and not your real baby because it cries all the time, it doesn't talk and it gets really ugly when it gets older. You can protect the baby from the trolls if you get it baptized right away. Maybe, Mama, we could baptize the baby in our stream as soon as it's born."

She tousled his hair playfully, and then hugging him said, "First of all, Michael, you're not a changeling. You were a very good baby, and you're now a handsome young man."

"I knew that I wasn't, Mama, because I could talk. But it was still scary, and I didn't dare stand up to Martinius."

"Secondly," she went on, "the baby will sleep in our room, close to your father and me. No troll, if there ever were such a creature, would dare get close to your father. And yes, my son, we will baptize the baby as soon as we can, but not in the stream. We will take the baby to the Presten. You are so sweet, and I love you very much for your concern and bravery."

Comforted and proud, Michael went to bed and slept peacefully. Of course, the little baby girl came and was protected and was baptized to ensure her place in Heaven before anything bad should happen to her.

Life at Glasè continued to be hard work for the parents, Michael and the other older children. Ole was forty-four years old and Thale was thirty-two when they began life on their own land. Everybody, with the exception of the baby and the toddlers, had a job to do.

Trees needed cutting, sawing and shaping, as there were other outbuildings to be put up and fences to be built around the animals compound so they could be out when the weather permitted. Wood for the fireplace was a constant need. There were also fields to plow, sow and harvest; barns needed to be cleaned; the animals had to be tended—including the team of horses, two milk cows, goats for cheese and sheep for wool, a pair of pigs and a few chickens; gardens needed planting, tending, harvest, and storage, including canning; cheese had to be made, butter churned and eggs picked.

Slaughter time came once each year. It was not uncommon, Michael recalled, for the children to become fond of the smaller animals. Though discouraged, it was a hard practice to prevent and, therefore, slaughter was a cruel practice the young ones neither understood nor appreciated. As they grew older, they learned not to make such attachments, so they no longer got sick at heart about eating a "pet."

It was work, from dawn until dark, but it was for their own family, not somebody else's benefit, so it was satisfying to work hard and go to sleep knowing that they controlled their own destiny. Michael became convinced that he, too, would one day have his own farm.

School was just down the road, a little less than a mile from his house. Like most Norwegian boys, he would continue his lessons until he was confirmed. Without the dreaded Martinius, school was a much more pleasant experience for him. He worked hard and made good grades, which greatly pleased his parents. He would find books wherever he could and bring them home to read in the evenings. If he could go to school after age fifteen, he would need to go quite far away to the hoyskole. He knew he was needed too much on the farm for that and the cost was too high, so it was never considered, let alone discussed.

The family continued to grow at Glasè, as Ole and Thale produced another daughter, Trine Ovidia, called Trina, and then another brother for Michael and Edward, Otto Thoralf. As Edward grew older, he tended the herd up near the little lake above the farm where the grass was green and lush. After milking in the morning, he and a pair of dogs would drive them up the slope, and in late afternoon back to the farm for another milking.

There was little diversion from the routine; days, weeks, months, seasons and years passed without change. More land was cleared, plowed and seeded; a few more animals were born. As Michael completed school, he took on more and more responsibility. His father was still strong and healthy, but was more at home on the sea than on land. Still they did well, and their acreage and livestock numbers grew.

From his school lessons and the other children at Glasè Farms, Michael learned that far across the Atlantic was a huge new country called America. This young nation was pushing its borders thousands of miles from its east coast to the west. In 1862, something called "The Railroad Land Grants Program" was initiated. It encouraged men with a lot of money to hire crews and lay steel track toward the west. Iron-wheeled vehicles, powered by steam engines traveling on the rails, would then bring people to settle the new land along with the goods necessary to help them survive and prosper. The young country's government gave away 128 million acres of its land to build these railroads between 1862 and 1871.

The new teacher, a woman named Agnes, also taught them that in 1863, to reach its goal of populating the entire nation, the government in America took additional action which greatly increased the odds of success for the railroad builders; it passed the "Homestead Act," which allowed anyone to file for what the Americans called a "homestead," one quarter-section of government surveyed land—160 acres—free. The land was yours at the end of five years if you had built a house on it, lived there, dug a well, tilled 10 acres and fenced a specified amount.

A farm that big just boggled young Michael's mind. Doing in America what they were doing at Glasè would earn them 160 acres of free land. He read what he could about America and talked to anyone he met who knew about it.

Michael remembered first hearing about this country in his catechism class. He knew that the first people to go there from Norway were a small group of religious dissenters. Way back in 1825, before he was born, the dissenters set sail on the sloop Restoration out of Stavanger, bound for a place called New York City. They were called "Liberals," because they opposed not only an imposed language change, but also the Danish imposed monarchy and the state church as well.

Also, in school, he had learned more about what his father had told him about people like his grampa and great grampa—the Norwegian cotters. Martinius had told the class about the problem in Norway of too many people and not enough land. For example, he had cited that in the 1801 census, Nord Trondelag County, where they lived, had 42,000 inhabitants. Now that number had almost doubled, but tillable land area remained the same. There was no future here for young people.

So news of those free 160 acres had reached young Norwegians who were desperate for land to till and a home to live in. Local newspapers advertised for "immigrants" who would leave Norway and other European countries and come to America and file homestead claims.

Every year more and more Norwegians from various towns, valleys and fjords were leaving Norway and sailing to America. Once they arrived, they maintained contact with each other in their new country through regional societies that published newsletters and held periodic reunions. They also sent information back to their friends and families in Norway.

The settlements Michael studied most began in a state called Wisconsin, both on farms and in the forest lands. As the railroad progressed, more people came and settled, and the frontier pushed west to Minnesota and was now moving into Dakota.

He remembered that the young Glasè couple, who owned the farm his father bought, had immigrated to America. From his brother and other Glasè family members he learned that several more of their family members had immigrated as a group to a settlement called Northfield, in a state called Minnesota.

When in Steinkjer, he learned that not far to the west, farm families and quite a few single people from the Stod and Ongdalen area had also immigrated to Minnesota. A large group of them settled along a lake in what was called White Bear Township, in Pope County, Minnesota. "County" was like the Norwegian "fylke," so Pope was like Nord Trondelag.

Thinking now, in retrospect, Michael smiled at the fact that as he was thinking of going to America, his future father-in-law, a farmer named Anton Holte, had already immigrated from Stod in 1858, settling first in Minnesota at Fillmore County. Anton's future wife, Ellen Wollan, emigrated from Ongdalen, not far from Stod, arriving in the Fillmore County settlement in 1860. The two were married in 1867 and moved to the White Bear Township settlement Michael had read about. When he was only seven years old, his future wife, Emma, was born there. *Thank God from whom all blessings flow*, he thought.

As the months went by, the young Michael thought more and more about his future, with strong consideration of America and the inviting attraction of those free 160 acre homesteads. He reasoned that his father was still a fairly young man and would probably live on the Glasè Farm for a long time before he retired. What was his future, to live at home?

While Michael had no special girl in mind, he knew that he would eventually marry and have a family of his own. Glasè couldn't support two families and he certainly did not want to be a cotter like his grandfather. If he farmed, he wanted land of his own. He was skilled now in building and could easily manage his own farm and make it prosper, but how would he ever get enough money to get started?

He had several conversations with his father about his future. His father applauded his plans and said how good it was for Michael to make sure he never got caught in the same trap of his grandfather and great grandfather, and he also agreed it was good to have your own home.

Michael decided he must first do his patriotic duty and serve in the Norwegian Maritime. He could have gone into the navy right after confirmation, like his father, but because there was so much left to be accomplished on the farm, he waited. By the time he reached eighteen, he knew he would enlist and serve for two years, since inscription was mandatory for all Norwegian young men.

By the time he completed his tour, he figured he would be 20 years old; his father would only be 53 and much too young to retire. Edward would be 11 then and could do what Michael was currently doing. In fact, he would have to start to pick up some of what Michael did when Michael left for the navy, and when he returned, there would be no need at all for Michael at Glasè.

He and his father talked a lot about sailing, and Ole was very helpful, explaining the pros and cons. He had loved being on the water, but was greatly bothered by all the time he was away from home after he married. He told Michael, because of all the skills he had learned about building at Glasè, it would not be a bad idea for Michael to volunteer as a ship repairman's apprentice when he joined the navy. It was what he had done, and it had paid off handsomely.

Chapter Four

Michael recalled that it was in November of the year 1883, three months before his nineteenth birthday, when he left home to enlist in the navy. The fall work was done, and it seemed the best time.

That day was carved into his memory like words chiseled into granite. Remembering it even now, over 50 years later, brought tears to his eyes. Little did he suspect that it would be the last time he would ever see his mother, feel her arms around him. No chance to once more tell her how much he loved her and thank her for all she had taught him. Thale would die young, just before her forty-fourth birthday, and be buried just as he was traveling home after completing his second year of conscription.

He remembered how, in turn, he had hugged the children: Hilde, now 14, more a grown up than child; Mattie, 11, a big help to her older sister and mother; Edward, 9, who would become his father's "right hand man;" Lottie, already 7; Trina, 5; and little Otto, only 3. His father hitched up the team to the wagon, they climbed on board, and Michel waved until they were out of sight. It was a good day's journey to Steinkjer, taking the cross-country route. Before he boarded the ship, he shook his father's hand, thanked him for all the things he had learned at his side and wished him continued good fortune on the farm. Both of their eyes became a little misty, and his father had to hasten away, he said, to get to his brother's farm along the Beistadfjorden before nightfall.

The ship he was to board and register on had been a steamer and, surprisingly, Michael had long ago forgotten its name. He remembered that he was welcomed by the deck officer who took him below to register, find him a bunk and generally acquaint him with the ship. Having only been on his father's little sailboat, he was astounded by the size of this vessel. Because the boat did not sail for another day, he had ample time to explore. He also asked the deck officer if there was a ship's carpenter aboard. The officer took him topside and introduced him to a sailor who at the moment was inventorying his toolbox.

Michael asked, "Could there be a chance that you might need an apprentice?" When there was no response, he proceeded to talk about the skills he had acquired at Glasè. The man looked and harrumphed, but said nothing. "So, who do I talk to about this?" Michael queried.

"You talk to me. I talk to the officer that just left, and he talks to the captain. I can always use help, but I prefer my help not to be quite so green. I don't have the time to be teaching you anything."

"If you have a small task you need done, show me what it is. If I fail to do the job to your satisfaction, I'll not bother you again. If you approve of my work, then say a good word for me to the officer. Agreed?"

"My name is Ole," he replied. "Follow me, and don't trip over anything on the deck."

"My name is Michael, and I thank you; I will watch my step." He thought about commenting on the man's name and then thought better of it.

The repair was a door that had pulled loose from the jamb in a high wind. It was OK if it was closed, but when opened it hung listlessly on one hinge, and the jamb was badly splintered. He asked where the supplies were, found what he needed, picked a saw, a plane and a hammer and screw driver from the tool box and went off to begin the repair. In less than two hours he returned the tools to the box, found Ole and asked, "Did you also want me to re-varnish the door?"

Before the ship sailed, he was informed that he would be the new ship carpenter's apprentice, and he was to report to Ole immediately after breakfast the next morning.

As the boat disembarked the second day, he was already hard at work on a damaged hatch cover, which would eventually leak water into the hold during high seas. Though he was busy, he had a chance from time to time to view the surroundings. They were sailing south to Trondheim before going out onto the North Sea. That's when his real adventure would begin. He was to make this trip four times before his tour of duty ended. He thought this was a good beginning to being in the maritime.

In his journal that night he wrote, "One cannot imagine how many naturally beautiful places there are along the coastline of Helgeland. There are a multitude of islands and islets on the outside of the ship lane, large and small in between each other, and on the mainland, green meadows and nice homesteads that are a joy for the eye to watch."

He had started the journal at Glasè and filled it mostly with poems he had memorized and recited out loud while working in the fields, chopping wood or any of the many other tasks he assumed. He was very impressed with poetry from his school studies and personal readings and thought it to be a wonderful way to express what one discovered, felt in their heart and stored in their mind. He loved to read and he loved to write.

As a young man, when he had the time and material was available, he remembered how he loved to read the sagas of Snorre Sturlassen, marvelous poems of historical significance. Oral tradition, or "word of mouth," his father had told him, was the ancient means of passing down historical data from generation to generation. He read other poetry and from time to time composed some verses in his head, but never committed them to paper, as he deemed them unworthy of print. He read a lot about the recent history of Norway, its struggles with Danish and Swedish domination. Some of the Norwegian kings became his heroes.

When the boat docked in Trondheim on a Sunday, he took leave of the ship after breakfast and walked the distance to Nidaros Cathedral, to visit the gravesite of one of his heroes, the holy saint and king, Olav. He was not prepared for what he saw. The steeple, which was his guide from the harbor, stretched to the sky. Inside the church itself seemed large enough to hold the total acreage of a community the size of Bartness. Gray stone upon gray stone reached ever upward, with arches filled with at least a hundred niches, each with its own chiseled carving. On each side there were huge towers, not quite as tall as the spire.

It was truly a battlement, if ever one was needed. From the towers you would be able to see the enemy while they were still at sea. Surely this church was a fit resting place for the king who had united the country and made it a Christian nation centuries ago.

A service was in progress, so he stood quietly in the back. When the organ sounded, he could swear the music came directly from heaven. Never had he heard an organ so beautiful and powerful. It absolutely filled the stone structure from top to bottom and from front to back.

When the service ended and all the people had exited, he asked a man who seemed to be some church official if it was all right for him to look around. He was told that, by all means, he should stay as long as he liked.

The church was built in the shape of a cross, with the nave, stretching forward for hundreds of feet. There were what appeared to be two large choirs off to the right and left. About two thirds of the way forward, he saw the marked gravesite of King Olav. He knelt and offered up a prayer of thanksgiving for the king and for his homeland, Norway, sought a blessing for his family and asked for safe passage on the sea.

As he turned around to exit, he was stunned. He first saw the marvelous brass pipes of the organ, and then, higher up, near the peak, the huge round colored window, sparkling like a thousand jewels in the reflected light. In later years he would learn that it was made from many pieces of stained glass. The morning sun, streaming through, heightened the reds and blues and greens in the scene. He counted sixteen pie shaped wedges, like flower stems out to the edge. At the end of each stem was what looked like a bud with a small white figure in each one. In the very middle of the round window was a small wheel, and in each wedge section going out, sixteen circles, again, with a figure in white in each. Below the round window were nine tall windows with arches at the top. In each of the windows there was a figure. He wondered if they might be depicting Jesus at various moments in his life. Whatever they were, it was the most uniquely beautiful work of art he had ever seen. He felt very humble.

He knew, from his readings, that the city of Trondheim was very old, started before the year 1000 by Olav Tryggvason. The wharf where they had docked had been built more than one hundred fifty years ago. Still, it was the most modern place he had ever seen. The images of that day would remain in his mind, as well as his heart, and those memories would last for many years to come.

So far, his limited experience in the maritime had been positive. He and Ole became good friends and complemented each other with their various skills. He was not prepared, however, for what was yet to come—the North Sea. As they left the quiet shelter of the fjord and entered the North Sea with its fabled high seas, he learned they were indeed "high seas." Sometimes, the waves crashing over the bow made it impossible to be on deck, let alone work there. On those days, he and Ole found projects down below.

It was humorous for the veterans to watch the new recruits like Michael find their sea legs. Each time the ship pitched, they would fly in the opposite direction, banging into a wall, the floor or even the ceiling at times. The veterans would laugh and slap their knees. It was amusing for Ole to watch Michael tie himself by his project with a rope so he could remain steady. It was several weeks before he discarded the rope and rocked and rolled with each pitch, with little more than a hitch step now and then.

From Trondheim they headed north. Each night he would record in his journal what he had seen that day. He would have such tales to tell the family when he got home. Unknown to him then, many years later he would use these words to write a description of Norway for his children.

So we take a trip along the coastline, sailing northward from Trondheim, to Narosland. I remember the names of two islands, that is Hestmand Oi, and Vego. There is a mountain on Hestmand Oi that looks like a man on horseback, after which it is named. Vego is a very large island with many inhabitants, and a market, and the steamroller ties to shore too, there, and a good harbor, namely Bronosund. Brono lies on the outside of sound and Alstadhaug on the mainland, where the priest Petter Dass lived and worked a long time ago in the 16th and17th century.

Once, when he was in school, Michael had been able to get a copy of some of Petter Dass' works. Dass, a Danish minister, became well known as an author and hymn writer, who lived and worked in the seventeenth and eighteenth century. For all the material he wrote, as much, or more was written about him. In legend, he was known to be the owner of the "Black Book," as well as being a master magician. In one story, on his way to a preaching engagement, he got a ride with the Devil. In return, he agreed to let the Devil have every soul that fell asleep during his sermon. The fable states that Dass, without any notes prepared ahead of time, preached a sermon like none ever delivered before. Satan didn't get a single soul.

Then we go farther north. There are many fjords that go into the country up north as well. There is a fjord that goes into the town of Namsun, and another one to Bodo, then we have Velfjorden, Saltenfjorden, Eidsfjorden and many, many more. But, there are more mountain masses along these fjords than there are father south.

Rorvar is the last docking place along the ship lane, then it goes to sea. There are many kilometers of open sea before you come to Svolvar in Lofoten. Svolvar is the eastern fishing area in Lofoten.

Then going westward along the Lofoten Islands, first we have the fishing village, Henningvar, then Brandsholmen and Mort Sundet, Balstad, Nusfjord and Sund. Post is the last and outermost fishing village. There are two villages between Post and Sund.

Between the islands of Post and Mosken there runs a sea stream that is called Norstrommen. Yes, there is a lot of noise. It roars and screams from it a long ways, when it goes out and in during ebb and flow. The frothing wave tops, and the foam goes high in the air. And painful it is for the ship or boat that comes there then. It is sure to go under!

There is a lot of fishing of the nice codfish in Lofoten throughout the winter months—January, February, and March. To take a meal of fresh codfish, cooked as soon as it is taken out of the saltwater, and with the accompanying fat, it is truly a magnificent meal. And it gives you strength in your legs.

Recalling that meal, Michael thought, *over here we get lutefisk.* Cooked properly and dipped in melted butter, it tasted almost as good. Unfortunately, the local stores only carried it during the Christmas holidays.

Now that we are so far north, we will continue and go to "Nordkapp" [North Cape] and admire the midnight sun. It is also a marvelous panorama for the eye to see the sweet sun ball that can be seen all night for a while in the summer.

Michael wrote the prose in his journal, but to him, all was poetry in his homeland. For him, it took verse, not narrative, to describe the awesome beauty and strength he saw. He recalled verses committed to memory, describing that which he was now seeing first hand.

The first we start with
Are hundreds of harbors in April.
There we meet soft thoughts,
When the fleet shall anchor,
And sixty thousand men on board
Carry Norway in their prayers around the world.

Sailing was a lonely avocation and he knew, early on, that he would not make it a lifetime job. One positive aspect was that he was clothed and fed and had nothing much to spend his wages on. He very seldom carried any kroner, but left them in the safe keeping of the bursar. The exception was buying gifts for his family at various ports they visited.

His first Christmas was his loneliest time. Without a calendar, there was nothing on board that told you the holiday had arrived. He looked forward to the day when he again would celebrate this holy time at home with family. Once he made it past that first Christmas, he could make it through one more. And then, come the third one, he would be home.

During his two-year tour of duty, Michael remembered he served on four different ships: two were steamers and two were sailing ships. After working with Ole for over six months, he requested appointment on another ship where he would serve as the ship's carpenter, rather than an apprentice. The request was granted, and there were two more transfer assignments after that. His final ship was a Norwegian bark, a sailing vessel, built in 1871.

He silently thanked his father many times over for suggesting he get signed on as an apprentice carpenter. He did not envy those who worked in the heat of the boiler rooms and stoked the furnaces. A couple times he had assisted the stevedores in loading and unloading goods. That was not for him either, but he did not allow himself to get soft. He worked hard and often, at days' end, his muscles would remind him of his physical activity that day.

All in all, Michael recalled that he saw a great deal of the European continent from the deck of his ships. He received a great education in geography, as his ships sailed as far north as Svalbard, in the Artic Ocean, and into the Barents Sea, along the north coat to Russia. Going back down the Norwegian coastline, he traveled past Denmark and Germany, through the English Channel, by France and around the coast of Portugal, through the Strait of Gibraltar and into the Mediterranean Sea.

While foreign ports were interesting, unless he was buying a gift he rarely took shore leave, except in Norway. While he enjoyed all these opportunities, his heart was partial to his native Norway. He loved the time he was able to spend in Oslo, the Viking capitol in the eighth century. It started as a little village at the top of Oslo Fjord. The modern city was attributed to King Harald Hardrade in about 1050 AD. There was so much to see there. He visited Akershus Castle, which the Renaissance King, Christian IV of Denmark, built when the old city of Oslo burned to the ground in 1624.

He also enjoyed excursions into Bergen, later dubbed, "The Gateway to The Fjords." Bergen was Norway's cultural center, giving birth to sons like Edvard Grieg, a composer, and Ole Bull, the famous violinist. On one stop, he got to attend the National Scene Theater, Norway's first national theater. What a thrill for this young country boy.

While there in Bergen harbor, he once trekked up Mount Floyen where he could view the city, the land and the fjords for miles in all directions. The mountain was steep; beginning at the harbor it rose to 320 meters. It was a weekend and there were many people there, many young couples with small children. Hiking was a favorite Norwegian pastime. He also walked a good distance to the west to Arne Fabrikker and bought a warm sweater for cold nights, and one for his father as well. While he knew he was following his father's example on the jaekt boat, being frugal in anticipation of the future, which for him would likely include immigration, this was money well spent.

In time, he had traveled the entire coastline of his native land. He saw hundreds of sights he had never seen before, and many he would never see again. His prize purchase during this time was his very own copy of a book of poetry by Bjornstjerne Bjornson. He committed a new poem, "Norge, Norge," to memory. The book became his prime possession, and from that day on, he took it with him wherever he went.

Blue up out of the grayish green sea,
Islands scattered around like young birds,
Fjords in tongues inward where it quiets down.
River valleys followed from the Mountains,
Forested ridge and mountain,
Long after, as soon as it clears by lakes and fields.
The peace of the holy day with temple in.
Norway, Norway. Cabins and houses and no castles
Joyful or hard.
You are ours, you are ours.
You are the land of the future.

Norway, Norway,
The shining land of the ski jumping run,
The harbor and fishing ground of the sea dog,
The road of the rafter,
The shepherds call of the mountain and glacial berm,
Fields Meadows, runes in the forest land, spread scars.
Cities that blossom, the rivers shoot out where it breaks,
White from sea where the swarms go.
Norway, Norway,
Cabins and houses and no castles
Joyful or hard.
You are ours, you are ours.
You are the land of the future.

It was an exciting day for Michael when his ship dropped anchor in Trondheim, the first week of December in 1885. He gathered his belongings, said his farewells, collected his wages from the bursar and went ashore. A free man again, he made the journey to Nidaros Cathedral to pray and thank God for safe keeping. Then he went back to the ticket office on the wharf and purchased his fare to Steinkjer. His boat would leave in two days, and Michael thought he could easily be home by Christmas.

At Steinkjer, he booked passage on the Beistadfjorden Ferry, a small boat hauling goods, mail and passengers as far as Vellamelen, the farthest stop north on Beistad Sundet, the last stop of the day. In the morning, the boat would backtrack the same route. After an overnight there, Michael would have a good breakfast, pack a little for lunch, put on his warmest clothes and walk the three or so miles to Glasè. With each mile traveled, his excitement grew; he was going home!

At Stavanger, weeks before he was to reach Trondheim, he had posted a letter telling his family he would be home soon. He told them his discharge date and his travel plans, but could not, because of exact sailing dates, predict the day or time, so he had simply written, *before Christmas*. He hoped the letter would reach Glasè in time and his return would not be a shocking one.

As the ferry pulled out of Steinkjer and headed west, he watched as they passed the Elnan farms, then north past his early homes—the Rones farms and Granhus. Next there was the school and church at Bartnes, Malm on the left, the Beistad parish back on the right, and finally, his destination; a lot of memories. Disembarked, he went to the local inn and had his supper.

Meals out of home were usually served smorgasbord style, with many choices from breads, meats and potatoes or dumplings, to preserved fruits and small cakes. Michael chose two "klub," potato dumplings with side pork. The dumpling was cut in small pieces, sprinkled with a little salt and pepper, and then the hot fat from the pork was drizzled over each piece. It was a heavy meal, and he would not go to bed hungry. In the morning he chose boiled eggs, bacon, fresh bread with butter, raspberry jam and, of course, coffee. He packed a lunch of bread, cheese, cold meats and a sweetbread made with cloudberries.

The sun had been up for about an hour when he set out for home. There was some snow, which was normal for early December; when it got deep, he just walked in the wagon ruts with ease.

In his duffel he had presents for everyone, items collected from all over Europe. As he walked, he inventoried in his mind the gifts that he had bought. For Hilde, there was a white lace mantilla and shawl from Spain; for Mattie, there was an ivory cross on a gold chain from the African Coast, and from France, a blue silk scarf that matched her beautiful blue eyes; for Edward, there was a fine hunting knife with bone handle from Russia, and a slingshot he had made himself from left over ship scraps; for Lottie, there was a warm wool scarf and cap with cheery bright colors from Scotland; for Trina, there was a little lamb he had carved from wood in the long nights on ship and a pair of warm mittens made of fine English wool. He smiled to himself as he remembered that Trina had once adopted and cared for a little lamb born at Glasè. For little Otto, there was a carved dog and a birch whistle he had made. He thought this would be a fine Christmas.

He had shopped long and hard for his mother and came up with a beautiful Norwegian solje brooch with gold spoons from Oslo. He also found a pair of ivory hair combs with inset rubies. He knew that she would exclaim how extravagant all this was, but her smile would betray her pleasure. For his father there was a fine pipe from Germany and a sweater like his own from Arne Fabrikker in Bergen. Yes, this would be a fine Christmas to replace the two he had missed in the Navy.

In two hours, he turned up the road that led north to the Glasè farms. He had made good time and would not need the lunch he had packed. He marveled once again at the beauty all around him. From each home a spiral of smoke lazed up toward the azure blue sky. The dark green pine forest was a perfect backdrop for the snow-covered fields. Livestock gathered at haystacks like children around the sweets table.

When he reached his home, he saw no one outside. He debated about whether or not to knock and decided to try the door and if it was not locked, just enter. He should have suspected that something was amiss with a black bow on the door. He walked into the kitchen to find everyone up and dressed; that was normal. When his sisters and brothers saw him, they got up as one, hurried to his side and hugged him. Hilde kissed him on the cheek and he saw tears in her eyes. "Mama's gone, Michael, Mama's gone!" Suddenly, all the children were hugging him and crying.

He could not believe his ears. "Mama's gone? Mama's gone? What happened? When did this happen? Was there an accident?" He found he could hardly breathe; his stomach was tied in a knot and he was unashamed of the tears that streamed down his cheeks. His beloved Mama was gone. He wouldn't see her and give her a hug as he dreamed many a night on ship. He wouldn't hear her voice saying how proud she was of him, and how glad she was that he was finally home.

Then he saw his father and was absolutely shocked. Ole sat staring at the welcoming scene, but seemed to see nothing. His hair was uncombed, and his face looked like it hadn't seen a razor in weeks; his clothes were rumpled. As Michael approached, he rose from his chair without a word, totally enfolded Michel in his arms and began to cry. As Michael embraced him, he felt the man's shoulders heave with each sob.

In those few minutes since he had entered the door, his heart had been broken twice. His Mama was gone and his father looked like the walking dead. Through tears, he managed to stammer out, "How, Papa, how?" And that was all.

It was a long time before Ole could speak. Finally he said, "We lost her just a week ago. We don't know what happened, she just passed away in her sleep. Oh, Michael, she just slipped away from us and there was nothing we could do. It was almost time for her birthday; she was only forty-three, Michael. God took your Mama when she was only forty-three."

It was a scene that would remain like a nightmare in Michael's mind until he himself passed away. This moment would change his life forever. As he remembered it now, so many years later, tears rolled down his cheeks.

Later in the evening, after visiting the gravesite, Michael and Ole sat by the fire and talked. "The farm has not done well while you were gone, Michael. The first fall we had a lightening fire that destroyed our whole crop and much of our hay supply. During the hard winter that followed, wolves came down from the forest and killed some of our sheep.

In the spring, there was no rain to water what had been sowed, and the heat of summer killed anything that might have sprouted. Without hay or feed, I had to sell off most of the animals to be able to feed what remained. It has been a hard time for all of us, but your mama seemed the most affected. Her heart was broken with disappointment. The more that went wrong, the harder she worked. I think she just worked herself to death."

"So, Papa, I'm home now. God willing, with the right weather, we can get back on our feet again."

"No, Michael, I have no stomach left for it anymore. This home is filled with a sadness that will never leave. I will find a buyer, and we will sell this place and everything but our personal belongings. I cannot stay here, and I will need money to find another place where the family can be together. I'm so sorry, Michael; as the oldest son, this was to be your place."

"Don't grieve for me, Papa. I hadn't planned to stay here anyway. I thought you too young to retire and me too ambitious to wait. While sailing, I heard again about all the people going to America to get the 160 acres of land their government is giving away. On board ship, I read letters that some of my shipmates had from their relatives and they were not disappointed. They received exactly what they were promised.

I have a couple destinations in mind in what is called the state of Minnesota.

They both have attracted people from our Nord Trondelag. Sometimes advertisements for jobs are posted in the newspapers. I will investigate them, and if they sound good, I will leave when the farm is sold. Like you, I have wages saved, and I will use that to travel and get started. If it looks good, maybe you and the rest of the family will follow."

"I think you are doing a smart thing, Michael. 160 acres is a lot of land, and to get it free is like a miracle. As for the children and me, we will see, we will see. I think you will have trouble convincing Hilde, as she has a sweetheart now. I suspect that it will not be long before she will marry. I will need to find someone to care for the younger ones. Your sister Hilde has been so helpful since Mama left us, and Mattie has pitched in, too. Edward has cared for the animals."

With that they embraced and retired for the night. Sleep was a long time coming for Michael. His mind was filled with all manner of memories of the past and thoughts for the future.

In the two years at sea, he had grown up a lot; the experience had both toughened and emboldened him. He thought, now, he could do anything he set his mind to. He would investigate and find out from neighbors more about their relatives in America and the settlement at Northfield. His circle would be wide as possible so as to get the most information. He would also go to Steinkjer and investigate emigration advertisements there, especially those from the area where the Stod and Ongdalen people had settled. He would also talk to port managers and find out about sailing dates and costs.

In the morning his father bathed, shaved, combed his hair and put on fresh clothes. It seemed as if Michael's homecoming had been like a tonic for him. No one said much or ate much for breakfast. The loss of mother and wife was too fresh. It would take time for wounds so deep to heal. In time they would, and life would go on.

Chapter Five

When Christmas arrived that year, Michael remembered how hard he and Hilde had worked to make it a true celebration. Michael took Otto with him and together they found the right sized tree, cut it down, hauled it home on a sled and brought it in. Mattie strung berries and popped corn and nuts for garland. She made an angel to stand on the top of the tree. The younger children made paper stars and snowflakes to hang on the branches. Hilde baked the flatbread Michael loved and some traditional sweets for the Christmas Eve supper.

When the day came, they put the candles on the tree and when the meal was complete, they all pitched in to clean up the dishes. Then, in family tradition, as Ole read the Christmas story, the two girls lit the candles with great care. They sang some Christmas hymns and Ole offered a prayer of thanks for the year and asked God to keep a close watch over his beloved family and also asked God to be good to their precious Thale. There were tears in everyone's eyes as they all said, "Amen," in unison.

Then Michael recited the verses from the Christmas poem he had memorized, "Jul der Hjemme"— Christmas Here at Home.

"Remember that Christmas, up there in the North,
With snow covered mountains and ice covered fjords,
With ringing bells which loudly sound
A message of holiday celebration to the hearts?
From the outermost islets and to the innermost valley,
From the fisherman's room, to the rich man's hall,
In cotter house and farm house,
All the way to the sailor at sea it reaches.

Do you remember the evening with mother and father,

The family gathered around the celebration table?
The peace and joy that reign there
Is truly my most precious childhood memory.
Do you remember the pine tree, which stood there so nice,
With lights and decoration on every branch,
Fruit and nuts hung linked together,
And a shining star high up at the top of the trunk?

Do you remember shining eyes and song?
How wonderfully beautiful it sounded in the room,
When all the siblings were with father and mother
Sounded the well-known Christmas choir.
Do you remember the wonderful frost clear evening,
The bright shining stars in the sky,
Silent and faithful they stand guard,
The symbol of him who was laid in the crib?"

Again, everyone applauded and said what a fine poem that was, and he was very pleased by their reaction.

Then he brought out his duffel and passed out his gifts to each in turn, beginning with the smallest. Otto blew his whistle until, holding their ears, the family made him stop. Then his dog became active, barking wildly as he chased the imaginary bear in Otto's mind.

After Trina modeled her mittens, she wrapped them around her lamb and hugged it to her chest. Lottie quickly put on her scarf and hat and kept it on even when she went to bed. Edward was so excited about his hunting knife, he didn't discover the slingshot until later. Mattie got tears of joy in her eyes when she saw her necklace and the scarf that her big brother told her matched her beautiful blue eyes.

When Hilde saw her lace mantilla and shawl, her mouth hung open with awe. Michael said, "I hear, young lady, that you have a serious suitor and might be thinking of getting married quite soon. Would you do me the honor of wearing these on your wedding day?"

She immediately blushed and then started to sob. She hugged him so hard, he was surprised by how strong she had become. *Just like Mama*, he thought.

She whispered softly to him, "I will be so proud to wear this with my wedding dress. Thank you, Michael, thank you. Mange tusen tak, many thousand thanks, and I so want you to meet my Arno. You will like him, too; he's such a hard worker." Then she donned her presents on head and shoulders. Everybody applauded and she curtsied grandly.

Everyone joined in the thanks and gave Michael hugs and a kiss on the cheek. Then Otto shouted, "Papa! What did you get for Papa? Did you buy Papa something? Let us see! Let us see!"

Michael reached in his bag and brought out the pipe first. He also had a package of Turkish tobacco that he'd forgotten about. "Papa, you work so hard that I bought you this pipe to make sure you will sit now and then to smoke it."

Ole immediately filled the bowl, tamped it down with his thumb and lit it with a brand from the fire. "Oh, this is a fine pipe, Michael, and the tobacco is like none I've ever smoked."

When he next saw the sweater, his eyes lit up like the fire and he had the girls undo the buttons and help him put it on. "Now I shall never work again. I will just sit by this fire in my beautiful warm sweater and smoke my pipe." The family all laughed, and it was a good sound.

Everybody knew what was next, but no one said a word. When Michael brought out the combs, he passed them around for all to see. "These are for Mama." There were numerous "Oohs," and "Aahs." "You may think me foolish," he said, "but tomorrow I will wrap these tightly in water proof covering, take a shovel and go down to Mama's grave. I will dig down a ways and lay these there, so they and Mama will lie together in the bosom of Mother Norway, and I will say, "Merry Christmas, Mama, Merry Christmas."

Everyone asked if they could come along. Pleased that they didn't think him addlepated, he said, "Yes, I want you all to be there with me to wish our mama a Merry Christmas."

Holding up the solje brooch, whose small silver and gold plated spoons shimmered in the firelight, he said, "This would have looked so nice on Mama's Sunday best dress. And I would have swelled with pride every time she put it on. Now you all know I have no sweetheart, but someday I will. I want a family just as fine as this one. I will keep this close until I choose a bride. On our wedding day, I will pin this on her wedding dress and Mama's spirit will be with us on that happy day."

Even as the tears fell, they jokingly taunted, "Michael's gonna get married. Michael's gonna get married." Even Ole chimed in, and then they all laughed and hugged him again. The healing had begun.

Michael remembered he had had mixed emotions as he recalled the selling of Glasè months later. It had been both the happiest and saddest place where he had lived both as a boy and then a young man.

By the time spring came, Ole had sold all of the animals that remained, except for one horse he would keep to pull the wagon. He had made arrangements with an auctioneer who said he would put up notices all around. The house, with a few exceptions, would be sold furnished. The auction would begin after lunch, to give time for people who had a distance to travel.

The next day, after the sale, everyone would help pack the wagon with their personal belongings and they would all go down to Ole's sister, Hanna. Hanna's husband, Joakim Granhus, had drowned on a fishing trip a few years before, and she had been trying to manage the farm herself, but found it a losing proposition. Having her brother, Ole, offer to come and live there to help run the place would be a blessing and she, in turn, would become the missing maternal figure for the children.

Michael's investigation of American homesteads had led him to two final choices of settlements, both in the state of Minnesota. The only problem was the word that most, if not all, of the more fertile homestead land was already taken.

One possibility was at the Northfield settlement where their closest neighbors had gone. From their neighbor, Michael had been able to get a summarized copy of the actual legislation carefully translated into Norwegian. It read:

THIRTY-SEVENTH CONGRESS Sess. II Ch. 75 1862. Chap. LXXV. -- An Act to secure Homestead to actual Settlers on Public Domain Be It enacted by the Senate and House of Representatives of the United States of America in assembled, That any person who is the head of a family, or who has arrived at the age of twenty-one years, and is a citizen of the United States, or who shall have filed his declaration intention to become such, as required by the naturalization laws of the United States, and who has never borne arms against the United States Government or given aid and comfort to its enemies, shall, from and after the first January, eighteen hundred and sixty-three, be entitled to enter one quarter section or a less quantity of unappropriated public lands, upon which said person may have filed a preemption claim, or which may, at the time the application is made, be subject to preemption at one dollar and twenty-five cents, or less, per acre; or eighty acres or less of such unappropriated lands, at two dollars and fifty cents per acre, to be located in a body, in conformity to the legal subdivision of the public lands, and after the same shall have been surveyed: Provided, That any person owning and residing on land may, under the provisions of this act, enter other land lying contiguous to his or her said land, which shall not, with the land so already owned and occupied, exceed in the aggregate one hundred and sixty acres.

Provided, however, That no certificate shall be given or patent issued therefore until the expiration of five years from the date of such entry; and if, at the expiration of such time, or at any time within two years thereafter; the person making such entry; or, if he be dead, his widow; or in case of her death, his heirs or devisee; or in case of a widow making such entry, her heirs or devisee, in case of her death; shall prove by two credible witnesses that he, she, or they have resided upon or cultivated the same for the term of five years immediately succeeding the time of filing the affidavit aforesaid and shall make affidavit that no part of said land has been alienated, and that he has borne true allegiance to the Government of the United States; then, in such case, he, she, or they, if at that time a citizen of the United States, shall be entitled to a patent, as in other cases provided for by law.

And be it further enacted, That the register of the land office shall note all such applications on the tract books and plats of his office, and keep a register of all such entries, and make return thereof to the General Land Office, together with the proof upon which they have been founded.

And be it further enacted, That if, at any time after the filing of the affidavit, as required in the second section of this act, and before the expiration of the five years aforesaid, it shall be proven, after due notice to the settler, to the satisfaction of the register of the land office, that the person having filed such affidavit shall have actually changed his or her residence or abandoned the said land for more than six months at any time, then and in that event the land so entered shall revert to the government.

And be it further enacted, That no individual shall be permitted to acquire title to more than one quarter section under the provision of this act; and that the Commissioner of the General Land Office is hereby required to prepare and issue such rules and regulations, consistent with this act, as shall be necessary and proper to carry its provision into effect; and that the registers and receivers of the several land offices shall be entitled to receive the same compensation for any lands entered under the provision of this act that they are now entitled to receive when the same quantity of land is entered with money, one half to be paid by the person making the application at the time of so doing, and the other half on the issue of the certificate by the person to whom it may be issued; but this shall not be construed to enlarge the maximum of compensation now prescribed by law for any register or receiver.

And be it further enacted, That nothing in this act shall be so construed as to prevent any person who has availed him or herself of the benefits of the first section of this act, from paying the minimum price, or the price to which the same may have graduated, for the quantity of land so entered at any time before the expiration of the five years, and obtaining a patent therefore from the government, as in other cases provided by law, on making proof of settlement and cultivation as provided by existing laws granting preemption rights

Approved, May 20, 1862.

Vol. XII Pub -- 50 page 393

Michael remembered that at first reading, it was just too much for his young mind to comprehend. There were too many words there. Overtime, he learned how to mark the phrases that matched what he had been taught and ignored the additional words that only confused him. His Glasè neighbor also reassured him that what he had marked was, in fact, what his brother and others had experienced.

His second focus, he recalled, was the settlement in White Bear Township. In retrospect, he often wondered if the hand of God had been with him in making this his choice. He ended up responding to an advertisement from White Bear Township for a man to clear homestead land. It was a perfect opportunity for him. There was a furnished homestead shack for him to live in. Michael thought this would be a good place to start, and his father agreed. It was a good opportunity to make a living while finding out where homestead land might still be available.

He wrote a letter immediately and told of his experience at Glasè. About 5 weeks later, he received a response. The man's name was Overby, and he offered Michael a job. He explained that work on the homestead had begun, but now he needed someone to clear more trees and till the new ground. He suggested once Michael had landed, he take a train west to a settlement in Minnesota called Willmar. There, Michael was to go to the local livery stable where a horse would be waiting for him, along with a hand drawn trail map. The homestead claim was about thirty miles north, and directions were for him to go to Indherred Lutheran Church and ask for Overby. The letter, as the advertisement had been, was written in Norwegian.

While he waited for an answer, Michael checked out arrangements in Steinkjer. It looked like he would sail to Kristiansund, where he would board another ship that would take him to a huge port on the east coast of America called New York. There, he could go west by train. His future, he recalled, had now been stretching out in front of him, and he was confident that his choices to date were good.

On the day of the auction the family rose early, had their breakfast, and then began loading the last of their belongings on the wagon. The bedding would be loaded the next morning. The house had been meticulously cleaned, as had the out buildings. Though the auction was not until mid morning, people began to arrive right after sun up. They were invited to inspect the home and the other buildings, which they did with many exclamations of, "Oh," "Look there," "I like this," and "You know what I think I would do here."

By the time the auctioneer arrived, there were about two-dozen people present and ready for the bidding to begin. The auctioneer warmed up the audience with a few humorous stories about Ole. Actually, he had only met Ole once and knew practically nothing about him, but he made it sound as if they were old friends and two of the most trust worthy individuals in Norway. Ole smiled and the smaller children hid their grins with their hands.

Finally, the auction began. "Who'll open the bidding at 2,500 kroner? Who'll start us off here with a decent offer for this fine property? Let's hear 2,500. 2,500, anyone? Don't be shy now; lets have a bid. I do believe, folks, the devil's got a hold on your tongues there. Who'll start with 2,500?"

"I'll offer 1,500," came a voice from the crowd.

This bid was followed quickly by "1,600," and then, "1,700."

"Well now, we're not bidding on Ole's shoes, my friends, we're looking at a whole farm here."

The crowd laughed, and a voice from the back hollered, "Are his shoes going to be auctioned, too? That's about all I can afford." Now, the crowd really laughed.

Bids started coming faster and faster, as the bidders warmed to the challenge. Soon it exceeded the 2,500 initial request, topped 3,000, and then settled down to a two couple contest. A tall, thin man with his petite, blonde wife, both still in their very early thirties and a slightly older gentleman, with a dark beard and mustache, and his short, cherubic faced wife were clearly vying for ownership in all earnestness.

"Let's hear 3,500. Yes! Now 3,600. Yes!"

The young blonde was hugging her taller husband around the waist, and every time he upped the bid, she squealed with delight and gave him a big squeeze, an obvious incentive to keep it up. The older couple's faces were set with grim determination. The auctioneer grinned and pushed the bidding up and up.

When it reached 4,000, Michael gave his dad's shoulder a squeeze. They both smiled, recalling the day Ole had purchased the farm for 2,800 kroner. As the kroners climbed, the two couples took longer and longer to reply, whispering between themselves and looking at their opponents to see if there was a glimmer of surrender. But the auctioneer was patient and waited each time. He knew he had a real contest going here. "Let's go 4,200. Don't lose it now, folks, after going this far. Another hundred kroner and it might be yours."

Finally, at 4,600, the younger couple shook their heads at the auctioneer. Their shoulders dropped in defeat, and the blonde wife's eyes grew misty. They had come so close and wanted it so badly. As the auctioneer said, "4,600, are we all done here? We're at 4,600, do I hear 4,700?" the young husband, his arm around his wife's shoulders, bent down and gently kissed her on the cheek. She whispered earnestly in his ear. He shook his head and she whispered again.

The young man straightened to his full height and called, "4,800 kroner. We're bidding 4,800 kroner."

The older couple looked as if someone had slapped them in the face. Obviously, this young couple had absolutely no common sense and didn't know when to quit. Everyone knew it was over when they turned on their heels and walked angrily away. The crowd "oohed" and the auctioneer said, "4,800 going once, 4,800 going twice, 4800 going for the third and final time. 4,800 kroner. Sold!"

The crowd cheered and clapped their hands. Those close to the couple slapped the young man on the shoulders saying, "Congratulations!" "Well done!" "Good job!" and wishing them both well.

Ole and the kids hugged each other in turn. It made it easier to leave their home knowing that this lovely young couple was going to take their place. The girls hugged the wife, who, with tears still in her eyes, now was all smiles. The men shook hands with the earnest young man who had won the bid when he agreed to give it one more try. Ole said softly, "Thank you. I wish you happiness in this place." It was a good day all around.

The new owner of the farm seemed compelled to explain his good fortune.

"I have worked every day since I was confirmed. In spring and summer, I work with my father, who is a cotter. In the late fall and winter months, I work for the logging company. I have saved every kroner I ever earned. My wife, Aslong, worked as a herd girl for her father and learned how to make good goat cheese, which she sells to merchants in the nearby town. She helped me put many kroner in the cupboard. When I quit bidding, she whispered to me to keep on. When I said, 'no, I need money for animals,' she told me her father had said, 'Aslong, when the bidding gets close, and you think you can go no further, remember that I will add up to 500 kroner to your dowry, if you need it.'"

On the way to Aunt Hanna's farm, the family stopped at Thale's gravesite to share the good news. Little Otto was first. "Oh, Mama, you should have been there. The nicest young man and his wife are going to live in our house, and Papa made a lot of money."

Michael was last. He knelt on the ground, his hand on the white cross that bore his mother's name. "Mama, I don't think I'll be able to come here anymore. I'm leaving on a ship for a place called America, far across the ocean. They say that I can get 160 acres of land for free, if I come there and become a citizen. I have to build a house on the land I want, till the field and live there for 5 years. That's all, Mama, for 160 acres of land.

I'm sorry I have to go that far, Mama, but I know your spirit will be with me wherever I go. Wouldn't it be nice, though, if our government would do the same with some of their high mountain land. I know you know, but I must tell you one more time how very much I love you. I miss you so much, but have such wonderful memories of you, and haven't forgotten all the things you taught me. Yes, I will be a good farmer. I will work hard like you and Papa. You keep your eye on me, and I will make you proud. I promise.

"Bye, bye, dear Mama," it hurt so badly to say that. "If you were here, I would not leave. But you are at rest now, and I must be about my business. I must leave now, so we can get to Hanna's before dark. Goodbye, my Mama, goodbye. Watch over me. Watch over me." With a huge lump in his throat and tears streaming down his face, he made his way to the wagon and climbed up beside his father. In his declining years, he would often pine for one more visit.

The road to Hanna's was pretty winding, but once under way, they made good time. They arrived just as she was lighting a candle in the window for them. The family all hugged her, and each child tried to shout over the other to tell about the auction. They had a good supper and, while Ole smoked his pipe, Michael joined him by the fire and the children all found the place where they would sleep in their new home.

Though both were tired, Michael and Ole talked into the late evening. Michael reassured his father that he had done the right thing. He told him the young couple was an assurance from God that he had made a good decision. He reminded Ole of how much Hanna would gain now that she had a man around the farm and a host of young people to assist with chores. He promised he would write letters and keep them all informed about his new surroundings and said when things got settled, maybe Ole could take some of his "small fortune" to come visit and see America for himself.

Michael remained with the family for a few days, helping his father mend some fences around the outbuilding that housed Hanna's few cows, goats and her one pig. His mind, however, was occupied by thoughts of what lay ahead. He had a small translation book, which he diligently studied. It contained short English phrases that he hoped might be helpful once he reached America.

Finally, the morning of departure arrived. Michael recalled rising early with mixed emotions of excitement, apprehension and sadness. He would catch the supply boat that would take him the first leg of his journey. In turn, he embraced each of his sisters and brothers and told them he would write about his adventures. He told each of them to write, and said he hoped they could visit him soon. Last of all, he bid farewell to his father, first shaking his hand and then giving him one last hug. "You must come visit me, Papa, once I get settled. Maybe you, too, can start over on a new homestead."

He took the lunch Hanna had prepared, waved to everyone and began his walk to the boat dock. He never turned around or looked back; it would have been too hard.

Chapter Six

Clearly, as if it were yesterday, Michael pictured himself, two days later, boarding the final ship in Kristiansund that would take him to America. As important as the trip was, to this day Michael could not recall the ship's name, but he could reel off all the facts he learned about it. It was a little over three years old, made of iron, 313 feet long and 40 feet wide; its hold was 30 feet deep. As a navy man, he had been impressed that its compound engines were capable of 2,000 horsepower. The hull was constructed of the best iron and was divided into five watertight compartments. It was also schooner rigged with three masts. On deck, it carried eight large lifeboats. The main deck was broad and particularly fitted for promenading, being guarded by high railings. It had a crew of 59 men.

At Kristiansund, it unloaded about 170 tubs of lard, 1,500 sacks of flour and 76 tubs of butter. Michael recalled thinking at the time that all of that would really make a lot of flatbread—if you could only find some potatoes.

Cabin accommodations were limited to 50 first class and 50 second class passengers, yet between decks, there was room for fully 200 persons in steerage. Michael had money enough for either first or second class, but decided he could better use the money when he got to America. He sailed in steerage, which was not totally unlike the crew quarters he had experienced in the navy. The ship sailed with 227 passengers, most of them in Michael's class. The trip took a little over two weeks, and everyone was on deck to cheer as the ship pulled into the harbor of New York

When he disembarked in New York, he spoke his first English words to the carriage driver: "railroad station," and to the ticket agent there: "Willmar, Minnesota." He was told that they could not ticket him to Willmar.

He shrugged his shoulders to indicate he didn't understand. The agent said, "You don't speak English, go to Norske window," and pointed left. Michael shrugged again.

The man pointed to the left again and repeated, "Norske, go Norske."

Michael backed away and walked in the direction the man had pointed. Four windows down, he saw a sign above a window that read, *Norske*. He waited behind 2 men and was glad to hear the agent talking to them in fluent Norwegian.

The new agent told him he would give him a ticket to a community called Minneapolis. There, he should go to another Norske window, where he could purchase his ticket for the Willmar spur.

The agent asked if he understood, and Michael answered, "Ja, ja."

The man then pointed him to track 7, and told him the train would leave at 1:00 in the afternoon, and he should get on car number 3. Michael again answered, "Ja, ja, tak."

Both the carriage driver and the ticket agent accepted payment in kroner, but urged him to go to the bursar's office and exchange kroner for dollars for the trip west. While he waited for his train, he did as they suggested. If he was cheated, he would never know. He had brought enough kroner with him to get him to the homestead, he thought. There he would write his father and ask him to send the rest of his savings.

The sight of his first train engine was an education in itself. The iron monster, belching black smoke from a big chimney, reminded him of a huge kitchen fireplace on wheels. Behind it was a car full of what here was called coal. It burned in an oven to heat up water and produce the steam, which then drove the pistons and powered the wheels. Michael thought it was remarkably similar to the steam ship. There were several cars lined up behind the engine; the last three were for passengers. Again, he chose to ride in 3rd class, car 3.

Compared to his native land, the scenery that unfolded as the train rolled west at about 20 miles an hour was unremarkable. What was obvious, however, was how much of it looked tillable. The land was relatively flat, with some broad expanses of tree cover. While there were no high craggy mountains, streams, waterfalls or fjords, it was beautiful in its own way.

When the train reached the state called Wisconsin, the rolling hills reminded him a little of the valleys in Norway, not as wide and deep as Gudbransdal, but very, very green. He had been told in one of his letters that his destination, Minnesota, would be as green as the Garden of Eden, and when the train arrived there later, so it was.

There were several other passengers on board who spoke Norwegian, but also knew quite a bit of English. He spent much time with them, not only to learn about the places they passed, but also to put in his mind as many

American words as he could. His seatmates had all been in his shoes at one point, and they were eager to help him in his struggle.

"Norsk is an easy language. English is not so kind," said one.

"Some words can mean many different things, and words aren't always pronounced like they are spelled, but you'll catch on."

The two other companions chuckled and nodded their heads in agreement. So he passed the time from New York to Minneapolis.

Dinner and supper were served in the form of bag lunches, with meat and cheese sandwiches, an apple or an orange, sometimes a cookie or small frosted cake. Coffee was always available, along with water. Breakfast was bread and butter, hardboiled eggs and cold sausage.

Sleep was accomplished sitting up, or if a seat was vacant next to yours, you could curl up and rest your head on your jacket. Most often, it was not hard to find such a spot. The only time it got a little crowded was the day's travel from a large settlement called Chicago to Minneapolis. There he said his goodbyes to his travel mates, after one of them assisted him in getting a ticket to Willmar, remembering the engine number and finding the track where the train would depart. They all wished him good luck.

Compared to his train ride so far, the trip to Willmar, despite the many stops, was very short—just a matter of hours. The livery stable was relatively easy to find, no more than a block or two from what railroaders called "the depot." He decided to spend the night in Willmar and depart in the morning. He walked one block to a huge two-story boarding house with a sign in the front window that said, *Rooms*. The Norwegian speaking smithy at the stable had recommended it, and gave him good instructions for the trip the next day, including a hand drawn map. The smithy himself had made the trip on many occasions.

The following morning, Michael joined some other boarders at 7:00 A.M. in the boarding house dining room. After a hot breakfast of cereal, eggs, bacon, potatoes and toast with butter and jam, Michael was off for White Bear Township. The trail was not hard to follow, and the countryside was a little like Wisconsin, with rolling hills, forests and, surprisingly, many lakes of different sizes. Now and then, he would see a homesteader in his field, and his wave was vigorously returned. So far, he felt good about where he was going.

When he reached his destination, he marveled at what he saw. Right in the middle of the lush green hills and the loamy black plowed fields was a beautiful sparkling blue lake. He would later learn its name was Minnewaska, a word from the language of the native people called Indians.

Standing tall beside it, with its steeple reaching halfway to the fluffy white clouds lazing overhead, was a big white church. It was not up to the standards of Nidaros, but certainly the most beautiful country church Michael had ever seen. Bartness Church was not very high and did not have such a peaked roof. It also did not have the beautiful steeple of Indherred. A painted sign in front read, *Indherred Lutheran Church*, the place he had been instructed to go to meet his employer.

He entered the church and looked around. He walked up to the front, and seeing no one, called out, "Hello," a greeting word he had added to his sparse English vocabulary. After three tries, he went back out the front door. Next to the church was a white two-story home. He decided to try there.

The lady who answered his knock was short and stout, her hair was the color of wheat, but her smile lit up her face and made Michael exclaim softly, "Vakre."

She said, "Pardon?" And Michael blushed. He had not intended to be so forward, and was glad she hadn't heard his compliment about her smile, "pretty."

In his best Norwegian, he said, "My name is Michael Glasoe, and I was told to come here to find my employer, Arnold Overby. Can you tell me where I can find him?"

The smile broadened, she turned and called inside, "Arnie, Michael Glasoe is on our doorstep." Other than hearing his name, he had no idea what she had said. Turning to Michael again, she replied, this time in Norwegian, "My husband will be so pleased you're here. We were getting worried that you might not get here in time to plant the spring crop. Almost everyone around has had their seed in the ground for over a week."

A trim man in a suit, with a vest and a white shirt, sporting a black string tie, stuck out his hand and said, in Norwegian, "Michael, I'm Reverend Overby, and I'm delighted you are here. Come in, come in, by all means." Michael followed his employer into the living room, where the Reverend invited him to sit in a large hi-back chair. He noticed little doilies on the back of the chair and wondered what they were for.

Michael explained in Norwegian and halting English that he was here to find his employer, but did not expect it to be a minister. "I will be working for you?"

In Norwegian again, the clergyman responded, "Indeed, Michael, indeed. My wife, Katrina, and I arrived here 2 years ago and moved onto a homestead that the church, with government approval, had reserved for us before I entered the seminary in Minneapolis. Like you, I emigrated to Minneapolis as a young man, but I was a late bloomer, and didn't decide to become a minister until I was past thirty and had two children.

"There are some very smart people in our congregation; one of them is in the State legislature. They figured out that offering a homestead to a seminary student would be a sure inducement to get prospective preachers to come here full time. In my first year, they offered me this homestead opportunity. They were right. In return, during the summers when seminary classes were suspended, I would come here and hold services, and we would stay in the sod house.

"The government was eager to go along with the agreement, as a settlement with a full-time minister would attract more settlers. That was what the homestead grants were all about, attract settlers who would stay and build the community.

"After I graduated and was ordained, we arrived here and we moved into the sod house on the homestead, which, except for the summers, had been occupied by a young member of the congregation for four years. We lived there a year and, like him, put in the crop to qualify so the land could be legally registered to us. In that time, the church built us this fine home. Thank God for that! By then we had 2 more children, and the sod house was not built for 6 people. Don't ever ask my wife what it was like."

"Will my job be to put in your crop and harvest it?" Michael asked. "That hardly sounds like a full-time job. How many acres do you have?"

"We have twenty acres tilled so far. You will tend that and clear more each year. We will supply you with food and goods and any tools or animals needed." And then with a smile, " Do you think that is enough to do?"

Michael grinned and replied, "Until winter comes."

The Reverend and his wife both laughed heartily. "We thought of that. We are proved up, so you don't have to live there in the winter."

"Proved up? What is that?" Michael asked.

"To get the land in your name, a homesteader must live there for 5 years and raise crops every year."

"Ja, ja, I have read that."

"In our case, the government made allowances for occupancy by a squatter from our congregation and considered our summers and one year living on the claim to fulfill the requirements. After requirements are met, you find someone to swear you have done what is specified. You get them to sign a piece of paper, take it to the Land Office and they will give you another piece of paper saying you own the property. You are 'proved up'. Is that clear?"

"Ja, it is as I learned in school," Michael replied.

"They teach this in Norwegian schools now?"

"Oh, yes. As you remember, there is very little land left to till in Norway. We get more people every year, but not more land. The Norwegian government is now encouraging young people to come to America and get free land. So they instruct teachers to tell their students about it. But, you said you lived on the claim in the summertime, and then, for only 1 year."

"In our case," Overby responded, "that's the genius of what the congregation worked out with the Land Office. The agent, who belongs to our church, persuaded the federal government to allow any member of our congregation to live there and farm for up to 4 years, but said we had to live there in the summer for those years, and then for the whole year of year 5.

"The whole idea of giving away land is to get settlers. Like I have said, having a church with a full time preacher, especially one who speaks both English and Norwegian, the government thought was a good way to make this settlement happen faster. You can see it's worked here. All the land is gone.

"The money we get each year from the crops helps to pay my salary and pay off the mortgage on this house and the one on the church. It's a pretty ingenious idea, I think. And that explains why you are here. You will clear and till more land each year so we get more crops, I get a larger salary, and we pay off the debt on the house and the church as fast as possible. Our church members are not used to being in debt, and they aren't comfortable with it."

"But the land is in your name?" Michael queried. "Why don't you get all the money?"

"I agreed to the government's and the church's terms. The land is mine. When the mortgages are paid off, a certain amount will be agreed upon as set aside for improvements. The net income will then be used to reduce the church's portion of my salary. Eventually, the crop money will be my income and, hopefully, some money for retirement. There are, of course, provisions for crop failure. Eventually, it is hoped that by the time of my retirement, there will be enough saved to build me a home. I will then pay someone to put in the crop and harvest it. That will be my retirement income."

"That is really complicated, but to be honest, I can't find any fault in it," Michael said.

"So, now, back to your living there in the winter. When the snow gets too deep to walk in and the winds blow colder than any place you ever lived, 2 of our children will double up in a bedroom and you will stay here with us. To keep you busy and help make you some extra money, you will become an apprentice to the man who built our church and this house. He puts up houses in good weather and then finishes them inside in the winter. Will that keep you busy enough, Michael?"

"It sounds like a good plan, but one more thing I don't understand, Reverend Overby, why the government doesn't just give you control of all the land in this parish like they did in Norway. There, you recall, the *preston* was very powerful. He decides who gets land and who doesn't. I suppose you would kind of be like your Land Office agent."

"Ah, yes, I remember Norway's history. I give the people property to farm and take away their freedom. We Norwegians here know that the Danes did a good job of taking over control of the Church in Norway. Here we may be poor, but my congregation is its own authority. No one! No one can tell us what to do!"

"I understand," replied Michael "and I agree. Now, if I may be so bold, Revered Overby, will I be paid? We never discussed that in our letter."

"Indeed you will, Michael. Half of what the land produces will be yours. Therefore, the more land you clear and till, the more you will make, and the more money the church will have. In the meantime, as I said, we will take care of all your needs. Also, if you wish to ride in some evenings, my wife will be more than happy to help you with your English, and we have plenty of books for you to read. If you prefer to wait until winter, that will be fine, too."

"No, as soon as I get organized, I will talk to you, Mrs. Overby. We can set up times for me to come in. I am very eager to get started."

Mrs. Overby then joined in. "That's a good plan. So, Michael, you will find a small corral in back. The water in the tank is for your horse to drink. You can put the saddle and blanket in the little stall. There is feed in the barrel inside the front door. Then come wash up and share supper with us."

"Tomorrow, I'll take you out to the homestead. It's little more than a half mile away." The Reverend stood and extended his hand. "Are we agreed, Michael."

"Yes," he replied, "we are agreed. And your offer is, I think, most generous, most generous. I think you are a very smart man, and I am a very lucky one." Then with great good humor, he winked and asked, "Do I get Sundays off?"

The two men rode out the next day with sacks of provisions to get Michael settled. Reverend Overby explained that there were two strong horses at the homestead being tended now by a neighbor's young son. They would stop on the way and meet him. "We pay his father to keep the feed bins full," he said, "and the boy gives the team water in the morning, then during the day stakes them out on the grass land and gives them water in the evenings. You will want to do the same to save on grain costs."

They arrived at the homestead less than an hour after leaving the parsonage, including the stop at the neighbor's place. Michael learned that in America, "Prestons" were often called Parson, or Pastor, or Reverend, and their home was called the parsonage or manse.

The sod home looked sturdy, and was totally shaded by two huge oak trees. It was a gorgeous site. They brought in the goods and Michael put the bedding Mrs. Overby had given him on the bed in the corner. A small loft overhead must have been the children's bedroom. He thought to himself that it must have been a really crowded place for a family to live.

Outside was a pump. Michael gave the handle 4 or 5 pumps up and down and the water ran clear. He took the cup hanging from a hook and tasted the water. It was good and it was cold. He handed the cup to the Reverend.

Michael saw the horses grazing not far away. They were extremely sturdy and looked like they could easily pull the large plow standing by the corral. The harnesses were neatly hung in the small barn.

The windmill was one of the largest he had ever seen. Unlike the huge cumbersome-looking Dutch windmills, these were small, trim, but sturdy metal structures. Reverend Overby explained that these systems were perfected in the United States, beginning with the Halladay windmill in 1854

The most important refinement of the American fan-type windmill, he said, was the development of steel blades in 1870. Steel blades could be made lighter and worked into more efficient shapes. They worked so well, he explained, that their high speed required a slow-down gear, which he pointed out to Michael. To turn the windmill on and off, there was a wooden arm that you pulled up to start and down to stop.

Michael noticed that behind the barn that there were several wheeled devices he didn't recognize. Reverend Overby introduced him to the disk harrow, the seed drill and the reaper. Michael, with hands on hips, just shook his head and laughed. "Now, isn't that something! In America, you get to ride while you work. Next thing you know, they'll come up with a device to tie the grain together."

Overby laughed and replied, "Michael, a man named McCormick has already done that, but I don't have one yet. We still bind and shock by hand."

Michael said, "In Norway, our farms are so small we could never afford to buy all these devices. They must cost you a pretty penny."

"Not a dime, Michael," said Overby. "These are all castoffs from congregation members who donated them to the church rather than use them for the meager trade-in they can get from the dealer. All I need to do is make sure they're kept greased and oiled. And here's another surprise. Several of the farmers have gone together to buy a thresher that takes the shocks, winnows the grain and loads it onto a wagon. They go from farm to farm. The women manage a cookhouse on wheels, so nobody goes hungry. I'm last on the list, but that's fine; they charge me nothing."

"Where do you store the grain?" Michael asked.

"We have no animals, so we don't," Overby replied. "At the south end of the lake, there is a growing community called Starbuck. We share horses and wagons, and I haul my grain there where a man buys it and ships it sometimes to the mills in Minneapolis, sometimes up to Duluth. The railroad profits by building more track and hauling more people and goods. The millers in Minneapolis profit by getting more grain to grind for flour and meal. Grain dealers make money by having more grain to sell overseas. It's a good scheme, Michael, a very good scheme." Again, Michael just shook his head in amazement.

Michael said, "So, will you show me the metes and bounds of this property, so I will know what to clear first, after I put the crop in."

"Yes, and don't forget every time you add 20 acres, you double your income. So, let's get our horses and we'll get right to it."

When they had surveyed all the markers, they took a couple benches from the hut, sat in the shade of the oaks and ate the lunch Mrs. Overby had sent along, washing it down with ice-cold well water. Then Overby helped him harness up the horses and Michael was set to turn over some land.

By the time the sun was fully over the horizon the next morning, Michael was done hitching the horses to the plow and ready to turn over the earth. Smiling as he climbed on the metal seat, he clucked to the horses and they began to pull him forward. He pulled on the right rein and they moved right, left and they moved left. Carefully, he tried out the depth handle, and it moved easily up and down. He was surprised by how dark and rich the land was. Before the end of the week, the field was ready for planting.

The neighboring farmer brought over the sacks of seed Overby had purchased. By Saturday night, the field was ready. As he unhooked the horses, the skies began to darken as if rain was predestined. That evening and into the night it fell softly, a good omen. By lantern light, he sat and wrote his first letter home.

May 14, 1886
Dear Papa and Family,
I have so much to tell you, I hardly know where to begin. My boat trip was long and uneventful. I arrived in a city called New York, and someone helped me board a train to another city called Minneapolis. The train is a big steam engine that pulls five or more things called cars. The substance they burn to create steam is called coal, which is harvested out of the ground. The steam created power pistons that turn the heavy iron wheels. One car hauled freight. The last three cars are filled with benches for people like me, riding from one place to another. It runs on iron rails that are fixed to large wooden boards called ties. Those are sunk into the ground and the rails are nailed to them by huge spikes.

Minneapolis is in the State of Minnesota, where I will work and live until I have enough money to look for a homestead of my own. From Minneapolis, I went by train to a town called Willmar. There, a horse was waiting for me, with a map to my employer in White Bear Township.

You will not believe this: my employer is the "Preston." In America, the government does not give them land and authority to manage it like they did in our country, but the church worked out a deal so the Reverend did get a homestead of 160 acres. His congregation built a new church and a new home for the family. They lived for a year in a sod hut on the land the government gave them. I will live in it until harvest is over.

Winter here is very severe. Reverend Overby says it is often 20 degrees below zero and can get to 40 below. After spending one winter in the sod hut themselves, they invited me to stay in their home for that cold season.

Although I have not yet met the man, I will be working for a carpenter during the winter. I am to be his apprentice, helping to finish the inside of houses he puts up in the summer.

Here's more good news: I will get half of the money from the sale of the grain I harvest. The more land I break up and plant, the more grain will be harvested and I will get more money. Now listen to this, I will also get paid by the carpenter in the winter and live with the Overbys for free. I tell you, these Americans have a scheme for everything.

Here, they do not store grain, but put it on the railroad. The train takes it to Minneapolis, where mills grind it up to make flour, or to a place called Duluth, where it's put on a ship and sold to other countries.

The church is very nice and has a good-sized congregation. The Overbys are very nice people. Not pompous at all. They have 4 well-behaved children.

They have machinery to use that is more advanced than what we had at Glasè. Would you believe it—I sit down to plow, I sit down to smooth the plowed ground, I sit down to sew the seed, and pretty soon, Overby said, I'll have a machine I can sit on to cut and bind the grain. It makes farm work so much easier.

This is a very pleasant area. Everything is very green. There are rolling hills and a beautiful lake called Minnewaska. I understand there is good fishing on the lake but I don't think I'll have time for that. I have to laugh, as everything here has "Minne" in it, Minnesota, Minneapolis, Minnewaska.

Now I am tired, so I will go rest. I think of you often and miss you.

Love,

Michael

Chapter Seven

That very first Sunday, as best he could recall, Michael was up early. The Overbys had invited him for breakfast before the morning service. He put on his best pair of trousers and a white shirt. He wished he had a string tie like Reverend Overby's. He would put it on his list for his first trip to Starbuck.

Breakfast was blueberry pancakes, and they tasted delicious when compared to what he had been fixing for himself. There was bacon and maple syrup that Mrs. Overby said she had made herself. It was all very good. Over coffee, he said he had written a letter and asked what he should put in as a return address so the family could write to him. She told him to write, *In Care Of Reverend Overby, Starbuck, Minnesota, USA*. Her husband would take it to the post office and also bring back any replies.

When the church bell had been rung about 15 minutes before the service was to begin, the Overbys and Michael walked next door. The Reverend continued around back and they went in the front door. It was a beautiful, clear, cool morning.

The church was only half full when they arrived, and people of the parish occupied the benches in the very back of the church, a custom he would become familiar with, but never understand. Mrs. Overby, the four children and Michael marched up to the front bench and sat right below the pulpit. She turned and motioned with her hand for people to move forward, but no one budged. She did not turn again.

A petite, young girl walked down the aisle and took her seat at the organ. She pumped the bellows with her feet a couple times, pulled buttons here and there and began playing softly. It was not a tune Michael recognized. What turned out to be the choir then marched down the aisle and took up the front two benches across the aisle from Mrs. Overby. The bell in the steeple rang three times, a few stragglers hurried in, and Reverend Overby took his place by the lectern. Michael thought the chair he sat in was not nearly as ornate as those he had seen in Norway, especially Nidaros in Trondheim.

The service was in English, although every one in the congregation would have understood it if it were all in Norwegian. "We are Americans now and must learn and use the language of America if we are to prosper," was the unspoken philosophy of every Norwegian settlement. Michael understood very little and recognized none of the psalms, which they here called hymns. He vowed that a year from now he would understand every word and sing every hymn. When the choir marched up to the chancel to sing, he was surprised to see Mrs. Overby walk up and direct them.

At dinner, which he had also been invited to share with the family, he talked to Mrs. Overby and they worked out a plan to meet twice a week in the evening for English lessons. She asked him if he could sing and he said, "Yes, I love to sing."

"Good, we need men in our choir. We will use music to start you out on your quest to learn the English language. I will work with you on the words of our song for Sunday. Then we will work on the tune. Then you will go home and study the words and the tune. On choir practice night, you will come in a half hour early and we will go over the music. Choir practice lasts about a half hour. And at the end, I sometimes like to introduce the next song we will sing. You can listen in, and maybe hum along a little and you'll be one leg up for next week's lesson."

Monday morning he began felling trees in an area that was sparsely populated with younger trees. It would take him at least a week, but should yield another acre or two and provide access to an open area that would double the acreage. The ax was nice and sharp and the work went well. Luckily, Overby had given him a pair of deerskin gloves. Even with those, his hands were sore by nightfall. By fall, they would be hard and calloused. For the larger trees, he would have to ask Overby for a good, strong bucksaw.

By the time the first snow fell, there were seven additional acres plowed. Michael had already marked off the next plot to clear. His hands were toughened and he no longer used the gloves unless the weather was a little cold. He moved into the Overby home two weeks before Christmas. As he looked back, it had been a short summer. He thought the time had flown by.

He had made great progress on his English and now was an established member of the choir, bringing the tenor section up to three voices. He also got to know the choir members and he found himself attracted to the pretty girl who played the organ, though she was only 15 years old. He learned that her name was Emma, and that she did not yet have a suitor. He had not attempted to engage her in conversation yet, but always said hello at choir practice. Her English was perfect, as she had been born here. He did not know if she knew any Norwegian. "Hello," was as brave as he dared get, but his resolve to master English became stronger.

As time went on, he was interested enough to pick up little bits of information here and there. Emma's father was Anton Holte, a charter member of Indherred. He had immigrated here over 25 years ago from Stod, Norway, which Michael knew was just north of Steinkjer. He had helped plot the church cemetery. Her mother was Ellen, and she had immigrated here in 1860. She originally came from Ongdalen, a place Michael knew was just to the west of Steinkjer. So, all of them had come from the same part of the county. That was a good omen, he thought.

He began working as a carpenter's apprentice just after the New Year. His employer's name was Anders Gullixon. He was twice Michael's age, and said he had immigrated here from near Oslo when he was 19 years old. The settlement, he said, was quite new then. He had a homestead halfway between the community of Starbuck and Indherred Church. He spoke in good English, but would compromise now and then on a word or phrase of importance and would use the Norwegian correlate.

On his first day, Gullixon took Michael to the Starbuck lumberyard. Michael was amazed. Here you could buy boards of many different sizes, already cut to a precise length and width. You could also buy big sheets of wood as big as 4 feet by 8 feet. He asked Gullixon how they were made and Gullixon said that soon he would take Michael to the local mill and he could see for himself how the original timbers were cut and dried and how the "plywood," as he called the large sheets of wood, were made. Gullixon picked out what he would need for the inside walls, added six doors with hardware, and many bundles of, what he had told Michael, were "laths." It was a real education for Michael and he marveled at how advanced everything was in this very young country. He would need to write his father and tell him about these lumberyards. His first day, Michael recalled, he began building inside walls. Gullixon told him to establish a base plate 2x4 and nail 8 feet 2x4's every 16 inches on center. Michael worked fast, and Gullixon was pleased with his work and complimented him at the end of the day. "I think, Michael, we will make a good team. You are, as I thought you would be, a hard worker with an eye for accuracy." He had to explain "accuracy" for Michael.

For three days Michael worked with the downstairs walls. Once erected, he would take the lath they had purchased and, as instructed, nail it horizontal to the 2x4s with just a slight gap between the laths. This, Gullixon told him, would provide the plaster enough space to anchor.

That went quickly, and after he and Gullixon built a rough stairway, Michael was putting up the walls on the second floor. Michael was comfortable working alone while Gullixon plastered downstairs. When those walls were up, Gullixon brought him back downstairs. He taught him how to mix the plaster using the right amount of water. There was a pleasing but pungent odor to the plaster. Michael would smell it as he walked into the house every morning. The smell lasted for a long time.

Taking a foot square piece of plywood with a three-inch, round dowel on the bottom of what he called his "mortarboard" (that, too, was a new term for Michael), Gullixon scooped up the plaster with a trowel and piled it onto his mortarboard. Then standing on a 2x12 stretched across 2 sawhorses, Gullixon applied the plaster to the wall. He started at the highest point of the wall where it reached the ceiling in one corner. He worked down to where he could later resume his plastering while standing on the floor.

Michael memorized "mortarboard," "sawhorse," "trowel," and practiced them silently in his head. Soon Gullixon handed him the mortarboard and said, "OK, Michael, my friend, let's see what kind of a plasterer you are." At first, as much plaster went on the floor as went on the wall. Gullixon coached, and soon Michael was losing less and less plaster. By the end of the second day, his arms and shoulders were a little sore, but he was able to smile as he looked at his work. Gullixon, by now, was following him, plastering from the midpoint to the floor.

By the time the downstairs walls were completed, Michael was sent upstairs to plaster those walls. Michael thought, *Gullixon must be pleased to let me go on my own.*

Indeed, Gullixon had been pleased, and told him months later, "It was my lucky day when you came to this town."

When the walls were all up and sufficiently dry, Gullixon had Michael hang the inside doors while he cut and hung the framework for the windows. This had involved another trip to the lumberyard to buy the finish lumber. Again, Michael was impressed at the wide selection of pine, maple and oak that was available, and already cut. Gullixon also selected the finished boards he would use for the cupboards.

In time, Michael began installing the doors upstairs and then the framework for the windows. Gullixon had begun to build and install cupboards, and soon Michael began cutting the boards to the sizes Gullixon gave him. He

94

thoroughly enjoyed his job, and told Gullixon so. He, in turn, was so pleased with Michael's work that he quickly asked him to stay on full time at a percent of what the homes they built sold for.

"With you, I can do one or maybe even two more houses a year. Do you know how to 'rough in' a house?"

Michael said he did, with logs, but would need some directions to build the way Gullixon did. Before he accepted Gullixon's offer, he said, he must speak to Reverend Overby. Overby not only gave him his blessing, but also found a replacement to work his homestead before spring rolled around. Michael began to learn how to build American houses from the ground up.

He moved out of the Overby's home, but continued his English lessons and, of course, he continued on in the choir. He helped the new homestead employee for just two days, to show him what he had intended to clear after the plowing and planting was done.

For his English lessons, he soon was working on a second grade reader and was becoming a little more fluent every day. Even though Gullixon understood Norwegian, they used English all the time, with the exception of a big word now and then that Michael had not yet learned. He occupied a room in Gullixon's upstairs, as all their children were married. He took his meals with them as well. He offered to pay, but Gullixon said, "You are such a hard worker, and I get so much more done now; I make almost twice as much money. The least I can do is keep you well fed for free."

For the next three years, Michael's life ran pretty much down the same road. He soon became as proficient as Gullixon at building houses. His English was much improved, and he had graduated from primers to books on many different subjects. He also liked to read the newspaper when it was available.

Starbuck was a nice little town and much of the house building was done there as businesses increased to meet the needs, locally, of the town and settlement population.

At the east end of the lake was another community called Glenwood, where he and Gullixon built a fine church. Since it was almost 10 miles away, the two found a rooming house and stayed there every night but Saturday. When the church was enclosed, Michael alone stayed there, but Gullixon continued to pay for the room, and came on Fridays and Saturdays to do whatever required two men. He was a very knowledgeable builder and Michael learned a lot from him, especially about furnishings. It was a combination of good teacher and good student.

When winter came, they spent some days in Gullixon's shop designing church furnishings. Gullixon had drawn plans for everything they built, even the church furniture. Together they built the altar, the pulpit, a lectern, and hardest of all, because it was so ornate, a baptismal font. Those items, together with the pews, required 2 men for assembly.

Michael built the parson's chair. It was also very ornate with several hand carvings. Michael did it in the evenings. He felt it was a fitting chair for the man who brought the Gospel. It was cushioned, but otherwise a plain design. Mrs. Gullixon cut out the pieces of wine colored velvet for the back and the seat and bought padding, which she shaped, so all he had to do was apply tacks on a ribbon of crocheted trim to hold the two pieces on. Gullixon looked at it and clucked his tongue in approval.

Michael was a quick learner and could have gone on his own, but he felt he owed it to Gullixon to stay with him. Often, as with the church, Gullixon would be building one place and Michael would be at another site. Whenever one needed help to put up trusses or whatever, they'd get together until the task was completed.

Michael was so pleased with his work on the parson's chair, that in his spare time, he built another for Reverend Overby. Four posts formed the legs of the chair. The two front legs were carved with the head of Harold The Fair Haired. The back legs were double the height of the front, with carved gargoyles going off at a 45-degree angle. Doweled into the front legs was a carved panel featuring vines with grapes and wheat stalks to symbolize the elements of Holy Communion. The two side panels were doweled into the front and back legs. The panels began just below the figure carved in the front legs and then curved elegantly up to where the gargoyles began. They were carved to resemble the round stained glass window he had seen at Nidaros in Trondheim. The back panel was doweled into the back legs. The carving showed 3 ornate crosses with the inscription *INRE* intertwined with the crosses. The seat was plain. He decided not to add a cushion. The chair was stained to match the other chancel furnishings.

He talked to the President of the Council to find out if he donated it, would the Council approve. After the President saw the chair, he not only approved, but also became very excited about how to present it. He told Michael not to worry about the Council; he was sure the Deacons would be very pleased and the Trustees would have no problems since it was donated.

On the first Saturday night after it was finished, the two of them carried the chair into the church. They moved the old chair to the opposite side of the chancel to be used by a guest preacher, when there was one. The new chair looked elegant, with a wide red ribbon with a bow tied just under the gargoyle heads. They could hardly wait to see Reverend Overby's face when he saw it.

They were not disappointed. As the pastor entered the chancel on Sunday morning, he walked toward the chair, saw the ribbon, knew it was different, stopped dead in his tracks and his jaw dropped wide open. Looking out at the congregation, he said, "What is this? Where did it come from?" As planned, Michael, in a fine new suit, came forward together with the President of the Council. Overby looked from one to the other.

Michael spoke first, in English. "Reverend, if it were not for you, I would not be standing here today. You were my sponsor, and when I arrived you took good care of me. I have built this chair for you out of love and respect. I would be honored if you would accept this gift as a token of my esteem."

Tears came quickly to Overby's eyes, and he clasped Michael in an embrace saying, "Thank you, my friend, thank you. I am proud to accept this work of art and will think of you every time I see it." The congregation stood as one and applauded. Now days the church was almost full every Sunday.

Michael returned to his seat, but not before Mrs. Overby stood up and hugged him tightly for a long, long time. She probably would have said something, but she was sobbing too hard to speak. She kissed him on the cheek before she stepped back and let him go.

Then the Deacons came forward. The Head Deacon had drafted a small service of consecration. When it was over, Reverend Overby sat in the chair and the congregation, led by the Council President, sang, a little more lustily than usual, "Thank God From Whom All Blessings Flow."

He, of course, was invited to the Overby's for dinner, and it was a joyful meal. Michael shared that he still checked the homestead frequently. He said the last time he visited the homestead, it looked like about 32 acres were now under the plow.

Overby said, "35."

Then he added that most of the standing timber now was large established trees. There was some concern on Overby's part about cutting it down. With the congregation getting bigger every Sunday, the need for additional income existed, but wasn't as crucial now. Every year the Trustees had sponsored a fund drive, and it looked as if one more would pay off the debt on that building.

Michael no longer took weekly English lessons from Mrs. Overby, but he still went to choir practice and was able to sight read the music, just like the other members. Emma, the organist, was now 18, and even though he was

24, he still pursued thoughts of wooing her. He knew she came early to practice her hymns, so he began coming to the church before the others arrived. On most evenings they would chat a little bit about this and that, slowly getting to know each other. She still did not have a boyfriend and Michael said he wasn't seeing anyone either.

He wished she lived closer by, as he would have liked to ask her if he could walk her home. Her parents' farm, however, was 2 miles northwest of Starbuck. She always came by horse and wagon.

One evening, out of the clear blue, Emma asked him if he had a horse and wagon. In fact, he had built a fine sturdy wagon that he used to haul his tools, lumber and supplies for the job he was working on. He had traded in his riding horse for a sturdier dray. When he replied that indeed he did, she said, "Do you think me too bold if I ask you next week, to come pick me up, drive me here and then take me home. My mother and father will be gone with the horse and wagon, and I do so hate to mount a horse."

Michael's heart beat like a steam engine at full speed. He replied that he would be more than happy to pick her up. He asked directions and told her what time he would arrive. She gave him the sweetest smile, took his hand with both of hers and said, "Oh, thank you, Michael. You are such a sweet man."

Michael's feet never touched the earth in the next seven days. Did she know that this little request was the very least he would be willing to do for her? Could he dare hope that she was as interested in him as he was with her? Was she growing a little impatient with him and priming the pump a little? No, that would be too hard to believe. On the day of choir practice, before he went to the house he was working on, he went to the livery stable. He engaged a horse and buggy for that afternoon and said when he'd be by to pick it up. He thought about bringing her some candy, but thought that might be just a little too forward for this occasion. If this worked out well, he would ask her out sometime soon, and then bring her a suitor's gift.

Even Gullixon noticed that Michael seemed more jubilant and asked why. When Michael told him, Gullixon laughed and said, "That's a fine family, Michael. Anton and Ellen were a couple of the first settlers here. They have worked hard on their homestead and are very much responsible for us having a church here in White Bear. If I'm right, I think they have about eight children. Good luck to you, Michael."

Michael quit working early and heated up some water for a bath. He shaved, for the second time, and put a little pomade in his hair. He wore dress pants and a white shirt.

He was at the livery by six and arrived at the Holte homestead earlier than he had said. Emma was ready and waiting. She was out the door before he had stopped the horses. She wore her hair up and looked quite sophisticated in a blue dress with a white lace collar, and a blue satin tie around the waist. While he usually didn't pay attention to such things, he even noticed that she wore white stockings and black patent leather shoes with a small heel. Michael suddenly had a very dry mouth and he wondered if her large blue eyes could see just how hard and fast his heart was beating.

He got down, went around to the other side of the buggy and offered his hand to help her up. She took it and said, "Thank you." When he got in again, she said teasingly, "Is this your wagon for work? It seems very elegant for hauling lumber."

He blushed and lied, "No, I thought in case it rained, this might keep us a little dryer." Then he teased her. "Since there's not a cloud in the sky, maybe I can just leave it off at the livery and go the rest of the way in the wagon. That would save me some money." She looked to see if he was serious, but saw his grin.

"No", she said, "I think I feel very elegant in this buggy and would prefer you keep it for the evening. I feel very special." And she patted his hand.

When he returned her to her home later that evening, she waited until he came around the buggy to help her down. She held onto his hands just a little longer than necessary as she said, "Thank you, Michael, you are such a dear man." Her hands squeezed his, and she ran up the steps and into the house. He had no idea how his chair, and its presentation to Pastor Overby, had impressed her.

All the way home Michael analyzed the evening. He thought that there might have been a little spark between them, which he admitted to himself, had set him on fire. He decided the true test would be *when* and *if* he asked her out. He quickly discarded the *if*. The church was having an ice cream social and pie auction in two weeks. He would ask her to go with him at the next choir practice. He went to bed a happy man. He was one step closer to having something in his life he'd never had before—a girl, pretty and petite, "en vakre liten piker".

As he reminisced, Michael chuckled to himself as he recalled how he never got up the courage to ask Emma to the church social, but he was there early and watched as the ladies brought in their prize winning pies to be auctioned. He watched carefully as Emma and her mother, Ellen, walked in with their pies neatly tied up in a dish towel, with the four corners knotted to make a handle. He prayed that they were each carrying their own pie. They carefully unwrapped them and set them on one of the tables. Michael mentally marked the location of Emma's pie. It looked like it could be apple, his favorite.

Reverend Overby acted as the auctioneer. He opened the social with the announcement that, in all, 23 pies would be put up for bids. He began by holding up a beautiful meringue creation. Bidding started at a dime and went up to thirty-five cents. "If this continues," Reverend Overby intoned, "it's going to be a bargain hunter's night. You're hardly paying for the cost of the ingredients, let alone the toil that goes into these delicious desserts."

At that, the bidding increased, ranging between 70 cents and $1.50. As Overby worked his way down the table, Michael's stomach began to fill up with butterflies, and his hands were sweating profusely. After Emma's mother, Ellen's, pie went for $1.60, Michael's mouth was so dry, he wasn't sure he would be able to get a bid out.

However, as soon as Overby picked up the pie Michael had memorized by now, he croaked out a bid. It came out so garbled, the Reverend had to ask him what he said. Blushing from head to toe, Michael managed to say clearly, "I bid $2.50."

A gasp came up from the crowd and Overby, grinning, said, "Two and a half dollars, Michael? Is that as high as you can go?"

"No," said Michael, not recognizing a tease, "I can go higher, Reverend. I bid $5."

As the crowd roared with laughter, Overby called out, "Five dollars is the bid; does anyone go higher?" To Michael's relief, not a single voice spoke up. "Before I sell this creation, would the maker of this $5 pie identify herself?" Emma hesitatingly raised her hand. "Sold!" Overby shouted. When Michael went up to retrieve his prize, the entire audience, with smiles on their faces, rose as one and applauded him. He blushed even more and noticed Emma's face was also red.

"Well, now!" Overby announced. "Now we've got some serious bidding going on. Let's keep it up." But none of the other pies got over $2.

As Michael exited with his pie, several of the men slapped him on the back with no comment, but total understanding. The women just giggled in shear delight. As he approached his wagon, he felt a tug on his sleeve. He turned and saw the love of his life, her eyes shining brighter than the stars overhead. She grabbed his hand, stood on tiptoe, kissed him on the cheek, and said, "You dear, dear, sweet man. You knew that was my pie, didn't you?" His blush became the answer. Then she added breathlessly, "Will you take me home after church next Sunday and stay for dinner with our family?"

He managed to get a "yes" out, and she squeezed his hand with both of hers before she turned and skipped off. When he got home, Michael ate the whole pie, washing it down with strong back coffee he warmed up. He hardly slept a wink all night.

The three days until Sunday sped by, and Michael worked at a feverish pace.

He again hired the buggy from the local stable and parked it close to the church, so everyone would see him as he and Emma left. She stopped practicing as he came down the aisle. Her smile was huge and warm as she watched him come nearer. "How was my pie, Michael?" she asked, beaming.

"It was the most delicious dessert I have ever tasted," he replied shyly. "I ate the whole thing before I went to bed."

Emma giggled with delight and said "Oh, you, Michael!" before she turned back to her organ and began playing. It was the sweetest music he had ever heard, both her voice and the organ. He sang with the choir anthem, but could remember nothing else about the service.

When the service ended, he waited while Emma gathered up her music and walked down the aisle with him. As they exited, it looked like hardly anyone had left for home. As he helped Emma into the buggy, he heard "Oohs" and "Ahs" from everywhere, and here and there a whistle. He sat straight and tall in the buggy seat, waving and smiling to the congregation members, who again were applauding him. It was obvious he and Emma, as a couple, had their blessing.

Dinner was not without some teasing from Emma's siblings. He blushed his way through it. Father Anton and Mother Ellen welcomed him warmly with a handshake, but said not a word about the auction. As he sat next to Emma, he hardly noticed the food he was eating. When it was over and the dishes were cleaned, he and Emma took a ride in his rented buggy. The day was perfect, with clear blue skies and a slight breeze. Michael thought, *If this isn't Heaven, then I'd rather stay right here, thank you, God.*

Emma asked him all about his family, and he told her of his days in Norway.

He told her of his beloved mother, who had died at such an early age. It was a day for getting to know each other and feeling comfortable about being together. When they stopped to water the horse at a stream, Emma again took his hands in hers and said, "I know you are very shy, and I waited and waited for you to ask me out. When the words never came, I'm sorry, Michael,

I got so bold as to ask you."

"Oh, don't apologize, Emma. I was dying to ask you from the very first time I saw you. I just didn't feel worthy. You were raised here, and your English is so perfect. You are so talented, and on top of it all you are beautiful and good and sweet."

"Oh, dear Michael, do you really like me?"

"I don't really know, because this has never happened to me before, but I think I like you more than just *like* you."

This time a light kiss on the lips, another squeeze of the hand, and she snuggled closer to him as they resumed their ride. She moved a ways away again as they neared her home. That day Michael stayed through the evening meal. Just outside the front door on leaving, where no one could see them, she put her arms around him and he responded by putting his arms around her and holding her close. She kissed him on the lips again and backing away while holding both hands, she said, "You are such a handsome man, Michael, and I fear I am falling in love with you."

He managed, "Ja, ja, me too." She gasped and hugged him one more time, then turned and went back into the house. On the way home, Michael wondered if what happened really happened, or if he just imagined it.

Back at the farm, Emma watched him through the window until she could no longer see him. Her heart would not stop pounding. In her thoughts she pondered the day. *I think I have found a husband—a dear, sweet, gentle, but hard-working man. Yes! Now, how do I get this shy gentleman to propose?*

It was the birth of a courtship that would go on for another year. Most of the time they spent together was church related, but often he visited her at her home. While they talked of marriage and family, and it was understood that they were a couple, Michael would not ask her to be his bride until he had built her a home. Working on it in his spare time, it took him until the fall of 1891 before he proposed. His courage came in the form of a letter he received from Emma, a month past her 19th birthday.

By then, Emma had moved out of her family home and was living with her best friend, Thomine Jorgerson. The two of them, together with other friends, Mary Thompson and Betsy Carlson, had a seamstress business that was doing very well. Their work was flawless and their reputation was outstanding. Emma had also been working on getting her brother, Adolph, interested in Thomine. One evening, sitting alone, Emma decided to work on getting Michael to propose. She decided to write him a carefully worded note hinting about marriage.

August 14, 1891 Starbuck, Minn.
Dear Friend Mikal,
Since I am sitting home alone this evening, I will write a few words to you, Mikal. Thomine went for a walk and I am sitting alone at home. I didn't have any desire to go along. I would rather be at home and write to you.

Tuesday evening there was a concert at the town hall. Thomine and I were there and it was very enjoyable. Tomorrow evening there will be a show again. I don't know if we will go.

Yesterday the Thali family was here in town. They were at Emma's and wanted to know if you weren't going to get married soon, so they could come to your wedding. Emma said that it was something she had never asked you so she didn't know.

Thomine is returning now so I have to quit for this time.
With loving greetings from your friend always,
Emma

Don't forget to send me a few words back to your Emma. Live well is my wish for you.

Unknown to Emma, he approached her parents a couple days later. They gave him their blessing: Anton with a smile and a handshake, Ellen with a warm hug.

On weekends, they were often together at the house he was building. Emma had no idea that he intended this one to be theirs. To her it was just another house and she loved to be close to him. She helped when she could and always made sure they had a good dinner to eat.

It was now just one week from the day he got Emma's letter. On that day the last nail was pounded and the last paintbrush put away clean, Michael took Emma outside and they sat in the shade of an apple tree, rich with fruit. This fall the apples would ripen and there would be fruit for fresh apple pie, and much more to can. Apple pie! Ja, it had won him a bride.

Picking a green apple, he handed it to Emma. "It was because of this fruit that we became a couple. So this is a good place for me to say something important."

Taking Emma's hand so gently, he said, "You must know by now how much I love you, and you must know I want to spend the rest of my life with you. My dear, beautiful, talented, wonderful, Emma, will you be my wife?" He was so proud he'd gotten all those words out in perfect English.

Her reaction was immediate, as she threw her arms around his neck, hugged him close and whispered in his ear, "Oh, my dear, sweet, Michael, I want nothing more in this world than to be with you. Yes, Michael, oh yes, I will marry you! And we will live together as long as God allows." This time the kiss on the lips was not just a peck. When she pulled back, she looked in his eyes and said, "Oh, Michael, your mustache tickles so!" And they both laughed until tears came.

Taking a new white handkerchief out of his pocket, he opened it to reveal the silver solje brooch with the shiny spoons. It glistened in the sunlight. Emma looked at him with an unspoken question in her eyes. He said to her, "Emma, I bought this brooch as a Christmas present for my dear mother, Thale. She died before I could get home to give it to her. I vowed on that Christmas that I would give it to my bride to wear on her wedding dress. Please, my Emma, keep this for me now as a token of our agreement to be man and wife. On our wedding day, I would like to pin it to your wedding dress to seal our vows, and that way, I will know my dear mother will be with us on that day."

Tears flowed from both of their eyes, and all Emma could get out as they embraced was "It is so beautiful, Michael. You are so beautiful. Oh, I will wear this with such pride to honor your love for your mother. Oh, Michael! Oh sweet, sweet, Michael, you are such a good man and I will love you forever. And, Michael, when we are married, I would love to have an apple tree just like this one in our yard. Then I can make you your favorite dessert. Every day I can look out the window and see the tree and remember your beautiful proposal and thank God for sending you to me."

"So, Emma, would you like to see your house now?

"Oh, Michael, you have found us a house to live in? Oh, yes, yes, let's go right now. I must see it! Maybe we can plant an apple tree in the yard."

"Well, that won't be necessary, it already has an apple tree, and it is filled with green apples that will soon ripen."

"Let's go, Michael, let's go. I can't wait another minute."

Taking Emma's hand, he led her up the walk to the house and ushered her through the door.

"Do you need to get something from in here? Oh, hurry, Michael. I'm on pins and needles to see our home. Please hurry."

"No need to hurry, Emma, no need to hurry. We're already there." Sweeping his hand from wall to wall and ceiling to floor he announced, "Welcome to the home of soon to be Michael and Emma Glasoe."

Emma's mouth dropped open in shear astonishment. "This house is our house, Michael? You're not fooling me are you? No, you would never be so cruel. This is our house? My heart is pounding so fast! Hold me so I don't faint."

Hugging her close, Michael said, "This is our house. We built it together and soon we will live in it together. Do you like it?"

"Do I like it? I have never seen anything so grand as this! It is the most beautiful house I have ever seen! Oh, Michael, why didn't you let me know?"

"Because I like surprises, and this was a good one. I will never forget the look on your face just now when I told you this was our home."

"I can't believe it! I just can't believe it, Michael. This is our house, our house! Oh, I must bring Mama and Papa here and show them. Oh! Oh! And I must bring Thomine here. I will tell her we're going to look at the house you're building, and I will bring her here and surprise her like you surprised me. What fun it will be. Oh, I love you so much, Michael."

In the days that followed, they began planning furniture for their home and ordered it from Sears Roebuck in time for early delivery. There was not much time—a week of August, the month of September and almost all of October. The wedding date was set for the 29th of that month. The furniture, they were told, would come in early October.

Young Michael had done well in this new land with its difficult language. He still was thinking homestead, but his carpentry business was going so well, he was reluctant to give up the nice income it provided. He had saved enough to pay for the materials to build their house, as well as the furniture they purchased. They bought only necessities, with the thought that he would supplement what they bought with whatever pieces he could build in his spare time. He started with beds for the mattresses they had ordered.

Of course he wrote home to his family in Norway to tell them about his Emma. He knew that they would be pleased that he had found a wonderful wife. He wished that they could all be there for the ceremony, but he knew he would have to be content with his memories of them. He promised them he would send a photograph of the wedding couple. He asked for their good wishes and prayers.

When the furniture arrived by rail from Chicago in late September, he moved into his new home. The thrill he felt as he came and left, day after day, was an unsurpassed pride in his accomplishment. Creating something, for him, was being in God's image. He got the same feeling when he turned the soil and planted the crop.

As the wedding day neared, he saw less and less of Emma. She was busy at home sewing her wedding dress. She wanted it to be perfect. Michael, of course, bought a new suit and new black shoes.

Chapter Eight

Two days before the wedding, Michael recalled, he had heard a knock on the door as he was finishing his supper. When he opened it, he got the shock of his life. There stood his father, Ole, his brothers, Otto and Edward, and his sister, Mattie. Michael couldn't speak, but greeted each of his brothers and his father in turn with a handshake and hug. He gave his little sister a hug so hard she giggled. There were tears in everyone's eyes.

They all jabbered back and forth in Norwegian for hours. It was like being home in Norway, except for the absence of his three other sisters, Hilde, Lottie and Trine. His father, at age 59, said he was here simply to see what this country, America, was all about. Edward, at the adventurous age of 17, was here to find a homestead when he turned 18, and Otto, age 11, would be living with him. Mattie, in the last of her teen years, was here to accept a job as a house servant in western Dakota.

They assured him they had eaten at the hotel before coming over. He made them coffee, which they sipped as they caught up on each other's past. Tomorrow, they agreed, Michael would meet them at the hotel and bring them and their belongings here to the house.

It turned out that his oldest sister, Hilde, had gotten married on the 10th of this month. The other two sisters would now be living with her and her husband, Arnt. Mattie said, "Oh, you should have seen Hilde, Michael. She wore your beautiful mantilla and the shawl you gave her for Christmas."

"That's all she wore?" Michael said teasingly. And everybody had a good laugh.

Mattie added sharply, "No! She also had her bunad and white stockings and black shoes, and underneath—I don't know." Everyone laughed again. "When will we meet your bride to be?"

Michael answered, "Tomorrow morning, before I pick you up, I'll drive out to Emma's parents' farm and tell her the good news that you are here. If she can't come right back with me, I'm sure she'll come later in the day. I can tell you this, she is going to be very surprised you're here and very excited to meet you." Then he asked, "How did you ever get here today when Hilde only got married on the 10th of this month?"

"It took a lot of planning and more than a little luck," Ole replied, "I can tell you that. After we got your letter, we all sat down and talked. Edward and Mattie had been planning to come earlier, but then decided they would wait six months so they could be at Hilde's wedding. Otto decided he would come along and be with Edward, rather than stay in Norway and live with Hilde. I have wanted to come here for a long time, but just never got motivated.

When we inquired about our tickets, the sailing date we chose cut it pretty close, but it all worked out fine. So—two family weddings in one month." They, of course, had all been at the wedding and two days later, boarded a steam ship for America. The crossing, they said, took only 10 days, one more day to get Mattie, Edward and Otto through their immigration process in New York, then four days by train to Starbuck.

A couple times, Michael found himself saying something in English, then stopped and continued on in Norwegian. Edward watched and listened carefully. "So, Michael," he asked in Norwegian, "Is it easy to learn this language?"

Michael laughed and replied, "No, Edward, it's not easy at all, but you have no choice. Immigrant communities, it seems, will not allow themselves the luxury of taking the easy way out, by speaking in the mother tongue. You have to learn English in order to survive. They are kind with you the first few weeks, when you are new in the community. After that, if you speak Norwegian, it's as though they can't hear you. Sometimes, in the beginning, I had to combine one or two words with many gestures. The minister's wife helped me at first, but now I do as much reading as I have time for, to increase my vocabulary and improve my pronunciation."

All Edward could say was "Oh," echoed by sister Mattie's "Oh."

"So, Edward, do you know where you are heading and when you have to be there?"

"I have been getting news from a community in North Dakota," Edward explained. "They say there is still plenty of homestead land available. I think it's a little late now in this year, but maybe I can find a place to work just like you did and then find my property as soon as the snow melts. I will be old enough to claim a homestead come my birthday in May."

"And how about you, Mattie?" Michael went on. "Where are you going, and when do you need to be there?"

"I am going to a place called Grenora, in the Dakotas. I saw an advertisement for a servant girl in our home newspaper and wrote to them. I am to write and let them know when I'll be there. How far from here do you think that would be, Michael? Maybe you could find a place for me here for a few days. Then I can go with Edward and Otto, but I will be going farther west, I think."

"Mattie," Michael said, "I have no idea, but tomorrow we'll go to the train station and look at the map. It would be good if the train would go there. Now I have an idea. I will need to talk to Emma about it, but what would all of you think about staying here with us through the winter. I could surely use the help in building houses. I have one house started and with the three of you helping me, we could get another one built. Then together, we could finish the inside of both of them during the winter."

Eyes lit up like Christmas candles, and almost as a chorus, "Oh, Michael, do you think we could, you just getting married and everything?"

Ole expressed further hesitancy, "Well, son, you know me. I'd be more than thrilled to help, but the timing, like Mattie said, we all might be too much for newlyweds to handle."

"Nonsense, all of you. I'll talk to Emma tomorrow. I'm sure she would appreciate Mattie's help around the house." Mattie beamed pure delight. "But, when she comes," he spoke softly, "you will all have to be on your very best behavior so she doesn't think you are rude or boorish." When faces went sober, Michael slapped his leg and laughed and laughed until they joined in. That was a good joke, he thought.

Michael drove them over to the hotel, hugged each one and said goodnight. "I have a good feeling about this. We are all going to help each other. I am so very glad you came. I have missed you so much. I can hardly wait to talk to Emma."

An early riser, he was at the Holte farm as they finished morning chores. Unused to impromptu visits, Emma's face registered concern. "Emma, you will never believe what happened at our house last evening," he said.

Now Emma's concern became more evident. "Oh, Michael, there wasn't a fire was there? After all your hard work and money."

"Oh, no, Emma, nothing bad. Instead—something good, very good! I had visitors. Try to guess who they were." Michael was playing the suspense to the hilt.

"Do I know them, Michael?"

"Well, yes, in a way? You've never met them, but you know about them."

"Oh, stop teasing, Michael, I don't have any idea who they would be; some people who want you to build something for them?"

"Oh, no. Better than that."

"Michael!"

"Oh, alright. Last evening when I finished my meal, there was a knock on our door. When I opened it...," he paused.

"Michael!!"

"On our doorstep were my father, my brothers, Edward and Otto, and my sister, Mattie—all the way from Norway."

"Oh, Michael. Oh, how wonderful! They came all that way from Norway for our wedding?"

"Well, yes and no. Father came for the wedding. Edward and Otto and are here for the wedding, too, but they also are on their way to Dakota to find a homestead. Mattie is here for the wedding, but is also on her way to Dakota to be a servant girl."

"When can I meet them? Oh, I hope they will approve of me. Could I come today?"

"Yes, today would be wonderful. Maybe you could stay to evening and show everyone what a fine cook you are. I know the wedding is so close and you're working hard on your dress..."

"The dress is done, Michael. I will come today and have Mama go through the larder with me and I'll bring the very best we have for supper."

"Oh, no, Emma, I can buy the food."

"No, no, it must be as I said. I want them to know how good I can be at taking care of you. I will come right after dinner. I will stay the afternoon and evening, but I want to start back home before the sun goes down. "

"Yes, that will be good. Now, Emma, I must tell you what I've done, but only if you approve. I have invited them all to stay with us through the winter. My father, Ole, and my two brothers would help me with the house building, and Mattie would help you with cooking and household chores. They think this is a wonderful offer, but are very worried that they will impose too much on us newlyweds."

"Nonsense. Just nonsense. They can stay as long as they can tolerate us. Oh, what good help you'll have, and I can help Mattie work on her English and prepare her for being a house girl. Nonsense, they must stay with us."

"You're right, they'll be wonderful help. I had already decided that if you said OK, we would frame up a second house before winter, so we'd have two to finish before the snow falls. That will mean more income for us, and wages for them. I must go to the hotel now and move them to the house. I will look for you right after the noon meal. You will like them, Emma, and they will adore you."

The ride back to the hotel was quickened by his eagerness to share the good news: Emma insisted they must stay through the winter. Life was good.

His family was waiting in the lobby when he drove up. He told them Emma would come in after the noon meal and would make supper. Then, clapping his hands, he announced that Emma not only approved their stay over the winter, but she insisted on it.

His siblings clapped their hands enthusiastically, whooped and danced around, until they drew the stare of other lodgers in the lobby.

They loaded boxes and trunks in the wagon. Ole sat up front with Michael, and the others scampered onto the back of the wagon. On the way home, they stopped at the depot. They trooped in to look at the map, and asked the agent a dozen questions. Yes, the railroad ran to Minot; it was a day's trip.

Emma arrived at the house with a basket full of food. Michael ran out to carry it in; the others waited nervously in the living room. Michael did the introductions. The men responded with an English, "Hello," and a handshake, but Mattie gave Emma a warm embrace and said in Norwegian, "Oh, you are just as beautiful as I imagined Michael's bride would be." The others echoed "Ja, ja."

Dinner was a baked ham, new potatoes, canned green beans and fresh buns that Emma had baked that morning. Everyone agreed it was just delicious. Then Emma mischievously produced 2 fresh apple pies, and as she dished out a slice for each of them, told of Michael's bid at the auction that had won him her heart forever. Oh, how they laughed at her story, and Michael blushed all over again. They all applauded when he added, "Ja, that may be, but that's the best five dollars I'll ever spend."

When Emma had left for home, the boys had enjoyed their second piece of pie and the coffee pot was drained. Everyone but Michael and Ole went up to bed. They sat and talked for some time. Michael got caught up on all that had happened since he left Norway. He, in turn, shared his experiences since coming to White Bear Township.

"Have you given up the idea of a homestead, Michael?" his father queried. "I know that was your dream when you left home."

"No, I've not given it up, but it's kind of been put out of mind. I like it here, but the available farmland around here was gone long before I arrived.

Like Edward and Otto, I think the nearest homestead land will be in the Dakotas. I understand the land there is flat and stretches out forever. Unfortunately, I hear the soil is not as fertile as we have here. The life of a prairie farmer can be a difficult one. While there are no mountains or fjords here, there are rolling hills and beautiful, clear lakes. Also, my building trade is doing so well, I'm reluctant to give it up."

"Well, have you ever considered doing both at once: finding a homestead, building your home and outbuildings, and then hiring someone to till the land, put in crops and harvest them, while you build houses?" Ole puffed on his pipe as Michael contemplated his thoughts.

"I must admit, Father, that I've kept myself so busy, I haven't given much thought to tomorrow, let alone next year. But your suggestion makes sense. I do miss turning over the good earth and harvesting the crops. I miss the animals, too." Michael continued, "You've ignited a spark, Father, but I think I will need to lay up at least a year's wages, if not two, to get from here to there.

"After Emma and I are wed, I will talk to her about our future. I'm sure she has some thoughts on that subject. She has been a farm girl, so being a farmer's wife shouldn't be too much of a change. It is so good to have you here with me, Father. You always give me wise advice and make me stretch out just a little farther. It will be interesting to see how it goes with Edward and Otto. I will keep in touch with them."

The next morning Mattie had hot cakes, leftover ham and fresh coffee for all of them just as the sun came over the horizon. Michael shared with his brothers his conversation with their father about homesteading, and they promised to send letters regularly when they reached Dakota.

The rest of the day was spent at the house Michael was working on, with everyone measuring, sawing and pounding nails. Even Michael was impressed with how much the four of them accomplished in one day. They would be a good team.

Thursday, October 29th, Michael remembered, was the day of his marriage to Emma. It had dawned clear, but with a sharp bite to the morning. By noon, the sun had warmed the air considerably, and by 2:00, the hour of the wedding, the day could not be described in any other terms but ideal.

The wagons started arriving just after one o'clock, and the churchyard was full as Michael and his family arrived. His father was pleased to see so many people in the church for his son's wedding, as he and his three children were ushered to the front of the church. Little did he know that many of them were Emma's mother's family, the Wollans, who had also immigrated here. In fact, they occupied a considerable territory, known informally as the "Wollan Community." Because of their numbers, the brothers had even achieved a certain level of fame when their picture appeared on the inside of a certain brand of cigars.

When Ellen Holte, resplendent in a beige lace dress, her dark hair brushed back to form a tight bun, had been seated next to her sons, Gustav, William, Adolph and Odin, the organ began the wedding march. Everyone rose as Emma and her father, his handsome goatee neatly trimmed and brushed, sporting a brand new three-piece suit himself, complete with a glittering gold watch chain across his vest, accompanied her to the chancel.

Emma, however, stole the show. She had spent hours dreaming about, and finally sewing her wedding dress. She had heard that sewing her own dress would bring bad luck, but she "poo-pooed" that "old-fashioned nonsense." Ever practical, she had designed a dress that could be her special Sunday dress after their marriage. Besides, she had a lot of help from her very good friends, Mary, Betsy and Thomine, "The Young Minnesota Seamstresses" as they called themselves. So, in reality, she had not really sewn the dress all by herself.

At first, she had thought of a white dress, but when she spied the bolt of beautiful royal blue fabric at the General Store in Starbuck, she immediately knew that would be her dress. She designed a fitted jacket with narrow lapels secured by velvet bows at the V-shaped waist. The long leg-o-mutton sleeves ended in delicate lace.

The night before her wedding she had crept out of bed and quietly stitched the waistline of the jacket even smaller, so that she could show off her tiny waist. She had worked in silence, scarcely daring to breathe. Her mama would not have approved of what she was doing, but Michael would. The full skirt of her dress was gathered at the hipline by more velvet bows. Under the jacket was a white silk blouse with a rounded collar.

Emma's one luxury was her veil. A cloud of white tulle had been gathered into a headdress and adorned with wild flowers that cascaded all the way to her shoulders. The veil floated along the floor behind her as she slowly walked down the aisle, beaming at Michael the entire way.

Her sister, Johanna, who had traveled all the way from North Dakota, was her Maid of Honor, and Gullixon, friend and mentor, was Michael's Best Man.

The service began with a congregational hymn. Reverend Overby spoke briefly to the couple of their commitment to each other, and to God, as they became as one. Vows were exchanged, and at that point, Emma handed something to Michael. He unfolded the lace hankie carefully to reveal the beautiful silver brooch that had sealed their engagement. As he pinned it on her, he said softly, "As I loved my dear mother, so shall I love you until the end of our time."

Katrina Overby, her voice both rich and full, sang "May God Watch Over You." The pronouncement of their marriage was made, and Overby introduced Michael and Emma Glasoe, "another young family under God," to the congregation.

The reception in the church basement was like a feast. Six tables gave witness to every kind of food imaginable: casseroles, gelatin salads in every color of the rainbow, sandwiches, pickles, homemade buns, lefse, flatbread, cookies and doughnuts. Mrs. Holte had made and decorated the wedding cake, resplendent with wild flowers that matched those on Emma's veil.

When it came time to leave, Ole noted the absence of Michael and Emma. Thinking they were probably already at the wagon, he and the children started in that direction. However, there was no one at the wagon. Edward noticed an envelope on the wagon seat. It was addressed to Ole. In Norwegian, he read, "Father, Do not be alarmed. We have decided to spend a few days alone. We will return shortly. Emma has sent a similar message to her parents. Thank you, thank you and thank you for being here for our wedding. We will see you soon. Love, Michael and Emma."

On the next day, Friday, a dray wagon pulled up in front of the Glasoe home. The driver knocked on the door and asked if there were any strong bodies that would help him unload his cargo. Ole, Edward and Otto accompanied him to the wagon. There he uncovered a beautiful new pump organ made of oak, burnished to the color of golden wheat. It was a struggle, but the four of them made it through the door and into the living room. There was one clear wall, so they placed it there. The drayman went out and returned with the matching oak organ stool with glass ball feet and a swivel seat that could be raised and lowered to various levels depending on the height of the player.

"So, who is this from?" Ole asked in Norwegian. He got no response, only a handshake and "tak" from the driver. Ole didn't know if the man understood his question, didn't know who it was from, or was sworn to secrecy. Ah, well, it was a beautiful addition to the Glasoe home.

The mystery was solved on Saturday afternoon when Michael and Emma drove up in a buggy. As Michael helped Emma down, he took a scarf from his pocket and tied it to cover her eyes and led her up to the house. By the time they reached the front door, everyone inside knew who the organ was from and who it was for. When the blindfold was removed, Emma gasped, and then burst into tears. Hugging him close to her, "Oh, Michael, Oh, Michael," was all she could get out. She also knew the giver. So, it was now assured, the Glasoe home would always be filled with music.

Oh, such music and singing, through the evening and again the next day when, after the church service, the Holte family joined them for dinner. What a joyous day it was, the two families together, singing in both Norwegian and English. Despite the fact the Holtes had been in America for over 30 years, they still were fluent in the language of their homeland.

Now everyone understood the reason for the secretive honeymoon. It was not impromptu, but carefully planned by Michael to ensure delivery of his wedding present to his bride, in their absence. He would later tell Emma and the families that the organ had been sitting at the depot since the time their furniture was delivered.

The weeks flew by and soon the first flakes of snow fell and the winter season arrived. Often, the first wet snows coated the barren tree branches like frost, and turned them magically into giant, glittering, crystal sculptures. When the clouds departed and the sun came out, the sparkling trees against the clear blue skies were a work of art no human could ever capture on canvas.

The men were busy every day except the Sabbath, working to complete the interiors of the two houses they had enclosed that fall. Sometimes they worked in pairs, sometimes all four together, depending on what needed to be done. The white-sided, two-story homes they built were typical of those around them. Downstairs was a generous kitchen, with lots of cupboard space and place for a table and chairs. Michael and Ole also made the cabinets. There was a small dining room and a generous living room.

Just inside the front door of the home was a small entry room, where food could be stored in the wintertime. Farm homes also used it as a place for their cream separators. While the room permitted cool air in the winter, it kept the cold air from the kitchen. On the back of the home, adjacent to the living room, was a small porch with screened windows, giving a great view of the backyard where flowers and fruit bearing plants often formed a lovely summer garden.

Upstairs, there were as many bedrooms as the buyer requested. The more rooms required, the smaller they became. It was unusual in those days for anyone to have their own bedroom after the first four children were born. As the family grew, the lucky first-born children acquired roommates.

Emma and Mattie kept busy at home. It was important that Mattie learned the skill of preserving vegetables, fruits and meat. The first priority was to can any fruits or vegetables that had ripened after the wedding. If small fruits were available, they made jams and jellies from apples and delicious apple butter with cinnamon and cloves.

Butter was churned every week, from the cream from their one cow. If they had too much on hand, they sold the excess to the grocer. Pickles came from cucumbers and beets.

Then they proceeded with chickens from their own coop, then a quarter of beef, and half a pig from Emma's parents: these all had to be butchered, cooked and canned. The men always marveled at how good it smelled when they came into the kitchen at the end of the day.

Much of the fat was rendered into lard, and the rest was used to make soap.

Of course, when the meat was fresh, for just a couple days they had roasts and chops and, once in a while, a steak. On very special occasions, they got a taste of their homemade wine—usually rhubarb or apple cider.

Then there was fresh bread to be made once or twice a week. White bread was standard, but a favorite was brown bread made with molasses. Buns were made for the men's sandwiches. It was a great learning experience for Mattie, and she and Emma enjoyed each other's company. It was also an opportunity for Mattie to learn English.

On one occasion, Emma's mother came three days in a row, bringing goat's milk and teaching the two young girls how to make cheese. On another day, she brought sweet cream and they learned to make "American" cheddar cheese. Now the sandwiches would taste really good.

When winter became severe, Otto stayed home to do the milking, pick eggs, chop firewood and clean the small barn. When she had the time, Emma would teach Otto English, while Mattie watched and listened. First came the alphabet, then simple three letter words and, finally, first readers. Like Mattie, he learned very quickly, and in the evening, passed his lesson on to his brother.

Also, as Emma rehearsed the hymns and the choir anthem for the Sunday service, she would have everyone sing along. To begin with, it was mostly Michael doing the singing, but as the months went along, his brothers and sister became full participants. Ole was content to sit and listen while he smoked his pipe.

The Advent season in Norway was traditionally the starting point for Christmas preparation, and social traditions in that country put a great deal of pressure on families to "do it right." There were special things to be done and a timeline for getting them done.

So Advent in the Glasoe household was a busy happy time. The house was cleaned top to bottom, even though they had lived there only one month. A wreath was made to hang on the front door to welcome visitors. Five pointed stars hung in every window. Decorations for the tree were made and stored until Christmas Eve when the tree would be cut and put in the living room. Garlands were made from cranberries and popcorn. Sugar cookies, in the shape of stars and trees, were hung with green and red thread. The boys, with Emma's oldest scissors, cut out ornate snowflakes. The crowning touch was the angel wearing a long, flowing satin dress. Below her, a satin banner had been carefully lettered, *Unto you is born...*

Now was also the time for making "goodies," as Emma called them. They included krumkake, a thin cookie rolled into a kind of tube while it was still hot and malleable; fatigman, rolled out thin, cut in diamonds, deep fried in lard and dusted with powdered sugar; sandbakkles, a favorite, made of butter, sugar and flour pressed into a fluted mold and baked; spritz, a small sugar cookie that the men ate like popcorn, or would have, if they could; and rosettes, made by dipping a flower shaped iron in batter and then into hot lard where it loosened and fried before being dusted with powdered sugar.

Christmas also meant flatbrod, a flour and potato dough, rolled thin and baked crispy on the top of the wood stove. And, of course, there was lefse, similar to flatbrod, but thicker and softer in texture. Oh, how good these tasted with fresh butter! Emma made a fruit cake, and for the Christmas Eve meal, kringle, a flaky yeast bread filled with raisins and nuts. Doughnuts, a favorite with coffee, were a household staple, but at Christmas time, a rising dough was made, the doughnut fried in lard and then glazed.

In Norway, Advent was the time for brewing beer, as mandated by the King. It had never been a practice in the Elnan home, however, as Thale would not permit it. Ole said the King was a Swede, and he was just trying to get the Norwegians drunk so they wouldn't be so ornery and hard to rule. It was not the practice in the new Glasoe household either, as Emma came from a family where strong drink was frowned upon. Emma said her coffee was better anyway.

Christmas Eve Day the men took the horse and wagon out to a pine grove and cut down the perfect tree to bring home and decorate. When they brought it in the door, there were enthusiastic words of appreciation for their efforts. Emma said, "That is the finest tree I have ever seen! How fitting to have it in our home on our first Christmas together."

The ladies spent the afternoon preparing the evening meal. They made meatballs from sausage and pork, and a tasty gravy to put on the mashed potatoes. There was creamed cabbage and mashed rutabagas topped with lots of butter. The lefse and the flatbread, made earlier, were brought out, along with the fresh buns the ladies had made that morning. It was a true feast.

After the Christmas Eve meal, everyone adjourned to the living room where the tree gave a heady pine aroma to the room. Everyone joined in the decoration process. The garlands were draped from top to bottom, the sugar cookies were carefully hung along with the ornate snowflakes. A small ladder was brought in so Emma could put the angel on the top of the tree and fasten the banner just below. Then they all put on the candles, careful to ensure they would not set a branch above on fire. Even though the tree was freshly cut to prevent just that, nobody wanted to take any chances on a fire.

Ole, as the patriarch, was given the honor of lighting the small candles from a larger candle held in his hand. Then Michael read the Christmas story from the Bible and as he finished, from the organ came the introductory strains of "Silent Night." Then Emma began at the beginning, and everyone joined in singing. Michael allowed himself the luxury of singing the Norwegian words along with his father, brothers and sister. "Glade Jul, hellige Jul, engler daler ned I sjul…"

Then came the strains of another Norwegian favorite, "I am so Glad." Again the small chorus sang in Norwegian, "Jeg er sa glad hver Julekveld, for da blev Jesus fodt." When they got to the 4th verse, "Det tenner moder alle lys…" "Then Mother trims the Christmas tree," Michael could go no further; tears filled his eyes, and the lump in his throat grew so big he could not get another note or word out. Mattie put both of her arms tightly around him and in a brave, clear and sweet soprano continued, "Sa ingen krok er mork…" "and fills the room with light."

When the song ended, Ole patted his head and said, "We all miss her, Michael. She has never left our hearts; not even for a minute. How she would have loved to be at your wedding and now celebrating this Christmas. And in spirit, I believe she was and is."

The rest of the family joined in, "Ja, ja," but there would be no more singing. Emma continued to play softly and everyone listened quietly, each thinking his or her own thoughts.

Christmas day was celebrated first at church, which was so full that latecomers had to stand, and then later at home. The meal that day was the preserved cod, the Norwegian favorite, lutefisk, that everyone agreed "stunk to the high heavens" while cooking, but tasted delicious when drenched in melted butter. There was also a baked hen with gravy for the mashed potatoes, the delicious breads with butter, pickles—both sweet and sour—and for dessert, Emma's "spouse winning" apple pie with coffee.

Stuffed to the gills, the family retired to the living room where the presents Saint Nicholas, or his tiny namesake relatives, the nisse, had left. The gifts were traditional knitted socks, gloves and handkerchiefs—small lacy ones for the ladies or oversized "honkers" for the men. Otto got a fine pocketknife and Edward, a pocket watch. Mattie received a beautiful hand crocheted doily and an embroidered lunch cloth for her hope chest; Michael got a fine Danish steel razor and Emma a set of Danish steel knives, both brought from Norway; Ole got a fine selection of American pipe tobacco. They all beamed in appreciation with many a "tak" uttered.

Later, while some napped, the others sat around talking about the "old days," as well as the future. Michael sat down by Otto, who was sitting alone in the corner. "So, Otto, you are going to be a rich American farmer?"

"You bet. I will have to work a few years yet, but I will be a big help to Edward and maybe he will pay me a little bit each year."

"Well, if you're going to be successful, you will need to know who to look out for and who to take care of so they profit you. Especially in this Christmas season."

"Who to look out for?"

"Oh ja. Years ago, when I lived with our grampa Benjamin, he told me of creatures and little people who could do you great harm or do you great good.'

"Grampa Benjamin told you?"

"Yes, many years ago now, when I helped him in the garden."

"What did he tell you?"

"Well, he told me about the trolls."

"We read about them in school, but our teacher said no one believes in them anymore."

"Is that right? Oh, that would be a big surprise for your grampa."

"Who did he say to watch out for?"

"Well many things during the year, but some things only at Christmas time, like the witch, Lussi, who flies through the air on a broom on December 13…"

"That's already passed."

"Ja, but in years to come, when you are rich and have many children, she will fly over your house and if she sees an unruly child, she will kidnap it."

"Then what?"

"Well, you must pay a big sum of money to get the child back. If you have many unruly children and she catches them all, it could cost you a fortune."

Suspicious, but still fascinated, Otto asked, "Who else do I look out for?"

"Julebukks."

"Julebukks?"

"They are half human and half goat. You must watch for them, because they will try to sneak onto your farm and drink the beer you have made for Christmas. If they find out you haven't made any, they will get terribly angry and do much harm to your wagons and animals. If they do get beer, they will fall sound asleep. Then you can drag them far into the woods and when they wake up, they won't know where they are."

"Which half is goat and which half human?"

"I can't say. Sometimes their heads and feet and arms and body get all mixed up. I assure you if you see one on your farm, you will know it, because it is such an ugly creature."

"What else?"

"Then there are the enforcers, who determine if you've done everything necessary for Christmas. Again, is the beer brewed, are the goodies made, is the house and barn clean, is there a wreath on your door and five pointed stars hung in all your windows?"

"What are they called and what will they do if everything's not done. Worse yet, what if we were all sick and couldn't help it?"

"They are the oskorei, and they are fearsome creatures, who ride through the skies like Witch Lussi, but instead of a broom, they are mounted on black, fire eyed horses. It doesn't matter to them why you're not ready. They will see your failure and try to terrify you and your family. If you're not ready, paint white crosses on your stable doors so their screams and shouts won't terrify and stampede the animals."

"They do that?"

"And worse! They may throw firebrands and burn up all your hay."

"Osko…?"

"Oskorei."

"You said there are good ones that help?"

"Indeed—the nisse. They are the guardians of the farm, generous protectors from the oskorei, julebukk and the witch. They also can be generous gift givers. They are very elfin, small, but they are very powerful. They wear short pants and long stockings. They have long beards and always wear a red stocking cap. You must be very kind to them. It is a good idea on Christmas Eve to leave a bowl of milk for them in the barn. Better yet, you can leave them a bowl of porridge with milk. Whichever, in the morning the bowl will be empty, and you may find they have left presents for the children."

By now Otto is staring right into Michael's eyes. His gaze does not waver with time and, eventually, Michael is doubled up in laughter.

With disgust, Otto punches his arm and says, "You are a julebukk! You are an ugly old goat who tells wild stories. What I need to watch out for at Christmas is you!" Then he laughed, too.

After the evening meal, which tasted as good if not better the second time around, they gathered around the organ and sang both English and Norwegian Christmas hymns. Emma had Michael surprise everyone with his fine tenor voice and perfect English, singing, "Away in the Manger," as a solo. When everyone was just about out of voice, they closed with "Et Barn er Fodt I Bethlehem," ("A Child is born in Bethlehem").

Before everyone went to bed, Emma brought out a bottle of their new wine. She filled each glass, and raising his, Michael proposed a toast. "To Mama, to Hilde and Lottie and their husbands, to Trina and all those I love in Norway."

Ole toasted the new bride and groom, and everyone said, "Ja, ja."

Then Michael, looking right at Otto, said, "And here's to the julebukks," and doubled up laughing again.

Emma poked him and said, "What's this all about, Michael?"

When he was able to speak he said, "This afternoon I didn't think Otto had eaten enough at the noon meal, so I fed him some baloney." He rocked with laughter again, but only Otto joined in. Everyone else just looked bewildered.

The day after Christmas, the tree was taken outside and set in a snowdrift for passersby to see. It also provided a feast for the birds. It was a delight to look out the window and see the many species of winter birds that appeared.

January was cold and hard. Some days the temperature got down to 30 below zero, and the men stayed home, rather than let the horse stand outside in that bitter cold all day at the building site. Ole remarked about the thermometer he saw in town. "There is a new way to tell the temperature in America, what do you call it here?" When Emma said, "Fahrenheit?" Ole said, "Ja, ja, that's it. In Norway we have the centigrade, but I discovered that when it gets down to 40 below zero, they both read the same. Isn't that a wonder?"

On a fair day near the end of January, they all went down to the train depot and bought their tickets. The agent was not able to book Ole's ship passage to Norway, but sold him train tickets and gave him directions on how to find the ship ticket agent in New York. It was right near the train station he promised, and they would tell him when the next sailing would occur. In the spring, the agent assured him there were many embarkation opportunities, as the ships were eager to get to Europe for more immigrant trade.

Mattie and her brothers bought tickets to Minot. Through the newspapers, the boys had found a man who was looking for workers who could speak Norwegian and maybe some English. He was a new homesteader and anxious to increase his acreage. He also needed help to put up some out buildings. He agreed to take them on, and they even agreed on a wage.

When Mattie got home, she wrote a letter to her sponsors announcing her arrival date and asking them to write back and confirm they would meet her at the depot. Everyone was set for an April departure: Ole, on Friday, April 1st; Mattie, Edward and Otto, for Monday, April 4th.

At the depot, Michael picked up a pamphlet entitled, *The Empire Builder*, for later reading. It turned out to be a brief history of the Great Northern Railroad and its founder, James Jerome Hill.

As he read it in the evenings after work, Michael would learn that the Great Northern actually began as the Minnesota & Pacific Railroad Company, in 1857. The state legislature, eager for railroads to be built in Minnesota, granted a charter to "construct a railroad in the direction of the Pacific." The St. Paul & Pacific ultimately failed, and after foreclosure in 1879, the properties were reorganized as the St. Paul, Minneapolis & Manitoba Railway Company, with a man from St. Paul, James J. Hill, its general manager.

Michael was impressed by the ingenuity of Mr. Hill. In no time, the tracks of his railroad stretched through Dakota Territory. What was most magnificent about the man was his business philosophy. The success of the railroad depended on bringing in settlers and then, providing them with good service. However, Hill felt it was his duty to help settlers prosper and remain in their new home, so he started showing farmers how to improve their methods of cultivation, including the concept of diversification. In order to increase his knowledge, he even started experimental farms, which eventually resulted in hardier strains of seed.

As the railroad continued west on its journey, through the mountains all the way to Seattle, Washington, the name changed to the great Northern Railroad, and James Hill became known as the "empire builder." *Yes*, Michael thought, *how I would like to be successful like Mr. Hill.* Though he was not aware of it, the seed was planted for a story Michael would write in his old age.

By the time April arrived, the men had finished building the two homes and had framed up a new one for Michael to work on. When Michael gave them their wages, the boys accepted with huge smiles. At least they wouldn't starve in Dakota. Ole absolutely refused any money. When Michael insisted, Ole took the money, then turned around and gave it to Mattie. "This is for all the good food, the fresh linens, the clean clothes, and your ever smiling face. Tuck it away, and let no one know you have it. And if you do take some out to buy something, think about your papa in Norway."

Saying goodbye to their father was the hardest for all of them. They all knew that he would not return to America; he loved his Norway too dearly. There was no future for him here. They also were aware they would probably not be able go back to Norway again during his lifetime. The boys hugged him and then hugged him again. Mattie clung to him and cried openly, her words of love were smothered in his shoulder, but he heard them.

Emma hugged him and kissed his cheek. "I am so grateful to our God that I got to meet you. Thank you for coming to our wedding. Give our love to Hilde and Lottie and Trina. I promise I will take good care of your Michael."

Then Michael held him, but no words were spoken. What was there left to say?

As they parted Ole reached into his coat pocket and took out an envelope which he handed to Michael. "Here, I almost forgot. This is the rest of your maritime wages you asked me to hold for you."

As he boarded the train, Ole turned once, his eyes still misty, and said "Jeg elsker deg. Jeg elsker deg! (I love you! I love you!)"

In chorus, they all echoed, "Jeg elsker deg, jeg elsker deg." They stood together on the platform as the train began to depart. They never moved until it was out of sight. Monday would be another day of parting.

On that day, before Mattie and the boys left, Michael said, "Now you write to us often, and let us know how things are. I can't stay here and build forever; there are fewer and fewer people moving in every year. All the land is gone.

"Emma's sister, Johanna, and her husband, Louis, are living in upper Dakota... I suppose I should learn to say *North* Dakota, but they only became a new state a couple years ago. Anyway, their home is in a place called Bottineau County. They will be writing to tell us how it is up there.

"Also, you boys be sure you keep in touch with your sister, and visit her if you can. It's going to be so very lonely for her with no family at all."

As the three boarded the train, they had mixed emotions. They had shared their apprehension, as well as their excitement, with Michael and Emma. They were off on an adventure that would shape their lives. Tears of joy rolled over those of sadness. Yes, they would see each other again. They were confident of that. Would they succeed? If hard work brought success, then the answer would be yes.

"God bless you and watch over you. Ja, ja, God be with you."

At home Michael took the envelope his father had given him and opened it for Emma. "Here is a little surprise. This is some of my maritime pay I asked my father to hold when I first traveled here. I had forgotten all about it. He gave it to me as he was leaving. Now we will figure out what to do with it.

Emma clapped her hands in glee as he counted out the kroner. "What to do with it will not be a hard decision. I think we should put it in the bank for a rainy day."

Chapter Nine

With much pleasure in the memory, Michael recollected that the next few years rolled along smoothly for the Glasoe household. He kept busy year round with his house building. Emma kept him well fed and in clean clothes. The community prospered, and the church congregation continued to grow.

The Minnesota Glasoes heard occasionally from the North Dakota brothers. They were in Minot, and Edward had a job working in a warehouse. Otto attended school and had a job delivering newspapers after classes. Edward's status report on homesteading land said that North Dakota had first opened 30 years ago and the Red River Valley land went fast. A man named Joseph Rolette filed the first claim in 1866. There were some really big farms that opened up, called Bonanza Farms. Edward also said that when he saved enough to get enough money for the 2 of them to live for one year, he was going to go west and find a claim.

Now, he added, most of the land up until Minot was gone, but farther west, especially in the northwest part of the state, he'd been told, there was a lot of land left. However, he went on, as soon as the railroad goes through an area, the land gets claimed fast. He hadn't been up there yet, as he also had heard that this was not a place of great beauty; there were no mountains or lakes, and the prairie land seemed to go on forever.

Mattie wrote that her employers had met her in a town called Williston and then they all had continued by horse and buggy to the middle of nowhere. The homestead was 3 miles from the border of the state of Montana and just 25 miles south of the Canadian border. You could not see another farm. It looked like when the railroad came farther west, just to the north of them, they would have lots of neighbors. Her employers were nice and everything she learned from Emma had come in handy. She said she was very lonesome, but busied herself and tried not to think about it.

Michael thought Mattie must be close to the area Edward talked about.

He hoped Edward would go out there sometime, look at the land and pay a visit to Mattie.

Emma's sister, Johanna, wrote that times were fine in Bottineau County. She suggested that there was a real need for house builders, as more and more people arrived. The land was not as flat there, and while they weren't big, there were mountains on the northern horizon. Because of their shape, they had been named the Turtle Mountains. She had also heard rumors there was a good-sized lake in the mountains.

About a year and a half after their marriage, Emma took Michael's hand one evening and placed it on her stomach. He looked at her quizzically, as she was usually not so bold. "Do you feel anything, Michael?" When he shook his head no, she smiled and said softly, "I think we're going to have a baby."

The emotion that came over Michael was so intense he thought he was not going to be able to draw a breath again. "A baby! A baby! We're going to have a baby? When, Emma? Do you know when yet? I didn't say anything, but after almost two years, I had all but given up hope."

"I can't predict for sure, but I think late fall or early winter—October or November. I am not very far along yet, so you'll have to wait a little while." Then, teasingly, she asked, "Can you do that?"

He hugged her to him and then stopped abruptly. "Oh, I must be careful not to squeeze you too hard."

"Oh my, Michael, don't be foolish. You can hug me whenever you want, as hard as you want. You will not injure the baby. But I have a request. Remember those oak pieces you had left over from furniture making? Do you think there are suitable pieces to make our baby a cradle?"

"Oh, yes. I will start tomorrow." Emma laughed so hard at his eagerness that she had to double over.

When she recovered herself, she said, "I don't think you need to start that soon. There are a still a few months to go by before it will be needed. But if you want, we will set it next to the coal stove to remind us that we are not just a married couple, but will soon be a little family."

October went by and while Emma continued to grow in girth, the baby was taking its time. Early in November, however, as Michael was preparing for work, Emma put her hand on his arm and said, "I think you had best go for my mother. I think our baby is ready to come."

Never had he saddled his horse so fast, or ridden her so hard as he did that morning. When he arrived at the Holte farm and knocked on the door, he blurted out the news to his mother-in-law, "The baby is coming! Hurry, hurry, hurry! Emma needs you."

He was surprised, as she calmly said, "Go to the barn and tell the boys to harness the horses and hitch them to the wagon. Then you go home to be with Emma, and I will arrive shortly. I've had a few babies myself, Michael, and unless your offspring is remarkably different, we have plenty of time, plenty of time. Now, off to the barn with you. I'll get some clothes together for the next few days."

Wednesday, November 8, 1893, was the longest day Michael could ever remember. Mother Holte arrived about an hour after he returned home. She and Emma went upstairs to the bedroom and Michael was told to wait downstairs; if he were needed, he would be called. At noon Mother Holte came down and started to put together some lunch. Emma was fine, he was told. She was progressing nicely, but it would still be a while. She warmed some soup on the range and made him a sandwich, and then took some soup up to Emma. He didn't think she ate anything herself.

In late afternoon, he heard voices coming from upstairs. As carefully as he listened, he couldn't make out a word. The voice got louder, and Michael knew it was Emma. Sitting on the bottom step, he could hear Mother Holte's softer voice. "You're doing fine, Emma, just fine. Now when I tell you, push hard." Then Emma's voice again, more a groan than a word. Michael closed his eyes and offered a silent prayer, asking God to care for his precious wife.

This went on for over half an hour, then suddenly he heard the baby crying loudly; then Emma's voice softly, "Oh, Mama, isn't the baby beautiful, just beautiful?" Michael suddenly realized he had been holding his breath. He sighed loudly, and for the first time that day, his whole being began to relax.

Mother Holte came down to get the water kettle off the range. "As soon as we get settled, Michael, I will call and you can come up."

"What is it—a boy or girl?" he asked.

"You have a wonderfully healthy baby," she replied. "I'll let Emma tell you if it's a son or a daughter. Just be patient a little while longer." An eternity later, she came down with a pile of bed linens and towels. "Go see your baby now, Michael. Emma is waiting for you."

He would never, during his lifetime, forget how beautiful Emma looked as he walked through the door. Her cheeks were rosy red, her eyes glistened with moisture and her smile as big and bright as he had ever seen. Cuddled in her arms was a small bundle wrapped in a white blanket.

"Hello, Papa Glasoe," she cooed. "Come here and meet your new son. It's a boy, Michael—a beautiful healthy little boy." As he drew close, she folded the wrap off his head and he saw the tiniest little face, its eyes squeezed shut, a tiny rosebud mouth making little sucking motions. He was beautiful.

He bent down and kissed Emma and said, "Thank you, dear wife, thank you. Today I am the luckiest, happiest man in this world. And, oh, how beautiful you both are! How do you feel? Are you all right?"

"Yes, I'm just fine. It was hard, but worth any pain I might have felt. I am fine now, Michael, just fine."

Mother Holte came into the room with a glass of milk for Emma. Setting it down on the bedside table, she turned and hugged Michael. "Congratulations, Papa. Now please ride out to the farm and tell them the good news. Take the wagon, with your horse behind, and tell them to come here for supper. Then if Emma's not too tired, they can see her and meet your new son."

Michael ate his supper upstairs and shared it with Emma. When he went down with the dishes, the others came up one at a time: Grampa Holte first and then the three uncles, from oldest to youngest. Then Michael said, "Goodnight, little mama, I love you so!" and Emma went right to sleep, the smile still on her face.

Mother Holte stayed until the weekend was over and Emma was able to go up and down the stairs by herself. Michael and Emma talked about names. They had talked about a few girls and boys names before their son was born, but now it was time to choose before the christening. They decided that since they were now Americans, they would not follow the traditional Norwegian naming practice. So, the boy would not be Ole or Magnus; he would have an American name.

On christening Sunday, the baby was dressed in the beautiful baptismal dress and cap, with the snow white knitted shawl his mother had made for him. As Pastor Overby dipped his fingers in the water of the baptismal font and sprinkled it on the head of the sleeping baby, he said, "Almer Mylo Glasoe, I baptize you in the name of the Father, and of the Son, and of the Holy Ghost." The Glasoe name would live on.

In 1895, Starbuck was fortunate enough to attract a doctor, a very good doctor—C.R. Christensen, MD, a new University of Minnesota School of Medicine graduate who had chosen to locate his practice there. Michael and Emma had gotten to know the young doctor and his wife well, as the Christensens joined Indherred Lutheran Church and they became fellow choir members.

The Glasoe children continued to be born in 2-year cycles. First came Edna in 1895, and then Edgar in 1897 and finally Hilda in 1899. Emma often joked about needing a year to rest up for the next one. Doctor Christensen delivered each one.

During those years, Michael received letters from both Edward and Mattie. Edward said he married a girl named Adeline. Unfortunately, she was not very fond of the idea of going off to the middle of nowhere to be a farmer's wife. Otto had found a good job and lived with them. Otto had told him when he saved up enough money and was 18, he was going off by himself to stake a claim. Mattie wrote that she, too, was married and was expecting a baby.

In 1897, 11 years after his arrival as an immigrant in that community, the doctor approached Michael and asked him to build a home. Michael explained that he worked for Gullixon and, perhaps, the doctor should talk to him. The doctor explained he couldn't yet afford the 2 of them and preferred to have Michael as his builder. Michael talked to Gullixon, who clapped him on the back and said, "Some day I knew I was going to lose you, and it looks like today is that day. You will do very well on your own, young man. I believe I will never find a replacement as good as you."

Sunday, after church, Michael made an appointment to talk to the doctor. He remembered he told him, "Yes, I will build your house, but we must set up a time to talk about a house plan and what you can afford to pay. As you well know, my family's growing and I will need to have some profit." It was agreed they would meet Monday evening after supper and as many evenings as necessary thereafter to finalize the plan. When all was agreed, they set a date for construction to begin. Michael felt very proud to be on his own and was anxious to start with the project as soon as possible. Gullixon had agreed to a two-week's notice.

In the year of Edgar's birth, Michael got a letter from his father, which first surprised him, then shocked and disappointed him. Ole, at age 65, had remarried—not a woman his own age, but a woman nearer the age of his oldest daughter, Hilde: his father's bride, Karoline Korneliusdatter, had been born in 1868. They were living in the house of her employer.

Michael felt that this marriage was an insult to his mother, Thale. He knew it was wrong to think like that, but he couldn't help it. He also was embarrassed by the fact that, with one exception, his father continued to find a place to live without buying a home. The exception, of course, was Glasè. Michael vowed he would not write his father back. He would ignore him.

When he shared the news with Emma, to his surprise she was delighted. When he tried to explain how old his father was, she counseled, "Michael, have you never thought what a lonely life it must be for your father. When he comes home at night, he comes to an empty house. When he goes to bed, he goes alone. He has no one to talk to, no one to share his thoughts or his dreams with. On the days while he is away at work, his mind is occupied, but the nights, Michael, think how long the nights must be. Now he has someone to share the rest of his days with. Losing your mother so early in his life was punishment enough. Don't punish him anymore. Write to him. Tell him how happy you are for him."

She was so sweet, and he knew that she was right. He hugged her to him and said, "Emma, you are a good woman. Sometimes I think you are too good for me."

"Hush, Michael. No more foolish talk like that. Find a pen and paper and write to your father."

He did write back and congratulated the couple. Two years later, he received a further surprise—another letter from Ole saying that he and Karoline had had a son, Torvald Petrus. Ole was 67. Michael chuckled to himself and said, "Well I'll be…"

After the doctor's house was finished, Michael got several other offers, but as the century mark was passed, building projects were pretty much drying up. Gullixon said he was thinking that maybe he would retire. The last year in Whitebear, 1901, Michael found only odd jobs here and there as a handy man. They began tapping into Michael's maritime savings.

The couple started talking seriously about moving somewhere else. It was an agonizing time. With three small children Emma was reluctant to move, though she knew it was inevitable. Thinking of leaving this house they had built, leaving their church, their friends, and especially her family, would be so difficult. *A daughter is supposed to live close to her parents forever.* It was an unspoken thought.

"Michael, I know you will do what is best for us all. Wherever you go, I will go with you. My sadness will be short lived." So Emma agreed to whatever was to be.

Word came from Edward that he had left his wife and, with Otto, had gone to Border Township in northwestern North Dakota and filed their claims. Border was located about 10 miles from the Canadian border and 20 miles from North Dakota's western border. Edward sent him a crude map of the two areas. The railroad, he wrote, was now moving west from a community called Flaxton, the place where they went to file their claims. Flaxton had already built itself up as the trade center for the area. It was a good day's journey by wagon. The rails were being laid just to the north of their claims. Michael and Emma talked for a long time about that.

Then came word from the Gorders, in Bottineau County, that the railroad was now extending west from there also, and people were coming in droves to an area they were calling Souris. Carpenters, they wrote, were in short supply. Imperial Lumber had now opened a yard in the community that was about 15 miles northwest of Bottineau.

Emma's brother, Adolph, had also heard from her sister, Johanna. When he found out the Glasoes were talking about moving there, he talked to Michael about going along. When Emma heard the news that Adolph, her brother, and Thomine, his new wife and her best friend, were talking about moving to Bottineau, too, she clapped her hands in glee. Maybe moving wouldn't be so bad after all.

Finally, Michael decided he would make a trip to North Dakota accompanied by Adolph. First they would go to Bottineau and then, if there was nothing there, he would go on to visit Edward in Border. Adolph agreed to the plan, and they talked to the ticket agent and found a way to get to Bottineau. From there, the men would rent a horse and buggy to get them to the new settlement.

Upon arrival in the Souris settlement, the men went down to the lumberyard and became acquainted with the manager, a man named Peter Boreson. Michael talked about his experience as a builder in Starbuck and also mentioned work was getting more difficult to find every year.

Peter told Michael that this was a good place for a carpenter to be right now. "There are a number of homesteaders, the last to arrive, who will want a house instead of a shack. Many," he said, "will soon want wood barns and other outbuildings." He told Michael that when he built the yard office, it was the first building in the community, but that the new town would grow quickly. "Small businesses will spring up and people will want to live nearby. I predict you can work here steady for the next ten years and maybe then some. In fact," he said, "just as soon as the railroad had begun to move toward Souris, Imperial Lumber, my employer, decided it would indeed be profitable to build a yard here."

Peter said he lived on a homestead near Bottineau. He stayed at the lumberyard during the week and rode his bicycle home every weekend. He said he was more than happy to recommend Michael to anyone in need of a carpenter; in fact, he had a customer looking for someone to build a barn, and he would recommend Michael. He told him to be sure and check back with him as soon as he was settled.

The men were gone over a week, and when they came home, the young couples talked together in earnest. They looked around the area for housing, and both found places to rent in a tiny new settlement called Carbury, not far from Bottineau and very close to Souris. The two men eventually agreed this would be a good place for them to settle. It was also agreed they should plan to move as soon as possible.

Before they left, they made a trip back to the lumberyard. Peter told them the homesteader was delighted to hear there was a carpenter available, and as soon as possible, to beat the winter, they would have to get together and have an agreement to build his barn. Michael said he would be back in less than 30 days.

On their return to Starbuck, Michael told Emma about the community, the man who ran the lumberyard and the offer to build a barn. He also said that there was a school nearby for Almer and Edna and Edgar. There was a church organized and they had attended a service at one of the member's homestead. Michael, chuckling, told Emma, "If my ears heard right, they needed a good organist. The girl who played the piano the Sunday I attended was only 12 years old."

And so it was decided—they would all leave. It was impossible to think of going by wagon because it was hundreds of miles, and heaven only knew what the roads—if there were roads—were like. So the Glasoes decided that they would sell the horse and wagon after their furniture was hauled to the depot. Michael would go first, while Emma stayed with her parents. In Souris, he would buy a new horse and borrow a wagon until he could build them a new one. He would move the furniture, so the house they would rent would be ready when Emma and the children arrived.

To diminish freight charges, they had an auction and sold off much of Michael's hand-built bedroom furniture that they didn't need right then. They sold their animals, including their horse; a Wollan cousin bought their house less than two weeks after they advertised it for sale.

When all that was complete, Michael brought Emma and the children to her parents' home where they would stay for a week. He hauled their belongings to the depot for shipment to Souris. He brought the horse and wagon to the new owner and got him to take him back to the depot where he left for Souris on the first train out.

By the time Emma arrived, Michael had already started his first barn, just a few miles out of town. He received a "builder's discount" for wood and supplies at Imperial Lumber. That was new to him, but it meant more profit.

Over time, the men became friends, even though Peter was over a dozen years older than Michael. Michael learned that Peter had come from Hedemarken County in the Gudbransdal Valley in Norway in 1866. He and his father, mother, brothers and sisters first settled in southwest Minnesota. His father, Borre Pedersen, had been killed in a logging accident. Peter said he had already left before the accident and had gone to a settlement called Hillsboro, in eastern Dakota; there he met and married his wife, Anna.

He was offered a job with Imperial in Bottineau and decided finally to homestead nearby. He, too, missed Norway, but agreed there was no future there.

Little did the two men expect that in the future, their children would meet and marry, but so it was that 4-year-old Almer, Michael's oldest, would marry Vera, Peder's youngest, but not even born yet.

The Holtes, who were now in their 60s, enjoyed the time with Emma and their grandchildren. If it was a happy time, it was also a sad leave taking. There were no guarantees that they would ever see each other again any time soon. They promised to write each other often. Like when Emma's brothers went off to work, so it was now, Ellen on the front step, her eyes filled with tears.

The train ride was long and tedious, especially with the children, and Emma wished many times that Michael were there. Luckily, the young couple just across the aisle, who obviously had no children, kept Almer entertained, or he kept them entertained. He even ate some of his meals his gramma had sent with them with the couple. Emma was grateful for the respite.

Seeing Michael waiting on the depot platform was a joyous sight; the worst was over. Emma hugged him longer than a normal hug would last. He hugged each child in turn. Now their new life would begin.

Their new home was not what they had in Whitebear; it was an older home and much smaller. After getting the children settled, the first thing Emma did was sit down at her organ. She examined it carefully and found not a scratch. Soon her music filled the rooms and a smile lit up Michael's face. This was not the best, but he had a premonition: they would not be permanent settlers here.

The scenery around Souris was somewhat similar to that in Whitebear, except for the ridge of high hills, "Turtle Mountains," to the northeast.

Boundary Creek ran through the community, north to southeast. It was, by all standards, a nice little settlement. Work was plentiful, and Michael soon was as busy as he had been in Minnesota. He still thought of finding a homestead, but again, he was just a few years too late. He knew, however, that the family would have to live there for a while, and it just never seemed to be the right time.

For Emma, having her brother, Adolph, her best friend, Thomine and sister, Johanna, living near, she was not nearly as isolated as she had feared. She eventually became the church organist and loaned her organ to the church until they could afford to purchase one. Except for the absence of her parents, her new life was much like the old one had been for her also.

The family continued to grow. Lillian arrived in 1901 when Edna went into first grade. Emma once laughingly remarked, "I no more get rid of one than I get another."

The surprise of 1902 was another baby—not for Michael and Emma, but, again, his father, Ole, and his "child bride," as Michael called her, Karoline. On July 13th, 1902, with Ole now close to 70, Karl Magnus was born.

In the newspaper Michael read that the new President, Theodore "Teddy" Roosevelt, had been a rancher in western North Dakota until the great blizzard of 1899 drove all the ranchers out. If western North Dakota was good enough for the President, maybe it was the place to homestead. He began seriously to think about it.

On Saturdays and in the summer, Almer went with his dad to the work site. Michael would find little things for him to do to keep him busy. By the time Edgar was old enough to go along, Almer was actually a help to his father. It was an exposure to a skill that he would turn to many years later in the "dust bowl and depression" years.

In the spring, Michael would plow a garden for Emma. In the fall, she would put up canned goods for the winter. Beef and pork were plentiful in the farm community and, again, they had their own coop for chickens. Their one cow was solely for milk and not for slaughter. Once a year, they would buy goat milk from a neighbor to make cheese. The larger the family grew, the more the food budget was strained.

When there were no more claims available and no new settlers arriving, the work began to dwindle for Michael again. In 1903, Adolph left to investigate the possibility of homestead land near the community of Mohall. Kari Thomine's sister, Helene, had homesteaded there and her mother and father had moved in with her. He would find work there and, depending on how things went, he would come back for the family. Michael wrote to his brother, Otto, to see if he was available to help with a little carpentry. Otto replied, yes he could come, but could Michael send him a ticket, as he was a little short on cash.

When he arrived, he and Michael talked long and late about the area where he had his homestead. Otto said it was no Norway, but the land was good for raising wheat, oats and barley, and more and more people were coming every day. Then, he added humorously, "Dakota's flat land is the only place in the world where you can stop for lunch, look back to where you had breakfast and look ahead to see where you'll have supper." They had a good laugh over that. Otto said he appreciated the chance to earn some money, but would need to be back before fall to tend his crops.

It was Peter Boreson's counsel that convinced Michael the time to go was now. Peter advised him to find himself a homestead and to continue to carpenter as well, as he was doing. "I tell you, Michael, it's the only way to keep up with the cost of a big family. Your boys are getting old enough now, so they should be able to help out with the farm work. My son, Ben, was behind the plow on his own at age 10."

Every day Michael wrestled with himself, wondering if he would wait until it was too late again. No, he had to do it now. Maybe if Adolph didn't find a claim in Mohall, he and Thomine and the kids would go along.

By the time he decided to share the news about moving, Emma already knew and said, "Let's do it, Michael, but I hope this is the last time. I am not getting any younger and neither are you. We need to get a little stability in our lives. Our children will begin to think we're gypsies."

She made him laugh. "Ja, sure—Norwegian gypsies."

When Adolph came back empty handed, Michael asked him if he was ready for the big adventure.

"And what, my good friend, is the big adventure?"

"I have decided I am going to go to Border Township and file a claim before I'm too late again. The railroad is nearby, and new homesteaders are coming every day. Emma knows and says what must be, must be. I'm leaving next week."

"I'm all for it. I was too late, also, in Mohall. A month there doing hard labor was enough to convince me, it's time to go to work for myself. I will talk to Thomine. If she knows Emma is leaving, she will want to leave, too."

The following week the men headed west to Border to stake out their claims.

Recalling that trip, Michael remembered a stopover in the Flaxton settlement. They had been told there were still not many farms there, but to look for a well-established farm owned by a man named Bell. Michael also had a rough idea of where Edward lived. When they reached Border Township, they saw only a couple settlements and immediately recognized the right one. It had a nice home, barn and a fenced area where various livestock were grazing.

They inquired there about homestead land and were told by the owner, William Bell, that west of his homestead, the land was unclaimed. He and his wife, Martha, were in their 40s. They had been the very first ones to settle in the area, so he was sure of his facts. The land had yielded them decent crops since they had arrived. "It's not beautiful until fall, but then as far as my eye can see, all is waving gold."

Michael said, "You were very brave to be the first to settle here."

"Not so brave. I knew that eventually others would come this way. It was just a matter of time. Welcome to Dakota Territory, or I suppose I should say North Dakota."

So, the weary travelers decided this would be it. The Glasoe family would stake their claim here, next to Bell's property. Adolph and family would stake out his claim as near as possible. Emma would be pleased to have her brother and sister-in-law as neighbors.

Bell showed them the line of his property, and they worked from there. They were very careful not to move Bell's markers. Michael told Adolf, "We don't want to become Boundary Ghosts."

"And just what is a Boundary Ghost?"

Michael, smiling, answered, "Land ownership is everything to the farmers in Norway since less than 5% of the land is tillable. Sometimes, magic rituals accompany the placing of boundary stones. Stealing land by moving them is severely punished. Often the guilty pilferer, even if he gets by with his crime, when he dies, is forced to come back, struggling in vain to return the boundary stone to its rightful place."

"And what Norwegian nonsense spinner put that story in your head?"

Laughing now, Michael replied, "An old huldre with an evil eye, whose name was Martinius."

"Huldre? Evil eye? As long as I've nothing else to do with my mind but measure, count and write down numbers, let's hear some more of your folk stories."

"Huldre lived in the mountains or hills of Norway or even right under the ground, in your cellar, your house or barn. The huldre are very human-like in appearance. They were often mistaken for men and there were often intermarriages. They can be very beautiful, or they can be ugly as sin. Sometimes they had a hidden feature—like a cow's tail. They steal babies, attempt to marry brides to be left alone at the summer farm in the mountains, kidnap people and might even share some dangerous food or drink with you. A huldre has the power of the Devil at his command and can do all sorts of evil things using spells and incantations."

"Incantations?"

"Things like reciting all the names of the Devil—Satan, Lucifer, Beelzebub—or like saying the Lord's Prayer backward while turning around counter clockwise."

"Evil things?"

"Ruin your crop, kill your animals or worse—your family."

"Oh, come on, Michael, the leg you're pulling is getting so long I'm starting to limp."

"Honest, Adolf, Martinius was so ugly, I was afraid to look at him for fear I'd turn to stone." With that he burst out laughing so hard he had to sit down. When he finally recovered he said, "Martinius was my school teacher. And this is gospel. I was so very, very afraid of him. I didn't dare look at him. I think he took delight in telling us these tales to frighten us."

So, in time, the metes and bounds were carefully measured and written down, first for Michael and then for Adolph. It was far from a professional survey, but in those days it would do. And it had, Michael thought, been fun.

The men had purchased lumber in Flaxton and worked feverishly to put up a homestead shack, so the women would have some place to live when they arrived. Michael chose a spot just up from a slough. He would eventually build his barn next to the slough, so the animals would have a place to water. There was no time or lumber for fancy siding, so the house was weatherized with tarpaper.

The shack completed, they went over to Adolph's homestead and put up a makeshift shack about 10' by 12'. It had no foundation and was not built for permanency, but fulfilled the homestead requirement of having a building on the site. They did not even bother to tack on tarpaper.

Then the men headed back for Souris, stopping one more time in Flaxton to file their claim. It cost each one $12 to file and would require another $6 to prove it up and get the certificate of ownership. .

That accomplished, they hoped to be back home in 3 days. There they were welcomed with open arms and the words, "What is it like? Tell me absolutely everything about it."

Michael said that, as expected, the land is very flat. They had counted about 5 homesteads. He said that the Bells, their closest neighbors, had a fine place and his crops were looking very good. He had not had time to visit Edward's claim.

He told Emma someone might be out to drill a well and put in a pump. It would be expensive, but there was no choice. The drillers would also be doing a couple other newcomers, so the shared expense would make it a little cheaper. Until then, Michael told her, he had made arrangement with Bell to deliver water to the house.

Chapter Ten

This time there was no money for trains, so the Glasoe family would have to make their way by hay wagon. Otto would drive their wagon and Gustav, a "volunteer" like Otto, would drive his brother, Adolph's, wagon.

One evening after making their decision to go, the couple had a long discussion. Since they would travel on 2 hay wagons, they must decide what furniture to take along and what to sell. As in their previous move, the decision was agonizing. From a houseful of furniture to only a wagonload would involve the sacrifice of many items. Michael and Emma decided that each of them would make a list of things they couldn't live without. Then they would compare lists and pare items down to what would fit on the wagon.

For a week they wrestled with their lists, putting things in, taking things out, adding and subtracting, reevaluating again and again.

For Emma, her number one choice was her organ. While it was not practical, utile or necessary for daily living, it was almost a part of her, an extension of her very being. She wondered if Michael would even list it. She hoped for it and even prayed for it.

Michael thought in terms of the practical: the stove for warmth and cooking, beds for the six of them, the frames being collapsible. Weight was a big consideration: how much could the horse pull day after day? The more people who could walk, the more goods they could load.

When Michael brought this up for discussion, Emma's heart sunk. The organ was the heaviest thing they owned. After a discussion with Otto, it was agreed that he would walk most of the way while driving the team. The 3 oldest children would trade off walking and riding. Emma, pregnant with her 6th child, Hilda and Lillian would ride. They would stop to rest both people and animals as they agreed on the need.

Finally the day came to compare lists and make their decision. After supper the two took out their lists and exchanged them. Michael saw the organ at the top of Emma's list. He smiled and shook his head; it was not a surprise. Next, he saw many of the practical items he himself had listed.

When Emma got Michael's list, she held it for a while, watching him as he read hers. Then taking a deep breath, she unfolded the paper with shaking hands, scanned the list and broke into tears. Sobbing, she put her arms around Michael and cried into his shoulder. At the top of his list was "organ."

The two families would wait until late May or early June to make the move, as winter, they were told, sometimes hung on longer in northwest North Dakota. The distance from Souris to Border was about 120 miles. At 20 miles a day, it would take one day short of a week to reach their destination.

The day before they left, the hayrack was loaded with everything except their personal belongings and their furnishings, including Emma's beloved organ. Emma had packed fresh breads and butter and brought the last of their canned goods. Thomine did the same. The women were sure they had enough to last. They would stop in Flaxton and buy more food supplies.

They had some hay in the wagon to feed the horse and also make the ride more comfortable for the family. The cow was tied behind. They had wired cages made out of lath for a few chickens to nest in and provide eggs. There was a solo crate for the rooster. At night they made a lean-to with blankets for sleeping.

On the day of departure, into the wagon climbed Emma, Hilda and Lillian. The three oldest children, Almer, almost 11, Edna, just turned 9, Edgar, soon to be 7, were eager to begin what would be a long trek.

The Holte wagon had no real heavy items and had fewer children. Married just 5 years, they had not had time to accumulate more than bare necessities. Thomine (or Kari, as she now preferred to be called) was also pregnant with their third child. Her 2 other children were Arthur, 3, and Margot, just 1 year old. It was agreed that if the Glasoe children tired, they could ride on the Holte wagon to rest. It was also agreed that every 2 hours Otto and Gustav would change wagons so Otto could rest. That would mean less rest stops.

The journey took almost a week, as anticipated. Driving sun up to almost sun down, stopping to rest and water the horses every three hours, eating their noon meal on the run, they made their 20 miles a day. Evenings they would have their meal as the sun was setting. Emma would softly fill the night air with music from her organ and once all the children were asleep, the grownups would lay down for the night.

They were a tired but happy bunch when they arrived at what was to be their final destination. God must have watched over them, they thought. Much rain had fallen in April, but they never got a drop on their journey to Border. Little did they realize how sparse the rainfall could be in western North Dakota: a little over 2.5 inches in the summer was average.

The family rested and recovered from their journey at the Glasoe homestead shack. There was not a lot of room, so the first night, after putting up the beds the Glasoes had brought, the men slept in the wagon.

Kari Thomine and the children were invited to stay at the Anton Roness shack to relieve the crowded conditions. There, on August 25, 1904, she gave birth to a second daughter, Alma, with Emma in attendance. Gust stayed with Kari Thomine and the children. Otto ate supper at the Glasoes and stayed through the night, then returned early the next morning to his homestead.

On September 13, 1904, Emma gave birth to the Glasoe's 6th child, Laura, with Kari Thomine in attendance. Her midwifery skills were severely tested when she had to remove a "skin cap" from the baby's head.

When Michael and Adolph stayed behind, they stayed in their homes until the auction sales. After that, the two men slept on straw beds with a sheet under them and one over them. The women both left one quilt, if needed, for cold nights. They cooked their own meals on a tiny range rescued from a neighbor's shed. Adolph would go out each morning to pick up the day's supply of food; expenses were kept to a minimum.

Michael recalled that in mid-October, earlier than anticipated, the house was finished. Michael collected his final payment, paid Adolph his wage and loaded his wagon with his tools and their personal items.

They went to the lumberyard and Adolph bought windows and a door for the sod barn he would erect. He was woefully short on cash and would have to conserve what he had to insure enough money for food.

Michael did the same for his sod barn, adding bags of cement for the foundation of the house addition he was planning. Both took one final advantage of Imperial's contractor discount. Michael bid goodbye to friend, Peter Boreson, who wished him well and reassured him he was doing the right thing.

Starting on the journey to their new lives, neither of them knew how brave they were to leave security behind and venture out to a place they knew almost nothing about. By now, however, the road there was becoming familiar.

Stopping in Flaxton one more time, they bought a few food supplies they would need. They would go as far as they could that afternoon, camp out and get home in daylight. Flaxton was a long, one-day ride, but they were close to home now and looked forward to reuniting with their families. Neither was aware that they had become fathers again in their absence.

Michael's arrival was greeted with whoops of joy from the children, who hugged his leg or whatever part of his body they could reach. When they had their turn, Emma shooed them off and hugged her husband. She shook her head and said, "You're early, Michael. You worked at night, didn't you?" No answer was her answer, and she hugged him harder. "Oh, I'm so glad you're home. Now come let me show you our well and pump.

"The driller could find nothing near the house or barn. He managed to put in a pump down by the slough, which we can use for the house. The animals will drink from the slough in the summer. In the winter, the well digger said, we'll need to install a big water tank in which to melt snow. We will need to dig a fire pit under the tank at one end, and then trench and rip rap with rocks to the other end to convey heat along the bottom. It's going to be a slow process, but I'm sure the boys can manage it, if you're out carpentering."

They walked down to the slough and Michael tried the pump. He caught enough water to get a swallow. "Umm, this is kind of sweet. I might not need any sugar with my coffee."

Then taking Michael's hand Emma said, "Now I must really show you something. Since your eyes appear so bad, I will have to let you get close." She took his hand and into the house they went. She led him over in one corner of the room, pointed at the cradle and said, "Obviously, you have not noticed my decrease in size, but this is your new daughter. She was still inside me when you left."

Tears came to his eyes—tears of remorse for being so forgetful and stupid not to have noticed and tears of joy for the tiny little girl snuggled in the blankets. "When, Emma? Oh, I'm so sorry. I forgot. In the excitement of seeing everyone again, I simply didn't notice. When did she come?"

"Six weeks ago, on September 13th—Friday the 13th—thanks to Kari. She was here as midwife and had to pull a "skin cap" away from her face. She has been just fine, and don't you feel so bad. With all you've had on your mind, we're lucky you found your way back. When she wakes, you can hold her. Now, outside we go to show you something else you missed."

"Oh, no, not more. I'm already so embarrassed, but don't ever tell anybody. Please!" he pleaded.

As the children came running up, Emma said, "Almer, show your father your surprise. His eyesight is getting pretty bad."

Almer pointed off to the west where Michael saw a beautiful haystack. "Edgar and me did it."

"Edgar and *I* did it," his mother corrected.

"No, you didn't, Mama. It was me and Edgar. Remember? Now see this, Papa," Almer said, as he led him to the back of the house.

Michael hadn't even noticed it, but as far as the eye could see, the land had been scorched—prairie fires. Michael had read about them. "I was out looking for arrowheads when I saw the fire. I first thought maybe it was a Viking ship with a fire-breathing dragon on the front, like you told me about. I ran home and told Mama, and she said, 'It's a prairie fire, and it could burn down our farm!'

"But, I saved it, Papa, me and Mama and Edna and Edgar and Uncle Gustav. Uncle Otto was at his homestead. I ran to Mr. Bell, but he was busy saving his place, so I ran back here and did what he did. We beat the fire out with wet gunnysacks. Then Uncle came on his horse and helped. We didn't lose anything, Papa, not a darned thing, not a consarned thing," he was so excited, he was out of breath. Neither adult commented on his language.

Michael hugged him and held on tight with pride, "Such a grown up boy you've become, and what a comfort for your mother. You did good, Almer. You did good."

With the other children now tugging on his leg, "Come with us, Papa, Come see what we found," he let Almer go and turned around. There, on the side of the shack was a huge stack of buffalo chips drying in the sun. "We found these all over, Papa. There are hundreds of them—maybe a thousand. We use them for fire; Edward said they burn good and hot, and they do. And they don't smell much."

"Well, my goodness! This place is just full of surprises. Anything else I should see?"

"You bet, Papa, follow us," and off into the house they ran. "Wait out here, Papa."

In less time than it took him to catch his breath, out they tumbled, each holding an arm full of horns. They fairly sparkled in the sunlight. "The buffalo lose these every year. We found them and shined them up. We're going to make whistles out of some of them and this winter you'll help us make hat racks. Right, Papa? You will help, won't you, Papa? Maybe we can sell them and make some money."

He laid back his head and howled with glee at their excitement. "You bet I'll help you. You bet. What a wonderful homecoming this turned out to be.

If I wasn't so tired, I might not be able to sleep tonight." He put his arm around Emma and said quietly, "You've kept them pretty busy this summer, little lady," and they both smiled.

"Now you kids run off and play. And you, my lady, come with me." He took her over to the wagon and lifted up a tarp underneath which lay a green tree.

"Whatever, Michael? We certainly need trees, but couldn't you have found more, so we could have a grove?"

"Well, yes in time I will do that. But this is not just any old tree. It's a very special tree."

"Really? And what's so spec—" She stopped in mid word, because she knew what it was. This was the apple tree she had told him she wanted years ago when they got engaged. "Oh, Michael you didn't forget. You didn't forget." Then she put her arms around him and gave him the sweetest kiss he could remember getting. "You are such a sweet man, and I will love you forever."

"Do you know why this tree is special?"

"Yes, because I asked for it so long ago."

"No, more than that."

"What, then?"

"Do you remember the tree in Starbuck?"

"Of course, I remember. It was so beautiful and gave us such good apples."

"This tree is grown from the seed of one of those apples you turned into a pie. I planted it after our first harvest. When it sprouted, I took it out to your father and asked him to watch it for me. I told him it was a secret and never to tell you. I said when it's big enough, I'll be back to get it and plant it beside our house. When your brother, Gust, came up to help move, your father sent it along with him. I hid it in the house I was building."

Tears in her eyes, she held both his hands, looked into his eyes and choked out, "I swear, you are the sweetest man that God ever created." Then trying to lift it out of the wagon she added, "Can we plant it now?"

He lifted it out, kissed her on the forehead and said, "Right now, my Emma, right now. You just show me the spot."

Otto came just in time for the evening meal. He was both surprised and pleased to see brother, Michael. "It is good you're home, brother. Your family has missed you," was his welcome. "Now I can get back to my own place. I've got lots of stuff to do."

"Not until you've eaten, Otto. Come sit down." Then, grabbing his shoulders, he said, "And thank you. Thank you for being there when I needed you."

After supper and after Otto left, Emma nursed the baby and then brought her to Michael, who rocked her to sleep, but then held her tenderly for a long time. They decided as soon as a pastor could be found, they would christen her Laura. They had church services here, Emma told him, but only when a circuit rider minister made it to their area.

Before the children went to bed, Michael brought out a gunnysack. As everyone crowded around the table, he took out a strange shaped silver covered thing and put it on the table. With his right hand, he unscrewed a little lid of the top. Again he reached into the gunnysack and took out a tin can with a little spout. He took the cover off the first item, then the cover off the spout and began pouring liquid from one to the other. Everybody wrinkled up their nose and said, "Uffda, that smells!"

Replacing both covers, he turned a handle on the silver thing and a little piece of material popped out of a slit on top. Reaching into his pocket, he pulled out a small stick with a red tip. Reaching under the table, the little assembly heard a scratching sound, and then saw the stick return; it was on fire. They all oohed and backed away. Touching the stick to the piece of material, a small flame appeared. Michael blew out the stick.

Finally, he reached into the sack and pulled out another sack. As he unwrapped it, they saw it was a tall glass with no bottom. He put it on top of the silver thing where it was held tight by four little pinchers. Turning the knob a little more, the whole room was full of light. Everyone together went, "Oooh!" and clapped their hands. Emma said, "Whatever is this?"

Michael said, "It's called an oil lamp. I got it from Boreson for half price. Instead of candles to read by at night, we'll have this device. It's much brighter. The glass top is called the chimney and the fire stick is called a match."

All the children said, "Can we stay up and read for a while?"

When Emma said, "For a while," everyone whooped and went in search of a book. They brought their father his Bible and their mother their favorite books. As Emma read out loud, the children listened intently. As the littlest ones laid their sleepy heads on the table, Michael took them one by one and put them to bed. As the older ones began to grow drowsy, Emma closed the book and said, "That's enough for tonight." Smiling sleepily, they toddled off.

When Emma returned, Michael was still reading. "Bed time for you, too, Mr. You've got a lot of sleep to catch up on."

"Just a few more minutes, Emma, and then I'll be with you. Isn't this lamp like a miracle?"

When Emma woke a few hours later, the lamp was still glowing. Padding over, she found Michael, head down, fast asleep on the table. Taking his arm, she said quietly, "How do you turn this thing off?" Smiling sheepishly, he cupped his hand at the top of the chimney, blew softly and then followed Emma to bed.

Michael slept so well, he wasn't awake until the sun was half risen and light filled the room. Almer and Edgar were already out feeding and watering the animals and milking the cow. Emma was busy at the stove and brought him his coffee as soon as he was dressed. Edna was mixing up hot cakes; they were going to give him a royal breakfast his first day home. The smaller children were still asleep, having learned that skill quickly, despite all the bustle in their one room home.

As meal preparation continued, he said to Emma, "Well, Mama, what is your pleasure first, another room off this end of the house for sleeping, or finishing the inside walls with lath and plaster?" When she said, "Extra room for bedrooms," he said, "Then as soon as I'm done with breakfast, I'm off to get the water tank, more lumber and windows, and seed for next spring planting. Also, make a list of food supplies you'll need for winter. I'm sorry to leave after just getting home, but it's obvious, dear wife, that you need more room. That accomplished, I'll start on the sod barn so the animals will be warm, too, this winter."

When the boys came in, they ran right over to him and said, "We're done taking care of the animals, and we have fresh milk for your breakfast. We're hard workers, Papa, real hard workers."

Michael smiled his appreciation and tousled both their heads. "So I've heard, boys, so I've heard. "Then, looking over at Edna he said, "The same goes for you, young lady," and she blushed with pleasure.

As anticipated, Michael was gone for 2 days. Returning late in the evening, they quickly unloaded materials and watered and fed the horse. Emma had kept a hearty warm meal for him, and he ate with relish as he talked about their trip.

Everyone sat and listened as if he were reciting a tale of adventure. "Are you ever going to stay here with us?" asked Edgar.

Before Michael could reply, Almer said, "When I grow up, I'm going to go off to make money for my family—just like Papa does."

"Me too," chimed Edgar.

Michael smiled and said, "I think my time of being away is over. There is so much to do here. I'll be busy for many years. So, let's all get ready for bed, we've got busy days ahead." The children slept behind two blankets fixed to a rope strung from wall to wall. Emma and Michael's bed was on the kitchen side.

With everyone tucked in, he drank another cup of coffee. "Tomorrow, I'll check early to see how Adolph's doing on their barn. Then I will be off to get the sand and gravel I need to lay the foundation. Luckily, it's not far away, so I should be back by noon. I will have the forms up by supper, and I can lay in the cement day after tomorrow. The walls will go up fast. Once they are up, I'll do the roof. Then, dear wife, I will put siding on the whole place, and you will finally have a decent looking home."

She kissed his cheek and said, "Come to bed now. You must be tired."

Adolph, with Gustav's help, had made fine progress with the sod barn. The walls were up, and they were putting in the windows and the door. Tomorrow, after lunch, they would go to Long Creek where there was a grove of trees to cut saplings for the roof. "It's about 15 miles, so we'll start out early. I'm anxious to get this done so I can get my family back."

Michael said, "Stop by my place on the way and, if my foundation's done, I'll go along to get some saplings for my barn roof, too."

Adolph surprised Michael by saying, "Until this thing gets finished so we can live in it, we're staying with your brother, Ed."

"Brother Ed? How is he? I must get over to see him."

"He's very excited that you are finally here. He knows you're going to be very busy, but he's anxious to see you."

As he was getting ready to leave, Michael noticed the absence of the shack they had built. "Adolph, what have you done with the shack we built?"

"Nothing. When I got here it was gone. I guess somebody came, saw it was empty and *helped* themselves to it."

"What a pity. That lumber would have come in handy for you." He shook his head and clucked his tongue as he drove off. *Poor Adolph; what rotten luck!*

When Adolph and Gust got to his place the next morning, Michael's horse was hitched to the wagon and he was ready to go.

That afternoon he unloaded the saplings and he and Almer trimmed them, then piled them up down by where the barn would be built. It was good that Adolph had found the Grove.

The next day Michael showed Almer how to cut sod, and the boy worked hard. Emma loaned him her gloves, which he used for about two weeks. Then he told her his hands were "worked in," and he never wore them again.

When Michael could help him, he did. The sod pieces were turned over and left to dry for a day. Then they'd load them up on the wagon, bring them to the site and lay them piece-by-piece, packing them down tight. At this point, Edgar had also wanted to help and he did. It was heavy work for the boys, but they never complained. At the end of the day, they would bring their mother down to proudly show her their progress. As the walls of the barn went up, so did the addition.

As Michael predicted, he got the walls and roof of the addition up, enclosed it, and then began the siding process. Then a cold spell set in and he focused on the sod barn. When that was roofed, a pit was dug for the water tank. Winter would truly test whether his building skills or if this water system, suggested by the well driller, would work.

When the first snowflakes flew, Michael was inside the addition beginning the inside finish work of lathing the walls. He followed with the plastering and, by Christmas, they moved the beds in. He put in some venting in the kitchen wall and, if everyone kept their doors open, there was sufficient heat on most nights. Michael and Emma occupied the bedroom farthest from the stove.

Emma had begun quilting before she even thought about marriage, so everyone had a blanket and at least a quilt or two to snuggle under. Most of the quilts were tied, simple patchwork blocks, made from discarded clothes. They were not fancy, but oh, how they kept off the cold. In spite of the covers, Michael still needed to make at least one trip out to the stove at night to stoke the fire.

Bell had showed Michael and Adolf where they could get good coal to burn. There was plenty not more than a mile and a half from their homesteads, and that was good, because it didn't take long for the buffalo chips to disappear and firewood was almost non-existent. With a pickaxe and shovel, they would bring home several wagons full. The box by the stove and the one in the barn never went empty.

Their first Advent and Christmas at the homestead came and went without much ado. They meant no disrespect to tradition, but everyone was just too busy. To the delight of the children, neither Lussi, the julebukk, nor the oskorei paid them a visit. Otto made them promise not to tell their mama what they knew, and then assured them all the creatures were just make believe. They did have a Christmas tree, but it was not much to look at. It was scrawny and sparse and anything but straight. However, with a little trimming, it didn't look quite as bad as when Michael had first brought it in the door. The parents vowed there would never be a Christmas as meager as this one again.

On Christmas Eve afternoon, the bath-taking brigade began, as it had every previous Christmas Eve. Emma warmed water on the stove, and the bathtub was her washtub. The youngest went first, with Emma doing the washing, Michael drying them off and Edna dressing them. The older children and the parents bathed behind the blankets hung from the ceiling. The whole process required three tubs of water, so it began early.

For supper there were the meatballs Emma had canned, good gravy and mashed potatoes along with lefse, flatbread and fresh butter churned the day before. They read the Christmas story, with each one of those who could, reading a verse or two. Michael recited his Christmas poem and told the children stories of his Christmases as a child in Norway. Then, as Emma played her organ, they sang Christmas carols in English. As a Christmas Eve treat, everyone feasted on the delicious sweets that always marked their Christmases.

The next morning after breakfast, while they lamented not having a warm church to attend, they dressed warmly and piled in the wagon, the children all huddled together, and drove over to Adolph and Kari's. Again, there were presents to give and get, to open and to "ooh" and "aah" about. Everybody marveled at how warm their sod barn was.

Then in a heartbeat, it was the start of a new year—1905. It was a hard year for the parents, with no children going off to school. Almer, Edna and Edgar would miss at least a year. The others, they hoped, would start in time, if a teacher could be secured soon. This was their first community with no school and no church.

Chapter Eleven

Who could forget that first winter on the homestead, Michael mused? January was a very bitter month, with huge drifts of snow, extremely cold temperatures and fierce prairie winds. They had never seen anything like this prairie winter. A rope had to be strung from the house to the barn as a method of literally feeling the way when the snow was falling so thickly that they were unable to see three feet in front of them. No child dared make the trip without a parent along. Often a drift would cover the rope, and when the wind died down, Michael would shovel a new path. Many times that winter he wished he had not built the barn so far away from the house.

There was no time off, however. The animals needed to be tended, and coal, water and milk had to be hauled to the house. The watering system worked fine when they could keep the fire going in the pit. When the wind blew strong from the wrong direction, snow would just sail in and put out the flame. On the first warm day, Michael fashioned a crude guard to keep the snow out.

They always made sure the barn door was secure, as coyotes continuously roamed the prairie looking for food. They often heard them howl, a spine-tingling sound that echoed in the still winter nights.

One night Almer was awakened by a tug on the arm of his nightshirt. When he opened his sleepy eyes, there was his little brother, Edgar, standing beside his bed. "Wake up, Almer, I think I heard the trolls outside." Almer was about to dismiss his little brother when he noticed his eyes were filled with tears and his chin was quivering.

"Do you know what these so-called trolls were doing?" Almer asked.

"It sounded like they were sweeping the porch. Do you think it's Lussi, the Witch?" Edgar whispered in a small, frightened voice.

"You are old enough to remember that trolls are just make believe. Remember? Uncle Otto told us so. It must have been a bad dream. Go back to bed," Almer reassured.

"Honest! I heard them. Is it all right if I sleep with you tonight," Edgar pleaded.

"Sure. Hop in and don't worry. Whatever it was, I'll protect you," Almer said in his most convincing big-brother manner.

Edgar climbed into bed and was soon sound asleep, cuddled next to his brother. Almer, however, stayed awake for the next hour, barely breathing as he listened to the coyotes brush against the bedroom wall, as they roamed the yard looking for anything they could chew and swallow. Better his little brother believe in trolls than in the wild animals that were just feet away. He wondered if one might be able to jump through the window. It took him a very long time to go to sleep.

The next day, the weather was clear and the older children got dressed in their warmest clothing, put on their "lubbas" (felt lined boots), and went out to see if they could follow the tracks of the coyotes. Usually the wind covered the tracks, but often not completely. Sometimes they would come upon the carcass of some animal, and the snow would be all packed down where the less aggressive wolves lay waiting for their turn as the strongest coyotes stood and ate. They never strayed very far away, and the older children were ever mindful to keep an eye in the direction the coyotes were heading, ready to run home if they saw one coming back. On their return, they delighted in telling their parents of their grizzly findings.

Winter finally gave way to spring. It was the most delightful snowmelt they'd ever seen, equal to the winter they had just endured. Despite the mud, the children reveled in being outdoors. Emma made sure that boots were off or shoes were scraped before they came in.

By that time, Michael had finished plastering the walls in the living area. He left space in the far wall for a door, as he intended to put another addition on that end of the house. For those too small to help, Emma taught their reading and writing lessons by the kitchen table in the morning and arithmetic in the afternoon. Even the littlest ones were included in the group. Michael had saved many of the books he used to learn English, and these were Emma's teaching guides.

As soon as the frost was out of the ground, Michael was out plowing. He had a good team of horses, and they worked hard to turn over the tough prairie soil. First he plowed east to west and then south to north. He had bought a breaking plow from Bell, as he said would not be breaking any more virgin soil; he had enough to take care of.

Stopping only for lunch, Michael plowed from breakfast to supper and turned over 10 new acres, as well as doing Emma's garden, which she wanted enlarged. Then, borrowing Bell's drag and seed drill, he prepared 7 acres of oats as feed for animals and 3 for wheat that he would take to Flaxton to have ground into flour. He called it his "lefse" field.

Then he taught Almer how to harness the horse and hitch up the plow. He remembered Boreson's comment about his oldest son behind the plow at age 10. Almer's job would be to plow up next to the hay field and, if he could handle the breaking plow, turn over sod to make the hay field bigger than last year. He walked a few rounds with him and showed him how to keep the plow deep enough, but not too deep. Then he watched a couple rounds and congratulated the boy on his work. He told Emma to call Almer in after an hour to rest, and then send him off for another hour after dinner. If the boy said he wasn't tired, let him go as long as he could.

When his crops were in, Michael spent the next six weeks building a house for a neighboring homesteader, Phillip Maigaard, who, with his wife, Anna, was living in a sod hut. He would use the money he earned to build himself a wood barn. He left home after breakfast and came back just before supper. Emma changed meal procedure and made the big meal at night instead of noon.

The first day he came home from the job, Almer ran to meet him so he could show Papa how much he had plowed. The rows were anything but straight, but he said to his son, "You must have worked a little longer than I thought you would."

"Yup, I worked for four hours, and then Mama made me quit. Tomorrow I will plow just as much. Did I do a good job, Papa?"

"You did better than good, Son. You did a spectacular job!"

"Speck what?"

"Spec-tac-u-lar. That means better than anyone else has ever done. How are your hands? Sore?"

"Nope. Mama loaned me her leather gloves again, and I wore them. My hands got all soft during the winter."

"Let's go get some supper, farmer."

"Ja, we're hungry aren't we, Papa?"

After supper, when the children were in bed, Michael and Emma talked about Almer's plowing. "He was so determined, Michael; he wouldn't quit. He wanted you to be surprised when you came home. Did he do a good job?"

"Yes, for his first time. The rows were less than straight and kind of look like he was trying to spell out Sivert Sivertsen's initials, but I told him he did a spectacular job."

Michael worked on the house that spring and summer, and when the house was enclosed, Philip said he would do the inside if Michael "showed him the ropes" a little.

After two days of working with him, Michael was off to get what he needed to start on his wood barn. This time, Almer and Edgar rode along. Like he had done when he and Adolph went together, the three slept under the stars in the wagon bed. Emma sent along many quilts that they used as mattresses, first on the wagon bed and, the final night, on top of the lumber. They could hardly wait to get home to tell the others about their "spectacular" trip to Flaxton.

Michael decided to do half of his barn this year and half the next, and he worked tirelessly in the heat of July and early August. Now they could increase the number of animals. Bell, who had been around about 8 years, was always looking for someone to sell his growing herds of animals to. Michael would buy another horse, a cow with calf, a sow and a boar.

Adolph borrowed the horses and plow when Michael and Almer were done with them to put up some hay and plow a garden for Thomine. Then he began work on the sod home. It would take a couple years of profit before they could afford to build with wood. The past winter had gone without incident, so they should be able to survive.

That summer the children wandered around the prairie again, looking for more buffalo horns and buffalo chips. They soon broadened that to include Indian artifacts—especially arrowheads.

The Indians that had occupied their land in the years before the settlers came were one of the Sioux tribes, the Assiniboine, or "Stone Boilers" as they were known. The name "boilers of stones" was given to them because of their extraordinary method of cooking meat. They would dig a hole in the ground and place a piece of buffalo-leather in it, which they filled with water and meat. Last came the "heat stones," blackened by the fires they were plucked from, which were thrown into the water to make it boil

The Assiniboine were a primitive tribe, basically hunters, eventually brought into the modern world through the introduction of horses. On horseback, the kill was much easier, so buffalo skulls, horns and bones might also be accompanied by the partially buried remains of the arrow that killed it. They often were in conflict with other Sioux tribes as well, and battlefields, if they could be discovered, were rife with arrowheads, sometimes spearheads and, once in a while, a tomahawk with a broken handle

Old Indian campsites were the favored place to find all manner of Indian relics. During the fur trading years, encampments were often as permanent as the meat supply. However, when the settlers began arriving, they moved often, and eventually all of the Assiniboine moved north to Canada, or west to what would be Montana.

In late August, Michael borrowed a reaper to bring in and bundle his wheat and oats, which the two oldest children built into shocks. He and the two boys later gathered the bundles in and piled them on the hayrack. He hooked the wagon on the back and drove a few miles to where a threshing machine was located. There were several wagons ahead of him, so he spent his time talking with the other drivers.

One of the men, Joseph Noistuen, said he was giving it up. Three years was all he could stomach. He asked Michael if he was looking for equipment, and Michael asked what he had. The man said he was going to sell his plow, disk and seed drill. They agreed on a price, and Michael got directions to the homestead.

The next day, he was there to bring first the disk home, then the seed drill. The following day, he brought the plow home in his wagon. They were only 3 years old and in fine condition. Michael got them all for what he considered a bargain price. He wished the man well and asked what he intended to do with the farm.

"Nothing," was the answer. "It isn't proved up; I've got 2 years to go. The one room house isn't much and neither is the sod barn. I've spent more on the machines than on them. I've sold my animals, except for the horse, and I'm keeping her and the wagon to haul our furniture. We have no children, so we have no problem there." When Michael asked where he was going, he said he had a job guaranteed with the railroad in Flaxton. Michael wished him well.

When he hauled his wheat into Flaxton, he stopped at the Land Office and asked what would happen to the man's homestead. He was told if someone got a quit claim notice from the previous homesteader, moved onto the property and farmed it, it would be theirs in two years.

Michael immediately telegraphed Pastor Overby in Whitebear: *Have abandoned, quit claim deeded homestead with house and barn waiting for pastor to file, live in the one room shack and start congregation here. Can you help? Telegraph me back a week from today. Michael*

He then asked the depot agent about where he could find Noistuen. The agent said that would be their new freight hauler. He pointed to the freight room door. Michael explained what he had in mind, and the man agreed to whatever paperwork necessary.

When he told Emma his plan, she was so excited. "Wouldn't that be wonderful, Michael! I'm sure there are enough people around to start a church."

The next few days Michael traveled from homestead to homestead, talking about his plan. He got nothing but positive responses and, "What can we do to help?" He replied he'd let them know.

At brother Edward's house, he was warmly greeted. As the two embraced, Edward said, "Well it took you long enough, brother."

"To get to Border or to your homestead?"

"Both, but you're forgiven. Otto told me that you had gone back to Souris to finish a house."

"Ja. Luckily, Adolph and I finished the job with 14 hour days, so we got home early. We both had lots to do here."

"Ja, that's what he told me. They stayed here, you know, until they got the barn built."

"Ja, Adolph told me. That was good of you."

"I must be honest. I enjoyed having family around again. It gets pretty lonely here by myself."

Edward had a small house that he and Otto had built. Michael admired the workmanship. "Well this is a solid little home. Have you convinced your wife to come out here?"

"About the house, thank you. I had a good teacher. About the wife, she divorced me quick as a wink. Adeline and I were not a very good match. She was greedy and I was poor. I have a new lady now. Her name is Alma. She's a Fagerland. I'm thinking of popping the question any day now. So what brings you here on this day?"

Michael explained about the pastor, and Edward said he could contribute labor, but not much else. Michael said labor was as good as gold.

Michael also told Edward that as soon as the pastor arrived, they would arrange a service at his homestead. He said, "I may not get back here to invite you, but you will hear about it through the grapevine." He gave him directions.

"I will be there, and if I can talk her into it, I'll bring Alma. You will like her. She's down to earth, just like your Emma."

In a week, he was back in the Flaxton telegraph office and got this reply:

Young man, just out of Augsburg Seminary this June, coming. Not married, no furniture. Will need help, but is willing. Arrive there on train November 1. I trust you to take care of everything and meet him. Overby

Back on the circuit two days later, Michael got promises of furniture, canned goods, men and machines to work the land, women to clean up the house, a cow, some chickens, a horse with saddle, harnesses and Michael agreed to build a wagon. People were so excited and appreciative of Michael's idea and its fulfillment.

When Michael got to the Maigaard homestead to see how the house was going, he was pleased to see the work was carefully done. To his surprise, he got an offer to build a barn. Maigaard also wanted to buy some animals.

It was already late fall, but Michael said he thought between the two of them they could get a good start on something, and if the weather held, might even get it enclosed. Shingles and siding would have to wait until spring. Tarpaper would have to do. The man was very happy about that; he thought he'd have to wait for spring. "Nope. First thing, after spring planting, I'll be here to finish it up."

"Well, Michael, I tell you this, if I find anybody who needs building done, I'm recommending you. You're the best!"

By the end of October, the temperature began dropping, but no snow. Michael took time off to go to Flaxton to meet the new minister. Emma and Kari spent November first at the pastor's homestead putting things in final order. Edna and Almer minded their siblings, who had been told to play outside. For noon, since it was a sunny day, they had a picnic in the wagon.

It was not hard for Michael to recognize the preacher when he got off the train late in the afternoon. Young, and dressed in standard clergy black, he was easy to spot. He was surprisingly tall and very lean. Michael grabbed his hand firmly and said how glad he was to have him here. The young man said, "Mr. Glasoe, my name is Martin Egdahl, and am I ever glad to be here. It was a long ride. I have nothing but my suitcase, and you might have to put me up for a while, until I can get some things organized."

"Putting you up will not be a problem, so don't worry about that. However, I'm sorry to report, your journey isn't over; we're still a day's ride from home, and tonight, unfortunately, we'll have to sleep in the back of the wagon. I'm praying, you hear, I'm praying, Reverend, that we won't freeze to death. We should be at our destination by suppertime tomorrow. "

The ride permitted the two men to get to know each other. Egdahl was not a stranger to farms, as he was born and grew up on one in southeast Minnesota,

156

where his father had come as a young man with his parents. As soon as his father was old enough, he staked out his own claim. Unmarried Egdahls on a homestead were not an unusual thing.

That first evening Michael drove a little farther than usual, with the blessing of a full moon. The young minister was already asleep when Michael stopped the wagon, fed and watered the horse and tied him to a tree. He, too, then crawled under a blanket and was soon fast asleep.

They were up with the first rays of the sun. They ate Emma's hard-boiled eggs, rusks with butter and cold sausages. Michael longed for a good cup of coffee. *Tomorrow*, he told himself, *tomorrow*. Lunch was a sandwich. By 4:00 PM, they were approaching the homestead. Wagons were lined up all the way into the house. Egdahl said, "You've got a lot of company, it seems."

Michael, himself surprised, returned, "A lot of company indeed." Emma had been busy. As they arrived in the yard, there were at least 30 men, women and a host of children to greet them. As the wagon stopped, Michael stood and announced, "People of Border, I am pleased to introduce you to our new pastor, Martin Egdahl."

"Praise God!" they echoed over and over again. Reverend Egdahl's face flushed. Never had he expected such a greeting. He was totally overwhelmed.

"Bring your suitcase," Michael said, as they exited from the wagon. Then he led him into the house, and as many people followed as could squeeze into the cramped quarters. The living area was filled with furniture; there were curtains on the windows, a cloth on the table with a vase of fresh wild flowers, almost completely overshadowed by the food dishes placed everywhere. No one would go hungry tonight. No one. Emma and Kari had indeed been busy, Michael thought.

"We are blessed by your presence and look forward to your service, for as long as you can remain with us. This is your home, Reverend Egdahl. May you live long and prosper in this place."

"My home? I thought this was your home, Mr. Glasoe."

"No, this is the home I wrote to Reverend Overby about. Everyone has contributed a little bit to make it comfortable for you. This is your home, pastor. This is your homestead. It isn't much, but we hope you like it. We will be doing the farming until this place becomes self-sufficient, and when the need comes, we'll enlarge the house.

"All we ask in return is that you bring God's word to us. We have been waiting to hear it again. We invite you to my home for your service next Sunday, at 11:00 AM. And it appears from the size of this crowd, we will have to hold it in the barn."

"We'll be there. We'll be there," was the chant from all who had heard Michael's invitation."

"And so will I," was the inspired reply, "and so will I. May God bless all you wonderful people. I am so thrilled to be here. I am happy to be home, but now let us sing the grace. I'm starving!"

As they ate, people visited, and word got around to bring a dish on Sunday and they would share their meal after the service. Everyone was very excited.

When the throngs had left and the children were asleep in the wagon, Michael, Emma, Adolf and Kari walked Pastor Egdahl through the little barn by lantern light. His pleasure was doubled. "How can I thank you, Mr. Glasoe? No seminary graduate I know has ever been received like this. I think from now on I must address you as St. Michael."

They all laughed. "No, Pastor Egdahl, we are the ones who are blessed," Michael responded. " We are like anyone starving; we long for the bread of life."

The ride home was a happy one. They all agreed that Border took a big step forward today. Tomorrow, they must find a schoolteacher.

In the days that followed, Egdahl visited as many homesteads as he could. He wanted to meet the families and personally invite them to the Sunday service. He didn't have to cook a meal all that week. Everyone invited him for morning coffee, noon dinner, afternoon coffee and the evening meal. Though he was tired in the evening, he would take the time to work on his sermon for an hour or two.

Michael spent the rest of the week working on Maigaard's barn. He made good progress and was pleased with his accomplishments.

On late Saturday afternoon, the day before the service, a wagon pulled up in front of the house. A man, a woman and 5 children climbed down and knocked on the door. Emma, busy with preparing a meal, asked one of the children to answer it. When the door opened, she heard a woman's voice, "Well, hello, young nephew, are your mother and father around?" When Emma heard "nephew," she spun around and almost fainted with joy. There in the doorway was Mattie. She flew across the room and the two women embraced, pulled back from each other and hugged again for a long time.

"Oh, it's so good to see you, Mattie! I'm so sorry we lost touch, but we were moving hither and yon and never seemed to know where we would be from one day to the other. I should have written you more often. Michael should have written you, at least to let you know we were here."

"No need for apologies, Emma. I am just as guilty and here are my reasons: children, say hello to your Aunt Emma. And Emma, say hello to Alva, Milo, Ellen, Cora and Elsie and then greet my husband, Sam—Sam Stenerson."

Emma greeted them warmly and then asked, "Whatever brings you here today?"

"Word gets around, Emma. We heard of your new pastor, and then we heard of Michael Glasoe's efforts to get him here. What a surprise when I heard 'Michael Glasoe.' 'That's my brother,' I screamed, 'and he is only 50 miles away.' Then when we heard the first service was to be at your house, we couldn't stay away. I told Sam, 'I don't care how long it takes to get there. We're going! We're going to be at Michael and Emma's house by Saturday.' And here we are."

Sam just smiled and said, "Ja."

Mattie was off again. "That's my Sam. So, we've brought some provisions, and just like in Starbuck, you and I are going to cook a dinner the men will never forget."

Emma introduced Mattie and Sam to Edna, busy at the stove. Mattie said, "Oops! You and I and *Edna* will make that unforgettable meal." Edna blushed with pleasure.

Emma said, "My two oldest boys, Almer and Edgar, are off with their father building a barn nearby, but they will be here soon. Let's go outside and get all these cousins acquainted with each other." When they opened the door, there stood all the Glasoe children in a row, mouths open in wonderment. The children were soon whooping and running off to show the Stenerson cousins their animals.

What a reunion when Michael got home! He opened the door and started to say, "Whose wagon is that...?" and then he saw Mattie. His eyes and his mouth fell open in unison and he held out his arms and said, "Mattie! Oh, Mattie, is it really you after all these years?" She ran to him and their embrace was long and tearful. Both realized how much they had been missed. "The children outside are yours?"

"Yes, 5—so far. I lost little Cora, or it would be 6. You have 6, too, I understand; but I haven't met the oldest boys who were off with you."

"You will, Mattie, you will. As soon as they saw new faces, they were off to join the fun and games."

The couples sat and talked after supper and well into lamplight, catching up on each other's lives since they said goodbye at the Starbuck depot. Mattie was thrilled to hear that brothers, Edward and Otto, planned to be there tomorrow for the church service. She was also surprised to hear Edward had married, and even more so, that he was divorced. Mattie confided that she had lost her first husband, August Swenson. His and the baby's death had been devastating. Then she patted Sam's hand and said, "This was my salvation. My sweet Sam. He pulled me out of the depths and gave me new reasons to live. I love him very much."

The small children all bedded down on the floor, happy as clams for the new experience. Sam and Mattie's children had all brought bedrolls. When the couples retired, they retired to beds.

Early Sunday morning, Adolph came over to load the organ on the wagon. He was as pleased to see Mattie as if she were his sister.

The three men were equal to the loading task and they drove the wagon into the barn. The skies were not cloudy, but Emma would take no chances on her organ getting wet. The men joked that she'd be playing a little closer to Heaven than ever before. Michael had made a makeshift podium for Reverend Egdahl to use. That, also, was placed on the wagon. The children had cleaned the barn the previous days, and the animals were outside in a small fenced pen that Michael and Almer had put up.

As luck would have it, Edward and his lady, Alma, together with Otto showed up early to see if there was anything Michael and Emma needed help with. What a surprising and joyful reunion it was for them and their sister. The both said many times, "Mattie! I can't believe it! Mattie! I thought I'd never see you again." Then when they found out she lived only 50 miles away, they clapped their hands and vowed this would not be the last gathering of the Glasoe clan.

In the excitement, poor Alma got lost in the shuffle, but Emma and Michael introduced themselves, greeted her and kept her in conversation until Edward remembered to introduce her. She just shook her finger at him and laughed.

The rest of the people began coming at 10:00 o'clock and kept coming right up to the time of the service. Some brought chairs, some boxes, some small kegs to sit on. Those who hadn't thought to bring something to sit on, stood around behind. Emma began playing the organ 15 minutes before the service. Her smile was a sign to all that this woman was in her element. She, herself, had never felt so inspired.

Pastor Egdahl climbed up on the wagon bed precisely at 11:00. He gave a brief prayer, "Oh my God, I humbly beseech Thee, prepare our souls to worship Thee this happy day. Purify our hearts from all vain and sinful thoughts; fix my affections on things above. Give me grace to preach Thy

Word. May those who hear, hear with good and honest hearts. Hear me, O God, for the sake of Jesus, our Savior. Amen."

When he had stopped at the Glasoe home during the week, he and Emma talked about what hymns would be best known. They agreed on three, and after the prayer he announced, "Now let us sing, 'Holy, Holy, Holy,' verse 1 and 3."

Emma played a few bars of introduction and then a strong baritone voice began singing, "Holy, Holy, Holy." Pastor Egdahl's voice boomed to the rafters, and even the most timid singers joined in. Tears were rolling down faces throughout the song, in gratitude for this gift that God had sent them.

"I am a graduate of Augsburg Seminary in Minneapolis. It is the seminary of The Lutheran Free Church. I have decided we will use the order of worship we use there. However, until we can get organized and get some printing done, I'll ask you to bow your heads and repeat after me. Almighty God, our Maker and Redeemer... we poor sinners confess unto Thee... that we are by nature sinful and unclean, and that we have sinned against Thee in thought, word and deed... Wherefore we flee for refuge... to Thine infinite mercy... and beseech Thee for Christ's sake... grant us remission of all our sins... and by Thy Holy Spirit... increase in us true knowledge of Thee... and of Thy will... and true obedience to Thy word... to the end that by Thy Grace... we may come to everlasting life... through Jesus Christ, our Lord. Amen."

Then in a strong baritone, he intoned what would come to be known as the Kyrie. "Repeat after me, God be praised for His glad tidings...

"Let us confess our holy faith," and he led them through the confession. Once more, the strong baritone voice this time intoned the Gloria Patria.

"Well, now, that wasn't so hard, was it?" A chorus of "no" rang out and Egdahl smiled. "Now let's try singing, 'O, God Our Help in ages Past' Verse 1."

His sermon was straight forward, the Gospel. Lost in sin, God sent His Son to redeem us. His life is our example. His death is our atonement. All our sins are paid for. His death set us free. We are forever children of God.

In closing, they sang "Beautiful Savior," and tears of joy and inspiration again spilled unashamed down the cheeks of men, women and children.

They prayed together the "Lords Prayer," and Pastor Egdahl, his hand raised, said, "The Lord bless thee and keep thee, The Lord make His face to shine upon thee and be gracious unto thee, The Lord lift up His countenance upon thee and give thee peace." Then to his surprise, Emma immediately played, and he sang, the threefold amen together with those who knew it.

So, the first service of worship in Border Township concluded. Many hands were offered to help the Reverend and Emma down. Handshake after handshake, pats on the back and words of appreciation accompanied him as he made his way out the barn door. Emma found Michael and hugged him so hard he said, "Uffda."

It was a happy group of people who shared their lunch together. It was agreed they would meet at Adolph Holte's again in a week.

When everyone looked like they had been served, Michael and Emma filled their plates and sat down at the two stools the Glasoe clan had saved for them. It was a happy meal, an enjoyable afternoon, and supper was easily made of leftovers. Edward, Alma and Otto left before the sun went down, with hugs all around.

Sam, Mattie and the children stayed a second night. The men had helped bring the organ in and everyone stood around it and sang until it was time to light the lamp. The children drifted off to bed one by one. Michael and Mattie sat and talked about their father and his new family and their sisters. Both remarked about Trina's death and agreed that she and their mother would be together in Heaven.

The Stenersons left after the breakfast, with promises on both sides to write more often. It had been one, big, marvelous weekend.

Chapter Twelve

As Michael remembered it, the next winter arrived late and turned out to be reasonably mild. He and Maigaard got the barn enclosed. Phillip purchased animals from Bell, and Michael added another horse to his list. Two teams would allow him and Almer to both plow at the same time, and would also provide Adolph with a team to use until he could afford to buy one. He had borrowed the team and the breaking plow the previous fall to turn over enough ground for planting in the spring.

The sod house at the Holtes was finished in late summer. That fall Adolph bought lumber and boarded up the inside walls, put up a ceiling and laid down a floor. Kari papered the walls and ceiling and painted the floor white.

That year Michael put together a make-shift sleigh from an old wagon that could be used to transport the family from home to church, to a neighbor's farm and back home again. Now and then he would take the family out for a "joy ride," just to break the winter monotony. They would take the seasoned heat stones the children had brought home, put them on the stove to get them nice and hot, then wrap them in gunnysacks and put them on the floor of the sleigh. The ride was "comfy" as the riders rested their feet on the stones. If they stopped for a visit, the stones came into the kitchen and were re-warmed for the ride home.

He also made his "fun sled," which consisted of just one long 12' board. Curved supports were attached crosswise and to them he attached two 4' wide runners. The riders placed their feet on the supports. They loved it when he got it going fast enough, then would make a sharp turn, and everyone, with squeals and bursts of laughter, tumbled into the snow. The children were especially fond of that experience. "Do it again, Papa, do it again!" Emma usually stayed home by the fire with the babies.

As he and Emma sat in the kitchen, she was knitting woolen scarves and mittens for the children, while Michael put together new "lubbas," the felt liners children wore in their boots. He had seen the material and pattern when he picked up wool for Emma at the Flaxton General Store. New patterns were a luxury, but always welcome as young feet grew. They talked about adding on to the house, and decided this year they would make the second addition. Michael agreed; completing the Maigaard barn would be his only outside job this year. He had the other half of his own barn to finish.

In March an early thaw began around the second week. By the middle of April, Michael and Almer had doubled the size of tilled land. With his own equipment, Michael did not have to wait for someone else to be done. By the end of April, with good rain, his field was sprouting. His new cow calved, the sow had a litter of three and the children were thrilled by the new additions.

Maigaard's barn was shingled and sided in no time. Michael began work on the other half of the barn immediately. By July he was laying the foundation of the new addition. By harvest time, it was ready for inside finishing.

This year Michael had a little extra grain to sell. That would help, since he didn't do any other work but Maigaard's barn. He invested in a pair of sheep and bought himself a shearing scissor. His livestock count was starting to grow.

The church was chartered, and Emma and Michael, along with 7 other families including the Holtes, were charter members. They decided it would be called Zion Lutheran Church. A Women's Society was organized in the Holte home. In the first year, membership grew to about 12 families, with two coming as much as 5 miles to attend the service. There was talk about a church building.

Michael then concentrated on establishing a school and corresponded with the State about a charter. Based on the information he received, he asked Pastor Egdahl to announce a meeting right after the service. He explained the procedures for a school, which were simple enough and included a building and a teacher. In the 1800s the qualifications for teachers in America had been an average of only 6 years of schooling. Now, to be a teacher required a high school graduation certificate.

Michael, remembering his own experience with Martinius, who was about as appropriate for young children, in his mind, as a "gorilla in the kitchen," lobbied hard for a female teacher. A selling point in his favor was cost. A male teacher would cost three times that of a female: $21 a month compared to $7.

The building site was selected, procured and certified by the state. They approved it at the cost of a survey and document stamp. Within months, volunteer labor had the school building ready, calling it "Dolphin Shack." All efforts were bent on making desks and finding a teacher. Desk dimensions were distributed, and each parent was to build their own. Many came to Michael, who built them for a little more than the cost of materials.

One of the homesteaders had a daughter, Agnes, who lived in Minot with her aunt while she went to high school. She was coming home this summer, and she agreed to take the teaching position. How lucky this new settlement was! She could have gone east to Fargo, and get half again as much in salary as she would get in Border. Emma knew that Agnes had missed her parents.

Emma told Michael in January that she was pregnant again. He chuckled and said, "You're right on time, every two years." On June 20, 1906, after 3 girls in a row, baby Arnold was born.

School began the week after harvest. The first day of school was a joyful one for parents and children. Unfortunately, only grades 1 through 6 could be accommodated. Almer, although he was one year older than the other sixth graders, was allowed to attend. He, Edna, Edgar and Hilda walked the one and one half miles to school. When the cold set in, Michael first used the wagon, and then his sled, to take the four plus as many others as he could pick up on the way.

It was agreed by everyone that until a church was built, services could be held in the school building. That would go on for quite a while.

Moral expectations of clergy and educators were extremely high in the new settlements. "They are examples in the community." While Border residents were a little surprised that the courtship of Agnes and Pastor Egdahl lasted only one year, they were pleased by the union, which, they hoped, ensured both a pastor and a teacher for years to come.

On their wedding day, the school was full to overflowing with settlers, which was, in a way, a good thing. It made the little community aware of how small the building was in relation to its mushrooming enrollment. That fall, after the harvest, they almost doubled the size. School that year did not start until November. The men in the community also built a bedroom addition onto the parsonage.

This was the year when Edward married Alma. There were, by then, three Fagerland brothers living in the community: Knute, Olaf and Ben. Again, Mattie and Sam visited, and together with Otto, Michael and Emma, it was a joyous family gathering.

In 1907, when Almer was too old to attend school anymore, he began confirmation, "reading for the minister," with Pastor Egdahl. He also became a valued worker on the homestead, as did his brothers in the years to come: Michael would build, and they would farm. When crops were in, the boys would also help build. The skills they learned under their father's tutelage would benefit them greatly as adults.

The Holtes traded hay for a team of horses. In time they began to prosper. The sod home was finally abandoned for a real wood frame home. Another girl was added to their family; Borghild Eveline was born in 1907.

Also in 1907, the stock market crashed, but no one in Border knew or cared. The talk in the community was all about Henry Ford, who introduced America to the Model T car. It sold for $850, and there were not many of them around in Border for many years. Nobody thought the invention would last: "Too expensive!" "Need roads!" "Runs on something called gasoline!"

In 1908 baby Agnes Theoline was added to the family, ensuring there would be no $850 for a car that year. As the children grew up, the years seemed to fly by for the Glasoes. Each year they tilled more land, produced a little more grain and made a little more profit. Michael continued to build— mostly barns—almost full time year round. The new settlers just kept coming.

Michael would be the first to admit that there were good years for the farm and bad, depending on the weather, especially the rainfall. In good years, the yield per acre was phenomenal, but there were years when the ground was so dry and so cracked that it looked like a jigsaw puzzle. In those years the tumbleweeds, like an invading army, would march across the prairies unimpeded. Other years, insects—especially the grasshoppers—sometimes wiped out entire fields.

In these interim years, as the Glasoe family grew, Michael recalled that the town of Fren, near Gillie's coalmine, became the supply community for the Border homesteaders. It consisted of a post office and a general store and was about half as far as Flaxton. The long two-day runs for food supplies were at an end. By 1910 the Village of Noonan had developed to 52 families, with about 185 individuals. Businesses started popping up to meet the needs of the residents and all the farms around it. Noonan was only about nine miles north and one mile west of the Glasoe farm.

That same year there were 50 families in Border and a total of 187 individuals. The majority came from Minnesota, a few came from Illinois, some from South Dakota and Nebraska and even one from New York. The largest group was of Norwegian descent, but there were a good number of Germans as well.

In that year the residents of Border and Noonan saw a phenomenon that scared some and amazed others. They were accustomed to the bright northern lights shimmering on the horizon, but the huge ball of fire low in the western sky, with its long tail of embers trailing west to east scared a lot of people. While it didn't appear until after midnight, its brightness woke Emma. She went outside to see what it was, then rushed back in to wake Michael. "What on earth do you suppose that is?"

"I haven't the vaguest idea, but it looks pretty far away. When it falls, I don't think it will hit us." Nevertheless, they stayed up all night, lest it land in their front yard. Later they would find out that what they had seen was something called a comet, discovered by a man named Halley. He predicted it would revisit the earth again in 75 years.

If the comet portended disaster for the Glasoe family, it would come to mean tragedy. In 1910 Emma lost her mother. Having just given birth to baby Olaf Erling five weeks before, she did not make the trip back to Starbuck for the funeral.

"I feel so bad, Michael, that I didn't go to my mother's funeral. Do you suppose she will forgive me? It will be such a sad day for Papa. She was his childhood friend, and they had so many years together. I know he will be so lonesome."

"If anyone would understand, it would be your mother. Like many homesteaders who left Norway, she knew she would never see her parents anymore. I think she will be proud to know she has another beautiful grandson. Your papa is a strong man who has endured many hardships, and he will find a way to cope with his loss."

"Do you really think so, Michael?"

"Of course, Emma, of course. Now forget about grief. Remember your mama and honor her in your heart. Sometimes that is all that we can do. These are hard times."

"I will, Michael, I will."

Later Emma would hear that when her mother was close to death, she asked to see her brothers. As the eight of them stood by her bedside, she told them what fine brothers they were and how brave they were to come to this country. She told them how comforting it was to always have them nearby. Then she smiled, closed her eyes and quietly slipped away. The brothers all cried as they knelt by her bed and prayed for the soul of their God fearing, hard working, patient and kindly sister.

Later, from Adolph, Emma learned her father had sold the farm, the machinery and all the household goods. He then went and lived with her mother's brother, Ole.

In the spring of 1911, Michael expanded his farming operation when he acquired brother Otto's homestead. On March 29, 1915, Otto, like his father, married Clara Siggerud, a landed woman, who had a homestead in Upland Township in 1909. Together, they built a home high on a hill, only to discover later that a well driller could not find any water there.

The second addition to Michael and Emma's home came in handy as the number of children grew to ten with the birth of George Lester LeRoy the following year, and in 1913, the last of the Glasoe children, Raymond Leonard, number 11, was added. Thirteen people in all filled the house to capacity: the parents, six boys and five girls.

As the children grew older and became eligible for school, there was much to do to get ready each school day. Each of the older children was assigned a younger sibling. They would first do their chores, wake their siblings and make their lunch for school, putting the food in pails that syrup and molasses came in.

One day Arnold grabbed the wrong pail, and when he opened it for lunch, he discovered he'd brought molasses. Everyone in the one room school laughed so hard, they almost fell off their desks. Then everyone shared with him so he didn't go hungry. It was always suspected that maybe brother Edgar had, for fun, pulled a "switcheroo."

In time, the school expanded from six grades to eight. Much, much later, as the community grew, a high school would be built in Noonan.

Both Emma and Kari were in much demand as midwives, and their reputations brought calls every time a new baby was due to arrive in the community. There were no doctors nearby, and calls came from as far away as 15 miles away. They were always "rush" calls, and often they were pulled out of bed in the middle of the night. While there, the women would help deliver the baby, then do house cleaning and laundry, as well as some baking. They were much revered and eventually got calls for other nursing duties.

In time, the building business was so good that Michael had to pair with another settler, Anton Roness, and his son, Einar. The Roness families came from the same area where Michael had grown up, the Rone's farms on Beistad Sundet. Michael's own mother, Thale, was the daughter of a Roness progenitor, Benjamin. Anton was a descendant of Benjamin's brother Einar.

The territory was now almost fully organized and was named Divide County, after a naming contest was held in 1911. George A. Gilmore, a lawyer from the Williston settlement, was the winner. That name was chosen because the Continental Divide ran through the county from northwest to southeast. Water to the north of the divide flowed into Hudson Bay, while the southern run-off went to the Gulf of Mexico.

The young community of Noonan was the first consideration as the temporary County Seat, but after a lot of politicking, it went to Crosby, 14 miles west of Noonan. Their Sagerty Hall was designated as the temporary Court House. Three Commissioners, Mac Colgan, Albert Makee and Charles Perry, appointed by Governor John Burke, made the final decision.

This "tug of war" was Michael's introduction to American politics. Michael had never met any of the men who were making the decisions, but since he and the other settlers in the county were pretty much responsible for towns popping up, he thought they should have a voice. Of course, the group never organized events where the homesteaders could speak; that just wasn't done. The Glasoes and Holtes were, of course, pulling for Noonan to be chosen. Sadly, Michael learned that no matter where you lived, those who have the money are those who have the power and those who make the decisions. It was a lesson that was not to be soon forgotten.

On the day the decision in favor of Crosby was announced, he told Emma, "I guess I sometimes just don't understand this country. So many fine things have been invented here, so we know there are intelligent people with great ingenuity, yet when it comes to making decisions that affect you and me, America doesn't look to the most intelligent. They let the rich people have all the power. Does that make sense to you, Emma?"

"Michael, dear Michael, I have no time to think such deep thoughts. My worries are healthy children, good food on the table, clean clothes that fit, a tidy house and then helping Dr. Smith when I can. I let you worry about the big things."

"In my perfect world, Emma, the decisions would be made by the dedicated, ingenious, hardworking, intelligent and God fearing members in the community."

"People like you, Michael?"

He blushed and replied, "I guess that's what I'm thinking, Emma. I guess that's what I'm thinking."

In the year that Crosby was arbitrarily chosen, it came very close to being wiped out by a cyclone. Luckily for the residents, while the storm cut a wide path, the major damage was to the northwest in Kermit, near the Ambrose settlement, another chief County Seat contender.

Damage in Crosby was limited to a cement block factory being blown down, along with a barn, killing several head of cattle. The rumor went around that God was voting for Noonan to be the permanent County Seat, as it was least hit by damage. Crosby fought back by saying the storm did more damage to Ambrose than to them.

The day of the storm, Michael had been working on a barn when the skies began to get very dark. "Let's get the tools put away, men, and head for home. This looks like it could be serious."

"Ja, ja, I agree!" was the hurried reply.

Luckily, they were only about four miles away from their homes. By the time Michael pulled into the barn, the sky was absolutely as dark as night, with an almost eerie greenness to the black above. After tending the horse, he shut the barn door and was soaked with rain by the time he made it to the house. "This one's going to be a big one!" he told the family and, with those words, the wind began blowing fiercely, hurling around anything outside that wasn't tied down.

When the house had been built, the boys had dug a small cellar under the kitchen floor. Emma pulled open the door in the floor and hustled all the children down the steps. "Almer, take this lamp. Your father and I will be right down. Edna, you take Lester and Elvira, you take Raymond. I've got Olaf."

The smallest voices by now began calling, "Mama, Mama!" and then the crying started. Hustling down the steps, as Michael followed with another lamp, she grabbed as many little ones as she could close to her and reassured them. "We're safe now, kids. We're safe down here."

"What is it, Mama?"

"I don't know, but it could be a tornado."

"What's a tornado? Is that the Indians coming back? I bet it's oskorei!"

Emma did not hear the last statement, but Michael did and he wondered how one of his children knew about oskorei. He'd never told them; in fact, he'd only told Otto. Then it dawned on him. Otto! Otto told the children when he helped move the family here. He could just see it. Around a campfire, when Emma was busy somewhere else, Otto had told the children what Michael told him. At first he was angry, but then, in time had to smile at his brother's "revenge."

"A tornado is a only a bad storm, with lots of rain and lots and lots of wind. We're safe down here," she reassured them.

Even in the cellar, they could hear the wind roaring. They stayed there until the wind noise stopped. Then Michael pushed up the cellar door, looked around and then cautiously went up and looked out the window. The sky was beginning to grow light again. Opening the door, he noticed the rain had stopped, but its fragrance filled the air. "Come on up now. The storm is over, and the sky is not so angry."

Michael and family, as well as their home and barn, got by with 3 exceptions: a haystack blown away, the outhouse overturned, and the most crushing blow—the loss of Emma's apple tree. Old and often suffering for lack of water, it was barely more than a branchless trunk. The gnarled limbs had simply snapped off in the merciless winds.

Adolph and Kari were also fine, but Adolph and Emma's oldest brother, Ole Hendrick, and wife, Ingeborg, who farmed up by Ambrose, did not fare so well. They lost their house and barn, and Ingeborg was badly burned when she was thrown against the stove. It was a week before Emma or Adolph heard the news, and by then Ole had already gone to Ambrose where he purchased lumber to build a new house.

Much later they heard that on the Truax farm, north of Kermit, one man was killed instantly and another died of injuries sometime later. The storm also claimed the lives of a man and his wife, but, miraculously, their baby survived.

In 1912 the campaign for a permanent County Seat got into high gear with Ambrose, the largest community in the County, Crosby and Noonan as the front-runners. Crosby had by far the most openly political strategy of the three.

While the Glasoes and Holtes had first supported Noonan, they also pulled for Ambrose, where Emma and Adolph's oldest brother, Ole, farmed. When Adolph gave Michael a ride into Noonan, they talked about the situation.

Michael said, "Adolph, can you believe the gall of those people in Crosby? I think they would sell their souls to the devil to win the county seat. The other day a man with a beard came to our homestead with some maps. He was wearing a suit and looked like an educated man. On a map he had showed me that the railroad, once it reached Crosby, would angle south and not go to Ambrose. I must admit that I thought he knew what he was talking about."

"Who was he, did he say?"

"Ja, he said he was a railroad engineer and was recommending that people in the county give their support to Crosby. I said that I particularly favored Noonan being the County Seat."

"Good for you, Michael. What did he say?"

"He said he hoped we were smart enough to know Noonan had no chance at becoming the county seat, and my vote would just be wasted. He said we were too far east. When I asked him what difference that made, he said that Noonan is just too backward to be in charge of anything. I asked which was it—too far east or too backward? He told me both. Emma was listening at the door, and I swear, I saw smoke coming out of her ears. It probably wasn't a Christian act, but I tell you, Adolph, I was so angry, I told that railroad engineer to "skidaddle" off our property or I'd sic the dog on him. He left in a hurry then. I lied. I don't even have a dog." Both men roared at that.

"Well, I tell you, Michael, they will pay for their tactics. I think the storm was a warning to mend their ways."

"Ja, ja. I said that to our Crosby visitor, and he told me that Ambrose had a lot more damage and even a few people killed and that maybe God was trying to say something about them. I said to him that Noonan had hardly any damage because we were too far east, so maybe God wanted us to be the county seat. He just snorted. I had him and he knew it."

"I'm glad he didn't come to our place. I do have a dog!"

Politics being politics, Crosby finally won out, and it was rumored they even gave a Noonan group $700 to reimburse donors who contributed to the campaign.

In the end, the communities accepted the Crosby win in good grace; there was more than local politics to absorb their attention.

In 1913 when the Suffragettes won the right for women to vote, Michael came home with the news. He railed on a little about women getting their nose into politics. When he said, "Well now, Emma, you can vote in the next election," he laughed, and expected her to do the same.

However, after following him from Starbuck to Souris to Border, after raising 11 children, while acting as midwife and nurse to most households in the community, after serving as church organist for more years than she could count, straight faced, she looked him in the eye and said simply, "It's about time, Michael. It's about time." He never brought the subject up again. Three years later they heard that Montana had elected the first woman ever to Congress.

It was in 1914 that Michael received a job that was unlike anything he'd ever done before. The growing community of Noonan contracted with him and his crew to build the town's water tank. It was no surprise to anyone that, when it was filled, nary a drop leaked out.

In 1915, Michael recalled that Emma's father, Anton Holte, at age 78, moved from Starbuck and came to live with Adolph and Kari. He would stay with them until he died 11 years later. Despite his age, he was still a vital man and kept busy around the farm. Adolph told Michael that the first fall they put him on the mower to help with haying, but that proved to be too dangerous, as he liked to have the horses "almost on the run" and they were afraid he might fall off and get killed.

So instead they put him in charge of the grove they had planted. While Anton carefully pruned the trees, Kari once confided to Emma, the trees prospered while her flowers perished. In the spring, before the flowers could bloom, Anton would pull up the "weeds" as he called them. No matter how many times she scolded him, he seemed to conveniently forget and would go out and do it again.

Emma, at one point, said to Kari, "Would you like me to ask him to stay at our place for a while? I think we could squeeze him in someplace."

"No, he says he won't stay any place but our house, because I make him mush and hot chocolate with marshmallows."

Anton had a favorite horse called Prince. He used to hitch him to the wagon and often went as far as his son Ole's farm, 18 miles away. So it also became his job to go places and bring home needed food and supplies.

Adolph and Kari had made it a practice to send all their daughters away to stay with relatives who lived in communities where there was a high school. Communities included Starbuck, Columbus, a few miles away, and Glasgow, Montana, where Kari's sister had settled. Most summers they were home again.

So, in 1915 when Lillian Glasoe finished 8th grade, she asked if she might go away to school like her cousins. Mattie, during one of her visits, had mentioned how happy she was that Grenora had a fine high school for her children to attend. After much discussion, her parents made arrangements for her to stay with her Aunt Mattie in Grenora and go to high school while she helped with the children and household chores. Like her cousins, she was at home during the summers.

It 1916 it was the thrill of Michael's life to be asked to build the new church. He had been a major factor in acquiring a pastor, now he would provide the church in which their shepherd would bring them the Gospel. Together with Anton and Einar, and on occasion his sons, he erected the new Zion Lutheran Church, including the furnishings. It was a labor of love for him, indeed taking him back to those early years in Starbuck. It was done with as much devotion as he had put into Pastor Overby's chair. Dedication day was a proud day for him, and it was surely a wonderful day for the patient homesteaders. With the surge of new pioneers, the congregation had grown considerably. In time, he would be asked to build another church in a nearby community.

It was also in that year, 1916, that the weather was perfect and North Dakota produced the largest wheat crop ever. It was a truly joyous year, worthy of celebration for this rural community.

It was around this time, Michael couldn't remember exactly which year, his brother Edward sold his homestead and bought the pool hall in Noonan. By that time, he and Alma had three children.

Sunday afternoons were dedicated to baseball. Border had a team, and they often played their games in the Holte's pasture. With the lack of any lakes nearby, it was about the only recreation the community had. The women and girls would dress up in their finest and bring lunch along. When the game was over, they would announce where the next game would be played. If it was away—and half the time it was—the family would pack up and go along.

The Glasoe boys, Almer and Edgar, were team regulars. They had no gloves, so they would begin tossing a ball around in the spring, firing it harder and harder until their hands were toughened in. Michael recalled that Almer was the catcher, and over the years had many broken fingers on either hand.

One day late in 1917, Michael received a letter, written in Norwegian. It was from his father's second wife. She wrote that his father, Ole, passed away on June 11th. He was six months short of his 85th birthday. Their son, Torvald, was going on 18, and Karl Magnus was 15. She remarked that Ole had talked many times about his visit to Minnesota. He was very proud of his American children, and he so enjoyed their letters.

In 1917, when the courthouse was dedicated in Crosby, a man by the name of Harris Baukol opened the Baukol-Noonan coal mine at the site where the homesteaders like Michael had "wagon mined" coal for their stoves. The new venture would provide employment through the bleak years ahead, and would help to keep the village of Noonan from becoming a ghost town.

In 1918, as surely as the Glasoe's children had seemed to be born on a schedule of one every two years, so it was again that they grew up, married and began their own families at the same rate. For the parents, it was a period of happiness mixed with sadness. The house emptied of children one by one. Michael and Emma saw it as a fulfillment of their obligation as parents, as they entered into a period of time where they would end as they had begun, alone, the two of them together.

In 1919 the Holtes had a sale and sold their farm equipment. They moved into Noonan and bought the Baukol house. Adolph used money from the sale to buy a half interest in the Lindstrom Hardware Store, which became Lindstrom and Holte Implement Company. His younger brother, William, came from Starbuck to rent their farm.

It was also a thrill in that year for the Glasoe family, when daughter Lillian became the first child to earn a high school degree. What an experience it was for Michael and Emma to see their first child get her high school diploma. They and the younger children made the trip to Grenora and stayed with Mattie and Sam.

As the Glasoes prepared to leave for home, they thanked the Stenersons profusely for letting their daughter live with them. Mattie graciously said, "Goodness, Emma, the girl was a marvelous help—minding the younger children, helping with cooking and baking and cleaning house. I tell you this, Emma, you surely trained her well in all those skills."

When Michael harrumphed, she added, "And of course you, too, brother Michael." It was a proud and happy time for both families. Michael's admiration of and love for his sister, Mattie, knew no bounds. Like him, she had come to America as a very young immigrant, and she had done so well for herself—so well.

As new businesses popped up, the town of Noonan just kept growing and flourishing. By 1920 it had grown to 97 families and 375 residents. It eventually had its own doctor, J. Allen Smith, MD, affectionately known as "Doc Smith."

In a short span of time, he discovered the reputations of Emma and Kari, who eventually became his right and left hands in the rural community, going with him on many occasions to assist as midwives and often staying on for days as a nurse for those who were severely ill. Almer was often his mother's chauffer. In 1921 Kari, herself, with vague complaints, went to Rochester, Minnesota, and went through the Mayo Clinic. They failed to find anything wrong with her.

After two years, William gave up on farming Adolph and Kari's homestead and moved back to Starbuck to the homestead. Art, their oldest son, was the next one to farm the land. He, too, lasted 2 years. He was followed by another Holte brother, Odin. By this time, Adolph had purchased two more quarters. Finally, in the 1920s, Adolph rented out the land to Holgrim Brootens, who remained there for many years.

While Adolph tended his business and managed the farm, Kari, almost by accident, began taking in patients at her home, which became a sort of "makeshift hospital." When Adolph's brother was taken ill on the farm, Doc Smith had him taken to Kari's home and, to her total amazement, he performed an appendectomy on her dining room table. Brother-in-law Odin became her first patient. While no major operations took place at the Holte home, it was common practice for tonsils to be removed there. Often Kari told the doctor she did not want to continue taking patients, but he turned a deaf ear to her complaints. "There is no other place to take them, Kari," he told her simply.

When inoculations became available, Emma, Kari and the doctor took advantage of them. That was a significant occurrence for the Border families, as they got the benefit of a healthy doctor, plus a nurse, when epidemics raged.

Diphtheria was a particularly dreaded disease of the upper respiratory system, usually passing quickly from person to person by coughing and sneezing. Symptoms began with a sore throat, fever, chills and loss of appetite. Sometimes a film would form in the throat, making it hard to breath. Diphtheria could also produce a toxin causing heart attacks and paralysis. It was particularly devastating for the young.

On one occasion, Emma was quarantined with one farm family for over three weeks, treating one family member after another. Miraculously, they all survived, and they never forgot the diligence of the woman who brought them back from the "valley of the shadow of death." The community was grateful to be spared an epidemic.

For her part, Emma was thankful that the family was spared the agonizing loss of life she had read about in one of Doc Smith's journals. She was particularly moved by the story of one family in the Red River Valley, who lost 5 children in 11 days. Being quarantined, no one could come in, and only the dead went out, usually passed through a window to coffin bearers outside. The father would use the bell on the front porch to alert a neighbor, and then hold his right hand up to signal the size of the coffin needed. The box would be delivered via the window; the grave would be dug in the yard, and the family who were well enough to be on their feet would watch the burial service through the window.

When Emma finally got home, her youngest, Raymond, hugged her for a long time and then asked, "Mama, is the Corn Team gone now?"

Holding him at arms length she repeated, "What Corn Team?"

"Daddy told us that you couldn't come home because of the Corn Team.

I remembered that when the threshing team comes, they stay a long time and don't leave until all the grain is threshed. I figured out that the Corn Team must be like them."

Enfolding him in her arms, with a huge smile she reassured him, "Yes, the Corn Team's gone, and I don't think they'll be back for a long time. In fact, I hope they never return."

Chapter Thirteen

In 1921 Michael started having problems with urination. He visited Doc Smith, who diagnosed an enlarged prostate. He recommended some medication and said Michael should come back in six weeks to see if the gland was back to normal. It wasn't, and 8 months later, Doc said he needed surgery. Michael hesitated at first, but when the doctor persisted, there seemed to no other choice.

As there was no hospital in Noonan yet, Doc Smith made arrangements for the surgery to be done at the Starbuck Hospital in Minnesota. Starbuck was chosen because it was one of only three advanced care hospitals in the area, completely outfitted for all manner of surgery and, more importantly, it was accessible by train. The other two hospitals were Fargo and Minneapolis.

The other reason, and perhaps most important reason for choosing Starbuck, was because Michael knew the doctor. Ten years after his arrival as an immigrant in that community, he was hired to build the house of Dr. C.R. Christensen, a new University of Minnesota School of Medicine graduate, who had chosen to locate his practice there. He had gotten to know the young doctor well. The Christensens had also joined Indherred Lutheran, and the doctor and his wife were fellow choir members. When little Edgar and younger sister Hilda were born, Emma chose to be under the care of Dr. Christensen.

Emma had packed a bag with the few things he would need. Son Arnold, age 19 and the oldest unmarried son, was freed up. He had been designated to be Michael's traveling companion. He would see to his needs in Starbuck and assist him on the trip home. It was quite a thrill for Arnold to be chosen.

When they arrived in Starbuck, Arnold sent post cards home to family members. One read:

Dear sister,
I am sending you a card about the hospital. The first X is Papa's room. The

other X is where I think they will operate. Papa is down there. They are
going to operate on him at 10 o'clock today. I hope he will be over it alright.
Sept 5, 1922.
Wishing you all a merry season.
Brother Arnold.

The card had a photo of the two-story hospital building. The surgery was completed, and a weakened Michael, with Arnold's strong shoulder, made the trip back to North Dakota. He remembered that his home had never looked so good, and Emma was loving and attentive. His recovery was slow, with house calls from Doc Smith, until he was able to return slowly to work. Michael continued accepting carpenter work, but depended on his crew to do the heavy lifting and the climbing.

Not long after that, Arnold was in an auto accident resulting in a head injury. He stayed with his aunt, Johanna, for a while, but eventually went to the State Hospital in Jamestown, North Dakota, and lived out his life there. It was a sad time for the Glasoe family as Arnold had shown such promise. They bowed to the will of God. He was not the only son Michael and Emma would lose.

Newspapers in the 1920s reported that prosperity was too unevenly distributed among the various parts of the American economy—farmers and unskilled workers were notably excluded—with the result that the nation's productive capacity was greater than its capacity to consume. News is simply news until it touches you. For the Glasoes and other homesteaders in Border Township, it meant that jobs became scarce and grain prices plummeted.

As they had watched their children marry, so they watched again as each child moved away. Almer was the first of the Glasoe boys to leave home to find work. He went to Landa in Bottineau County, where he worked as a salesman for his uncle, Louie Gorder, at Gorder and Olson's hardware store, since Louie and Johanna had no son. While working there, he met Peder Boreson's youngest daughter, Vera, at church choir practice. The courtship ended with their marriage in 1923.

When Michael discovered that his son would be marrying Peter Boreson's daughter, he was overjoyed. "Emma, we will need to go to the wedding. Mr. Boreson was such a help to me in Souris. He was the one who suggested I claim a homestead and then keep on working as a carpenter."

"Of course, we will go. Almer is our first son to take a wife; I'm more anxious to meet that young lady than her father. What was her name? Did you hear?"

"Vera, I believe. Ja, Vera."

As the day approached, they packed up their car, bringing as many children as possible. They made arrangements to stay with Louie and Johanna, Emma's sister.

The wedding day was perfect. The Glasoes were surprised that the church in Landa was full. Peter and Anna, it turned out, were well known in the community, and it seemed like everyone in town had gathered together to help them celebrate. After the service, the Boresons held a reception at their home and served up a full chicken dinner for all the guests.

When Michael shook Peter's hand, he said, "Well, Michael, whoever would have expected this when we worked together in Souris? It is a pleasant surprise, and I may well have influenced it when I asked my daughter to pick up your son for church choir practice."

"On my part, Peter, this was not something I ever suspected. I thought I had seen the last of you when our wagon headed for Border Township. How did you end up here?"

"Well, when the railroad extended on to Landa, Imperial wanted me to open up a yard there, which I did. It has been as successful as Souris. I sold the homestead and bought me a few quarters out here. It's been good land so far. How goes it with you?"

"I filed my homestead claim, but heeding your advice, I continued to carpenter. I added another quarter to my homestead in 1911. My building business got so good, I had to hire a couple men and then got help from my boys when they were not busy on the farm. Our land is not quite as good as yours, but we have had some good crops. 1916 was our best year."

"Ja, mine too."

A wedding guest that Michael didn't know approached them as they were talking and said, "You know when I look at you two, I can only think of the Norwegian comic characters, *Ola han Per*. You, Peter, are so broad and tall and you, Mr. Glasoe, are so short and slight."

Laughing, Peter said, "Well thank you, Christ. I will take that as a compliment."

"And I," Michael answered, "I take as an insult, Christ!" And then they all laughed.

Emma had a brief time to talk to Vera and thought she was very nice. She asked how the two of them met.

Vera said, "One day my father said, 'Drive down south to so-and-so's farm'—to this day I can't remember their name – 'and pick up Almer Glasoe to sing in the choir. He's a fine tenor, and we need tenors'. So I did, and I guess the 'love bug' rode along, because now we're to be married."

It was a lovely wedding, a delicious dinner and a happy time. Getting to visit with sister Johanna again was a bonus for Emma.

After the wedding, Almer had farmed the home place, as the farm was called, with Vera's brother Gil on the sizeable Boreson farm for one year. His first son, Harland, was born there. In time the young family moved to a small house in Landa where he operated a dray line service. After selling that business, he purchased a truck, hauling gravel to make a living.

The 20s were difficult times for the prairie farmers. World War I had destroyed the European grain market for them. It would take years to recover. Lower grain production and sales meant people on the prairie had less money "to do with," and thus, businesses in small towns like Landa and Noonan also suffered.

After adding two more children, a son Doran and daughter Nola, and trying to scratch out a living in Landa, Almer, his wife and three children returned to Noonan in 1931. Their oldest son, Harland, years later recalled that trip from Landa to Noonan. It closely paralleled the trip Michael and Emma took 27 years earlier.

Harland wrote of that experience: *What a trip that was! We loaded up the truck with our belongings and headed for Noonan, which took us all day. As I remember, it was dark when we arrived. Dad, Mother and sister Nola sat up front in the cab. Brother Doran and I sat up on top of furniture in the open air. Dad had such poor tires that they would develop bumps or lumps on the tires. Believe it or not, he would get out, saw them off, and away we would we go again.*

Back in Noonan, Almer found a job at Henry Staflin's Service Station. The automobile that settlers had at one time decried would never make it was now a flourishing business. Almer manned the gas truck that hauled fuel to the farmers who also had discovered tractors.

On one occasion he had to make a trip to Flaxton; there the truck broke down. Arranging to have it repaired he called Vera and said he was having trouble with the truck in Flaxton, so come and get him. He told her, 'Now, be sure you don't pick anyone up along the way.' It was the wrong thing to say. When more than an hour went by, he got tired of waiting and started walking. He saw his wife coming and started waving his arms to attract her attention; she drove right by him. She found his truck in Flaxton, but no Almer. She guessed he must have found a ride, so back home she went, passing him, his arms waving again, for the second time. This story was told more than once at family gatherings. Everyone would laugh and Vera would blush and say, "Well, he told me not to stop and pick anyone up and that's what I did." Everyone would laugh again, this time pointing fingers at Almer, who just shook his head and laughed along with them.

While in Landa, Almer had continued to play baseball and was glad to see when he came home that the Border community still had a team. It was composed mostly of Glasoe brothers: Edgar, Olaf, Lester and Raymond, with several other local players. After Almer raised the Glasoe total to five, they called themselves the Glasoe Team.

Almer would stay with his family in Noonan for several more years, but then, for lack of work, he would leave again.

So it was with a little sadness, but a lot of pride, that Michael, in his musings, remembered the fine family he and Emma had raised, their children's happy marriages, their sad farewells and the grandchildren who, over time, numbered more than 40. If that was not a legacy, Michael thought, then nothing was.

As he approached his 60th birthday, Michael often thought of the advice he had received from Peder Boreson about having a second income, especially in his last years of farming. Without income from his carpenter work, trying to live off the farm from the time of World War I would have been done only with the assistance of bank loans, the fate of many homesteaders. The weather on the plains was often brutal enough, but Michael and his neighbors battled other demons.

No matter how much they increased their crop acreage, no matter how they mechanized their farms, the income remained meager. The millers refused to pay increased prices for the grain, but charged higher prices for their flour. Attempts to build co-ops and join together to demand higher prices did nothing to improve their struggle.

As the depression gripping the country deepened, it became tougher and tougher for farmers to make a living. After the World War in Europe, there was no foreign market for their grain. Michael talked to Emma about his frustrations.

"I remember when I returned home from the navy. I intended to help my father and mother on the farm for a while. My mother had died, and my father had had some losses. There was not much left and when I offered to help, he told me no, 'I have no stomach for it anymore.' I tell you, Emma, neither do I."

"What would you like to do, Michael? You know I have always believed in you to know what is best."

"Well, I will soon turn 61. I've never been as strong as I was before my surgery. I would like to concentrate on doing a little bit of carpentering, but I would like to sell our equipment, rent out the farm and find a house in Noonan."

"So it will be then. I will not mind retiring a little bit myself, and Noonan is getting to be a nice little town. Just plant me an apple tree and plow me up a garden plot."

And so it was decided in 1926 that Michael and Emma, after a lifetime of struggle, hard work, sacrifice, sweat and tears, took out a mortgage on a house in Noonan and left the homestead. The children had all married and established their own lives and families. All they had to take care of were each other. Michael would soon be 61 years old; Emma was 55. They rented the farm out to sons-in-law, Gust and Einar Roness.

In that same year there had been a glimmer of hope for Divide County farmers when a Montana driller with an 85' rig drilled 1,600' in search of oil on a site just north of Noonan. The Northwest Oil Company was chartered, and shares were sold to finance the project.

There wasn't a homestead couple who didn't talk about, dream about, or pray about finding oil on their property. Michael and Emma were no exception.

"You know, Emma, I wouldn't be surprised if they came and drilled down by our slough, they would strike oil."

"What makes you think that?"

"Well, the sweetness of the water tells me that things are just not right there. It could just well be that it's caused by the oil farther down."

"Oil makes the water sweet?"

"Well I don't know, Emma, but it just has always seemed strange to me."

In 1927 the only site drilled was abandoned, and no another attempt was made nearby. It didn't mean there wasn't any oil, but that the operation ran out of money and when no more cash could be raised, the operation was discontinued.

There were, of course, rumors that they actually found oil, but capped it in hopes of coming back in a while to get the land for little or nothing. There were even rumors that a man in Colgan used oil from a trench dug in his basement to operate his light plant.

Michael, now with time on his hands, would follow the news religiously in the *Noonan Miner*, the *Divide County Journal* and on his $5 Sears and Roebuck radio. The news continued to be bad.

In the 1920s Michael had read about all the banks that were opening at a rate of four to five per day. However, with few federal restrictions and poor management, most of them became highly insolvent, and between 1923 and 1929 they began closing at the rate of two a day. Eventually, 11,000 of America's 25,000 banks failed. In 1929 the United States slipped deeper into a depression.

He also read and heard that after the First World War many of the countries that had borrowed money from the United States couldn't pay their debts, plus they had no money to buy American goods. The lack of a European market just got worse and worse and almost destroyed the farming industry. It was not just in Border, it was all over.

It wasn't just the economy going bad, the homesteaders now had to also deal with the weather. In 1931 one of the bleakest periods for the prairie states began with a severe drought hitting the Midwest. As the crops died, "black blizzards" occurred, when topsoil from over-plowed and over-grazed land began to blow away in the high, dry winds that never seemed to quit. The following year there were a total of 14 storms, increasing to 38 in 1933. By 1934 drought covered 75% of the nation.

Between 12 million and 15 million Americans, about 25 percent of the work force, were unemployed. Millions of people had lost their life's savings. Many had lost their homes and lived in makeshift shacks. Many more stood in long lines for free soup and bread.

One evening Michael said to Emma as she sat darning socks, "Today I heard on the radio that 30 percent of the people in Minnesota have no jobs, and in northeast Minnesota, it's as high as 78 percent. It makes me wonder how Lillian and her family are doing down in Minneapolis. With less wheat to grind, I worry about Al's job."

"Well, don't spend too much time on it. I'm sure if things were too tough, they'd let us or somebody know."

"I also worry about our friends in Whitebear and Starbuck. The radio reports that there were breadlines everywhere in the Midwest, and homes and farms here are being abandoned. The farmland is just blowing away. I thank the good Lord we were able to retire before it got this bad. We struggled, I'm sure you would agree, but it was nothing like this."

"Maybe, Michael, you should stop listening to news on the radio and reading about it in the paper. I think it only saddens you. Why don't you do some writing? Write letters to the kids who are away. Instead of all the bad news, maybe you can write about good things happening to people. Ja, that's it, you need to be writing."

"Maybe you're right. For a long time I've been thinking about writing down some of my favorite poems about Norway and giving them to the children. Like you, they have no idea of what a wondrous place it is."

"Oh, I think I know a little about it. With my mother and dad and all my Wollan uncles from there, I've heard much of Norway's beauty. Interestingly, never anything bad was said, everything was always good and beautiful. Are you sure you and my parents didn't come from heaven?"

"Oh! So now the secret is out, Emma, all the more reason for me to think that it would be a good thing to think about and write down. Tomorrow I will get me another notebook."

Emma replied, "Ja, and when the dirt blows, you just pull down the shades and light your lamp." Then she chuckled.

Michael still had one ear tuned to the radio, he couldn't get away from it; it was too important. His eyes, however, remained focused on his notebook, filling one of them with poems.

The first one he chose to write down was entitled "Fedresland Sang," (Song of the Fatherland).

The evening he finished it, he asked Emma if he could read it to her. She, of course, told him, "Yes," and listened quietly to his recitation, as he knew it by heart.

He began,

"There lies a land against the eternal snow.
In the crevices there is only spring life to see,
But, the sea is there with historic roar.
And loved is this country, as mother is by son.

She took us in her lap, that time we were,
And, gave us her saga with pictures.
We read until the age became big and wet.
Then the old one smiled and only nodded her head.

We ran down to the fjord. We were staring at
The stone gray monument, old where it stood.

She stood there, an elder, and said nothing.
But, stone piles lay round in a ring.
She took us by the hand and accompanied us
Away from there to the church so quiet and low
Where the fathers humbly have bent there knees,
And softly she said, 'do as them.'

She spread her snow over steep hillsides,
Then asked her boys to cross it on skis.
She crushed the calm water of the North Sea with her,
Then asked her boys to raise their sails.

She put the most beautiful girls in a row,
To follow our sport with smile and song.
And she sat herself on her high saga chair,
With the power of the moonlight under her chair.

Then there sounded a forward, forward, still
In the language and mood of the father,
For freedom, for Norwegian-ness, for Norway,
And the mountains themselves shout, hurray! hurray!

Then the rolling sound of enthusiasm loosened,
Then we were baptized by her powerful spirit,
Then over the mountain stood a glowing sight,
Which afterward urge us until our death."

When he finished all the verses she said, "What are sagas, Michael?"
"They are the soul of our country, Emma. They are Norway's poetic history, passed faithfully down from generation to generation by mouth before writing was invented. My father urged me, early on in Norway, to read them all."
"You know, Michael, in this country if something isn't written down people either think it's not true or it's probably not important. That's why I'm urging you to write instead of listen to the awful news on the radio."
"Now you sound like Martinius, my old teacher in Norway. Sagas are written down now and I read a lot of them. I've also started to write my life down."

"So, this poem is about those sagas, right?"

"Yes. The first verse is about the physical country of Norway, but the following verses are about our Viking heritage. Then Mother Norway holds us on her lap until we are big enough to learn of the Viking chiefs who ruled our country. They would meet in a special place called a Ting. The spot was marked by a large stone monument and then around in the circle were large rocks where the chieftains sat to discuss important matters affecting their kingdom in Norway."

"So, they were kind of like the government here where men write the laws in Washington?"

"That's right, Emma. The last of the Viking kings tried to force everyone to become Christian and threatened those who denied baptism with death."

"Oh, how awful. There really was a king like that?"

"Yes, he meant well, but he used Viking tactics and the people would not have it. It took King Olaf to Christianize the country. Remember the words, 'She took us by the hand and accompanied us away.' Mother Norway forsook the Viking violence and led us to the place where the 'fathers humbly bent their knees.' She wanted her people to embrace the Christian faith."

"I say, Michael, you see more in that poem then I saw."

"Yes, Emma, and from there she sprinkled us across the land and urged us to fight for our freedom, for our Norwegian-ness, for Norway. Oh, it is a beautiful and powerful poem, don't you think."

"Yes, when you explain it to me, it is. When you explain it to me, it is very wonderful. You are a true son of Norway and you miss it, don't you?"

"To that question, I will respond as my grandfather did when my father asked him if he ever wished he had become a sailor. Grampa Amundson said, 'Every day, Ole. Every day.' Yes I miss Norway, and I would so have liked to take you there one day."

When he finished writing his poems, he began writing down what he remembered of glorious Norway. His heart became so full of longing, he would have given anything to go back. *However, when you have nothing,* he thought, *giving anything is also nothing. Multiply any number, no matter how big, by zero and the total is zero; it would never happen.*

In the evenings he would read to Emma what he had written that day. She would ask questions, and he would give answers. It was almost like a geography lesson, a history lesson and a social studies lesson all in one.

One night, after the last page had been read, Emma teased, "Where were you when I was trying to teach the children before we had our school?"

One day, an idea for a story hit him. He'd never written a story, so this would be a real challenge. The story he thought up was, what would have happened to all the poor immigrants if they'd never had to leave Norway? What if Norway had come up with a homestead program and granted some of the State lands high up in the mountains to Norwegian young people like those he read about in the conservation corps?

At dinner the next day, he said, "Emma, listen to this. What would you think if I tried writing a story about a young Christian man in Norway, who convinced the government to start a homestead program?"

"Homestead in Norway, I thought there was no more land to be farmed? Is this a make believe thing?"

"Sort of. I think in this country it might be called a fantasy. The land would be good land, high up in the mountains, where timber would have to be cut and stumps pulled so the land could be tilled. The lumber would be used to build a house, a barn and a granary."

"Is there such land?"

"In my story there will be; people, and even the government, just never noticed it. They only thought of farming in the valleys."

"If it keeps you away from the news, then I say do it. And make it a long story."

"I will. I've already decided to name the young man—Ole; and, like my father, he will be the son of a cotter. He will work hard both summer and winter, so he doesn't become a slave for the rich farmers."

"Ja, ja. I will be interested to hear what you write. You have already surprised me with how well you handle the pen and paper. I thought I married a carpenter, then a farmer and now, I find myself spending my days and nights with a writer. Maybe, as you write, you can read it to me in the evenings, like the poems and the description of Norway. Then, if there is a woman in the story, I can help make sure she's not just another pretty face. She be can be comely and sweet, but above all, she must be a hard worker who helps her husband."

The next day Michael began his story. Little did he know, it would take him almost 2 years to get it just right, so he could make his final writing in new notebooks. True to Emma's urging he made it a long story.

While he wrote, he still kept one eye on the news. One bright light on the dust- obscured horizon, at least for a few, had been a joint conservation work program for young men aged 18 to 25. Under supervision of the army, it was estimated that they began with 1,000,000 young men working 40 hours a week, planting trees to stop erosion and reclaiming land that had been abandoned.

The Corp provided clothing food and shelter and paid each man $30 a month. Most saved $5 for their own expenses and treats at the canteen and sent $25 home to parents and siblings; what a blessing that was.

In those days, a steady $25 a month came in handy. Bread was .05 a loaf; butter, .19 a pound; eggs, .25 a dozen; potatoes, $1.35 for 200 pounds; round steak, .26 a pound; bacon, .22 a pound; chicken, .22 a pound; ham, .31 a pound; pork chops, .20 a pound; and flour, .99 for 5 pounds.

The Corp was not the cure, but it was a step in the direction of protecting and conserving America's farmland and provided Michael the seed of an idea for his "Ole" fantasy. It was a positive note in an otherwise discordant prairie symphony.

It would not be until 1939 that the rains would return to the plains, finally bringing an end to the drought. Farms once again produced crops. By that time, however, many homesteaders had given up in despair. Non-farmers were still forced to scratch out a living anyway they could. It would take until World War II for the economy to return to a semblance of normalcy.

Chapter Fourteen

It had been in the spring of 1939 that Michael had finally finished his story. He had given his final rewrite to his friend, Ole, for a final proof read. He had also started to write down his life story for his children to read and had been pleased with his good start. Now, as Christmas approached, he hadn't written so much as another word. He was just too tired most of the time.

By now the Glasoes had a phone, so they were not isolated any more than they wanted to be. Still, with a lot of the family gone, it got lonely at times and they longed for the old days, when the house was full of hustle and bustle.

That Christmas the Glasoes received a letter from their granddaughter, Ellen, who had left Minneapolis to "go out west". They were pleased that she had thought of them in this holy season. While Michael was reluctant to reveal to the next generation that having learned the spoken English, he, after all these years, could not write it, he wanted to thank Ellen for remembering them. In Norwegian, he wrote the following:

Noonan, North Dakota
December 10, 1939

Dear Ellen:
A thousand thanks, Ellen, for the letter you sent us. It did us good to see that you remember us who are old. I wish I could have written this letter to you in English, but you will have to find someone who can read it and translate it for you.

Now it is not long until the great festival of Christmas which we celebrate each year in memory of the great salvation provided for us sinful human beings. Let us this year celebrate it appropriately with thanks to God for the wonderful grace He has shone toward us.

As to our health, it is about the same as when you left us. One day we are up and around and the next may be in bed, but patience overcomes all things.

I hope, Ellen, you will soon find a well paying job and be able to set aside something to repay you for all the work and studying you have done in school.

There will be a Christmas festival and program at Zion Church during the holidays. They are now practicing with the children and met for the first time yesterday. I believe Rose Fenster is the leader of the program.

No doubt you have seen many wonderful and beautiful things out there in the West—something different than here in barren North Dakota where Russian thistle and grasshoppers thrive so well. I wish I could have seen some of the wonderful scenery in the West, but that will never be fulfilled.

It is so quiet and still here, not even a fly to disturb me, but still I cannot think of anything new that would be of interest to you. I must be a dumb-cluck, I believe.

Next Saturday, if I live, I can celebrate my 74th birthday. There will be many years, Ellen, before you reach that age, but time flies fast and before we know it we have gotten old.

Tiden rinder, tiden aviner hastig bordt.

Tenk paa evighed I tide om den ei skal vorde sordt.

Ja hvad er egentlig livet? Et pust I sive;

En Strom of kraefter som higer efter en evighed.

(Time flies, time hastens on.

Think of eternity in time, if it will be dark.

What is real life? A puff in the wind;

A stream of energy reaching out to eternity.)

Yesterday your mother and father were here awhile. They had been to Crosby and stopped here awhile afterward.

This is the first letter I have written to any of my grandchildren. You must save it as a remembrance of your old grandparents. Perhaps it will be the last, too.

Now it will not be long before there will be lutefisk and lefse. Ha! Ha!

You asked in your letter if I had finished the story I was writing. Yes, it is now finished, and Ole Joraanstad has it to read. I began another one, too, but have not written any more for some time.

I think it is best that I close now, as perhaps you are long since tired of

this letter, Ellen. Live well and write to us again. Greetings to all our acquaintances out there.
  A friendly greeting to you from your grandparents,

Grandpa and Grandma Glasoe

Because of Michael's health, Emma decided to invite the family, those that still lived in Noonan or close by, to their house for dinner. It would be crowded for sure, but how comforting at Christmas to be close to the ones they loved. She would buy and cook the turkey, and each of the families would bring the bread and lefse and flat bread, side dishes of corn casserole and canned beans and corn and sweet potatoes. If Michael's health was good, they would go to church on Christmas and listen to one of Pastor Waage's "hour-long" sermons. It would be a festive time.

It was, indeed, festive. The women began arriving early with their requested part of the dinner. The things that needed to be kept warm were wrapped tightly in all manner of heat conserving trappings. They would sit on the top of the stove until the stuffed turkey came out of the oven. Then they'd be reheated. The potatoes would be cooked fresh and mashed with lots of butter and cream, as Emma made her delicious, mouth-watering gravy from the turkey drippings.

By a little after one-o-clock, the famished group was sitting down to eat. Michael, whose appetite waxed and waned from day to day, swore he was as stuffed as the turkey had been. There was much laughter and conversation around the table, and everyone was in a holiday mood. It was good for Emma and Michael to have family in the house again.

When the last of the leftovers were put away and the last dish washed and dried, everyone gathered in the living room. An adult occupied every chair, and the floor was almost totally obliterated by the grandchildren sitting there. Michael asked if he might recite one of his favorite poems and surprised everyone. No one knew he read poetry, let alone memorized it. In chorus, the children exclaimed, "Yes, Grampa!"

"When I was a young man in Norway, I read a poem about Christmas that I liked very much. At our home on Christmas Evening, I would recite it after the tree was trimmed. I learned it in Norwegian and I recited it in Norwegian. Now that we are all Americans, I will do my best with the English translation." The room was totally hushed in anticipation. "The poem is entitled in Norwegian, 'Jul der Hjemme,' or 'Christmas There at Home.'

"Remember that Christmas up there in the North,
With snow covered mountains and ice covered fjords,
With ringing bells which loudly sound
A message of holiday celebration to the hearts,
From the outermost islets and to the innermost valley,
From the fisherman's room to the rich man's hall,
In cotter house and farm house?
All the way to the sailor at sea it reaches.
Do you remember the evening with mother and father,
The family gathered around the celebration table,
The peace and joy that reign there?
Is truly my most precious childhood memory."

His voice wavered and his eyes clouded with tears, but he continued on with the rest of the verses. Emma's eyes were brimming also, as she thought of her mother.

"Do you remember the pine tree, which stood there so nice,
With lights and decoration on every branch,
Fruit and nuts hung linked together,
And a shining star high up at the top of the trunk?
Do you remember shining eyes and song?
How wonderfully beautiful it sounded in the room,
When all the siblings were with father and mother,
Sounded the well known Christmas choir.
Do you remember the wonderful frost clear evening?
The bright shining stars in the sky,
Silent and faithful they stand guard,
The symbol of Him who was laid in the crib."

Then he signaled to Emma at the organ, and she played a few introductory bars before Michael's clear tenor voice began to sing, "Silent night, holy night"…and every one joined in. It was "the well known Christmas choir," raising its voice one more time.

Then he held up a quieting hand, and in a voice as strong as it had been almost 50 years ago in their first home in Starbuck, he sang the verse again in Norwegian. By the time the last word was sung and the last note faded, there was not a dry eye in the room.

It started with soft clapping from a few of the younger grandchildren and was soon picked up by everyone in the room with shouts of "That was beautiful, Grampa," "Will you teach the Norwegian words to me, Grampa?" "Thank you, Dad." "Thank you, Michael, I will never forget this evening?" Pleased with the reception, Michael rose on love strengthened legs, folded one arm behind his back and one across his front and performed a perfect bow. It was a day to remember. Forever!

Michael and Emma ushered in the New Year quietly in their home. For 49 years they had done the same. For supper Emma cooked rommegrot in hopes that Michael would finish his bowl. He could not.

"Leave the dishes until tomorrow, Emma, and come to the living room with me. When they were seated, he said, "I have another poem I think is appropriate for this day. It is titled 'Ved Arshiftet', which, you know, means, 'Turn of the Year.'" His voice was still strong, but his recitation was soft in reverence.

"A year has passed
And, once again, disappeared,
Swallowed up as everything else, in the sea of time.
Shall everything pass?
Shall everything disappear?
Shall everything be lowered into the tomb of oblivion?
What is there to find,
What have we in mind,
That hasn't, with time, entered his journey?
Does the soul have a longing
Which over its entrapment
And over its prison has will and power?
When all has passed, and everything has disappeared,
Swallowed up as everything in the sea of time.
Eternity shall live,
Eternity shall become,
It shall never be lowered into the tomb of oblivion."

"That was a beautiful poem, Michael, but so sad."
"No, not sad, my Emma, it is a poem about hope; 'Eternity shall live,

eternity shall become, it shall never be lowered into the tomb of oblivion.' Remember, Emma, our risen Savior said, 'Behold, I go to prepare a place for you… a place for me… a place for you… a place for us.' His resurrection ensured eternity. The poem is not about sadness it is about hope and joy, the joy of everlasting life. Eternity shall live!"

Emma did not reply. The lump in her throat was so large she could not utter a sound. Tears trickled down her cheeks, but Michael never saw them, his eyes were closed.

True to his words to Emma, he stopped punishing himself for what he did not write down. He thanked his God for what he had committed to his notebooks.

Dr. Smith's treatments did not stem the onslaught of his illness. While he was still able to be up and around, he slowly, painfully planted the garden. The garden was harvested that fall, and Emma went through her familiar routine of canning her vegetables. His pen, however, never again touched paper, and no further biography was written. The creative skill of the once young, courageous, hardworking pioneer was stilled for all time.

The good health that Michael enjoyed for most of his life dissipated. Within a few months, he was bedridden. The granddaughters still around came and helped their grandmother set up a cot in the dining room where she could keep an eye on him. He asked his Emma to be sure that the things he had written would not get thrown away. She promised they would not.

Pastor Waage visited often and was a great comfort to Michael and Emma. He would read their favorite passages, and then they would pray together. Once in a while, at Michael's request, he would sing softly in Norwegian: the Norwegian folk-tune, with music by Edvard Grieg, "Den Store Hvide Flok Ve Se."

"Behold a host arrayed in white, like a thousand snow-clad mountains bright, with palms they stand—who are this band before the throne of light? These are the ransomed throng, the same that from the tribulation came, and in the flood of Jesus' blood are cleansed from guilt and shame, and now arrayed in robes made white, they God are serving day and night, and anthems swell where God doth dwell, mid angels in the height."

Michael told the Reverend, "I read in one of my Norwegian newspapers that Grieg passed away in 1907." Then with a broad grin, "Do you suppose he will be there to greet me?"

Waage replied, "Without a doubt, Michael, without a doubt. And watch for Ole Bull to be playing his violin." He brought great comfort to this couple of strong faith. They loved him dearly.

Emma gathered all of Michael's blue notebooks and put them in a box. On all sides in large letters she wrote, *DO NOT DESTROY*. Taking the box to his bedside, she inventoried each notebook to ensure she had them all.

"Were there any more notebooks, Michael?"

"No. I believe you have them all. I would like it each day, if you would read to me from the story of 'Ole, The Mountain Farmer.' I am so very pleased with that story." And she did; faithfully she read each page and found joy and comfort in the smile on her husband's face.

Always the busy one, she now sat beside Michael for hours during the day and often came at night to check on him. When she wasn't reading to him, she would play her organ and try to sing, and he would try to join in. With her back to him, he could not see the tears. Every morning and every afternoon, she would make him her best coffee, but in the end, the best he could do was to suck on the sugar cubes dipped in coffee.

One day Michael asked Emma if she would read the poem "Norge, Norge" for him. She found the poetry notebook, turned the pages until she found the requested verse and she began to read...

"Blue up out of the grayish green sea,
Islands scattered around like young birds,
Fjords in tongues inward where it quiets down.
River valleys followed from the Mountains,
Forested ridge and mountain,
Long after, as soon as it clears by lakes and fields.
The peace of the holy day with temple in.
Norway, Norway.
Cabins and houses and no castles
Joyful or hard.
You are ours, you are ours.
You are the land of the future.

Norway, Norway,
The shining land of the ski jumping run,
The harbor and fishing ground of the sea dog,
The road of the rafter,
The shepherds call of the mountain and glacial berm,
Fields, meadows, runes in the forest land, spread scars.

Cities that blossom, the rivers shoot out where it breaks,
White from sea where the swarms go.
Norway, Norway,
Cabins and houses and no castles
Joyful or hard.
You are ours, you are ours.
You are the land of the future."

"You know, Emma, when I lived in Norway, I often saw the Beistad Fjord where my father plied his jaekt boat. It was beautiful, but small; instead of tall mountains rising above it there were high hills, much like the Turtle Mountains.

"In the Navy, I went to bed one of the first nights. When I woke the next morning, I went up on deck, and what I saw took my breath away. For the first time ever I gazed up at majestic mountains, reaching into the clouds. When I looked down, I saw the mountains again in the mirror smooth waters. Neat farms were on the peninsulas, with buildings freshly painted red and white. Now and then there were tiny waterfalls released by the sun from the mountain top snowfields.

"The sight, my Emma, was so gorgeous that it brought tears to my eyes. 'Norway, Norway, blue up out of the grayish green sea'. As you read, I closed my eyes and I was Ole Fjelbonde, standing in the clearing beyond my farm, looking down from my high post at the calm waters below. It was a gorgeous view, a gorgeous view and I thought, I have just seen heaven."

"You still love Norway very much, don't you, Michael?"

"Ja."

"And you miss it very much?"

"Every day, Emma, every day."

"Would you like me to read another poem?

"Ja"

"Which one?"

"I never found out the name, but it starts, 'Look at Norway's flowering valley.'"

"Ja ja, here I have found it…

"Look at Norway's flowering valley,
Farewell you stuffy corner.
The wild pine tree forest

Stand now so comfortably cool.
Tra-la-la, yes so delightful it is in the north
Amongst mountain and mountainside and fjord.
On fresh green meadow
Flowers stand white, yellow and blue,
And, cheer up all large and small,
And ready make a delightful bride's bed.
Tra-la-la, yes so delightful it is in the north
Amongst mountain, mountainside and fjord.
If we happen to get a shower,
Some rain does the farmer's field good.
We never shun wetness,
It is against our nature.
Tra-la-la, yes, so delightful it is in the north
Amongst mountain, mountainside and fjord.
Listen to the proud waterfall of the mountain,
It breaks the silence and need of the winter.
Now it proceeds freely on its way,
And rumbles deeply in us.
Rumble, rumble, rumble, yes, so delightful it is in the north
Amongst mountain, mountainside and fjord."

Finishing her reading, Emma, too, was beginning to feel a sadness at never seeing her parents and her Michael's Norway. The poet had made it seem so beautiful. "Were you Ole again while I was reading, Michael?"

"No, I was Michael."

"Was your young bride, Aslong, by your side?"

"No."

"No? Were you alone?"

"No."

"Who was with you?"

"You, Emma, my young bride. You were there, with apple blossoms in your hair."

Emma had to leave the room in a rush, so he would not hear her sobbing. "Oh, Michael, I love you so much, and I am losing you. God give me the strength to go on." She dried her eyes and returned with some sugar lumps dunked in coffee.

The children around would visit often and, on occasion, the grandchildren would come. The house would bustle again during those visits, as his home had done years before, when his own children were little. Their giggles and laughter were a tonic for him. He loved his children so, and wished that, like Ole Fjeldbonde, he had done more for them.

When he could talk, he would reminisce with Emma about their life together. "I truly believe, Emma, that I was led by God to Whitebear. We were meant to meet and get married. And we had a good life there in Minnesota. I often wondered how it would be if we stayed. I know it was so very hard for you to leave your mother and father. Just like my mother, you have always been so strong and brave. I don't know what would have happened to me if I didn't have you." And the tears would fall.

"Are you afraid to die, Michael?" she asked one day.

His voice strong, he quoted his favorite preacher, Petter Dass, "'Death is not hard for those who have lived well.' No, my Emma, I have nothing to fear, only the regret that I must leave you."

As autumn turned to winter and the first flakes of snow began to fall, he said, "I'm going home to see Mama again, my Emma; what a reunion that will be! Then I will see my papa and my sister, Trine. We, and your dear parents, will wait for you to join us." Sitting on the bed, his head was resting in her lap; stroking his hair, she held him silently until he breathed his last breath and then for a long time after, willing him to return; but he was gone. Finally she called her friend, Dr. Smith, and asked him to come.

Michael's illness and death had a profound affect on Emma. Though she was only 68 years old, she felt like 100. His death left her totally numb. She had trouble going to sleep. She would wake often during the night to stare into the darkness. In spite of all the months she spent sleeping alone while Michael had his bed in the dining room, their bed now seemed so empty.

Grief became a long journey through tears, and then anger; why had God chosen Michael, he was such a man of faith; he was a loving husband and father; he was a hard worker, a good carpenter, a good farmer; he wrote beautiful things. Anger led to guilt, and she dreamed up things she should have done for him, but didn't. She remembered every angry word she'd ever spoken to him. Slowly, she slipped into depression. No matter how hard the family tried to help, she withdrew deeper and deeper into her sadness.

Overwhelmed by loneliness, all hope died within her. She stopped eating when there was no longer an appetite. She stopped caring about her appearance, with no one around to see her. Her own health began to decline rapidly. The only good moments were when, like Michael, she allowed herself to remember.

    She lasted only 10 months after Michael's death. Then, on July 24th, two weeks after her 69th birthday, she, too, passed away. No one was surprised. The family's double grief was tempered by the knowledge that their mother and father were together again, as they had always been. The doctor pronounced that she "suffered a stroke." Her children knew she died of a broken heart.

Postscript

In the process of sorting through her parents' personal belongings, one of Michael and Emma's daughters found the box with the instructions *DO NOT DESTROY*. Shaking it, nothing rattled, so she didn't bother to open it. Years later, she would dig it out of her front closet and give it to her youngest brother, Raymond, who had not been able to be there when his parents' things were meted out. She said, "I'm not sure exactly what's in here, Raymond. I've never opened it, but I thought you should have something to remember the folks by."

He was very pleased that she had remembered him. When he finally got it home and got around to opening it, he chuckled. What a prize! Inside were a bunch of blue notebooks filled with Norwegian writing.

As the last born, he knew much less Norwegian than his older brothers and sisters. He looked through some of the notebooks and recognized a word here and there, but not enough to get even the vaguest idea of what they were. Good judgment caused him to put them away; at that moment his curiosity level was not that high.

Many years later, while discussing family, he got them out and showed them to his oldest son, who volunteered to take them and try to find a translator. What he did not know was that, by then, most of the people who might be able to do it were gone. They were written in the "Old Norsk," not the language of Norway today. He kept them for years, and then, not wanting to throw them out without knowing what they were, he finally passed them on to his sister, who in time passed them on to another brother living in the State of Washington, about as far away from Norway as you can get in this country.

After the turn of the century, with the notebooks now at least 60 years old, that brother received a request for copies of the notebooks from another Glasoe cousin, who said he wanted to include the writings in a family history he was writing. It took time to get the notebooks and the translations copied, but in time they were bundled up and mailed off.

As the author of The Immigrant's Treasure, I was the eventual recipient of those notebooks. The story of their discovery and my acquisition began with my efforts to discover my ancestral roots and put the information I gathered into a written family history.

Genealogy has probably been around as long as there have been parents and grandparents. Genealogists have labored over the centuries to record family history. One of the more diligent searchers for family history turned out to be me. From the day I first received a regular paycheck, I became a lover, collector and restorer of antiques. My appetite for family history was soon as all-consuming as my appreciation for the antiquities I gathered over the years.

In time, I would come to read the words of Knute Hauge and be smitten with the need to know who it was that gave up this beauty to come to the plains of America, not the names—I would know them, but the person; what was my heritage and why? Hauge had written: *Ingen er barn av idag, du er barn av dei tusen ar. Djupt gjennom lag etter lag—rotende gar.*—You are a child of one thousand years not merely a child of today. Your roots extend through time, generation to generation.

I am indeed the product of all my Norwegian ancestors, but what did I know of their lives? Born too late to know them or establish any kind of knowledgeable relationship, I wondered who were they; where exactly did they come from in this land; why did they ever leave such beauty; what did they do?; who am I and what do I owe them? Finding the answers became my challenge.

I've already chronicled most of the details of my search for my family roots in Norway. I have poured that information into a family history that I gave to my children, my brothers and sister, their children and, finally, to each cousin who requested a copy. Its title came from the verse above, *Children Of One Thousand Years*.

The story of how the notebooks got from my cousin in Washington to me is brief, but interesting. To cousins, whose addresses I possessed, I sent copies of the initial draft of my family history for purposes of editing, correcting names, dates, places, or events, adding or deleting material.

One evening, after I had gone to bed, my wife received a phone call from my Uncle Raymond Glasoe's oldest son, who had received a draft history. I was awake enough to know it wasn't our children, and pondered who had called. I was still half awake when my wife came to bed, and I asked, "Who called?"

She replied, "I can't tell you."

"What was it about?"

"I can't tell you."

"Why?"

"If I tell you, you won't sleep all night."

In the morning, almost breathlessly, she told me the call was from a cousin who knew of the existence of a half dozen, blue, spiral notebooks, filled with Grampa Michael's writings.

"They are all in Norwegian, so nobody knows what they say. Three different cousins have tried to get them translated, but so far they haven't found anyone who can translate the old Norse."

"Who has them now?"

"Your cousin on the West Coast."

"Do you have his name and address?"

"Yes."

A letter went out that day with a request for copies of the notebooks. I stated my intent was to contact friends in Norway who might be able to translate them, copy and postal charges would be reimbursed.

There was no answer, but one day in late April, UPS drove into our yard and delivered a box to our door. When I opened it and saw it was filled with copies of handwritten, Norwegian script, carefully clipped together, and labeled Book 1, Book 2, all the way to 6. I knew exactly what it was— Grampa Michael's writings. The big surprise was that the box contained not only the writings in Norwegian, but their translation as well. I was absolutely overwhelmed; not only did they exist—I now had them in my possession. What a family treasure, our grandfather Michael's writings!

It was an expectant grandson who started to read Book 1. Curiously enough, I didn't recognize any of the names. I went up to the computer, clicked on the Family Tree icon and looked for them in the sea full of names that I had accumulated. Nothing, except for the name Ole, his father. So who were these people Grampa included in his writings, Ole and Aslong? Ole was married to Thale Margarete. My wife was more resourceful, leafing through all the packets until she found an Epilogue.

"Listen to this," she said. "This fantasy picture is written…" Instead of a continuation of my grandfather's biography, Grampa Michael had written a 60-page story about a heroic young Norwegian named Ole Fjeldbonde. Ole, the mountain farmer and his bride, Aslong. Unbelievable!

Searching through the rest of the material, more surprises were found. There was a beautiful narrative description of Norway and, finally, a notebook filled with poetry, which I first thought was a collection of my grandfather's original works. I was amazed at his poetic skill. However, after some searching it turned out to be some of his favorite poems. Still, all I could do was shake my head; my grandfather was not only a gifted farmer and carpenter, but also a writer.

I couldn't get the handwritten pages into manuscript form fast enough. Being a one-finger typist, however, it took me a "week of days." As I worked, I thought about what I should do with these original works. I decided I would add them at the end of my family history narrative, which was near completion.

Later, I hit on the idea of writing *The Immigrant's Treasure* and submitting it for publication; that way Michael's writings could be read and remembered not only by our family, but also by descendants of other Norwegian-Americans who share the common experience of pioneer ancestors. It was with this purpose in mind that I wrote this book.

In this world, I believe there are treasures more precious than gold or diamonds. There is "Family," past and present, and now—the writings of my grandfather, Michael. M. Bernhard Glasoe.

Epilogue

The following pages contain the writings of my grandfather. I treat them as a separate work, under his name. I have taken the liberty of formatting it as I imagine he would have, if he had the luxury of a word processor. It is what he might have sent to a publisher, had one been readily available.

I have not attempted to edit his work for grammar or spelling. I did add a few punctuation marks and developed paragraphs, as there were none in his work. Grampa Michael, like all good frugal Norwegians, used every inch of the notebook to put down his thoughts, top to bottom, margin to margin.

I have taken the privilege of giving a title to Michael's description of Norway.

Bracketed words or phrases are the work of the translator.

These are the actual writings of Michael M. Bernhard Glasoe, my grandfather.

THE WRITINGS OF MICHAEL M. BERNHARD GLASOE [1865 – 1940]

A Narrative Description of Norway
and
A Work of Fiction

Norway! My Norway!

By Michael M. Bernhard Glasoe

"Norway! Norway! Cabins and houses but no castles," so says a Norwegian poet. And it is indeed true. There are not many large castles in old mother Norway, but nevertheless, she offers so much natural beauty that not many other countries can show.

First we will mention all these narrow fjords, which extend into the country from the sea. On both sides of the fjord there lay well maintained farms, mirroring themselves in the calm sea. And up above them lies the green pine tree meadow, to make the beauty even more beautiful.

Look at the pine tree, raised so proud and beautiful on the mountain's highest peaks, where its green crown bravely stands and waves in the stormy wind.

And a little farther in, the birch tree forest grows luxuriantly down to the riverbank, where it mirrors its leaf rich crown in the crystal clear water. In some places alder, rowan and bird cherry grow; the rowan with its red berries and the bird cherry with a blossom of white flowers in the spring.

And in the forest there grow a lot of wild berries, such as lingonberries, blueberries and raspberries and not to forget the wonderful cloudberries, which grow in the mountain marshes, which are collected in the fall. They are remarkable, as taste is concerned.

And then there is an abundance of fresh water or mountain lakes where you can fish for the wonderful mountain trout—the best, well tasting fish in the whole world, much better than the fat salmon.

Then we cast our eyes out across the fjord again. There we see boats of all types: sailboats, motorboats and rowing boats. Some are out to fish, some are sailing for pleasure, but all are out to enjoy the wonderful fresh nature.

So we take a trip along the coastline, sailing northward from Trondheim [a city midway up the Norwegian coast] to Narosland. The ones who have not traveled there cannot imagine how many naturally beautiful places there are along the coastline of Helgeland. There are a multitude of islands and islets on the outside of the ship lane, large and small in between each other, and on the mainland, green meadows and nice homesteads that are a joy for the eye to watch.

I have, myself, traveled there four times, two times with steamroller and two times with a sailing ship. But it is now fifty years ago, so I have forgotten the name of all the places. I remember the names of two islands, that is Hestmand Oi [Horseman Island] and Vego. There is a mountain on Hestmand Oi that looks like a man on horseback, after which it is named. Vego is a very large island with many inhabitants, and a market, and the steamroller ties to shore, too, there. And then I remember a good harbor, namely Bronosund. Brono lies on the outside of sound and Alstadhaug on the mainland, where the priest Peder Dass lived and worked a long time ago [16th-17th century].

Peder Dass was a poet and large soul maker. I have read one of his poem collections, namely, the Nordland's Trompet [Northland Trumpet]. I remember only one stanza of that. He was, in fact, one time out in his parish and had to stop over for the night at a place. And when it was close to bedtime, and the wife of the house was to make the bed for him, so he says in his poem, "When it was into the evening, in came mother Guri with the hide, the hair of the hide was plentiful and long foreign rides, hiding therein. They rode not on saddles, those men, my back had to pay for that." It had to be something in the hide that hurt his back.

Then we go farther north. There are many fjords that go into the country up north as well, but I cannot remember the names of them all. There is a fjord that goes into the town of Namsun, and another one to Bodo, then we have Velfjorden, Saltenfjorden, Eidsfjorden and many, many more. But there are more mountain masses along these fjords than there are farther south.

If my memory serves me right, then Rorvar is the last docking plate along the ship lane, then it goes to sea. There are many kilometers [1 kilometer = .6 US miles] of open sea before you come to Svolvar in Lofoten. Svolvar is the eastern fishing area in Lofoten.

Then go westward along the Lofoten Islands. First we have the fishing village, Henningvar, then Brandsholmen and Mort Sundet, Balstad, Nusfjord and Sund. Post is the last and outermost fishing village. There are two villages between Post and Sund, which I cannot remember the names of.

Between the islands of Post and Mosken there runs a sea stream that is called "Norstrommen" [Norwegian stream]. Yes, there is lots of noise, it roars and screams from it a long ways when it goes out and in during ebb and flow. The frothing wave tops and the foam goes high in the air. And painful it is for the ship or boat that come there then. It is sure to go under!

There is a lot of fishing of the nice codfish in Lofoten throughout the winter months, January, February, March. We get it here served as lutefisk, and it is very well tasting in and of itself. But take a meal of fresh codfish, cooked as soon as it is taken out of the saltwater and with the accompanying fat, it is truly a magnificent meal. And it gives you strength in your legs.

Yes, now that we are so far north, we will continue and go to "Nordkapp" [North Cape] and admire the midnight sun. It is also a marvelous panorama for the eye to see the sweet sun ball that can be seen all night for a while in the summer.

Can you forget old Norway?
I cannot forget it,
These proud cliff castles are
And will remain my birth land.
—Kan Du Glemme Gamle Norge

Yes, in not so long a while, you can drive by automobile all the way from Oslo to the northern most tip of Norway. And, if you want to, you can take some of the spurs up through some of the fruitful valleys, of which there are so many, with a long running river in the center and well maintained farms on both sides of the river all the way from the sea to the high mountains, with fields and undulating meadows of sweet clover and timothy. And one can see milking cattle, sheep and goats grazing up through the valley. In a few of the rivers there are great waterfalls, but most of them are now controlled by dams. Large power stations have been built by them, which bring electrical power to city and village.

Yes, there is hardly one farm now without electrical lighting and motor power to run all kinds of machinery, namely grinding stone, milk separator, circle saw and harvesting machine.

Yes, there are truly remarkable advances that have occurred during the last fifty years in motherland Norway, in all areas. It is proof that the people love their land.

And will forward its progress
From the border out to the drifting net.

There is enough sun and there is enough cropland, if only they! If only they! have enough love. Yes, it would be too extensive for me to describe and give a complete account of all these valleys.

Only a little from the rich "Gudbransdal Valley," with its old historic memories.

I remember from history about the times of King Olaf, The Sacred, when he introduced Christianity in Norway. He had come as far as to Gudbransdalen, where the giant "Dale Gudbrand," lived at "Hundtorp" with his false god, and was not willing to the Christian faith. He could talk about how much his god could devour in feed every day, and how much help it could give him.

King Olaf told his men, "Early tomorrow, at sunrise, when I get Gudbrand to turn his eyes against the sun, then beat his false god [statue] to pieces." As said, as done. At the same time that the sun rose over the horizon, the king said, "Look, Gudbrand, there comes our god with shimmer and warmth and will destroy your god." At the same time, the king's men then beat the statue of the false god to pieces. And there crawled a lot of mice and rats out of it. It was they who had eaten the feed that had been brought. Gudbrand became angry at first, but then he surrendered, and promised the king his faithfulness. It is maybe after him the valley is named.

And we have read about that time when the Scottish attacked the valley to plunder and pillage. What a reception the farmers gave them. One famous legend tells how the men of Sinclair were chased out of the valley by the farmers who, without many weapons, used rolling rocks and logs down the mountain sides as ammunition. This episode is called the "Sinclartoget"— Train of Sinclair. Not a single soul came home that could tell how dangerous it is to visit the ones who live in the Norwegian mountains.

I think now we will have to put some provisions in our backpack and head up to the high regions, namely the high mountain plateau. There are now automobile roads built quite high up, and there are nice hotels where you can get refreshments and lodging for the night, if you wish.

But this last section of the trip must be done on foot in order to come to the highest peak. But you will be rewarded for your hard work when you have reached up there. There your eye meets the wonderful and naturally beautiful panorama. That, you cannot forget for a long time afterward.

I cannot, with my pen, paint the grand view you will get to see. It is something that will lift your soul up to Him who has created the beautiful things in nature. You will be tempted to sing with the poet:

I live in the high mountain,
Where a Finn shot a reindeer with his rifle, on skis,
Where a natural spring trickled,
And where the grouse were playing in the bushes.
The top of the mountain that carries the pine trees,

Cheerful souls, freedom home.
The busy sounds of the valley never reach my sky high residence.

Then we leave the high mountain plateau and walk down to the valley. There we then meet something gorgeous, and we will again exclaim and sing:

I live in the valley
Between scenting fields,
and where the river runs clear through leaf rich trees...

There we hear the lark singing, and the cuckoo crows its "koo-koo" on the ridge.

Yes, it doesn't matter where we walk, either in the mountain or the valley, or along the fjord. It is something so uplifting and beautiful to watch everywhere we travel in the Norwegian nature, something that makes one fresh and healthy, both in soul and body.

There are, of course, many who look at Norway as a small, poor country. It is not large, but it is not poor. No, there is no one there who suffers now today. Everyone is taken good care of. The old, who have no property, get a yearly pension, and the sick get help if they need it, and the suffering also get help. And there is no unemployment among the people. No, they are much better off there than in America.

There are many branches of the economy such as grain farming, cattle breeding, dairy farming, forest. Yes, there are many thousands of kroner worth of wood products, which are harvested every year from the forests during the winter. And there is mining, and fishing, which brings large sums of money to the people every year. There are canneries of fish and herring, and many large factories of all kinds, which make what is necessary for industry.

And the country has a large shipping fleet. Some are in daily runs along the coastline north and south. And some go abroad as to England, America, France and Spain; yes, across the whole world.

"Norwegian Nature"

So, we sing on our journey
Through the wonderful nature of Norway.
Let the song peacefully extend

As colors rocking forward,
On the fjords, against beaches, and forests, and mountains,
And mix with the marvel of nature.

The warmth in the need of the people.
The strong, deep in its song,
Here it turns the eye toward you,
And gave for the meeting it got,
A look of all its love.

Here, the history first awoke.
Here, Halvdan's heart dreamt the biggest
In the look he there saw rise.
He sensed the whole kingdom.
And Norway stood up and gave him message,
And the waters shared farther out.

Here the song must bring forth,
The whole picture of our home.
Let the storm into the quietness,
Let the power into the soft.
When the country gathers, each,
Will see that our history it is.

The first we start with
Are hundreds of harbors in April.
There we meet soft thoughts,
When the fleet shall anchor,
And sixty thousand men on board
Carry Norway in their prayers around the world.
Look at the coasts of bare rocks,
With seagulls, whale and fishing villages,
And ships in under the islands.
But boats out across the sea,
And nets in the fjords and seine,
And white roe across the bottom.

Look at the Lofoten's wild struggle,

Where the cliffs stand in the middle of the sea,
And the fog drifts around the peaks,
While the sea swells around the base
And all is dark myth and fear.
But, in the middle of the struggle, a boat fishing.

There you see the icebreaker,
In snow and half-light, he pulls himself
From the stream it soon masters.
And the boat hauls toward the ice,
And shot after shot, and seal after seal,
An marrow and courage, in body and soul.

Then we are to recede for the night,
Where the whole village is in the mountain,
On the mountain farm with the milking chores.
In the mountain castle, under the cliffs,
And where calling song awaiting,
Is answered by a great wilderness.

But hastily we must go,
If we are to be anywhere,
In the mountains where the rocks are mined,
In the mountains, where the reindeer is hunted.
And to here, the river, white with froth, leads,
And the rafter stand on his wood boards.

And if we once again stop here,
We will grow attached to the wide villages,
Whose farmers so gently bear
The faith, which is our honor,
And to which great men of the fatherland have,
Which glitter our morning red were.

So, we sing on our wonderful journey,
Through the wonderful nature of Norway.
Our toil shines before our eyes.
Our past from the ridges reminds us.

And future shall come from the country,
Assure as the God it relies upon.

Yes, we love this land that towers
Where the ocean foams;
Rugged, storm-swept, it embowers
Many thousand homes.
Love it, love it, of you thinking,
Father, Mother dear,
And that night of saga sinking
Dreamful to us here.

This land Harald saved
With his giant rule.

The translator wrote: *Michael added this note: Harald Hardrada, Harald the Hard Ruler, the first Viking to rule all of Norway as one country.*

Ole Fjeldbonde

(Ole, The Mountain Farmer)

A Work of Fiction by Michael M. Bernhard Glasoe

Chapter One

Ole was born at "husmandsplads" [cotter's farm] to poor parents. They had a cotter's farm under the large farm down in the valley. Ole's father had to work for the farmer almost every day, all year, and the work at home on the little piece of land he had, he had to, for the most part, do at night. The family grew and the food stretched thin many a time. Ole was the oldest and had to go out to herd for strangers when he was eight years old and had it difficult many times, but he was a strong and robust boy, and he did not give up, even if he got a little punishment some times.

The years went by and he became old enough to become confirmed by the priest. He had his book with him and did his homework while he herded the creatures.

In the fall he became confirmed and became number one of the boys, something unheard of for a son of a cotter. But he was a good learner and was a very astute boy, big and robust was he, too, for a boy his age. None of his friends could frighten him if it came to a fight between them.

After he was confirmed, he served at a farm there in the town, and he served for the same man until he was twenty years of age. The farmer liked the boy very well and wanted to keep him longer, but Ole had gotten ideas in his head and thought it was best for him to end his service. Ole and a daughter of another cotter had fallen in love and he started thinking about getting a home for himself and Aslong—that was her name. But after having decided that he did not want to be a cotter, not for anything in the world, he had seen enough of his father's miserable life. No! He would much rather clear himself a piece of land up on the mountainside and become his own master.

He had wondered about a lot in the forest and the mountains, and there was a place out in the government common land that he had seen that would be a fine homestead if it were cleared. There was a large fishing lake nearby, and there was a river running out of this lake and just past this area that he had picked out for his homestead.

But it was far from town, out in the wild mountain. He was wondering if Aslong would like living there in such lonely surroundings in the wild mountain. But he continued in his thoughts; *if she loves me she will follow where I go. I would at least speak with her about this. I like this area very much and I think I will write the Norwegian Government to find out if I would be allowed to clear a homestead out there. I will first talk to Aslong, however, about this and hear her opinion.*

He then presented this plan to her and she answered him, "Ole, wherever you build and live, I will come with you and be with you and help you all I am able to, both in good days and bad days, in difficult times and in good times."

"It was wonderful for you to think that way, Aslong. It shows me that you have confidence in me and love me. A thousand thanks for your promise. It will help me, over time, to become an independent man with the help of God."

So he wrote to the Norwegian Government and presented his plan to them, asking if they could grant him the right to clear and build himself a home out in the mountains. After some time passed, he received the answer that he could clear as much land as he wanted up there, and all the timber for the house he could freely cut. So, now that this task is completed, he thought it was time to start doing something. I will start immediately this summer.

He had a few "kroner" [Crown - $1 = 7 kroner] of his salary when he served with Tobias Oppegaard, and clothes he did not need. In the time ahead, he thought, *I will buy myself some tools that I need for house building and some for farm work, and then I need something for the kitchen, such as a coffee pot and frying pan*; but he thought, *how can I carry all of it on the back so far?*

But Ole was not the type of man to give up halfway; had he started something, it was sure to be completed. The heavy load did not frighten him. *But I will first go to my Aslong, and tell her about how things have turned out for us. The fact that the State has said I could clear and build, and free timber for the houses. So now we have the choice to begin, if we want.*

"I have almost made up my mind to start immediately this summer, but as you know, it will be a long time before I have a little and built the house that we shall call our home. Will it be too long for you, Aslong, to wait, maybe one to three years before I can take you as my bride?"

"No, Ole, you know I will wait if it were to be six years. Go and start what you have made up your mind to do. I will wait and pray to God that He will bless your work, so you will succeed. And when you arrive there in the wilderness, God is the only one you can talk to. Pray to him, Ole, and He will give you strength and inspiration and bless your toil so it succeeds. Go, in God's name. The Lord protect you. Do not, by all means, worry about me."

Ole left her with the best hopes, went ahead and got himself what he needed, and had to carry all of it on the back. It was a heavy load, but he did not think of it. He was strong as a bear, and in good spirits all the time, and that helps to overcome all that seems impossible for us.

In the afternoon he came to his designated spot. The first thing he did was build some stones for an oven for the coffee pot he would use to make coffee for his meal. The coffee made, he ate, rested a bit, then went around to find a good place to build something to live in overnight and to use as storage for his things. As he went and looked around, he came to a little "aspeland" [aspen grove]. He made a decision: *I will cut down a few of these aspen, it will be quickly done. Then I will raise them up like a "Finne gamme" [Finish turf hut]. One to four kind of large, with a fork in the top and the rest smaller. I will build it so big I can use it for living quarters until I get my house built.*

He started to cut and raise these aspen trees, the forked ones first, and then the rest around. He dug the bottom ends into the ground a little. Then he laid "torre" [sod] all around and up to the top. He did not get more than halfway to the top that day, but he decided to move his things inside and sleep there over night.

He made a little opening to come in and out through, but he had nothing to do a door out of. But he cut a few pine branches to close the opening with. Then he went to rest, the first day had come to its end. So the ground was to be his and Aslong's future home, where they would live as free people and not as bondsmen/slaves for others, and bring up their children to become good citizens of their country.

When Ole rested, he carried in some grass or hay for a bed. Then he closed the door opening and after that he kneeled down and prayed to everyone's Father in heaven to be with him and his, and protect them against bad things and bad luck. Thereafter, he went to bed and slept well until the next morning.

He got up and said his morning prayer and made himself some breakfast. Finished with that, he began his work. He laid in more sod, all the way to the top; then he put pine branches from below and birch/willow tied it all together. He did it for if there would become strong and hard rain, he did not want the sod to be washed down. He dug a small ditch all around his hut, as close as the door opening. He did it so as to keep the water away from his floor. He made a tour around to see his domain because he would first choose a suitable place for his house, for that was the most he wanted to do, to clear a parcel for the house.

He walked around for a long time and looked at the surroundings. He had already decided where the building place would be. It was a small hill to the south, not far from where he walked, and the thought came to mind that he would go up there and look around. While he walked back and forth up there, he noticed that a few water bubbles came up out of the ground. He went closer and found out there was a spring that day lighted there.

He seemed to have made a great discovery. He tasted the water and it was outstandingly good. He said to himself, "The first thing I will do is to dig around this spring and lay stones around it, and make a lid over it. Then I can have good drinking water, much better than the water in the river. And who knows, with time I can lead the water down to the houses. There is plenty of fall relief for that."

The next day after breakfast he completed the well. He started clearing a site for the house and digging a cellar. Done with that, he carried stone for the foundation wall. It was strenuous work, but he wanted to have a foundation wall under his house, no matter how long it took him.

After many days of hard work, the wall was done. Then he took his axe and started to cut timber to build with. It was good pine wood around his building spot, so he didn't take long to carry the timber. But to carry it, he had to, there was no other way around it.

He had laid out his house eight "alen" [an archaic measuring unit = two feet] one way and twelve "alen" the other way, only one room and one tier high. But, nevertheless, it was many timbers to carry on the shoulder, but courage and strength overcame anything. Neither did he forget to pray to his God for patience and strength to complete what he had set out to do.

When he had built several days, he started to carry the timber forward. So, after some time passed, he began to cut it up for the walls. He laid the timbers up around and laid moss between them. He thought about casting it both on the outside and inside with clay.

He worked with the timber a while. Then he cut more timber and carried it forward. Like this he continued several weeks, until he had the walls up. But then his mind was at ease. Now it was time to put the roof on. He wanted to use birch bark and sod for that, but he needed wood planks under first.

"Where am I going to get wood planks from? I need planks for the floor as well, and for a door and the windows. I think the only thing I can do is make a trip to town and get myself a hand-saw, but can I handle it myself? No, I don't think so. I think I need to get someone to help me. Maybe my father could ask for days off from the work for the farmer to help me. I will go to town tomorrow and try my luck."

The next morning during sunrise, he left and at dinnertime he was at home with his parents. But as customary, his father was at work down on the farm. He then went down there and met his father and explained to him what he had in mind.

"Yes," said his father, "I will come with you to help you, if the farmer will let me free. I will go right now and talk to him." And so he did.

The farmer answered him, "It is some nonsense your son is up to up there, but I will nevertheless let you free for four days, on the condition you make up the lost time."

"Yes," his father promised, and with that everything was in order.

They were then able to borrow a saw from one of the farmers, and Ole bought some supplies. They needed something to eat if the work be accomplished with the hands. He also got himself some glass for the windows on the house. There were actually two of them. He would try to make the frames himself, as soon as he was able to cut enough wood for the floor and roof and miscellaneous other things.

The next morning they headed up the mountain trail, up to Ole's future home. They came there at suppertime. They made coffee and ate their dinner, rested a bit and they walked around, looking at the surroundings before they started their work.

After some time passed, his father uttered, "It is a magnificent and beautiful homestead you have found, my son. If only it had not been so far up in the mountains."

Ole answered, "This was of no importance, but to live as a free man was more important. If you live some years into the future still, Father, you will soon be able to see great changes around here, if God will stand by me and give me strength to complete what I have set out to do. Without His support, I can accomplish nothing. I must live with his blessing if it is to succeed for me."

"Yes, that is correct, my son. Do not forget your great benefactor, but always trust His omnipotence and mercy, which last forever for the people who believe and pray to Him."

They each then took their axe and the saw and went out into the timber forest. They chose a place where there was good timber and there they built a scaffolding to cut on, and thought it would be easier to carry the planks forward after they were cut than to carry the timber. They finished the scaffolding that afternoon and also cut some timber. They cut the timber exactly to the length required for the roof, so it would be just to nail them onto the roof beams without cutting any further.

Yes, so was their first working day over. They went home to the cabin to make their supper. Ole had brought with him a fishing net, which he had put at the mouth of the river. He said to his father, "I will go and see if there are any fish in the net, while you make the fire and put some pots on so they can begin to cook."

Ole found quite a few nice trout in the yarn and returned home with them. He and his father helped each other to filet the fish while the potatoes boiled. After they had enjoyed their good evening meal of fried mountain trout, potatoes, "flatbrod" [flatbread] and good black coffee, they lay and conversed about various things.

Ole then shouted, "Do you see, Father! Here we can have fresh mountain trout every day if we want, while down in the village, they have to eat the salted, pickled herring." Then he added, "I think all I can accomplish this summer is to finish the house, but if I can finish it this fall, I will be satisfied. I have thought about building a chimney or a fireplace in one end of the house. Should I build it before I put the roof on, do you think?"

"Yes, I think it will be best for you to build it before you put the roof on."

Ole continued, "There is a place where I have seen very good rock, but it's quite far away. It will be too hard to carry it forward. I wonder now when I have cut the wood if I could not make some kind of wheelbarrow out of boards and roll the rock on. You know we have to cut a few boards for the floor. I could lay them out as a runway to roll on. Then I could bring quite big loads at a time."

"Yes, I think," said his father, "that will be the only way to go about it, to make yourself a wheel barrow."

"I have seen pretty good clay somewhere. I will use that and put the rocks in so that the chimney will be nice and tight."

It was now so far into the evening that they wanted to rest after a completed day of work. They prayed their evening prayer, and if God would give them a good night's sleep so they could continue again the next day.

They woke up the next morning early, stood up fresh and healthy. They prayed their morning prayer and thanked God for His protection through the darkness of the night. They made themselves breakfast and ate it, went then out into the forest and started to cut boards. They cut and sawed timber that whole day and the next day.

And at dinnertime the third day, his father had to return to the village that afternoon. Ole thought that he had more than enough boards for the house. After having eaten dinner, the father got ready to go home. He took with him the big saw to bring it home to its owner.

Ole thanked his father and said, "You did me an invaluable big service, Father, to help me. I hope I sometime can pay you for that. May God be with you, and say hello to my mother and siblings from me. If you see Aslong, say hello to her, too. Tell her how you liked it up here. Live well, Father! Take good care of yourself."

After his father had left, he started making arms for his wheelbarrow. The wheel he thought about making out of two plank thicknesses, like a "korbe enle" [?] wheel, with wood axel through. He had no iron to reinforce with, it all had to be made out of wood. After a day of hard work it was done, to be put to use.

He carried forward a few boards and made a runway up to his rock quarry. After this was done, he began to roll rock forward, but his wheelbarrow made all kinds of screaming, ghostly noises. Wood was rubbing against wood and made this ghostly music. *I will have to find something and lubricate it.* With this thought, this he did. It helped for a while, but then the same roar started again. "Yes, it can scream all it wants to," he said to himself, "it doesn't disturb anybody but myself anyway."

When he had rolled rock for two days, he started to roll forward some clay. When he thought he had enough of this, he made himself a kind of churn to work the clay, so it became sticky and good to work with.

Then the masonry work started. He laid rock after rock, with clay between. He had never tried work like this before, but he was encouraged and he thought he could handle it. If it wasn't going to be first class, it was for himself he was doing the work. After many days of hard work, he managed to complete the chimney. Said he to himself, I am just as happy as when I started it, only a little richer in experience. Yes, life is a school and you never become fully learned.

From his mother he had learned that, as a prerequisite for advancement in life, come prayer, work and diligence. Prayer without work does no good, work without prayer leads to no real blessing. Neither prayer nor work will do much good if no diligence is shown in both prayer and work. These were his mother's teachings and he tried to live up to them.

Done with the chimney, he began to put a roof on the house, nailed boards onto the roof beams. Only after this came birch bark and sod onto the top of that. The roof completed, he started making frames for the windows and molding for the door and windows.

It took him quite some time, but he got it nevertheless put together quite well, and even though he was no carpenter, got it put in. So now the task was to lay the floor and seal the wall with clay.

Now the fall started to come upon him and he worked to be done as soon as possible. If the earth was not frozen before he was done with the house, he would work up a piece of land to plant potatoes in the spring. He would find out if they would grow so far into the mountain.

After two weeks passed, he was done with his house and the ground was not frozen yet, so he decided to dig up a piece of farmland before he went home. He also made a chest for his tools and put it down in the cellar so no one would find it if someone would happen to come there during the winter.

There were a few boards and planks left over. These he carried inside the house and laid them against a wall. He picked up his fishing net, dried it, and put that in the chest.

Despite all the chores he had to do in his cabin, he worked relentlessly for a whole week on his potato field. Then he closed the door to the house, took his backpack on his back and said goodbye to his new home.

He went home to rest a while until he was to start logging. He would work in the timber forest all winter long and earn something so he could continue next spring again and build on his mountain house.

He had still a few crowns left that he would use to buy food for his parents. He went down to one of the farmers and there he bought a sack of flour and a medium pig, which he took home to give to his parents. The pig they were to slaughter for Christmas, he said. Also he went on a trip to town and bought some things he needed for himself, like leather for a harness because he would get a shoemaker to sew it during the winter; he had decided to get a horse in the spring and take it with him to the mountain to haul timber to his "uthuses" [outhouses/sheds].

He talked then with his father if he would make sure to get a packsaddle made and two panniers, so they would be ready for him when he came back from the timber forest in the spring.

"Yes." His father promised to make sure of this. "It might be that I could make it, too, in the evenings during the winter. In any case, they will be here when you come home."

Then he went on a trip over to speak with Aslong. He had bought something for her as a Christmas present. It was still a month until Christmas, but he wanted to give it to her before he left, and at the same time say goodbye before he took off. He met her at home and remained for a while. They spoke together about their future and made plans.

"Aslong," he said, "if everything goes as well as it has so far, and God gives me health and strength to work, I believe we can move into our new house in a year and a half from now."

"Ole, you know I'll wait until the time is convenient for you. God be with us until that day."

He gave her a beautiful silver brooch as a Christmas present. She thanked him and gave him a kiss. Now he had to go home and get ready for the trip the next day. Then they said goodbye to each other and she said, "You know I will be faithful to you when God separates us. Good luck on your journey and may the Lord protect you until we meet again."

"Thank you, Aslong. I will keep your words in my heart." He wished her a merry Christmas and went home.

He and his parents then sat and talked into the night about many things. He gave his mother five crowns and told her to buy something good for the Christmas holidays. He wanted them to have a very good Christmas. She gave him two pairs of wool socks and gloves that she had knitted herself for him.

He took his mother by her neck and gave her a kiss and said, "I can never thank you enough for all the things you have done for me since I came into this world. May the Lord bless and protect you in your old days." They were both emotional and tearful.

He also embraced his father and thanked him for being so kind to him. "I have to thank you, my parents, for what I am, and I will not forget you as long as my blood passes through my veins."

He packed his backpack so it was ready for the morning after, because he wanted to take off early the next morning. He woke up early and his mother had breakfast ready for him. He said his morning prayer and table prayer, ate, and was then ready to leave. He took farewell of his parents and wished them a merry Christmas. Then he wandered off.

It was far to the forest camp, so he rushed to come there before it was dark, because darkness sets in early that time of year. He walked without stopping until dinnertime. Then he sat down on a rock and brought out the lunchbox his mother had sent with him, ate it and rested a bit. Then it was to continue again.

Around four o'clock, he had arrived at the camp. It was a large logging company that had bought a stretch of forest that was to be cut that winter, and they had built a camp out in the forest for its workers. Ole worked all winter long and had no accident.

Chapter Two

The last days of April that he was home greeted his parents just as strong and healthy as when he left them.

He rested himself a few days and then started looking around for a horse, having earned quite good money throughout the winter, and having many crowns in his pocket.

First he went to see Aslong. She was happy to see him healthy and strong and back home. She shouted, "You look better now than when you left last fall. God has really been good to you."

He told her he was going to take a stroll around the village, "to get a horse that I can bring into the mountain this summer. And likewise a dog, so it doesn't become so lonely as it was last summer, when I have these animals around me. I will come to see you again before I go up there." So he left her and headed down to the farms.

He soon found out that there was a farmer who had a horse for sale. He then went over to him to find out if they could agree on a price and do business. Ole said, "Hello," and explained his errand.

The farmer answered, "Yes, I have thought about selling one because I have more than I really need." They then went to the stable to look at it. They were all well-fed and fine animals.

Ole said, "Which one do you want to sell?"

"Oh, it doesn't make much difference, they are all good horses," the farmer replied. Ole thought he wanted one that he could trust in all respects, and not too old. "This one here is six years old and a good horse in all respects," the farmer said.

"How much do you ask for it then?" Ole asked. The farmer named a sum. *Isn't that too high a price*, thought Ole?

"Can you pay all cash?" the farmer asked. Ole confirmed that. "Yes, then I will reduce the price to twenty-five crowns," he said.

Ole had seen that there were two beautiful dogs at the farm and said afterward, "If you give me one of these dogs as a part of the bargain, I will buy," Ole said.

The farmer stood and thought about it for a while, then he said, "All right, let it be so." Ole got the money out and paid. The farmer then said, "You are getting a trustworthy horse, and a good dog as well. I wish you good luck with them."

Ole took the horse and the dog and led them home to his parents' place. He thought he had gotten a really good bargain by getting both animals in the same deal. Now he went down to the shoemaker to pick up his harness, paid for the work and went home.

The next day he put the harness on his horse and took off to one of the farms to borrow a wagon to go to town with. There were miscellaneous things he wanted to buy. He borrowed a wagon and then went to town.

He bought himself a few cups and plates, as well as a kerosene lamp and a jar of kerosene, coffee, flour and potatoes, cured ham and cured meat, sausages, butter and cheese, salt and some spices and a can of syrup. He wanted syrup water for his evening porridge instead of milk. *I need food,* he thought, *if I shall be able to work. I can't have fish every meal, but I will use it instead of herring.*

Then he bought nails of all lengths, a lock for the house door and a rope to tie the horse with. He could not let it loose out there. Likewise, two wool blankets for his bed and some cloth to make a mattress with. *I will get Mother to sew it together for me,* he thought. *I'll cut some hay to put in it so I can lie as well as a king, because I will make myself a bed when I come up there. I don't want to lie on a bare ground, as I did last summer.* He also bought a scythe and sharpener, a rifle and a few bullets for it, a plane and a saw.

While he wandered around in town he realized that it wasn't long until "Syttende Mai" [seventeenth of May, Norwegian Independence Day]. *I will probably not have the opportunity to celebrate Syttende Mai this year because I have to leave for my mountain home right away. But, I know what I will do so I can honor Motherland Norway on her Independence Day together with everyone else anyway. I will buy myself a big flag and take it with me up there. I will raise a tall flagpole and then raise the flag to the top on that day, so I will also help honor her even then. I will do it alone. I think my capital will be enough to do that.* He then went to buy a flag, a little block pulley and flag rope. He was now done with his errands and started to load his wagon to go home.

He came home in the evening, unloaded his load and put it in the "stabburet" [traditional shed] set above ground on columns to store food, then brought the wagon home to its owner. The next day he started packing his panniers while his mother sewed together his mattress.

She would also bake some flatbread for him. He had bought quite a lot of rye crackers in town, but he also wanted to have flatbread. He had bought a whole sack of flour, but let his mother have most of it. He took only enough to make porridge because he got a heavy enough burden for the horse as it was. He would also carry some on his back.

Done with the packing, he went over to Aslong to take farewell with her. They sat a long time and talked. He told her about what he would do this summer. First and foremost, he would make some things for the house, like a table and a couple of benches, a corner cupboard and a kind of bed. And he would have to build a plow for the horse to pull and many other things.

He would also build a barn for the goats that he thought about getting when she came home to him. "You see," he said, "I have to make it so that you have something to tend to, so you don't become lonely. The goats are what will be our main income. It is them that must give us what we need to support ourselves."

"No, I will not be lonely," she answered, "I will probably find something to do so that time passes. By the way, you probably will be home most of the time, too."

"Yes, I will be at home to work on the houses and the field, except the trips I have to make to town with the goat cheese," he said. "Maybe one trip every month. But you will always have the dog for companionship and I will not be gone more than a day at a time."

It was now so late that he bid her farewell and left. She wished him all good luck with his tasks and that the Lord would be with him and protect him against evil. "Thank you, Aslong! Live well until we meet again."

The next morning he put the harness on his horse, took the dog and the horse by their reigns, bid heartily farewell with his parents, and then went away.

He finally came to his house and home a little after dinnertime. All seemed to be in the same condition as when he left it. He took the harness off the horse and carried it inside, tied the dog, and then took the horse down to the creek and let it drink, tethering it down by the marsh. Then he went ahead and cut some dry wood, carried it inside and made a fire in the fireplace and put on the coffee pot. He had to have something to eat before he did anything.

After having eaten his dinner and given the dog something to eat, he started making a table. Done with that, he made two small benches and afterward a corner cupboard in one corner of the house. Now, he thought, he had enough furniture for a while. *I can now sit next to a table in my own house, and eat my meal in God's name.* He kneeled down and prayed to God and thanked Him for what he had done for him, so far, and asked Him to be with him still.

This day was then so far into the night that there was no time to do much more. Therefore, he took his fishing net, went down to the creek and put it out. Now it shall taste good to get a meal of fresh mountain trout again. On the way home he walked past the horse and moved it, went home and made his supper.

After having eaten his meal, it was dark. He remembered his lamp, unpacked it and filled it with kerosene, lit it and put it on the table. He then found his little Bible, sat down with it at the table, and read in it for a while, then said his evening prayer.

Next morning he awoke at sunrise, stood up and read his morning prayer first and thereafter made his breakfast, ate it and went down then to the horse to move it and to give it water. Done with that, he went to see if there were any fish in the net. Yes, he got a good catch. *It will be more than enough food for a meal for me and the dog,* he thought. Then he went home again, and started cleaning the fish so it would be ready when dinnertime came.

Now he came to think that it was the sixteenth of May today and that he should have his flagpole put up. Then he took the axe and went out into the forest, saw a really nice tall pine tree, cut it down and cut the branches and bark off. *Then,* thought he, *if only I could manage to carry it forward to the house. I have the horse, but I don't have anything that it could pull with. I will try to carry it myself because I need to get it up today, because tomorrow it is Mother Norway's holiday.* He raised it and put it onto his shoulder. *I think I can handle it,* and he wandered off with the tall pine tree on his shoulder. When he came up to the house, he leaned it up on the roof of the house.

I now think I will go inside and make myself a really good cup of coffee and something to bite into after this hard toil. I am so happy I got it here.

After his snack, as one would call it, he started to dig a hole in the ground for the flagpole. He dug quite a big hole and deep, too. He dug it only a little ways from the house. He thought that was the only way he would be able to raise it. Let the top rest against the roof of the house and put the bottom end into the hole. The hole was now done, but now it was time for dinner.

Then he went inside to make the dinner. Done with his meal and the dishes, he rested a little, read some in his prayer book and spoke with God. It was for him just as important as food for the body; he also sought food for his soul.

Now he was invigorated and in good spirits to begin again. First he went down to tend the horse.

Now he made a ball for the top of the pole. This done, he took it and the little ring with him up on the roof and fastened it to the pole and put the line through it. Now it was ready to be raised to its position. He put the bottom end down in the middle of the hole. Then he drove a few sticks next to the end so it wouldn't move. That done, he cut four suitable rods to support it with when it was turned upside down, and fastened one of them with a nail loosely, a ways up on the pole, so they could be moved. Now it was time to try it. If it would succeed would depend on the circumstances.

Then he put his shoulder against the pole and lifted and moved the rods at the same time. The first pushes were heavy, but he made it without a problem. After it was somewhat in balance, he supported it upside down. The rods, so it couldn't fall down, went from a ways up the pole, and in all directions supported it, as they were legs. Then he said, "I am glad it stands there now."

Now it was to fill the hole. He threw in a few rocks first, then a little soil likewise, layer by layer until the hole was filled. "So now that has been accomplished," he said to himself. "Tomorrow the dear Norwegian flag will blow in the wind on this pole. And this shall be my symbol that I am a free man and live in a fee and independent country. And if my king or my country calls me to duty, I will do my fair share. Yes, die if necessary."

The day was now almost over and he thought he had accomplished a big piece of work. that day. "Yes, tomorrow it is a holiday. I will do only the most unavoidable tasks and celebrate the day together with my God."

In the morning, the seventeenth of May, he arose early, carried out his morning prayer, had breakfast and went down and took care of the horse, did his house chores, then went out, took the flag with him and hooked it up on the pole. It unfolded magnificently in the beautiful morning wind.

He stood there as an admirer for a while. Then he shouted, "I thank you, good God! I feel I am standing on holy ground. You let me find this place and have been with me all days until now. And also my people and my land you have protected and given them freedom and independence. We have become a free people.

"Yes, hard times we have endured, sings the poet, and that is true. After a 400-year stand still during the union with Denmark, and then finally the 100-year-long political struggle during union with Sweden for complete freedom. These struggles and troubles have not weakened our people; they have put iron in them. You, oh God, be certain we are one of the most free people in the world."

And when he stood there he remembered the song, "Noreg," by Arne Garborg. He knew it by heart and sang it aloud while he stood there. He took off his hat and sang:

"God bless the land of Norway,
Every house, every valley, every beach,
Every grove and field.
He let it never die,
He protects village and island,
He protects man and woman
until eternity.

We got it high and free,
We got it friendly and whole,
With ocean and mountain.
It stands so well and secure,
It stands so clean and blue,
Just like God's castle
With sunshine on it.

It is our love on the earth,
It is our best word,
Our comfort and welfare.
Magnificent men they were
Who brought it to us.
It is our inheritance,
The village of freedom.

Much work is put down
For the country's peace and might.
From time to time
It cost a thousand years,

In struggle from spring to spring,
In fight so long and painful,
Until we are free.

Here they lie,
Grave after grave,
From field down to ocean
Those who struggled so.
God bless every honest "Svein"
Who sleeps there under stone.
God bless them each and every one
Where they are now.

But the country they turned around,
That we will protect devotedly
Until the end of time,
Our love and best behavior,
Our life and all our might,
Will be on Norway's guard
Until the end of time.

In love warm and mild,
We lay effort to it.
Then it grows forward,
Then the flower will grow,
Then it will stand wild,
And always remain free
For man and creature."

He lifted his eyes up to the flag, then went inside. He took his Bible and read in it for a while.

He had not planned to do much that day, but then got to thinking how hard it was to lie on the floor. *I really think I have to make myself a bed this afternoon*, he thought.

Then he made himself dinner and, after that, went down to tend the horse. Then he started nailing together a box for a bed with feet on it. That done, he took the mattress cover, went down to the marsh, and cut some old grass and filled it. Then he carried it home and put it in his bed, took out a sheet and two pillows that his mother had sent with him, put it down and the wool blankets on top. So, now the bed was made. Now after this time, I can lie like a king.

Just now he thought that he hadn't planted any potatoes. *It may be late,* he thought, *but I will try to dig some down anyway.* He rook a bucketful, cut it up, went out and planted it. There was not enough for the field so he planted another bushel. Yes, now they are in the ground, it will depend on if God will give it growth.

It was now evening, so there was no time to start anything else that day. He now had to make his regular chores and take care of the horse. "Yes, now then is this seventeenth of May over. I have done what I could to celebrate it, to my country's honor and glory. And for the first time I planted seeds in the land that will be my home."

After his customary evening prayer he went to sleep and slept as a king in his castle.

Next morning after ending morning chores, he started making a kind of sled and plow for the horse to pull. It took him that day and most of the next day before they were done. Then he began to cut timber for his goat house. He cut several days, then he took the horse and began to pull it to the homestead. Then he hauled rock forward for the foundation. He thought he now had enough of them, so he began the masonry work.

He wanted to build the goat house and the stable house under the same roof. He would have a room in between the goat house and stable for hay. The stable he would build big enough for two horses and three cows. With time, when he got another stable, he could take the whole building he put up now for the goats. It was his plan to fence in a piece of land around the barn for them to be in the summer, but a house he had to have for them in the winter. He thought in time that he would get as many as fifty goats, but would start with ten next spring.

He now worked with the foundation a few days. It finally done, he began to lay timber, rolled up trunk after trunk and cut them together. But after a while he ran out of timber and had to cut more and pull forward. After a while the walls were tall enough anyway. He now put on the roof beams and made quite a lofty roof on his building. Because he didn't want a hayloft, he constructed only a few beams clear across to hold the building together. Now he had come so far he could put the roof on. Instead of boards, he cut up aspen trees and put the flat side up, then put bark and sod on. It took much time and heavy toil it was, too, for a man to do everything alone. But he didn't give up; he had decided to have it done this summer.

Yes, the one day slipped by like the other, the same toil from morning to evening. He had to make his meals three times daily, wash the dishes and keep it tidy in the house, went down every morning to his fishing net after fish, and the horse needed grooming. But he never forgot his prayer with God, morning and evening.

The dog was a true friend to him. It followed him everywhere he went and during the night he let it be inside the house.

Now it was already the month of August, but the stable was ready. Then he began to cut timber again and to pull forward for a small milking shed. He needed a room to store milk and cheese inside. At the end of August this was also completed.

He told himself he would begin to work up a piece of farming land. He wanted to plant more potatoes the next spring because the ones he had planted this spring had grown well and were very big now. He also wanted to seed a piece with rye. He wanted to find out if it would grow and become ripe this high into the mountain.

He worked on the field all the month of September. Now it was time to take up the potatoes and store them. He dug them up and got five sacks full. He thought it was a magnificent crop he got. He thanked God for His mercy toward him, then carried the potatoes down into the cellar and covered them with hay and sod so they would not freeze through the winter.

The next thing was to gather his belongings and get ready for the journey home. What he was not going to take with him he brought down into the cellar and hid it as well as he could. Bedspreads and all utensils he was going to take with him, and he packed them into the panniers. The harness he also took with him. He wanted to let his father use the horse during the winter while he, himself, was out logging.

The next morning after breakfast, he went down to the horse and took it up to the house, put the harness on and thereafter the panniers, put his axe into it, and took the rifle on his shoulder, called the dog and with that, they departed to the village. He thought to himself about the rifle he was carrying, *I really haven't made much use of. It is strange; I have been up here two summers, but still haven't seen any wild animal of any sorts. But, it may be useful to have in the future.*

They came home to his parents a little into the afternoon. "Yes, so has yet another summer gone by and disappeared in the course of time, with struggle and toil to sustain life. But, thanks to God, I feel myself just as strong and healthy as before. And I will continue," he said.

He greeted his parents and they conversed for a while about his doings up there on the mountain plateau, then he got something to eat. Actually, he rested the rest of the day because he was not going to the logging camp until the beginning of November, so he had all October to get ready.

The next day he went over to Aslong's house to greet her. He remained there into the day. They spoke together about how far he had come with their future home and laid plans for the future.

"This fall," he said, "I will go to the forest one month earlier, but then I will be back one month earlier in the spring. I will be back around the first of April. Then I have thought about, if you agree, giving notice of our "banns" [marriage], and having our wedding so we could come up to our house the first of May, so I can get my rye sowed as early as possible."

"You know, Ole, that I agree and I am glad that it will not be so long until I can come and help you."

"I'm sure there will be many things you will miss out there in the wilderness," he said. "We will not come to church as often either, but we have our Bible and prayer books. We will use them. We will be able to hear God's words and commandments anyway. Yes, may God be with us, His will come true."

The next days he wandered around among the neighbors. He wanted to find out if there were any of them that wanted to sell him some goats for spring. Yes, he found out that he could have as many as he had thought about buying.

He was then at home for a while, helping his mother with miscellaneous things until it was time for him to leave for the forest. Now the day had arrived and he took some snack food in the backpack, his axe and the rifle and the dog he wanted to have with him. They had become such good friends that they could not be separated.

Then he took hearty farewell with his mother and left. There is now not much to tell about until he comes back again. He came to the logger's camp in good shape.

Chapter Three

Then this winter was over with also. The first days of April he was back, just as healthy and fresh as before, even though he had worked like an ant all winter through. He was paid so much for each dozen timbers, so the more dozens—the more profit. He was home with his mother one day or so and then went out to see Aslong and talk with her.

She was glad to see him back again. They agreed that Ole should go to the priest and ask for the banns. He so did, met with the priest at home, and it was decided they were to announce their marriage the first coming Sunday. It had to be announced three Sundays after each other before they could have their wedding.

So the first Sunday, it sounded from the pulpit after the sermon was over. "It is announced the marriage for the first time for bachelor, Ole Thormod Mikalsen Pladsen, and batchelorette, Aslong Bertine Knudsdatter Haugen."

Ole went and bought then what he thought about taking with him. He got hold of ten goats and one buck, two sheep and one ram. Everything was bought very cheap and he could not pick them before he was ready to leave. Now to get ahold of two good cows. He had to have a cow's milk to mix in with the goat's milk in order to get good cheese. He went around to miscellaneous places, but there was none that thought they had more than they needed themselves.

But at last he ran into a man whom, he felt, could sell two. He needed more money he said, "And if you can pay in cash then I shall sell it quite cheaply." Ole said he could. The farmer said, "I have two good cows. They had had calves two months ago and is with calf now." Yes, that was as Ole wanted to have it. They went and looked at them and Ole liked them well. They were in good shape and looked like great milkers, not old, just the right age.

The farmer mentioned a sum that he wanted to sell them for. Ole paid for them and said, "Now the cows are mine, but you can have them until one week or two before I pick them up."

The farmer answered, "That is in order," and thereby was that item OK and done with.

Ole then went to a smith. He wanted to get some iron furnishings made for himself because he thought about making a plow to plow his barley field. Next day he went to town and bought food supplies and miscellaneous other things that they had to bring. Among other things, a big pot to make cheese in.

Aslong had a busy time these days, to sew her wedding dress. Ole had given her money for this. She was a pretty good seamstress herself, but now she had gotten another seamstress to help her to be done a little earlier.

Ole now thought they had everything he would bring with him this time. They had to wait another week or more before they could have their wedding. Now it was announced for the third time that they were to be married, and Ole went to the priest and talked with him about marrying them one day that week. The priest said they could come to the church on Thursday at ten o'clock.

On Thursday Ole and Aslong went to the church, and their parents were with them—both his and hers. The priest made a beautiful wedding for them and said, among other things, that "The ones who take God with them in everything they do will have luck and overcome anything. No matter how dark it looks, many a time, and that love overcomes everything. Love toward God is the great commandment. The only king I know, stay in love and you have God's peace, because God Himself is love."

Ole put the wedding ring onto her hand and now they were man and wife. They then went home to Aslong's parents' to have a wedding dinner together. Ole had bought them miscellaneous things, among those a wedding cake. After the dinner was over, they sat a while and talked about this and that until it was time for Ole's parents to go home. Ole stayed there until the next day, because then he and Aslong would go around collecting the creatures he had bought.

The day after their wedding, they headed out to accomplish this task. It was almost evening by the time they came to Ole's parents' place with the goats and the sheep. Aslong then stayed there overnight, because the next day they were to bring home the cows they had bought. The next morning they then went down to get them. Into the afternoon they were home. Now they had collected everything. Now it was time to pack the panniers.

They first had to go to Aslong's house to collect her clothes and belongings. They took the horse with them and went over there. They collected her things that evening, but he realized he could not get everything with them because she had so much, among other things, a spinning wheel.

The next morning they took farewell with Aslong's parents and went over to Ole's to pack the rest of what they had to bring. Now they were finally done with that, they took farewell with his parents, and let the creatures loose and collected them for the trip. The dog was of great help. Aslong led the horse and Ole and the dog chased the herd.

It went reasonably well up along the path. Into the afternoon, they had arrived. Ole said to Aslong, "Now we are almost at our new home."

She said, "I can see no houses yet, only a white pole that reaches up above the trees."

He then said, "That is my flagpole, and today we shall hoist the flag in your honor."

There was pine forest all around the houses, so they could not be seen at a distance. On the south side, there was only a thin strip of trees. Otherwise, there was thick pine forest around the houses. But where the house was, he had cleared a large, nice yard. Now they had arrived at the house.

Aslong tied the horse to a tree and helped Ole to get the creatures in. Then they took the pannier packs off the horse and carried them into the house. Ole said, "I will take care of the horse and bring a little dry wood so we can make coffee. I think we need something to strengthen ourselves with after the long journey."

Aslong started to unpack from the panniers and clean up a bit in the house. Then Ole came with the wood and started the fire, went down into the cellar after the coffee pot. At the same time, he checked to see if the potatoes were OK. He could not find a single one that had frozen over the winter, and he was glad for that.

Now the coffee pot was put on, Aslong washed the table off and put on something to eat with the coffee. She would cook something warm for supper, she said.

After having eaten, they went out and milked the cows, but the goats they let go until the evening. Ole thought he would let them out to graze throughout the evening. He would watch them, he said, so she would have time to wash the milking cups until the evening, and clean up a little in the house.

She washed and scrubbed all evening, carried milk cups and all that was needed for milking over to the milk shed. Then she scrubbed the floor in the

243

house, and cut green pine needles and sprinkled over it. It became fresh and cozy in the house.

Now time passed into the evening and she hung a pot with milk over the fireplace; she thought she would make a really fine milk porridge for supper. After a while, Ole and the dog came home with the herd. Then it was time to milk, but Aslong thought they should have supper first.

Ole came into the living room; he stood startled and didn't know quite what to say. Then he uttered, "Aslong, how nice and cozy it is in our living room now." He embraced her and gave her a kiss. She had put clean clothes on the bed and a white tablecloth on the table and a glass with beautiful flowers. She had put on the table cured meat and flatbread and put out good milk porridge with fresh milk.

Ole exclaimed, "Again, you have made a real feast, Aslong."

"Yes, it is our first day together here in our new home. You and I will remember this day as long as we live," she said.

Then they sat down to eat and read their prayer and ate. Ole said, "It is the best porridge I have eaten in a long, long time. You are a real chef, Aslong."

When they were done with eating the evening meal, they went out to milk the cows and the goats. That done, they carried the milk to the shed and strained it into cups and put them on the shelves in there.

Now Aslong went into the house to wash up after the evening meal and Ole went out to cut wood and carry it in, so it would be ready for the next day.

Now the toil was over for this day. Ole took his prayer book and said their evening prayer. The also sang a song together, the well know Psalm, "With all his trust in the Lord, his house stands on solid ground." Then, they went to sleep.

The next morning, it was the same all over again. They got up, had their morning coffee, milked and put the milk away, had their morning prayer and breakfast, and let the creatures out. Aslong would take care of them today.

She took her yarn with her; the dog walked next to her and the creatures. She was in her right element now. She knitted and sang all morning. Sang so it sounded across all the ridges around. Now she sang, "Saterjentens Sondag" [Shepherd Girls' Sunday].

"On the sun, I see everything moves forward.
Soon it is the time of the mass.
If I could only once wish myself home to people

Who walk on the church's path…"

The morning passed so quickly for her that she didn't even think about the fact that it was almost midday. Now, she turned the creatures on their way home. Ole had ended his work around eleven thirty, went down to get fish and take them home, made fire in the fireplace and put the pots over the heat so they would be done by the time Aslong came, filleted and cleaned the fish so it was ready to fry, chopped more firewood and took in.

Now she came. He heard the cowbell and went to help her get the herd in. Now, the pots were cooked and he began to fry fish while she put on the table the things that would go with the meal. He asked her how she liked to herd and she said, "The morning went so fast that before I knew it, it was already midday."

The lunch over with, they went to milk. He helped her with the milk. Then he went to his work. She tended to the milk and the rest of the things to do in the house. It was necessary to keep the creatures locked up for about three hours in the afternoon and then let them loose again. Then, they let them loose again and herded them.

Ole thought he would finish his plowing that day so he could plow and sow the next day. Now it was the evening and the plowing was done. He spent the rest of the day chopping wood because he knew it would require a lot of wood when Aslong started to make the cheese and cook "primost" [spreadable cheese].

Now he heard the cowbell again. Aslong came with the herd and he went with her to help. When they were in the barn, he said, "I will begin to milk while you make supper." That he did. When she was done in the house and came to help him, there were only four goats left to milk. Now they were done and went inside to have their supper.

That day was passed and it would be the same over and over the next few days. Ole told her that he had the plow ready now, and tomorrow he would sew his barley. "When I am done with the barley and the potatoes have I that in the ground, I will watch the herd for you."

The next morning, after the customary morning duties were over with, Aslong went away with the creatures and Ole put the horse before the plow. He plowed and sowed his barley and then plowed it again. He only had one sack full, and that he sowed. In what was left of the field, he sowed potatoes. He planted a little over a sack. Now he was finished with the planting this spring. The first thing he would do now was to fence in a parcel for the goats around the barn. Then was this day, with customary toil, over with.

In the evening, after they were done with their prayer, they sat and talked a while. Ole had thought about getting a "gjetergutt" (shepherd boy). "You, Aslong, will have more than enough to do aside from the herding, to make cheese and cook primost, and take care of the house. I think," he said, "when I go to town at the end of this month, I will look for one."

"Yes," Aslong said," it would be good to have a boy. You will also have more time for your work when you don't have to help me so much."

"I don't think Einar from Stenseng has taken permanent service yet. He was confirmed last fall and has worked a little around at the farm. I think he is a very able boy, and if I can get him, I will pay him quite well. At least I will find out when I go down there."

Then, the one day went like the next one with the daily toil, until the month of May was almost over.

Now Ole had to go down with a load of cheese and primost. They both had a hectic time packing the panniers. They had to have wax paper around every cheese so it wouldn't spoil.

The next morning he left and Aslong became alone. But she was not concerned; she had the dog for company.

In the afternoon, he was back and had Einar with him, the son of Gunder Stenseng. They had agreed he would be there to herd for a couple of years, for one hundred and twenty crowns, and do the herding this summer.

Ole had also gotten with him two pigs and a lot of other things. He said to Aslong, "I think we have made it really well this month. The cheese brought in one hundred and twenty-five crowns. I think it was splendid for this month."

Yes, now there was one more in the family. They had no bed for him, but Einar thought that he would make his bed in the hayloft. At least he could sleep there through the summer. And that's how it was.

The next morning he was up early. They didn't have to call him. He helped with milking, was inside the house for prayers and breakfast. He got to see Ole's rifle hanging up there on the wall and asked if he could take that with him. "Yes," said Ole. "You can have it every day if you can carry it with you." Now, he let the creatures loose, took the dog with him and disappeared through the woods.

Ole went to make the fencing for the goats and also had to cut some wood. Then he could continue to clear more acreage until the time that he had to cut the hay and stack it. They now carried on, each with their own work, until the end of June. Then Ole had to go down again with a load of cheese.

Yes, now they were ready. He took the horse and left. Aslong then became alone because Einar had to go with the creatures. She said to him, "I will have the dog at home with me today, so it won't be so lonely." That's the way it was.

Einar thought today he would bring the creatures to an area where he had not herded them before. It was a ridge between two large marshlands that went down to the river. Along the river there were a lot of deciduous trees, and an ideal spot for the goat. He let them follow this ridge and then came down to the river. Here, there was a real treat for them, grass and leaves in abundance.

Einar went around looking at the creatures as they were gorging on the luscious grass. But there was also something else that now caught his attention. His eye had focused onto some brownish animal that came wandering through the brush. He knew what it was—a bear. Rapidly, he took the rifle off his shoulder. *I know I'm no bear shooter*, he thought, *but I will try anyway.*

Now it had come so close that he gave him a bullet. Yes, it hit because it roared and rose onto its two rear limbs, against him. But now Einar sent him a bullet right into his chest. It gave it the final blow; it fell over and was dead. *This has to be an exceptionally good rifle*, he thought, *otherwise I could not have hit it.*

Now, he took his knife and started to skin it. He would take the pelt with him home. *Yes*, he said to himself, *you probably thought about getting yourself some fresh goat meat, but you miscalculated this time. This "krag Jorgens" beat you to it.* He now took the skin off and put it together, tied a birch around it to carry it with. He was quite proud of his courage.

When Ole came home that evening and got to see the bear pelt, he was totally surprised. "Yes, I must say, that was well done, Einar."

"I couldn't help it. It came all the way up to me and I carried this rifle. So, I had to try it, and the outcome was good."

Now it was late into the summer, and Ole had to collect the hay for the livestock for the winter. He then started to cut grass. Aslong was with him some of the days to rake it together into piles. They let them lay that way until they became dry. Then they raked it, put it in haystacks and finally the hayrack. He had cut hay now for a long time and thought maybe it was enough. He would get Aslong to herd for Einar a few days when she didn't make cheese, so he could help him to put the hayracks together. Then, after two weeks hard work, he thought he had enough.

Everything now proceeded in its old rhythm again; Aslong made cheese, Einar herded and Ole worked in his field. It went that way for a while again. Then Ole had to go down with a load of cheese. There was now only one week left of July.

They now made the harness ready this evening, and the next morning he left. Toward the evening he was back, well satisfied with the trip. The last trip made him many crowns more than the other two.

He calculated together all three trips and said to Aslong, "You soon will make us rich with your cheese and primost. They are well made and I get premium for it, and the highest marks. You are a valuable wife, Aslong, and all I can do is give you this." With that said, he embraced her and gave her a kiss. "I can tell you that these three trips down with cheese have brought in quite a nice sum for three months by ten goats and two cows." Yes, Aslong was happy and satisfied.

Now everything went along as usual for a while with the daily routine, day after day, until the end of August approached. Then Ole began to think that he should build some kind of house for his barley. He thought for sure now that it was ripe. He would first make the trip down to the town; then he would make a decision when he came back again.

Yes, now he had made his trip to town again and was back. Also, this time it went well. He got a better price for his cheese every time. So it was very promising for him and Aslong. They got ample compensation for their toil, and they didn't forget to thank God for His mercy toward them. They gave Him the credit for everything going well with them.

He had now decided to build a kind of house as a grain bin. That is to say, he would use it as a barn for a while, but otherwise he would use it for a carpentry and smithy workshop. *I should start right away*, he thought, *if I am to get it done by the end of fall.*

He then started to cut and pull forward timber for this house. Toward the end of September, he had it done with the exception of the floor. He would put down a concrete floor in it, he thought, if it wouldn't get too cold.

Now it was time again for the trip to town this month. So he got ready to leave the next day. This day, while Ole was in town and the dog was at home with Aslong, Einar had another visit by a bear. This time, it took a goat from him. He didn't notice it until it had killed the goat, but it did not have time to feast on it. Einar gave it two bullets, one right after the other, and it rolled over dead. He took his knife and skinned both the bear and the goat and carried the skins with him home. Now he had killed two bears this summer.

That was quite an accomplishment for a youngster like him.

Now Ole was back again and became very surprised when he heard that Einar had shot a bear again. Aslong thought the bear came on the days when she had the dog at home. So after this time, she would let it follow the herd every day. "Yes we did lose a goat, but it would have been worse if we had lost one of the cows."

Ole had brought with him home some sacks of cement and would now put down the floor in his temporary hay barn. Done with that, he began to cut the barley and put it on the hayracks to dry. It turned out to be a very good crop he got on this little field. He thought it would be enough for flour for the year and enough for seeding the next spring. He was well satisfied with his trial acreage and thanked God for giving him His blessing so that all his endeavors succeeded so well. His potatoes, too, looked promising. He soon had to take them out, too.

When he had dried his barley, he took a sickle and went down to the deciduous woods down by the river and cut some leaves and tied it up with a string. It had to be cut while it was green. He worked with that for three days and then took the horse and pulled it home and stacked it. He wanted to have it to give to the goats once and a while during the winter.

Now it was also time to take the potatoes up, so he began with that. Aslong helped him, too, when she could take some time off from the house chores. They put them into sacks and drove them up to the house and they put them in the cellar. They got a big crop with very large potatoes.

He said to Aslong when they were done, "I am more than satisfied with this year's crop. I would never have dreamt that everything would grow so magnificently up here in the mountain, but thanks to God. It is He who gave it growth. We work well, and do our share, but if God was not with us and blessed our toil, then we could not get anything. When I get my barley into the barn, I will then have a thanksgiving day. We will then promise and thank the Lord for His grand mercy toward us."

He now helped Aslong with different things around the house, cut up some firewood and made a bed for Einar to sleep in the house. It would soon be too cold to sleep out in the hayloft. And Aslong put up a curtain around the bed and made it cozy for him.

Then the first summer passed of Ole and Aslong's life together here on "Fjeldbo," as he would call his farm. The fall arrived and the winter came closer, but they were happy and well satisfied. They hoped that God would still be with them and protect them throughout the cold winter.

Ole now drove his barley crop in and stacked it in one end of the house he had put up as a hay barn. He would thresh it later in the winter. Now the end of October was nearing and Ole had to make a trip to town. Maybe it would be the last this fall; he didn't really know. If the weather would remain nice throughout the month of November, maybe he would make one more trip.

Now Ole was back after the end of his trip to town. It went well for him also this time, and he brought with him necessities that were needed to live through the winter. Aslong had also sent after seeds to plant in springtime. She planned to plant a kitchen garden, and likewise, a few flowers.

This day was Sunday, and after the dinner was over and Aslong was done with the dishes, Ole said, "I think we should congregate around God's word a while and make this a thanksgiving day for all the good that God has blessed us with through this summer."

They sat down, all three at the table, sang a psalm and Ole read a prayer. He thanked God for all the mercy that He had shown them so far, and asked Him to be with them still. They sang a psalm again and Ole read, "The Lord's Prayer."

Time now passes, as customary, with the daily chores. It was a nice fall and Ole was to town again for a trip at the end of November. It would be the last for this summer and fall.

Now he began to thresh his barley, banged a few out at a time, and then shook the straws up and carried them out into the sled that he had standing outside the door. When it was full, he drove the load over to the hay barn. And, like this, he carried on until all the grains were off the straws. Then he gleaned them by throwing them with a "Spjeld" [wood bat] from one end of the house to the other.

When that was done, he collected the berries and carried them away. The lightest grains he put into a bin. The best he filled into sacks and put them up against a wall. He got quite a lot of barley out of the little field he had. So now that work was over with.

Now, it was time to drive wood and chop it for the Christmas weekend. So they started, both Einar and Ole, to cut wood in the forest and drive it forward. They now had many loads collected and began to chop them up. They sawed and chopped a long while until, they thought, there was enough wood for half the winter.

There were now only three days left until Christmas. Aslong was busy with baking and decorating the house. Ole now went to find a little pine tree for a Christmas tree that they wanted to have for Christmas Eve. She decorated it, and so it was completed, except for lighting candles on Christmas Eve.

Time passed quickly and now it was Christmas Eve. Ole helped her with miscellaneous things. He chopped fresh pine needles and spread onto the floor, carried in wood for her, and water and other things. Now he went to put up a sheaf in the barn for the little birds. He had saved a sheaf for that.

They completed the chores in the stable and barn early that evening, filtered the milk and did what was to do in the milking shed, then went into the inside. They washed themselves and dressed up for the holiday. This was the first Christmas Eve they celebrated at Fjeldbo. But they enjoyed many more with the blessings of God. So, the Christmas season had started. Ole read the gospel of Christmas, and they sang one of the well-known Christmas psalms, "Jeg Singer Julekveld" [I Sing a Christmas Song]. Aslong now put the Christmas food on the table and they sat down at the table. They read the table prayer and started eating. After the holiday meal was over with, Ole helped Aslong with the dishes. Then they lit the candles on the Christmas tree and sang again some Christmas psalms.

Ole had bought something for Aslong and Einar in time, as a Christmas gift for them. He gave it to them now. Aslong had knitted something for them each. It was a real Christmas spirit over them and they felt happy and content.

"You, old one, who live now on this side of 'blaamyren' [blue marsh], do you remember how they celebrated Christmas there at home with the mother and father? I will here recite the song by Bernhard Gabrielsen, 'Jul Der Hjemme,' [Christmas, There At Home.]

"Do you remember Christmas up there in the north?
With snow covered mountains and ice covered fjords,
With ringing bells which loudly rings
And brings the message of the holiday to the heart?
From the outermost rocky coast to the immense valley,
From the fisherman's living room to the rich man's hall,
In cotter's cottage and farm,
Even to seamen on the ocean the message reaches.

Do you remember the evening with father and mother?
The family together at the holiday table?
The peace and happiness that rule in there
Are truly my most beautiful childhood memories.
Do you remember the pine tree that stood there so beautiful,

With light and decoration on each branch?
Fruit and nut hung linked together,
And a lit star high at the top on the trunk.

Do you remember lit eyes and singing?
How joyfully comforting in the living room it sounded?
When the flock of siblings with father and mother
Sang the well known Christmas carols.
Do you remember the wonderful frost clear evening,
The sky's magnificent stars?
Silent and faithful they stand guard
The symbol of Him that was laid in the crib."

The family on Fjeldbo didn't get an opportunity to go to church on Christmas Day with church bell sounds as they did down in the big town, but they had a very nice holiday. They gathered around God's word, read and prayed and sang Christmas psalms. They felt happy and lucky in their situation.

Chapter Four

The days until New Years they didn't do any other work than the daily necessities. But after New Years, they started to cut timber. Ole and Einar were in the woods all the time, except the time it took to tend to the creatures. They continued that way throughout January and February, cut timber and drove it down to the river. Ole had decided to build a dam this summer down in the river and put up a small saw and saw mill.

The first days of March, he decided to take the horse and the sled and go down to town. He would bring the saw home and the things that went with it, and likewise two small millstones. "I will probably be gone two or three days," he said to Einar. "Could you do the chores at home while I'm gone."

"Yes," Einar said, "you can take the time you need. I will take care of the chores at home. I think we have enough hay in the shed for a weeks time or more, so you don't have to worry about that."

Ole then went the next day. It went well on the trip down. He was now making the rounds to get hold of what he was determined he would need. He bought himself also another horse and harness, a good long sled with frames on and a good plow. He now had two loads and two horses to bring with him home. It took longer for him than he thought, but after four days passed he was home in good shape.

"I think now," he said to Einar, "we should drive home some hay, fill up the hay barn again so we have it for a while. After that, we will drive forward some wood and chop up. We will chop so we have enough for the whole summer. There will be enough time for that now." Then they drove the hay barn full of hay, and afterward pulled wood forward.

"We will find ourselves a really tall pine tree and cut it down, a huge one because I want to make myself an 'agerulen' [field roller] out of it." They walked around and looked until they found one that he thought would be suitable for that. They cut it down and sawed it to the appropriate length and pulled it home. He said to Einar, "While you chop up the wood, I will make myself a larger harrow and roller."

It was now into the month of April and Ole was done with the harrow and agerulen. Then he helped Einar a few days with the wood, until he thought it would be enough through the summer.

Ole, now said to Einar, "As you know, it is not long until the year that I hired you for is over. I should like to know if you want to be here longer to work for me, or if you have decided to quit? I have to go to into town after the seventeenth of May, you see, and then I have to get another man if you don't want to be here one more year."

Einar replied that he liked it here and that he was willing to work another year for him. "I will," said Ole, "pay you two hundred crowns for the next year, and you don't have to herd. I will get myself a young boy to watch the creatures, because I want you to dig trenches down in the marshland this summer. "Yes," Einar said. He was pleased with the pay and would do his best to compensate for it.

The sun started to shine warmly now and the snow melted quickly. So, it was not long until Ole could start to work on the field and do his spring plowing. Now the frost is out of the ground, and Aslong said to them that they could help working up a piece of land close to the house for her garden; and likewise she would like a flowerbed around the flagpole. They both started digging, and after two days passed, both pieces of land were completed and ready to plant in.

Ole now thought that the acreage was dry enough, put his horses to the harrow and started harrowing his rye field. He thought it was pleasurable to walk behind the harrow now. With two horses in front of a large harrow, he could do so much more a day, and better work, too, he thought. Now after a few days passed, he was done with the rye field; then it was time to plant potatoes.

Einar had helped around the house and taken care of the creatures. Now he had to help Ole with the potato planting. They drove out some dung for the potato acreage. After they were done with all the planting, they drove out the dung that remained and put it on the rye field.

Aslong also had her kitchen garden planted now. She worked with that every spare moment she had from the household chores. Now, after this, she wanted to work in her flower garden. She would arrange it very beautifully. She made the flowerbeds around the flagpole, divided them up into small triangles with passage walks between them. In the round circle, she put down small round rocks and the walkways she covered with nice gravel. Around the pole itself, there was a passageway with gravel. She rolled dung from the goat house and worked it into the soil before she planted the seeds. Today it was the sixteenth of May and she wanted to finish the planting today, for tomorrow they would celebrate the Seventeenth of May.

This day it was Mother Norway's liberation day, Seventeenth of May, and Ole took the flag out and raised it on the pole. Aslong and Einar stood there, too, and looked on. Ole said, "It probably will not be much celebration for us, other than to fly the flag for the day. I will anyway, read the first verse of the Fatherland's Song:

"Yes, we love this country,
as it comes forward.
Furrowed and weathered over the waters,
With the thousand homes.
Love it, love it and think about
Our father and mother
And the storybook that lowers
Dreams onto our soul.

"Hail you, you fresh, you beautiful, you mountain high North. God keep our king and our dear Fatherland and our people. Honor to you, our benefactor and protector. Then also, we have taken part in the celebration of our Norway's Freedom Day," he said.

They went each to their individual tasks for a while. After dinner was over, Ole went down to his barn to clean in there because he wanted to use it as a bedroom for the two loggers that were to work for him during the summer. He had secured them ahead of time, and they should be ready to come with him when he came down in May. He made a kind of bed and put in there a small table and two benches. He wanted to make it as comfortable for them as he could.

Done with that, he made a stall in the goat house for his two calves that had come a while back, two beautiful cow calves. He had them in the barn with the cows, but now needed that space for the ox he wanted to buy when he went down to town. Later in the afternoon he packed the cheese into the panniers so it was ready the next morning.

"Yes," he said in the evening, "we have had another Seventeenth of May, and yet another year has passed of our lives. Yes, year after year rush ahead and never come again."

Early the next morning, he went with the horse down to the village in town, and got what he needed to take with him home. Also, he bought five good goats and an ox, one and a half years old.

Then, he went over to a homestead where there was a boy that he wanted to have to herd in the summer. Arne was his name, the son of Anton Moen. Ole said he would pay him well if he wanted to come with him right away. Yes, the boy was very willing to go with him and the parents concurred. So, then all was taken care of. The boy pulled his clothes together and was ready in a short while.

Ole then went to meet the two men that he had promised to work for him through the summer. They had waited for him, so it didn't take long for them to get ready. At last they were ready for the trip up to Fjeldbo.

He got one of the men to lead the horse and Arne chased the goats and Ole the ox. The other man helped in moving the crowd. It went remarkably well with them, but it was late in the evening before they arrived.

After the creatures and the horse were out in house, they went in and got their evening meal. After that, it was time to go to rest for the night. Arne followed Einar to the hayloft, to lie together with him. Ole was with the other two to show them their room. "You have to lie in an out house," said Ole, "but it is the best I can do for you, my house is too small." They answered that this is as good a sleeping room as we need at this time of the year.

The next morning Ole went with them down to the river. He also took a horse with them. They walked around and looked over the location and then chose a place where they wanted to build the dam. It was a good ways from where Ole had cut the timber so he had to drive it again to the place where he wanted to build.

After a few days, Ole said to Aslong, "I see it will be too much for you to do all this work alone, cook for five men, all this and then milking in addition. I will get Einar in my place tomorrow so I can go down and get sister Anna up here to help you through the summer." Aslong also thought it was maybe the best to get some help.

So the next morning, he put on the lady's saddle on one horse and went down to his parents. He met Anna at home and explained to her what he had come for. Yes, she was immediately willing to come with him. She packed her clothes and was ready. He talked with his mother and got a little to eat and then it was time to head out again. He put Anna on the saddle and tied her clothes onto the horse. He led the horse himself.

Into the afternoon, Aslong heard them come and went out to greet Anna. They greeted each other and Aslong said, "It was good of you, Anna, to come up here to help me. I hope you like it here. You know it is not like the village. There is no entertainment of any kind, only work, and more work. Come inside now to get some refreshments.

Anna said, "I think it is nice and beautiful up here. The truth is that I like this place, so I'm sure I will enjoy it here."

The day after, Ole started helping down at the river again, and Einar went to his work on the marshland. Then one day went like the other throughout the summer. In June, Ole was back in town again and Einar helped the loggers in his place. Now it was already so late in the summer that the hay had to be done. The men who were building the dam thought they could continue without Ole and Einar's help for a while, so they started with the hay.

It was now close to the end of July, and they were done with the hay collection. Ole went to town again and Einar continued to dig ditches down at the marsh. Ole was down at the river again and helped. That was the way they kept going throughout August and September. Ole went to town twice during that time.

Now he had to cut his barley and store it. In the middle of October the loggers were through with their work. Now then, one of his dreams had come true, now he had a saw and a mill.

He could cut wood and boards for his houses and mill his own flour at home. It had cost him many crowns and a lot of toil, but he was well satisfied. He did not owe anything and he had more than enough to pay for everything. He now settled with the men and paid them the salary they had been told before they started. He gave them a "saeter skrukke" [knapsack], as they called it, for a job well done. They contained two goat cheeses, some butter for both of them, and one thigh of ham. They were both family men so that came in handy. They thanked him for the payment and likewise for the gift. They thanked Ole and Aslong for the good heart they had shown.

One of them said, "We have worked on different places through the time, but never such good room and board as here. Yes, I say, it is nice to work for such people who know to appreciate the work, and treat a worker as a peer and not a slave. Thank you for all the good you have shown towards us and God be with you and reward you for that."

Ole said, thereafter, "We have not done more than is the duty of man. When one blesses us and our toil, then the purpose is that we should do good things with it, both to ourselves and our fellow human beings. I did not come here to dig in some field and put crowns on the bottom of the chest, but with time, to get a nice home. That is why I had you here in the summer. It was necessary for the start of my 'Flam.'"

The day afterward he took the men and their tools down to the village. Also, he had some cheese with him. After coming down, he bid farewell to them and added that maybe in a few years, if we are all alive and that, maybe I will need your help again.

The next day Ole and Einar started to take out the potatoes. He was now up by the house with a load to put in the cellar. Then he heard that Aslong and Anna were singing in there, sang so it really sounded good to him. He went in and stood a while, until the song was ended. Then, also, he started a song and they sang with him.

"Sing only in your childhoods spring,
In your bright summer.
The song itself from the heart goes
And to the heart comes.
Sometime your teenage song,
Will, when the fall arrives merrily,
Come to meet you.
The hair makes the hair gray itself.
Floats more peacefully,
Floats, before you know it yourself
In your memory,
As a voice both sad and happy,
Your teenage song sound
In the silent times."

Ole then said, "It made me feel so good to hear you both sing so beautifully. There is nothing that calms your spirit and livens your mood as the song does. And I like to see you both happy and in good spirits." Then he went about his work again.

Now the potatoes were in the house, and Anna and Aslong had harvested the crop from the kitchen garden. Aslong was well rewarded for her toil. With it, she got a good crop of many things. Her nice flower garden, which had been blooming throughout the summer and was a treat for the eye, began now to wither and fade. The frost had already advanced.

Yes, this is the way it is all through nature's cycle, everything grows and blossoms for a while. But then fall arrives and the healthy growth ends, and everything withers and dies. This way it is also with humans. They blossom and live for a while, but then they start to wither and fall away. At last the fall of death comes.

Ole now had gotten his barley crop into the house. So now, all his produce salvaged for this year, he was well satisfied.

Throughout the month of November, Ole and Einar worked to fill in the ditches down by the marsh. They made wood boards first to make room for the water to flow in, and then pine needles and thereafter, filled soil in them. They were just done with this before the earth froze. Throughout the time before Christmas they were in the forest and cut firewood, drove home and then cut them up.

Ole asked Anna one day if she would be with them over the winter, then he would pay her for a whole year, he said. "Yes", she said, "I like myself well here, and I don't think I would find a better place." The thing is, she liked Einar and wanted to be close to where he was.

"That is wonderful," Ole said, "We will surely need your help."

Now it came close to the holiday season. They slaughtered, baked, brewed and cleaned up. Everyone was busy from dusk to dawn. Arne was not there now, he had to go home in the fall when the school started, but he promised to come back next spring to herd through the summer.

Now, the holiday had arrived and everyone prepared to celebrate it, as it is customary. Christmas eve is the focal point of the whole Christmas holiday. They were all dressed up and gathered around the holiday table. Ole read the Christmas gospel and prayed to God, thanked him first for all the good that they had been blessed with throughout the year that had passed. And then he gave thanks next for the savior who was sent down here to save mankind from sin, whose holiday we now celebrate in memory thereof. They sang a song and Ole said grace. Then the meal started. After the holiday meal was over with, the candles were lit on the Christmas tree. And all sang Christmas psalms and gave presents to each other. They had a really joyful and formal Christmas Eve.

On the first day of Christmas they gathered again to a celebration dinner and around God's word. They could not get to any church, so they had a sermon about Christmas at home.

Chapter Five

Then, after the New Year again, everything went back to normal, with timber cutting and hauling through the whole winter, until the snow started letting go in the spring. Then they released the saw and cut wood and boards until the time came when they had to start the fields. And likewise they milled enough flour for the year. Now, the time had come for the spring season. So, Ole started to plow and roto-till and sow his barley. And after that had been done they planted potatoes.

Aslong said to Ole that day, "I don't feel well now so I think it is best that you go down to get my mother." He knew what it was about so he threw a saddle on the horse and away he went. It didn't take long to get to the village that day. He explained to his mother-in-law what it was about, and she got ready at once and accompanied him. She sat in the saddle and she led the horse. In the afternoon they were at Fjeldbo. In the morning, on the seventeenth of May, Aslong gave birth to a son and everything went well. Ole thought that it was a strange coincidence that his first-born son was born on Independence Day. "I will now have to go raise the flag in honor of Mother Norway and my son's birthday," he said.

Anna had planted the kitchen garden and the flowers this spring, so everything was now in the ground, if only God would give it growth now through the summer. Arne had also come back again to care for the creatures. When Aslong's mother had been there a month they thought she could go home. Ole then took her home.

After this, everything went on its own rhythm again. Ole and Einar continued still with the work down by the marsh, one digging ditches, the other plowed. Rotated and rolled, they kept going this way the whole summer. But next summer they were all overgrown with red clover and timothy. So was another of Ole's dreams come true.

When their son was six weeks old they took him with them and baptized him. He got the name Harald.

At Fjeldbo everything went along as usual, day after day, winter and summer, two years ahead. Harald, this summer, was two years old. Ole had built himself not a big one, but an efficient barn. It was this summer that Ole got to see the fruits of his toil dry up the marsh. He got such a large field of hay that it was something to envy. There was stack after stack along the marshland of the red clover hay. Yes, he thought to himself, that he got rich reward for his work.

We will now go four years into the future. Harald will be five the coming spring and Ole has achieved great things through the four years that have passed. He has built up new buildings, stable, barn and a "stabbur" [elevated storage house], all built rather fast. He also now has a big herd of all kinds of animals.

Einar now has been at Fjeldbo seven years and faithfully served his master. But, now he wants to quit this spring. He said to Ole, "When my year is over with, it is my intention to quit for you. I have decided to get a home of my own, and Anna will share it with me. I will clear and build myself a home out here only a little ways from your homestead. I have received the same conditions from the Norwegian Government as you received. So, we will become neighbors in the future."

"I take great pleasure in hearing this," Ole said, "and I will wish you the best in your choice, both of wife and homestead. You can stay here with us while you build your home. I think there is food enough if there is one more in the family. Likewise, you can have a horse to haul your timber with. The saw you can use when the time comes that you need board." Einar thanked him for the offer and was more than pleased.

It will now be appropriate to mention that in the period of time that we passed, Harald got a brother and a sister. Oivind is now three years old and Agnes one year.

The two last years Arne had been at Fjeldbo, both winter and summer, after he was confirmed. Before this, he was only there in the summer. Now, Ole asked if he could take Einar's place as farm helper because Einar would quit now in a few days. Arne was now seventeen years old and a good boy, thought Ole. He liked having him there.

Arne answered, "I like working here for you, if you are pleased with me and what I do. I thought we would get along well, so there is nothing to talk about."

"I will try to get ahold of a young man to work the creatures in the summer, as you did before," Ole said.

Now the seventeenth of May had arrived again, and Ole raised the flag up just as he had done every year before throughout the time they had lived at Fjeldbo. The seventeenth of May had become like a double celebration day for him since his first son was born that day. We will now note that his second son, Oivind, was also born on a significant day for Norway, namely the seventh of June.

Now Ole had been to town again and came home with a new shepherd boy, Odin Fladberget [flat mountain]. Ole and Arne's work now consisted of putting up a fence. He had been doing that the last summers in between spring and fall planting season. He thought they would be done this summer and then all of his property would be fenced in, both the highland, not cultivated, and cropland. So in the fall, when all the harvest was in the barn, he would let the creatures loose in there and didn't have to watch them for a while.

Hay harvest did not take such a long time now on Fjeldbo as before. Ole had bought himself a "Dering Slaamasjein" [harvester], and a tiller. But there was a lot more hay to handle. There was so much that each year that the hay bins were filled up in the barn and stable, they put up many stacks outside. Ole had cleared a large area in the forest, a way from the house, and put a fence around it. In there he stacked the hay that he could not get into the houses.

When all the harvest was in the houses in the fall, and when the frost and winter hit, then Ole and Arne had to start in the forest again, cut wood and timber, and when it was close to spring, then to sawcut boards and planks, down on the saw. Ole had decided to build a new house in the near future, so it was important to get materials for that.

The next summer it was his intent to build a cellar and get it cemented. He would have cellar under the whole house, and wall all the way around from the bottom to the top.

So then all of this summer and winter had passed on, or rather one year, and a new spring was coming up. The sun was shining warmly and the snow was melting. Water started to flow in the river. Ole and Arne were down at the saw, at full work to cut boards and planks for the house that he would build. They continued there until it was dry enough on the fields to do spring sowing. Now, the time was then ready to plow, sow and plant. They continued doing this until the middle of May, and then they were done with that.

Then after that they started to dig on the cellar. Today it was the seventeenth of May again and Ole raised the flag up, but there was no celebration that day. But there was something that happened that day anyway that had its influence on the surroundings there. In the afternoon three young men came up there to Ole, each with a backpack on their back. All three looked to be around twenty years of age. They said to Ole that they came to find a homestead and wanted to clear and build themselves a home up here.

Ole guided them the best he could. Two of them decided to settle in the outskirts of the forest, west of Ole, and the third a ways east from where Einar was. So then, he got four neighbors, two on each side. Yes, that was more than he had thought would happen, but he was glad for that and there was room for many more.

They continued their work on the cellar a while again, but it was quite a large cellar so it took a long time. But now it was pretty much completed and they hauled rock to it. Ole was now on a trip to the village in town again, and came back with two bricklayers who would complete the cellar wall that summer.

Einar now had his house complete to move into, so he and Anna would go down to town and have their wedding. Anna had now been with Ole and Aslong seven years, just as long as Einar. Ole now had to find someone to take Anna's place, because Aslong could not manage to do everything alone. She had the children to take care of also.

Ole then went down to the town and was gone for two days, but came back with two maids. Now Aslong would get good help. The one would take care of the cooking and the other would make cheese and take care of the milking, he said, but Aslong had to be the one to give them guidance.

Yes, now the hay harvest was coming up again, and Ole and Arne had to work with the hay. There was a lot of hay this summer, too. Yes, it was now fall again, and all the harvest at Fjeldbo is in the house, and the wall on the house was done, too.

We will now let the work at Fjeldbo, summer as winter, go on as usual for a while. In the summer the house was being built and the fields were being worked on, and during the winter they continued in the forest.

When Harald was seven years old, he was sent down to Ole's parents in the fall to go to school during the winter, and was there every winter until he was confirmed. Likewise Oivind, when he was old enough, was at Aslong's parents, and his sister Agnes, likewise. This way it went year after year, in a hectic manner at Fjeldbo.

This summer, Harald was fifteen years old and was to go to the priest to study to be confirmed. And the Fjeldbo family moved into their new large house the same summer. It took many years before it was completed and shining white. And well built in all parts, with a bath and central heating, warm and cold water. There was a deck on both sides with a balcony over.

Ole had not only completed this house through the years, but had also built three other houses at the farm at the same time, namely a pig sty and hen house in the same building, a tool shed for farm equipment and wood storage. He also had built a new and modern milking shed around a small dairy with cool room for milk, butter and cheese. There was also put in a water pipeline to all the houses from the water spring he found the first spring he was up there.

He had a furniture maker work for him for a year and a half to make furniture for the house. It was now the middle of this spring since Ole started cleaning up there. Now that he saw the change that had occurred and everything that had been accomplished during that time, he felt thankful to God.

And so this dream of his had become realized. But there was one thing still that he had planned and that was to get a road built down to the town. The rumor had apparently spread widely about Ole's success up here, because in the last few years more and more people came to settle on both sides of him. If they achieve as much as Ole has, only the future will tell.

Harald was now confirmed this fall. His father wanted to send him to a Hoyskole, college. He wanted Harald to learn a subject so he could work with head and hands, as he called it. Harald decided to go to engineering college, and after Christmas he then was sent to the school.

The last summer there was a shortage of hay. The farmers had heard that Fjeldbo had more hay than he needed for himself. And some of them decided to go up there to buy hay, and at the end of March a large crowd of them were up there.

When they came up there they asked Ole if he would sell them some hay. "Yes," he answered, "I have maybe a little to spare."

"What are you asking for your hay?" they asked.

"Oh," he said, "I don't know what it would be worth." Then he said, "You can pile up on your sleds as much as you can put on for five kroner per load."

Yes, they were happy to get that much hay so cheap. It wasn't even half price. They put on their loads and were ready to go home. They were all satisfied and thanked Ole for the service. Ole wasn't a man to take advantage of the difficult situation of his fellow man, just to enrich himself. Some days afterward, another group came up there and wanted to buy hay. He also let them take it on the same terms.

He said to himself, *isn't it something odd that this has happened, that, I who would live up here in the wilderness, would come to sell hay to these well-to-do farmers down in the village?* Yes, there are many things unthinkable that go on in this world.

The next day the last farmers had been there. He said to Arne, because Arne was still there, "I think there must be a good road down to the village, now, after so many have driven. I think we will load up two loads of hay and take them with us to my parents and one to Aslong's."

They did this. He took with him miscellaneous other goodies for them also, such as flour meat and butter. He had brought something every year. Yes, several times throughout the year. He was very good to his parents, and didn't forget to make good toward his parents-in-law, as well.

This spring he sent a request to the Norwegian government to have a road built from the new establishment and down to the village. He explained to them that there was now a complete large village up there that needed this road. And likewise, what great advantage it would be for the state to have the road built. There was a timber forest there that the state owned, worth many millions of kroner that could be harvested if there was built a good automobile road from there.

The whole summer passed but he didn't hear from the government. In the fall he decided to go to Oslo [capitol of Norway] and speak verbally with them. He did that. He decided not to give up until he got either a yes or no answer.

After two weeks passed he was back. He told Aslong that he had gotten a promise that next spring an engineer and two men would come and start planning the roadway, and had good hope that it would be completed.

So after a winter had gone by and the spring had come with spring birdsong, all creatures held a busy life. It was a lot of activity in the forest, in the outback, and at home. They all are useful in their own way and they all sing praise for the creator.

In the month of May, the engineer came by there. They wanted to stop at Fjeldbo for a while. They now started to survey a line where the road would go. Ole thought it was a good start for his dream to come true. They worked with that all summer, into the fall, they were then done. Their map and calculations were now turned into the Department of Road Building. Ole didn't hear anything for a long while. But surely, two years later he got a message that the decision had been made to build this twenty-kilometer [twelve US miles] long roadway. The work would start next spring.

Harald had come home from school with his examination diploma. He was now a fully trained engineer. His father told him about the decision by the government to build this road, and said, "You, Harald, should try to get the position to build this road. I will do everything in my power to help you get it. You should take your recommendations and go to Oslo and see them about that. I will write a letter to send with you." Harald then decided to go to Oslo right away.

Oivind was sent to farming school after he had become confirmed, but now had two years left there before he could take his exam. He was studying to become an agronomist.

Harald was now going to Oslo, and his father wrote a letter to send with him. He asked the Norwegian Government to do him the honor of hiring his son to build the road that was decided, if he had good enough credentials from the school. There was more in the letter, by the way, but we will avoid mentioning that here.

Harald then went down and had a meeting with the government. They looked over his credentials and his father's letter. And, they agreed to let him have the position to build the road. Harald went home happy in his mind because it went so well, and his father was even happier when he heard about it. In a week or so the work had to start.

He now went down to the village to get workers and a good foreman. They were to start down at the village. He got the tools and equipment that they needed. It wasn't long before he had a workforce of fifty men. He divided them into two crews, each with its foreman.

It was certainly a good thing for the unemployed in the village that this road was built. It created work for many every summer over the course of three years. Harald was busy every day the whole summer through. When the fall came and the frost started, they had to finish working. They were then home, each by themselves, until spring came and they started again.

They continued on that road for three summers. In the fall, the third year, the road was completed. Now, there was a nice automobile road from the village up to Fjeldbo. It went along the south end of the big forest up there, almost past every residence there and continued eastward a little farther than it was developed. Then, it turned into the great timber forest a while. And, farther west went a gravel road for horse riding into the forest. Those spurs into the forest were apparently meant for timber traffic later on.

Harald was now home through the winter, and likewise Oivind was now done with school and had gotten a job as an agronomist for the state and was to run some farming projects. Agnes was home also, until after Christmas, but then had to go to school again. She had one year left until she was educated as a teacher.

Chapter Six

Ole Fjeldbo was now forty-seven years old that fall when the road was completed, and his big dream was fulfilled, that dream that had now been in his mind for twenty-seven years, or since the first spring he started up there. He thanked his God, because he had been with him and made everything so well for him.

Then, one more winter was over and the spring came with a bird whistle and singing by the lark, and the cuckoo uttered its koo-koo over in the hills.

This spring some of the high state representatives came by to look at the road that Harald had built, and inspected all parts of it, and opened it for traffic. They came all the way up to Fjeldbo, and observed with amazement what Ole had been able to accomplish there in twenty-seven years. They complimented him highly on what he had done for his Fatherland. They also complimented Harald. They said that he had done excellent work down to the last detail. They didn't find anything that was not correct and they gave him good grades.

They gave themselves a lot of time up there at Fjeldbo, looked around and were also along on a trip far into the timber forest. Aslong offered them the best that she had, good goat cheese, primost, good flatbread and preserved meat, and even malt beer. They thanked her for her hospitality and bid farewell, and then invited Ole and Aslong to come visit them.

After Ole was done with the spring planting, he went down to town and bought himself a Ford truck. He thought that times were long gone when you had to climb up on the horse's back. During the last years he had to go down three times every month. Now, he thought, he could get all that down in one load every month. Ole had a lot to bring to the market now during summer and autumn: butter, cheese, wool, and sometimes he sold his sheep for slaughter, and calves he had nursed, and got good money.

He told Aslong one day, "I thought I had built enough houses here so that

I would have enough of them, but now after I got this Ford machine, I do believe that I should have a house for it, too. I think I will clear up in the tool shed, and make room for it there, first, until I manage to arrange materials for a new house. When I build I will build it big enough for a passenger car, too."

There ware many of Ole's neighbors who had children who were old enough to go to school. Lately, they had begun to talk about a schoolhouse. They agreed to have a meeting at Ole Fjeldbo's and discuss what they could do about that. They then met and Ole was elected president of the board.

Ole said, "I don't have any children to send to school, now, but I will nevertheless do everything I can to have a school house built. It will be of great benefit and comfort to our community out here. But it is too late this summer to do anything about it, and we should have had school this winter. I will make a proposition to you. You see, I have a large room on the upper level of my house that I will let you use and conduct school there a couple of semesters, so we will have much more time for our building project. It will just be to make desks and chairs, but that I will make sure to do. I will give them to the school, and the room shall cost you nothing. You can come with us up to look at it."

Once arrived, they all exclaimed, "But it is a large hall!"

"I have five bedrooms up here, so I let this be one room. I thought it might be handy sometime as a congregation hall." They all thanked Ole for his good offer and were glad that they would have a school this fall.

Once returned again, Ole said, "Now that we are congregated here, we might as well decide where the school house should be built. Axel Solberg said it should be built as centrally as possible. Einar Stenseng said, "I will give a parcel of my land for it up to the property line between me and Ole." They were all satisfied with that, and so it was decided.

"Now," said Ole, "we must organize the school district and give it a name. And then we must elect representatives to look after the school. You can suggest as many names as you wish, and then we vote. We will take the name that gets the most votes."

There were a whole lot of names nominated, but the name Solberg got most votes. So it became Solberg's, by Fjeldbo. "So then, we must elect a secretary," Ole said. Aksel Solberg was unanimously elected to that post. "So then, there is treasurer who must be elected." It became Einar Stenseng. "And then we must have a custodian." They all voted for Ole Fjeldbo. His duty was to write the Government to request state funding for their school.

It was Aksel Solberg who had to arrange to get a schoolteacher. "Now," Ole said, "I believe it will be best if we pay a sum, each of us to the treasurer, so he has enough in the cash box to pay a teacher's salary with. I believe that if we all pay twenty-five kroner, it would be enough for that." Everyone agreed with Ole and did as he suggested.

Aksel Solberg knew that Agnes Fjeldbo was at home and was an educated teacher. He went over to talk with her and asked if she would hold school for their children throughout the winter. She asked where they would have the school. "Here at your father's place," he answered.

Agnes was completely perplexed. "This is something quite remarkable for me to hear," she said. "Yes, I will do the best I can to teach your children."

Aksel Solberg said, "We cannot pay more than fifty kroner a month to you for this semester, if you are satisfied with that." Agnes said that was good pay and was well satisfied.

Aksel now went back to the others and told them that he had engaged a teacher for the school, namely Agnes Fjeldbo. They were all very happy about that. So now everything was arranged for school. It was then decided that school should start the first of October and go on for seven months. They then separated to go each to their own, with understanding that they would meet one day later in the fall when they were done with harvesting their crops, to clear the lot for their school house so that it was ready.

Ole was done with the building of his houses, he made a yard on the south side of his house, fenced it in with a nice fence painted white. On the inside of the fence, there was planted two rows of nice deciduous trees, and then a row of red currant bushes and many cherry trees.

In the middle of the yard there stood the new high flagpole, and around it a nice lawn. Around the lawn there were all kinds of beautiful flowers planted. On two sides of the flag pole, a little ways away from it in each direction, a water fountain was installed, which when the faucet was turned on sent a shower of water across the whole yard. Yes, it was truly something remarkable to see this far up in the mountain. It showed what diligence and thoughtfulness could lead to.

After the road had been built past his home, he worked on the entranceway at each end of the yard and house, one on the east, and one on the west side toward the house. And on the outside of each entranceway a hidden garden was made, both fenced in with white fence.

Ole grew more in these gardens than they needed for their own consumption at the farm. So he took a load into town each fall and sold what they didn't need. It also increased his savings substantially.

Along the road and in between the two entranceways there was also a beautiful pine tree orchard that went all the way up to the fruit tree garden. There it was nicely cleared and sowed with grass. Inside the orchard there were two benches painted white, where they would sit in the shade in the summer under these green pine trees, breathe the lovely mountain air and look across the large plains.

Ole had now decided to go to town to get a hay compressor. He would compress and sell the hay that was left over each summer. The fenced-in storage area was now full of haystacks, so there was no room for more.

The next day they started compressing hay, and kept doing that for a long time into the fall. Now they were done and Ole started hauling it down to the market. He made three trips each day, but still it took several days. But when he was done, his savings had increased to many hundreds of kroner more.

Agnes Fjeldbo had now run the school for two and one half months. Before the school started her father had bought a small cheap organ and put it up in the classroom, and she played on it to lead songs with the children. Likewise, she got her father to make three little tables that she put up farthermost down in the classroom, and two benches for each table. There were twelve children, you see. She wanted to have four at each tables when they had their lunch. She taught them to say their grace before they started eating, in a chorus, and a prayer of thanks after the meal.

Aslong, Agnes' mother, brought the children something warm to drink with their sandwiches each lunch throughout the winter—sometimes warm soup, sometimes warm milk, and sometimes "dravle" [warm milk with goat cheese in it]. And each time they got the dravle they mumbled, "Num, num, it tastes so good."

Aslong Fjeldbo was a philanthropical and loving woman, who wanted to do good deeds toward each and everyone she came in contact with. This way was the whole family at Fjeldbo. They were good hearted and welcoming against everyone, and they tried their best to make others happy.

Many of Ole's neighbors could come to him for advice and direction, but almost every time he answered, "When all is said and done, I don't know any more about this thing than you do, but I give you good advice anyway, that has always helped me. And that is, trust yourself, believe that you can accomplish it, and then pray to your God to receive inspiration, and his blessing. Believe deeply and fully that he listens to you and you will succeed. My mother always said to me, 'remember that diligent work and diligent prayer bring happiness.' And, I fully and deeply believe she was right."

The great holiday season—Christmas—was now approaching, and Agnes Fjeldbo had a busy time to teach her school children the Christmas program. She had decided to have a Christmas tree celebration in the school on the second day of Christmas. She asked parents who had children at home, about four, five, or six years old, to bring them to the school so she could practice with them so that they could participate in the program. They did this, took them up there several times as Christmas was approaching.

Now the holiday season had arrived, and they would for the first time celebrate a Christmas tree celebration in the new development around Fjeldbo. They now went, both great and small, to the celebration with great expectations, and were not disappointed. It was a remarkable and great holiday celebration for everyone. Agnes had surely worked diligently to achieve such a beautiful program. Everyone agreed it was the best they had experienced in a long time.

After the program was over, all the children and the adults were treated with apples, candies and nuts. At the end they asked the congregation to join in the psalm, "Now all thank God with their heart, mouth, and hands, who mercifully give us, who from mother's life and childhood, have given all necessities."

Aksel Solberg stood up and thanked Agnes for her sacrifice and diligence that she had put into arranging this celebration. "It made me very joyful in my heart," he said, "to sit and see all these children's faces and hear them sing these lovely old Christmas psalms. And I think the others also agree with me that this is the most wonderful time we have had in a long time. But there is one thing I think is not fair, that our teacher should bear all the costs of the celebration. It should suffice that she has done all the work and should not have monetary expenses as well, I believe. I think we should get together and change that."

Agnes stood up and said, "It does my heart good to hear that you enjoyed this celebration, but any contributions for expenses I have incurred, I will not hear about it. I did it to teach the children, and I have had just as great a benefit from it as you have. God be with you, and he blesses this celebration for all of us."

Chapter Seven

Now another winter was over with, and it disappeared in time's bottomless sea, and a new spring was approaching. The sun shone warmly and everything in nature started a new life. The grass started to sprout and the flowers peeked here and there in the greens. The birds chirped and sang in the orchard. All suggested that summer was coming.

The residents around Fjeldbo started making their acres ready for planting. It was crucial to get the seeds in as early as possible in the spring. It was their decision that when they were done with the planting and the rest of the spring chores, they would start to build their schoolhouse. They had cleared the lot last fall and throughout the winter they had cut timber and hauled it to the side. They had also made boards for this spring.

So now the work starts on the house. Ole Fjeldbo had two men for a while to build a new house for his truck and passenger car that he now wanted to buy. The house was painted white, as the other houses at Fjeldbo.

Ole now was on a trip to town, and then came home with a passenger car. He said to Aslong that now they would have the opportunity to get to church every Sunday throughout the summer.

There was one thing that Ole had had in his thoughts for may years now, but now he started to think more and more about it, it was to have electrical lighting and power for their village up here. There was a cascade far down along that river that Ole had his saw and mill, which would suit perfectly for a site for a power station and dam. But, the question was, if there would be water enough year round. There was another river, a little farther south, and Ole had decided if it proved possible to lead the water in that one to their river, that there would be enough water.

He wrote the Government to request that they send an engineer up there to examine the circumstances, and if state would support them to build this power station. In the summer Harald Fjeldbo came up there, he was sent by the Government to carry out observations in regard to his father's request. Harald was now permanently employed by the state as an engineer, and lived in Oslo.

He now stopped by his parents' on Fjeldbo, while he carried out his surveying and calculations. He had two men with him who helped him. It took the whole summer before they were done. *Yes, now there is a start accomplished on this project as well*, thought Ole to himself. I wonder what the result will be.

Harald talked a little with his father about this project. He felt that it could be accomplished satisfactorily if the Government decided to proceed with it. Harald now took farewell with his parents and went back to Oslo.

When it was into winter, first in March, a letter came along with papers to Ole from Oslo. They said in the letter that if the residents up there were willing to sign the contract that they sent, then the state would build this power station and complete everything that would come under this project. But everyone has to pay a sum each year for twenty years. If they all agreed to this condition the work would start in the spring.

Ole now called his neighbors together and told them how the situation was, and explained the conditions for them. He would like to know what they meant to do about that. They were all excited about getting electrical lighting, so they unanimously signed the contract presented by the government. Then that was arranged and Ole sent the contract back to Oslo.

In the spring, Harald came back up there again to start the work. Yes, there was a lot of activity up there this summer. A little into the project there were over a hundred men that were working under Harald, some on the dam, and some on the house that was to house the dynamo. Some put up poles and others the electrical cable. A large "kattepilar" [Caterpillar] steam hoe was needed to dig the ditches. It took a lot of men just to get wood and water to it.

When it was close to the middle of summer, Harald said one day to his father, "If the work proceeds forward after this time, as it has done so far, then I believe strongly that it will be completed this fall."

He also said that he was ordered by the state to build electrical line along the road that went into the forest, because into fall it was the intention that a foreman was to come with some men to build a camp at each side road, a cabin with two large rooms, and stables on the two locations. He said that they would begin next winter to cut timber that is located in this area, and in the summer hauled down with trucks. They will keep doing that for three years at the very least.

"So you will have the opportunity, Father, to get rid of some of that hay you have left over." But his father said there were many more than him with hay to spare. Because there were plenty of his neighbors who had dried up marshes and planted grass and had grown a large quantity of hay.

They also got their schoolhouse completed this summer and electric lighting was installed there, too.

Now, it was getting close to the end of October, and Harald was now done with the work down by the dam. He had laid off his men, all but two mechanics who were there to correct a few more things. They now tried running and tried the machinery, and everything worked satisfactorily. "Before you leave," his father said, "you will have to help me install three motors that I want to have. First, I want you to calculate how big they need to be before I go down to get them. You see, I want one for the threshing machine, and one for the circular saw to cut wood with, and one for the milk separator."

Harald said he would take his two men with him up there and get them installed. He then calculated how powerful they should be and made notes for his father. It didn't take Harald and his men very long until they were installed and in contact. "Yes, I am well satisfied," Ole said, "this is one more of my dreams fulfilled."

There was now electrical lighting in every house and every room on Fjeldbo, and power to carry out the heaviest work at the farm. Ole sent up a thank you prayer to God, who so mercifully stood by him through all these years and blessed his projects, and so they succeeded for him.

Harald now had to go to Oslo again, and therefore took farewell with his parents. "Maybe," he said, "I will come to visit you during Christmas again, if God will let me."

They were now well along with the building of the cabins for the timber camps. The intent was that there would be twenty-five men in each camp to cut and haul throughout the winter. These undertakings brought a lot of work for people around there. First the road and then the power station, and now— this timber traffic. They ought to be thankful to him for his vision and spirit of enterprise.

Agnes Fjeldbo had now started her third school semester up there, two at home at her father's and now the third in the new schoolhouse. But she thought that it would be the last winter she held school now, because she had become engaged with a farmer's boy down in the village, and was to be married next summer. His name was Ragnar Oppegaard, the grandson of Tobias Oppegaard, the farmer who Ole served for five years, from his fifteenth to twentieth year. After that time, he started clearing and built a home for himself and Aslong.

Ole probably never thought when he was at Tobias', that he would become a relative with him, but this is the way it goes, many unthinkable things happen. Old Tobias was a long time dead now, and his oldest son had the farm now. Ragnar, his son, the second in a row, was not heir to the farm. Agnes and Ragnar were just about the same age.

Ole and Aslong's parents were too old to go and toil for these farmers anymore. So he invited them to come up to them, and be there during their old days. He told them, "We have room enough for you and food, too. You don't have to have any particular housekeeping because I will have you at our table at meal times. And neither would you have to do any work. I want you to take it easy the last years of your life. I believe you have toiled and suffered enough throughout the times."

After a while they decided to move up to Fjeldbo to stay with Ole and Aslong. Both of their parents would come. They would take with them the dearest to their hearts, the rest they would sell. When they were ready to come up, Ole traveled down there with his automobiles to pick them up.

Aksel Solberg had gotten the idea that he would get a telephone up there, and they then started a shareholding company, and started building a telephone line. The switchboard ended up at Aksel Solberg's place. Yes, they now had telephone and electric lighting and all good things up there. But there was one thing they did not have yet, and that was a church and a priest.

Ole had thought a lot lately about how to get a priest to serve them and build a church. They probably could manage to build a church, but there was not enough to pay salary for a permanent priest. But he arranged it with the State Department for Church Matters, that they would get a priest to serve them every third Sunday, and the meetings would be held at Fjeldbo. The priest would also take care of all the children who were old enough to be confirmed. So then, they had to accept that for a while.

Ole Fjeldbo got from the government, some years ago, ownership of the land he had worked and fenced in, so it was his complete property and he could do with it as he pleased. Ole's both sons, Harald and Oivind, now had started families and had good positions that gave them good income, and both lived in Oslo. They came up to Fjeldbo to visit their parents now and then, but Ole understood that they didn't have much interest to become farmers.

Agnes now became married this summer with Ragnar Oppegaard. Her father talked to her and he wanted them to stay here at Fjeldbo, together with them. They would not need to start any new homestead. He said, "If you live here and help, then I will let you have half of the income every year. And when the time comes that I myself am unable to take care of it, then this home becomes yours, if you help us and take care of us in our old days."

The father's words made Agnes start crying. She assured her father that she would stay at home and do the best for them when old age came to them.

We have neglected to mention that there was, every year, a festivity at Fjeldbo on the seventeenth of May. Ole's neighbors came there almost all the time, every seventeenth of May, and celebrated the Independence Day. The flag was hanging from the pole, and they sang patriotic songs and gave speeches. If there was nice weather, they had their festivities down in the beautiful pine tree grove; if the weather was sour, up in Ole's congregation hall. Aksel Solberg, excited about his neighborhood and his Fatherland, could hold good, funny, and patriotic speeches that captivated his audience. They could have a really good time without dance and strong drinks.

Epilogue

This fantasy picture is written to show what the son of a cotter, at home in Norway, could accomplish with diligent work and sacrifice. He had to sacrifice all the temptations of youth, such as dance and cinema, and all other calls to pleasure. Instead, work, more work, late and early. But he took his God with him in all his doings so it was not heavy for him to forsake.

Down in the village, in daily talk, they called him Ole Fjeldbonde, the Mountain Farmer, instead of Ole, Cotter's Boy. Yes he was a farmer in the true meaning of the word. But he was more than a farmer, he was a liberal, Fatherland loving man. He didn't inherit his farm and land, but started with two empty hands and worked his way up to prosperity, and got himself a nice home, where his family lived in harmony and took their God with them in everything.

If Mother Norway would foster many sons like this one, the land would get built from the border out to the drifting net. As it is written in one of Bjornstjerne Bjornson's songs:

So, we rest ourselves in the evening
Where the whole village is in the mountains,
At the mountain farm with the milking chores,
On the mountain castle under the cliffs,
And where a yearning call awaiting,
Receives answer from Grand Nature.